# EVERYTHING THE SUN TOUCHES

# ALSO AVAILABLE

## THE SUN & FLAME DUOLOGY

Volume 1: Everything the Sun Touches
Volume 2: Everything the Flame Heals (publishing in Spring 2027)

## THE SLOE MOON SERIES

Volume 1: Tall Trees
Volume 2: Stoneharp
Volume 3: Crooked Hill
Volume 4: Eastbay
Volume 5: Halfway
Volume 6: Goldenlake

## NOVELLA

The Boy Who Played the Queen

# CONTENT WARNINGS

strong language, religious trauma, injury detail

# EVERYTHING THE SUN TOUCHES

## SUN & FLAME
### VOLUME ONE

## C. M. KUHTZ

WOLLSCHWEBER
PUBLISHING

Wollschweber Publishing

www.wollschweberpublishing.com



## CREDITS

Copyediting: River Ari, Better Than Sex Editing

Production: C. M. Kuhtz

Cover design: My Lan Khuc (LaolanArt)

Logo design: Dorit Osang

Map and interior illustrations: Ken Turner

A catalogue record for this book is available from the British Library.

ISBN 978-1-06831-962-4 hardback
ISBN 978-1-06831-963-1 paperback
ISBN 978-1-06831-964-8 ebook

# DRAMATIS PERSONAE

## Pronunciation Guide

*Vowels*
A—as in 'marvel' (ā)
E—long, as in 'elusive' (ē) or short and flat (ə), as in 'energy'
I—like ee, as in 'feel' (ee), though sometimes more like a flat e (ə)
O—round, as in 'over' (ō)
U—like oo, as in 'moon' (oo)

*Consonants*
C and Q—like k, as in 'crown' (k), but sometimes soft (s)
J and Y—like y, as in 'yay' (y)
S—soft, as in 'zebra' (z)
W—like v, as in 'village' (v)

**Bjell da Relian** (Byēll dā Rēlee-ānn; he/him)—First Bull in Seagard

**Brother Rago** (Rā-go; he/him)—a priest of the Star

**Cisir da Fewell** (Sisir dā Fyoo-el; he/him)—a young man, newly appointed secretary to the First Sun of Seagard

**Eravis na Eloven** (Ērāwəz nā Elōwen; she/her)—a young woman in Seagard

**Garalis Wolf** (Gārāləs; she/her)—Gia's mother

**Giannis (Gia) Wolf** (Gee-ānəs [Gee-ā]; she/her)—Qonna's best friend

**Guardsman Jark** (Yārk; he/him)—a handsome member of the Royal Guard

**Hevo** (Hē-vō; he/him)—a young man employed in the House of the Sun

**Lauron Wolf** (Lau-rōn; he/him)—Gia's father

**Hilvis da Ozanil da Nileon** (Heelvəs dā Ōzā-neel dā Nee-ləōn; she/her)—Noa's mother, third wife of Nivael da Nileon

**Nian da Nileon** (Nee-ān dā Nee-ləōn; he/him)/**Lilyis Sun** (Ləllyəs; she/her)—a Prince of Crooked Hill, founder of the Company of the Sun

**Nivael da Nileon** (Nee-vā-ēl dā Nee-ləōn; he/him)—a Prince of Crooked Hill, founder of the Company of the Sun and Noa's father

**Noalis (Noa) da Nileon** (Nō-āləs [Nō-ā] dā Nee-ləōn; she/her)—daughter of Nivael and Hilvis

**Nurin da Nileon** (Noorən dā Nee-ləōn)—the king, Noa's uncle.

**Pjer** (Pyēr; he/him)—a young man in the employment of the Applebeck Temple

**Qattir (Qatt) na Qes** (Kattər [Katt] nā Kəz; he/him)—Qonna's oldest brother, one of a set of twins.

**Qes na Qarim** (Kəz nā Kāreem; he/him)—Qonna's father, First Sun in Seagard

**Qitli na Qes** (Kətlee nā Kəz; he/him)—Qonna's youngest brother

**Qonnamaris (Qonna) na Qe**s (Konnāmārəs [Konnā] nā Kəz; she/her)—a young woman growing up in Seagard

**Qonna's mother**—a trader's wife in Seagard

**Qov na Qes** (Kōf nā Kəz; he/him)—Qonna's middle brother, one of a set of twins.

**Rilk da Relian** (Rəlk dā Rēlee-ānn; he/him) he/him)—Bjell da Relian's secretary

**Rinald da Relian** (Ree-nāld dā Rēlee-ānn; he/him)—a member of the Company of the Bull

**Sloe Moon** (Slō; they/them)—a famous wizard in Birkland, Qes' half-sibling and Lilyis' partner

**Spark** (he/him)—a dog

**Yoren** (Yō-rēn; he/him)—a young man employed in the House of the Sun

# THE EIGHT KINGDOMS

TH
EASTCLERE & NORTHWOOD
GREENCLERE
Northcastle
Greengard
Woodgard
WHITERIVERS
Pietwood
Crooked Hill
Eastbay
ROSEVALE
HILLAKES & SOUTHCLERE
Rosegard
Seagard

# BOOK ONE

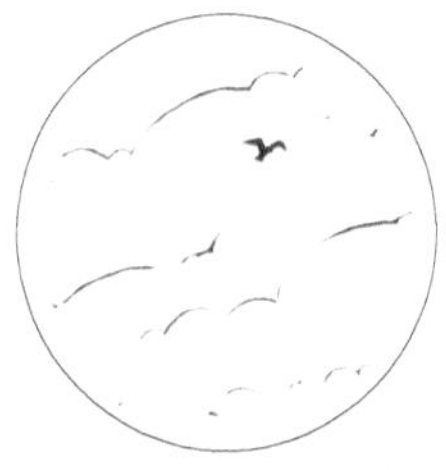

# QONNA

## *hint at more*

Don't be such a fucking hypocrite, Dad." Qonna clenches her fists while a shocked silence settles over the room. It isn't the first time she's used this kind of language around him, but it's definitely the first with her mother present, and as usual, it changes everything.

Qonna draws herself up. She only has half a hand's breadth on her father's height, but he manages to make her feel small when his brows knit together and his face flushes under its short dark beard.

"Would you care to repeat that?" His voice is tightly controlled.

Qonna's fists shake. She may look so much like her father, and have a similar temper, flaring up at any given provocation, but while he's had the time and experience to learn to handle his emotions, Qonna is far too easily baited. "I'm not going to this *fucking* dance. Uncle Lauron said it's no more than a meat market."

Her father's jaw tenses. "When did you see Lauron?"

*Oh no.* Qonna forces herself to take a deep breath. *This won't be the only mistake you make today. Just get through it. Just get out of the room.* "A few days ago."

"Damn it to all Eight Hells, Qonna!"

Her mother whimpers. She's used to her husband slipping the occasional curse word into the conversation, but she draws a firm line at blasphemy.

He shoots her an irritated glance. "How many times do I need to spell it out for you? You're not to go within five fucking feet of the *Rotting Pear* when you're on your own. It's not safe in the Triangle."

"You've taken me to the *Pear* plenty of times."

"That's different," he says.

"Is it?" What he really means is, it's unsafe to walk through town without a man—an official protector.

"Anyway, that's another conversation. Your mother put your name on the attendance list months ago. You're going to the dance if I have to wrap you in the upstairs carpet and drag you."

Qonna squares her shoulders, broad-built and far more muscular than is useful for the life her parents have planned for her. "I'd like to see you try."

Her father isn't a hitter, but by the Star, she can see it in his eyes when he's tempted. It takes all she has to still the trembling in her fists and stare him down. A low growl forms in her throat.

"That's enough." It's been a long time since her mother forced herself to intervene in one of their stand-offs. Usually, she isn't present at all. On this day she pushes the embroidery frame away, its spindly legs screeching across the wooden floor of the room she prefers to spend her time in.

*You're such a stupid cow*, Qonna scolds herself. *Never ever allow these talks to escalate outside of the study.*

"The seamstress has been paid," her mother says as she rises to her feet, delicate slippers poking from layers of the finest linen to be had in Seagard. "You are attending the dance."

"Mother …."

"Everyone put in a lot of work to prepare for the occasion." While her husband and daughter are tall and fleshy, Qonna's mother is slight, the bones of her wrists as thin as a sparrow's, with every single hair covered under the elaborate construction of pins and starched linen deemed fashionable these days.

One of the few adornments Qonna ever sees her mother wear is a golden star pendant large enough to stretch across her palm, with a semi-precious stone set in its centre the colour of a tightly furled rose bud. Whenever her mother's voice reveals the core of ice that long ago settled in her heart, Qonna's gaze slips down and fastens on the jewel, as if the words are uttered by the golden shape itself. "We will not discuss this further. The carriage has been ordered to await you at the sixth bell."

Qonna's mouth falls open, but before she can get in another squeal of protest, her mother swishes out of the room. It's a trick. A fool-proof method to claim the last word.

The door shuts behind her mother with an ominous clang, not exactly violent, but still forceful.

"Oh fuck." Her father rubs his forehead. "I can't remember the last time she actually stood up to make herself heard. Why did Lauron say it was a meat market?"

Qonna's heart sinks like a stone. "He didn't use those exact words. He said, 'those dances are an excuse for every man in the city to ogle his friends' daughters.' It makes no sense for me to be there. You promised you wouldn't make any decisions about my engagement until my twentieth birthday."

"Your birthday is only seven months away. We've given you a lot more time than most city people would've." Like Qonna, her father is quick to anger but soon to cool off. The colour is already gone from his face, the fire from his dark eyes. While Qonna resembles him in so many ways, she didn't inherit those eyes—the one feature she would truly love to share. Everything else—the thick straight brows, the upturned nose, and soft cheeks—she has from him, plus the propensity to overall hairiness, if she didn't spend so much time with the pair of bronze tweezers her mother gifted her when her first blood arrived. Qonna's eyes are blue, and not even a captivating blue, but dull, like a sun-bleached pebble.

She huffs in frustration. "It's not enough time, Dad. What was the last dance you came to with us? Do you remember the utter misery of standing around waiting until the torture was over? No one has ever asked me to dance, and no one ever will. None of the city men fancy twirling around the room with a woman who can spit over their heads."

"Someone might surprise you one day."

"I don't want to be surprised. I don't fancy them either."

"None of them?" A glint of worry flashes in his eyes, a worry she's started to feel herself sometimes.

"Not a single one. They're all obsessed with their horses and swordfighting lessons." She glares at him. Another sore point.

He rubs his face again. He tends to do that a lot around her, as if the existence of his daughter constantly puts him in situations he'd rather avoid. His three sons likely never make him feel like that. All their time together is spent in much more pleasurable pursuits: riding out of town to do business, fishing, or attending the races and other sporting events. All of them have already enrolled in the Company of the Sun, with the twins starting their apprenticeship this summer.

As the eldest of the siblings, Qonna has been excluded from these activities ever since her first blood drew a line under her childhood.

"Dad …." *You sound so whiny. He never responds well to that.*

Something new falls across his face, something more unwelcome than the anger he faced her with only moments ago: sorrow.

Qonna has always known about her heritage. How could she not, when the whole city was set on reminding her every single day that her father might try to slot himself into society with as few ripples as possible, but that neither of his parents were natives of the Kingdom of the Hillakes and Southclere. Even if he had chosen a wife from one of the most well-connected families in Seagard, no one made it easy for him or his children, though since the death of his father, Qes na Qarim has done his utmost to find a place among the citizens.

When he's in a good mood, Qonna can sometimes squeeze more information out of him than expected, but he always has to be a little drunk, something that happens less and less. One of the reasons for his renewed effort of temperance is the disapproval of her mother.

Qonna had heard her brothers whisper the shameful fact that their grandfather was given to spells of heavy drinking whenever life became too much to bear. Her father might've been secretly happy the spirits claimed Grandfather Qarim but is clearly worried about being tempted by the same.

Qonna remembers when all her father's children sat around him after one of the celebratory meals that came every month or so, and listened to him tell the stories they hoped for: Grandfather Qarim crossing the mighty ocean to find love on the other side of the world with nothing more than the clothes on his back, a stranger in one of the youngest cities in the whole Eight Kingdoms. Sometimes it was a romantic tale and sometimes they watched in dismay as their father, quick to anger but hard to bring to tears, tried to cover his breaking voice with a crooked smile.

Neither Qonna nor her three younger brothers can rely on their mother to dig deep. She prefers to do the opposite: keep as much hidden as she can, as if once she was fooled into marrying someone unsuitable and now lives with painful regrets.

They know more than they want to about their mother's side of the family, the lineage tying them closely to most of the merchant families in the Southclere district. Their mother diligently stitched her family's emblem on anything that would hold still: handkerchiefs, bedlinens, sashes, woollen hose. It's stamped into the leather of the chairs and woven into countless tapestries around the house—a dove-grey animal curled into the round, its twisted horn closing the circle by barely touching its own bottom.

The day Qonna realized she wasn't likely to see a unicorn in the flesh was painful like a deliberate betrayal. Why choose an animal for your house you don't possess? None of her uncles kept one in a special section of their stables, none of her aunts had seen more than endless reproductions of its form on cloth, leather, wax, and parchment.

Qonna cried herself to sleep that night on a pillow crested with a unicorn, and sometimes she believes the general feeling of disenchantment that rules her life stems from that very day.

As the only daughter among four children, she spends most of her days trying to avoid the extracurricular activities her mother deems necessary for her to blossom into a young woman of Seagard. She's quite happy to oversee the accounts and draw up meal plans for the household, and she's grateful for any moment she's allowed to sit in her bedroom with one of the three books she's allowed to keep—

all suitable enough, though some of the Rosegardian poems hint at more. Usually, she must make time for these pursuits: rise an hour early, before the maid thinks about waking her, claw the gunk out of her eyes, and try to concentrate on the pages.

Whoever copied out the poems might not have understood their secret meanings, only concentrated on the shape of ink on parchment. But if they saw what was hidden there? Sometimes she longs for someone to share a sly grin with, however many years ago they put their quill on the line.

On these cold mornings the house has its own noises. Some days her brothers are already up, preparing for an expedition to the harbour bridge or other meetings they need to get used to. They clomp around above her head, unbothered about disturbing their big sister, undoubtedly excited and glad to escape into the city.

In time they'll be directed to attend their own share of dances and be wooed by flocks of merchant's daughters. None of it is fair. She often wonders whether her father at least is aware of how much she loses out on. It would've been different if Grandfather Qarim had found someone to love at home in Birkland and not dragged his sorry arse all the way to the Cities to subject his granddaughter to infinitely boring evenings waiting to be taken pity on in a dress that will inevitably stain upon first contact with a bowl of tea.

She longs to be allowed to stay home, to be still for a while without any responsibilities tugging at her, without her mother pointedly nudging her own embroidery frame at her, because the world doesn't have enough bloody chair covers.

Qonna rises on her elbows. Her bed is too short; she can barely move without rolling onto the floor. This has always been her space on the first floor of the house she was born in, the home once coveted by many young women eager to become its mistress, that bears the promising name of *Pomegranates*. Like almost everything else in Seagard, it's comparatively new, but the beams have started to darken and the floors to settle. She knows this building like the back of her hand, every finger-width of its walls.

The dress she's going to wear tonight hangs off a wooden frame by the door. It's blue, she knows that it's blue, but in the dim light of the small room it seems drab and sack-like, and the dreaded headdress is perched next to it, already folded and pinned into the shape her mother prefers for her.

Only seven months until her twentieth birthday—and who knows what'll happen then? Everyone seems keen for her to find someone to marry and leave the room with the small window that must've been meant for storage, not to shelter the daughter of the house. There's a chair and the small pile of her books next to a clay jug with prepared goose quills, the inkhorn, and a bowl filled with yet more pins. Scraps of paper are pushed into a pile, although she takes care to hide most of what she writes at the bottom of the chest that holds her winter skirts. It's not much and, at the same time, a lot more than most people have.

As the daughter born into the house, she was always destined to remove herself from it, but if there's one thing she already knows, it's that there won't be someone waiting for her at the dance. No one who miraculously appears, ready to be enchanted against his will by someone who carries her heritage in the very shape of her body, however many wimples her mother tries to hide it with.

# CISIR

## *new suns*

The man Cisir has been allocated to is late to reach the House of the Sun. By now the traffic has died down so much it can't be an excuse for his tardiness, but Cisir was warned: Qes na Qarim comes and goes as he pleases.

Qes won't often need his secretary to accompany him, so a large part of the position will be waiting around for Qes to appear, dictating a few letters, and filing away the mess he leaves behind. To think that only a few weeks ago, Cisir was ecstatic at the prospect of making a new life in this city. Today he feels stranded again.

Outside, soft spring sunshine spills over the cobbles, and waves roll into the harbour. He's been staring out of the window for what feels like hours. After the usual morning rush, things around the harbour bridge have quietened. If he sticks his head out as far as possible, he can't see the quay from here, not even the very tips of the masts.

At times, the House of the Sun itself seems to hold its breath. During the last years it sprawled outwards, taking over the buildings to its right and much of the yard, and although it's painted every so often, Cisir recalls being appalled at its weatherbeaten yellow frontage when he came for his interview, the salt-bleached banners at its door.

This morning, he crossed the threshold for the second time in his life, into the dark interior of the part accessible to customers, filled with mingled fragrances oozing from the shelves, with bags, baskets, and little packets heaped upon the counter. Today he wears the uniform of the Sun, the yellow tunic with its sewn-on emblem, and who knows how many years he will wear it.

He flinches as the door swings open.

Someone enters, someone tall, with a cloud of curly blue-black hair and a deep frown. "You're the new boy."

"Yes … Master."

The man snorts, shrugging off an ochre-coloured cloak with fox fur trim, much too warm for a sunny day in late spring. He holds out the cloak for Cisir to take and as his new master steps close, his thick brows separate and lift. Qes na Qarim must not meet many men who are as tall as him, maybe a little taller if Cisir would stand straight. "Hailing from where exactly?"

"Windyhill, Master."

"Windyhill? That is …."

"Northeast from here, close to the Rosevale border, Master."

"I didn't know they made them this big up there." His new master scratches the chin beneath his cropped beard. Silver threads mix into the hair at his temples. They might be of similar height, but Qes na Qarim is twice as sturdy, heavy in chest and shoulders.

They say he's been in the House of the Sun since its foundation. They say he became tired of it long ago. Qes studies him as if he hadn't expected to find his new secretary waiting for his arrival, though very little goes on in the House of the Sun without him being informed.

Cisir swallows, aware that more questions are coming his way.

"What sort of place is Windyhill?" his new master asks.

"Smallish."

The dark brows arch and Cisir blushes. Windyhill doesn't incur a large amount of interest, and generally no one wants to know much about Cisir, either.

"Smallish and …?" Qes prompts. "I assume your family had enough funds to provide you with a decent education and make you follow a career in the Companies. Do they have a big house up there?"

"Windyhill Manor, Master. I suppose it is of reasonable size."

"You suppose?" Qes' brows do most of the talking for him. So far, he's clearly not impressed.

Cisir takes a pained breath. "Compared to other areas of Southclere; there are not many families of consequence who choose to make their home so close to the border."

"Though the treaties have kept the peace between the Eight Kingdoms for such a long time?" Qes asks.

"It doesn't feel that long, Master. You wouldn't know it, this far in the south."

"Were you trained in combat …?"

"Cisir, Master."

"Cisir …?"

"Cisir da Fewell."

"*Da* Fewell?"

Cisir shudders. Most people react a bit strangely when they become aware that, at least a long time ago, Cisir's family was noble. There can't be many aristocratic scribes in such a new city as Seagard trying to gain employment with the Companies. Seagard is a place of merchants, of trading families. "Whatever riches there were, they've long been spent," he says flatly. He feels the urge to cross his arms, to do anything to protect himself.

Qes na Qarim surprises him once again. He shrugs. "Isn't that always the way?" He tilts his head. "You were tutored from an early age?"

"Yes, Master."

"Including combat?"

"They tried, but I'm afraid I'm not very good. I've always shown more aptitude for accountancy. And calligraphy, but that's … that's probably beside the point."

"As I was never properly trained, I'll enjoy my records being extremely readable." Qes gives a deep huff, perhaps trying to make Cisir more comfortable. "Every new face coming into the Sun has an interesting story to tell, but not too many names begin with *da* so far, so you might be congratulated on that. Do you feel much deprived?"

Cisir blushes again. "Deprived of what?"

"If there was money for training and tutors, you didn't suffer terribly growing up." Qes' black eyes narrow. Compared to most men in Seagard, Cisir's new master is of darker complexion. Cisir was told stories of the man's parentage, but he thought them to be malicious rumours, spread by agents of the Company of the Bull.

"I never felt hunger growing up," Cisir answers cautiously. "No one could call me deprived."

"You don't have a bone to pick with anyone? No enemies?"

These are far more questions than he was asked during the initial interview. Even if his master wants to be especially thorough, much of it is laughably pointless. "No enemies. That I'm aware of."

"Did you bring some samples?"

"As requested." Cisir notices with dismay that his fingers are shaking as he hands over the scroll of ratty parchment, scraped and used again and again. The only kind he's been able to afford for exercises.

"Extremely readable, indeed." A grin flashes upon Qes' face. He quickly smothers it, giving Cisir a sideways glance. Cisir wonders what he takes notice of. There's the height, but also the big nose with the bump on it, the fact that he can never get the knife sharp enough for a good shave, and that his curls do need a trim. They've started to hang past his collarbone, something Cisir's father would've deeply lamented. He looks unremarkable enough, one of many sandy-haired men in Seagard, even if he has the biggest nose of all.

"When did you come down to Seagard?" Qes asks.

"A few weeks ago, Master."

"Specifically for the job?"

"Yes," Cisir admits.

"Are there no scribes needed in the north?"

"It seemed the best opportunity to …."

"… to get as far away from home as you could?" Qes finishes.

"Yes." Cisir swallows again. "Master."

"To escape your father or your mother?"

"Ehm, both of them?"

Qes narrows his eyes again. "Can you dance?"

"What?"

"All that combat training, all those calligraphy exercises—did the tutors provide you with dancing lessons too?"

"They have. Not that I'd call myself particularly gifted, mind." He glances down at his soft shoes. "My feet are very big."

Qes na Qarim sighs as he hands back the scroll. "Fine. It would've worked out too well—the gods never tend to be this generous."

"Why?" Cisir's question rushes out before he can keep it in.

"I need someone tall enough to dance with my daughter."

That sounds weird enough to be the truth. "Does she want to be danced with?"

Qes blinks. "Not many young men would ask that question, Cisir da Fewell. I'm not sure that she does, but it's time. As a daughter of the Cities, she has her own duties to fulfil and attending the first dance of the season is among them." The frown is back. "Actually, I know she's less than keen to go, but I assume that's because she's headstrong and hates standing about."

He obviously isn't aware how long Cisir has waited for him today, doing exactly that.

"Know what? I'll send a messenger. Perhaps she'll be more inclined to attend if she knows someone is willing to stand up with her." His gaze drills into his new secretary. "Would you be willing?"

Can Cisir deny the man he was given to work with? "Is it part of the job?"

"I can make it part of it." It sounds like a threat.

Cisir's shoulders slump. "I'm willing, but I must stress that I really can't dance."

"Surely enough to sway around the room once and then have a cup of wine?"

"Maybe enough for that, Master."

"Excellent. I'll send the message now and let you know what she says. I'll meet you in the stores in half an hour."


'The stores' are the room where the most precious goods are kept under lock and key, and personally counted out by the highest-ranking member of the Sun.

Cisir perches on the edge of the packing table, hugging the scroll to his chest. How can he have landed himself in yet another complicated situation within hours of starting his new position? He knows exactly what will happen: he will fall in love again.

He always falls in love, and it always ends in humiliation. He might have a name that raises interest, but as soon as the woman in question realizes there's no coin coming with it and that the only thing he has to recommend himself is indeed *himself*, it goes wrong. Why did he ever believe that when he left Windyhill, he could leave himself behind?

Seagard is so new; it seemed the best option to reinvent himself, but here he stands with a stomach as sour as sorrel vinegar and all nails bitten to the quick.

"There you are." His master materializes, appearing self-satisfied enough for Cisir to wonder what exactly he promised that daughter of his. *A young nobleman, fallen on hard times. Nothing much to look at, but with a very legible hand.* "It always helps when they can follow instructions."

'They' probably means new Suns. In the last years Qes must've seen many men arrive, helpless with awkwardness but eager to grasp the chance at a new life. Cisir can't be the only one who felt pulled to Seagard for that very reason: because it was more open to new ideas on how to live than anywhere else in the kingdom.

He straightens up and waits for more of said instructions.

Qes na Qarim pulls something folded from the inside of his tunic. It's the first time Cisir has seen an actual piece of paper. He heard it's becoming widely available in larger Cities and is commonly used in Birkland. Made from flattened grass fibres, rough to write on and cheap, but easier to carry around than the wax tablets Cisir learned on. The ink spiderwebbed across the page can't hide the severity of his master's unschooled script. Cisir suppresses a shudder; he needed all the warnings he received.

Qes na Qarim seems barely civilized without the fur-lined cloak, someone with a lot of curly hair and a beard on the verge of growing out of control, in a dark-green tunic and riding boots, with a broad belt spanning his waist. It has a short blade strapped to it horizontally behind the back. Is Cisir supposed to be armed?

He feels the soft wingbeat of rising fear. What is he supposed to do here? Stare at his master until needed? If he really takes so long to read a short list, how can he bear all that lost time? Cisir lifts his right hand to his mouth, but he's gnawed his nails down as far as he can. Anymore and he'll start to bleed.

Qes' gaze whips up. "Right, that should take us less than an hour, if we're smart about it." He presses the note into Cisir's hand and rifles through the small bag on his belt, eventually unearthing a cluster of spirally keys. "Can you ready the scales and call out to me what's needed?" His master points to a wooden box housing the scales, gleaming dully in the light of the single oil lamp he brought with him.

Carefully, Cisir unpacks the instrument. It's beautifully made and covered in etchings that have something foreign to them. With relief, Cisir notices his hands have become steady. He was given a task he knows how to do. He sets out the weights, then flattens the paper next to them. It feels rough under his fingertips, the scrawl of oak gall ink telling him the Company needs a better recipe for it—or that, though he'll handle the most precious commodities the Sun trades with, the Company needs to save coin.

As Cisir lifts his head, he realizes Qes na Qarim has tracked every one of his movements. Qes' face is pulled into a thoughtful expression, as if he's working on a plan for him.

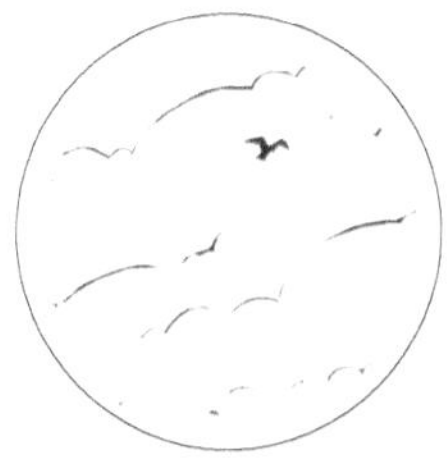

# QONNA

## *appropriate circumstances*

Qonna's feet remember the way. As a child she walked it nearly every day—another thing that was snatched away, something she mourned for years without being aware of it. Back then, times were different, everything much more informal, and on the days Uncle Lauron came to meet them, he often brought Giannis with him. They would spend many afternoons playing among the treasures of the Sun, unbothered by the clients who came in to order their bits and pieces. It changed with the years; with every young man apprenticed there was less space for little girls who loved to roam through the stores.

The cobbles of the main road leading from the Eastown to the harbour still feel familiar under the soles of her shoes, and at least here they're swept several times a day. The sunshine charms many people out into the open. Maids working in the big houses lining the road step out to chat, and everywhere in the yards behind the colourful facades, miles of washed linens must be hung up to dry.

Qonna's resentment bubbles up like a sulphurous spring. These women have much more pressing problems to deal with than a father with the oddest ideas of how to solve an awkward situation. She sees them at one of the rare times when they can actually take a breath, squinting up into the warmth and laughing with their friends and neighbours. Whatever Qonna witnesses in this moment is a precious respite from their lives.

Still. She would so love to make her way to the Triangle and unearth Giannis from the *Rotting Pear*, sit on the wobbly bench in its yard, and have a good moan about absolutely everything. But Gia surely has her own list of things she needs to do, now that her mother has developed the ambition to transform the *Pear* into the most respectable house in the quarter. The last time Qonna saw her, Gia's palms were covered in blisters from all the scrubbing she was made to do. *But,* says the little mean voice in the back of Qonna's head, *when she's not scrubbing, she can go where she likes. Or she could be, if she wasn't so comfortable where she is.*

Qonna's strides shorten. *Is this a good idea? Perhaps going into the Triangle will get me in less trouble.* She grits her teeth and continues. She will finish what she started.

Around her, the main road narrows into a gentle curve leading down to the bridge. From up here she can see five ships anchored in the harbour, some of them smaller vessels built to keep close to the coast, but one is immense, as big as the ships sailing across to Birkland, its red sails rolled up neatly. It has pride of place at the quay, and its sides are painted with the silhouettes of charging bulls.

Qonna sucks in her cheeks and bites down. This usually means her father will be in one of his volatile moods—and probably explains this morning's escalation. Though her mother has declared herself averse to any Company talk at home, Qonna knows what it means when the Company of the Bull returns such a capacious vessel to the kingdoms. It's packed with everything they need to have a record year. It's so early, months away from Shortest Night, and the Bulls are already raking in profits. None of the Sun's ships have made it back yet, and at some point, the House's stores will start to run low.

She turns her back to the red ship as soon as she can. Though the Bulls own a few warehouses at the harbour, their headquarters lie further from the quay, and the House of the Sun claims its space on the bridge, painted yellow but a bit shabby after last winter. The vertical banners fixed at both sides of its entrance appear battered, their seams ripped.

As always during business hours, the door is propped open with a piece of reddish-gold sandstone carved into the likeness of a small dog with a lolling tongue. It makes her smile involuntarily. *Don't slow down now, dammit. He needs to see you angry.*

As she ducks into the spice-scented interior, she catches the Sun keeping watch over the wares cleaning his nails with a penknife. It's been so long since she felt moved to storm down she doesn't recognize this one.

He looks alarmed. As he should. "I'm sorry?" he asks, flushing.

Qonna ignores him. "Dad?" she yells at the door leading behind the public part of the house. "Dad, I know you're back there!" She takes up her skirts; the Sun tries to block her, but she shoulders him out of the way ignoring his horrified yelp.

"Don't you dare fucking hide!" Her voice echoes through the corridor. However many Suns are on staff these days, they'll all hear her loud and clear. She can be loud when she puts her mind to it. "Daaaad!"

"Back here." He sounds resigned and holds open the door until she reaches him. "Was that necessary? A return message would have sufficed."

"What on earth were you thinking?" She steps into the small room that holds the pricy things, the spices that travelled furthest, the silks and special teas. In the corner stands someone tall and gangly with a lengthy mop of blond curls. "Is that him?"

Her father sighs. "Qonna, this is Cisir da Fewell, my new secretary. Cisir, this is my daughter, Qonnamaris na Qes. I'd hoped for you two to come together in more appropriate circumstances."

Their eyes meet. *Damn him, this is the blue I've always wanted! Like the brightest of dragonflies.*

He blushes and cringes away from her.

None of the young men she was made to curtsey to at the dances ever reacted like that. Perhaps this is because he's on his own and not in a protective gaggle of other men, but though he's taller than her father, he reminds her of a yearling in its awkward phase. As if he hasn't quite grown into his limbs yet.

"Nice to meet you," she says.

"Charmed to make your acquaintance." It's a gallant phrase that would've sounded smarmy coming from many other people, but he manages to expel it in such a way he echoes his education, not a genuine feeling. They stare at each other for a few heartbeats before her father interrupts them by clearing his throat.

"He says he was trained to dance."

"I don't need you to find dance partners for me, Dad. It's not only embarrassing, but creepy."

"But you said …." Her father scowls. "Oh. You said that purely for your mother's benefit?"

"I need her to get off my back. Just because Birkland people tend to be of a different body type …." In the corner of her eye, her would-be dance partner is squirming. He clearly wants to be anywhere but here. Having him witness one of her parental discussions might come in handy later, though. "Have you never felt out of place here?"

Her father crosses his arms. Qonna knows he doesn't want to talk about that—how hard it was for him to grow up in the city, being of mixed heritage, with a father who was often drunk and a mother who left them both behind as soon as a tempting opportunity presented itself. His history is one of the reasons people stare at her so much. In a city addicted to gossip, all inhabitants know of the astonishing rise of Qes na Qarim, a bastard brat from one of the grottiest taverns in Seagard who became the First Sun in residence at the Yellow House, as it is commonly known.

"All the time," her father croaks out, a confession she isn't prepared for. "That's why I want to help. To at least try and make up for all the things you're missing out on because you were born on this side of the ocean and not in the west." He rubs his own arms as if to soothe himself. Or to keep from hugging her. "I'm sorry about this morning, Qonna."

"I know. But jumping in with weird plans to smuggle someone onto the guest list is not helpful. Did you ask him if he wants to attend something so mind-numbingly boring as the Annual Spring Festival Dance of the Westown Guild of Braid Makers? There are so many more diverting options to spend an evening in Seagard. He could explore the Triangle." She shoots Cisir a grin, and he must've had enough time in town by now to understand what she's alluding to. His face resembles a boiled beetroot.

"He was willing," her father mumbles.

"Of course he was willing—he works for you. Only recently joined the Sun, I'd say? He's still on his best behaviour."

As both father and daughter fix their gaze on the secretary, his shoulders collide with the shelf behind him. Right at the top, a wooden box dislodges and tumbles down. It hits him square in the forehead, and with a muffled shout her father's employee crumples at her feet, followed by more boxes raining down on him, bouncing off his back.

Her father stares down, then begins to laugh, while Qonna, attacked by guilt, flings herself down to remove the containers from the poor man. Thankfully they were all locked and none of the spices spilled out. Cisir managed to pull his arms up to shield most of himself, but between his sandy brows the first box' sharp corner has imprinted itself with a deep notch. Blood seeps to the surface, which finally shuts up her father.

"Oh gods." His hand shows dark against Cisir's stubbly cheek as he's about to touch him, but then Cisir's lashes flutter. "Thank the Star. When we promise adventure in the service of the Sun, we don't mean getting knocked out on your very first day. Help me, Qonna."

For such a thin man, Cisir da Fewell is surprisingly heavy, even with both of them heaving him up. When Qonna slides her arm around his back, she can feel him trembling. "I didn't want you to get hurt. Just not dance with me."

"I understand completely." He sounds a bit slurred, and her father keeps his own arm wrapped around him in case he keels over again.

Qonna loosens the outer wrapping that hides her pinned-up braid and starts to dab at the blood.

Cisir whimpers, tries to dodge her hand. "I'm fine."

She pulls a low stool from behind the door and positions it behind him with her right foot. "Sit down. You need to let me see properly. Dad, can you get me some of the apple brandy you keep for when the princes come to visit?"

Her father darts out of the door as soon as his secretary has planted his lean arse on the stool, his knees poking up at sharp angles like a grasshopper's. When she tries to dab again, his hand darts up to catch her wrist. "I'm fine," he repeats. "But thank you. Also, for trying to get me out of the obligation. I didn't know how to deny him."

"He can be thoughtless at times, but usually means well. Which can be more infuriating. Is it very painful?"

"It's …."

"Don't say 'fine.'"

"… bearable? It wasn't such a heavy box."

"It came down with enough force to sweep you off your feet, and you're bleeding. Is this really your first day?"

He blinks. "Yes." He only now seems to notice he's holding her wrist and the blush rushes back.

"Apple brandy!" Her father bolts through the door waving a leather flask. "Took me some time to find it. It's been a while since a Prince of Crooked Hill darkened our doors."

Qonna pulls out the stopper and suppresses a cough as the sharp scent rises. The fumes are enough to make her dizzy as she wets the linen. "This will sting a bit," she warns the man sitting in front of her, his bony knees drawn up to his chin. Sure enough, when she touches his skin with the soaked cloth, he hisses like a cat but tries his best to stay put. His face screws up and the blush leaches away. It's astonishing how quickly he changes colour. "I owe you something for that," Qonna says. "If we don't dance, then perhaps a tour of the city? There are many nooks and crannies you don't get to see if you're new in town. Where are you lodging?"

"At the *Hungry Unicorn* until I can find something cheaper and long-term."

"The *Unicorn*?" Her father sucks air through his front teeth. "That is indeed pricy."

"It was the house recommended by the Sun who interviewed me, Master."

"Huh. He must've seen your name and made the wrong assumption. A friend of mine has recently started renting out rooms and it's not that much further from the bridge."

Qonna frowns at him. "Since when has Uncle Lauron changed his tune? I thought he was dead against taking lodgers?"

"Well, Cisir would be his first. And Lauron is only one part of the whole operation."

"So, *Auntie Garalis* wants to start renting out?" Qonna clarifies.

"They have the space," her father says with a shrug. "Might as well make some money off it."

"Right," she says. "In that case let me be of use and bring him to the *Pear*."

"But I have more hours to work today," Cisir protests.

Qonna glares at her father, daring him to contradict her.

"No," Qes says. "You're done for today. If anything gets you out of packing orders, it's almost being killed by the spice boxes." Her father's mouth hitches up in a smile as he adds, "Take him away, then. We can finish up tomorrow."

# CISIR

## *dearest friend*

It feels as if someone is jabbing him between the brows with every step he takes. The brandy might've cleaned the wound, but it left its sting behind. Cisir's vision flickers. It's like walking through one of those dreams in which nothing makes sense, yet he follows along unquestioningly.

His master's daughter strides beside him, her linen skirts making a soft swishing noise against her legs and sometimes brushing the back of his own. She's tall and the spitting image of her father, with many of the same intonations to her voice. She pushed her sleeves up to reveal strong wrists and muscular forearms, and because she used the outer wrap of her head covering earlier, the loops of her dark braids are visible beneath the thin linen cap she wears, secured with a bow at the nape of her neck.

She should feel naked with her hair almost on display, but she seems utterly comfortable, walking along so confidently. The main road rises beneath their soles, winding its way up from the harbour bridge to the upper quarters, the stretch where the largest houses jostle against each other in an ostentatious show of carving skill and expensive pigments. On his arrival, coming down from the northern gate, Cisir admired all these frolicking animals, flowers, and stars worked into the beams, but on this day they seem painfully bright and feverish.

When his master's daughter turns to squint at his forehead and the scab forming there, she stills. "You're very flushed," she says. "I'm a fast walker, apologies."

He tries to take a measured breath, but it sounds like a pained gasp.

"We'll rest here before we go on to the Triangle." She reaches out to steady him. "You need to take it slow for the rest of the day."

"That wasn't supposed to happen," he groans, barely noticing her hand on his elbow, on the sleeve of the yellow uniform with the embroidered emblem of the sun above his heart. "I was supposed to be a competent scribe today and impress my new master with my diligence and foresight."

She snorts. "Strange how that never works out, hm? Don't worry. My father is no monster. Most of the time he's kind and understanding, and though I really want to strangle him sometimes, he has a much better grip on the situation than my brothers, or my mother."

"You don't get on with your mother?"

"Show me any daughter of marriageable age who truly does? And we live in one of the bigger houses. I can't imagine how it must feel if there's only one room for everyone to sleep in."

Cisir studies her: the soft face, the dark brows. "Do you often try to understand what other people's lives are like?"

"You don't?" She smiles. "Maybe that comes with living in the city proper with all those people milling around. That said, my mother would have a fit if she knew I was running about with my hair on show, and that my father sanctioned a walk into the Triangle after taking such objection to it this morning. He must believe me well-protected with you at my side."

"Not in the state I'm in, surely."

"Oh, he thinks he's done something clever, sending us off together. He must actually believe the only reason I haven't agreed to get myself engaged is because everyone in Seagard is a foot shorter than me."

"That's not the reason?"

It's her turn to blush. "You can't choose who you fall in love with, can you?"

Her words feel like a kick to the heart. "No," he says. "I never could."

Her face brightens. "Have you got someone waiting for you at home? Until you've secured your position and attained the first salary increases to pay for the wedding?"

He frowns; it hurts as the skin between his brows wrinkles. "There's no one who wants to marry me." His throat constricts, but he can't start to sniffle on one of the most prominent street corners of Seagard, in front of his master's daughter. He bites down on his lip to stop the treacherous trembling.

"Oh dear." Her fingers squeeze his elbow. "Trust me to put my foot in it. Everyone has their reasons to come to the Cities. For some it's lack of money, for others lack of love."

"I'm not always this … weak."

"You got thumped in the head today. You're allowed to be anything you want."

He wipes his other sleeve across his face. "That's a lie."

"I only want you to feel better," she says.

"You want to feel less responsible."

Her eyes narrow at him. "Yes."

"I think I'm good to walk on."

"Wait, why did you say that?"

He sighs. "It seems like you feel guilt towards a lot of people. Even if there's nothing you can blame yourself for."

"You know me all of one hour and that's what you come up with?" She sounds taken aback.

The hairs on the back of his neck lift. "It is wrong?"

She stares at him. Her eyes are of the lightest blue, like the underside of summer clouds. *I could've danced with her tonight. Instead, I had to injure myself and fuck it all up from the start.*

"I could say something really mean to you now," she grits out, "but that would hardly be fair. I think I'll wait until we know each other a little better to bring out the big blades."

His heart skips a beat. "You still want us to know each other?"

"If you decide to move into the *Rotting Pear*, we can't avoid it. Uncle Lauron's daughter Gia is my dearest friend."

Cisir has heard much of the Triangle. Its reputation had made its way up to Windyhill, one of the reasons his father never would've accepted this scheme. He would've been sure to see his eldest son buckle under the temptations on offer. Now that Cisir is here, the Triangle seems a bit less clean than the other quarters he's visited so far, but nothing points to the wealth of depravities his parents envisioned. In fact, it's disappointingly empty.

"Where is everyone?"

"It's early," Qonna says. "You'll have to be a bit more careful when you come back from work in the evenings, unless you plan to spend most of your starting salary on dubious pleasures."

*Does she know what she's talking about? And what that does to me?* "I don't plan on that."

She gives him a little shove, clearly forgetting he isn't too sure on his feet. As he stumbles, she blanches. "Oh, shit. Sorry."

He's never heard a woman use such coarse language, but then his master does as well. "It's fine," he says once again, and earns a stern glare.

"I think you need to stop doing that. Nothing is fine. Your forehead has a massive bloody bump on it, for one, and I can't risk you fainting away in the streets. Here we are."

She points to a building that looks as if it's crammed into a space much too small for it; it bulges outwards, ready to spill over. Its roofs are covered in blooming moss and under a recent coat of white paint, a multitude of patchy repairs are visible.

Above the door hangs a wooden shield, festooned with the outline of a pear that has a worm poking out of it. There's a smug smile on the worm's face.

Cisir swallows. "Here we are."

"I'll introduce you to everyone." Again Qonna reaches out, to pull him over the threshold.

The inside of the *Rotting Pear* is painted too, in the same white, against which the dark furniture appears sparse and somehow sophisticated, though scarred from long use. The floor is swept, apart from a sprinkling of dried rosemary on its stones. Clearly no one is expected to spill their drink here. It's oddly clean, but everything points to the fact that this is a recent development.

"They're not really open for business yet," his master's daughter explains. "Gia!" She truly has an excellent voice for yelling. It echoes deep into the *Pear*.

Footsteps on stairs answer her, and in the backdoor of the house appears another young woman, much shorter than her and with a headdress a bit too elaborate for an innkeeper's daughter. Against the cream-coloured linen, her cheeks are darker than anyone else's Cisir has seen in the kingdoms. She's round and soft and beautiful in a way that's wholly unexpected. He watches Qonna and Gia embrace each other. They seem delighted to meet. Jealousy boils up in his stomach, fierce and irrational. He doesn't know either of them. He shouldn't feel so left out. Hopefully, he can blame it on the pain. He's never had a friend who was this glad to see him.

"I bring you my father's latest secretary," Qonna says. "He needs a room to rent, and Father said your mother had the idea to start taking in lodgers."

Gia's gaze lands on his face. "What happened to him?"

"Something fell on his head and he's a bit shaken up."

"Sit down." Gia lays a warm hand on his shoulder and presses him onto a bench. His knees buckle before her.

"I cleaned it up already," Qonna says, and now she seems to be jealous too, of the attention that falls on him.

"You did an excellent job of it," Gia says with a kindness that makes Qonna beam. "We should cool it and try to get the swelling down. I'll get some fresh water from the well." She bustles out, the scent of rosemary wafting, and it only takes a few breaths for footsteps to return—but it isn't Gia who enters the common room. It's a man, lean and with slightly lighter skin than hers, his long brown hair falling down his back to his belt.

"Poor little fucker." In his hand is a scrunched-up piece of paper with Qes na Qarim's scrawl on it. "He's swelling up like a pig's bladder."

"Uncle Lauron, don't make him feel worse." Qonna shifts in front of Cisir, as if he needs shielding.

"Gia will have him fixed up in no time. I asked the boys to move a bed into the spare room for him." His dark-brown eyes latch onto the cut on Cisir's face. "Can't promise you'll find it as comfortable as the *Unicorn*, boy, but at least it won't cost you an arm and a leg." He leans in and pats Cisir's cheek. "I can ask Qes to pay me directly, if that's easier."

"No, that's fine, I'll …." Cisir's mouth has gone dry. Too many beautiful people have poked and prodded him today.

"Father!" Gia smiles at Lauron as she joins them, carrying a bowl and a folded piece of linen. She has the most charming dimples—because Cisir's day isn't rough enough as it is. "I've given the boys blankets and fresh sheets for him."

"Perfect," Lauron grunts. "He looks as if he could use some ale."

"Just water, please," Cisir manages to say.

Lauron grins. "Just water, it is."

His daughter soaks the cloth and squeezes it almost dry. "Hold this against your face."

The linen is deliciously cool, as if his skin is on fire. It strains against his touch, and he goes cross-eyed as he tries to glance up at the three people standing around him. He longs to be held by every single one of them, and if Gia's mother is as warm and gentle as her, he'll be in so much trouble.

*It was supposed to be different. Why can't I be different?*


The room they prepared for him is small, but like most of the house, astonishingly clean, with scrubbed floorboards and a painted wall cloth depicting a pattern of running wolves. The bed is narrow but comfortable, and they've given him a chest for the belongings he needs to collect from the *Unicorn*. It reminds him too much of his room at home in Windyhill, but by this point he's almost given up on reinventing himself anyway.

Qonna sets a jug of water on the windowsill. "Will you be happy here?"

He presses the wet cloth to his face. "I'm never that happy anywhere," he says, before he realizes he meant to say something far less personal. "Thank you. I'm sure you hadn't planned on minding someone who doesn't have enough sense to dodge a spice box today." He turns to Gia and Lauron before Qonna has time to protest. "Thank you," he says again. "This is very nice."

"Then we'll leave you to it. Rest, sleep, get back on your feet," Lauron says. "Girls—" He pulls his daughter away from the door. "Give him space to breathe." He closes the door after them and for a few moments Cisir hears frantic whispering behind it, then finally the women's shoes and Lauron's boots on the stairs.

Cisir takes a deep, shivering breath. The room has a different smell than the common room below, like dried rose petals and other sweetly scented flowers, and it's bright compared to the wood-panelled cell he could afford in the *Unicorn*. It even has a window.

When he steps close to its shutters he can see many roofs, all thatched with straw, but in different stages: some as mossy as the *Pear's*, others much newer, and a few with golden patches where leaks have been repaired.

He stuffs the cloth in the jug to refresh it, watches it unfold in the water with dream-like slowness. This is not what he expected his future to be.

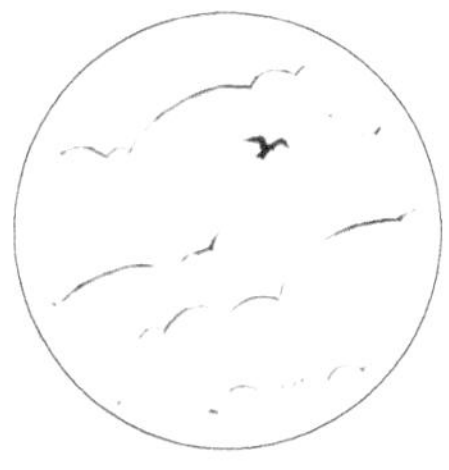

# QONNA

## *tainted by association*

If Gia was with her, they could be talking about what happened at the *Pear* today. Whatever she can say about Cisir da Fewell, never has someone come into her life who brought such a rapid string of events with him, someone who made himself so vulnerable and was so easy to talk to.

She glances along the young men on offer.

The Annual Spring Festival Dance of the Westown Guild of Braid Makers is traditionally held in the guildhall a few steps from the oldest guesthouse in the city, the *Hungry Unicorn*, and somehow it feels strange to know her father's secretary has his effects stashed away in a room there.

*Should I suggest collecting them for him? The* Unicorn *should be open until late. It might provide a great excuse to once again leave early.*

As they like to do, the male dancing partners stand in a big cluster at one wall of the hall that has been decorated with a wealth of flower garlands; its high window shutters were thrown open to let in as much natural light as possible, to avoid lighting the candles and oil lights too early, which would make everyone sweat.

All these men are impossibly young. Most of them must be apprentices of the various dependencies of the kingdom's guilds, but they've been allowed to wear their private fashions for the night, with only the Braid Makers sporting brass pins in the form of a knotted ribbon, the emblem stencilled on every conceivable surface of their hall and woven into the bench covers. The Braid Makers must once have paid a hefty sum to the royal family to secure themselves such an auspicious date for an annual dance, on the eve of an important festival when everyone delights in letting their hair down.

Or almost everyone. Cisir will spend his evening shut away recuperating in the *Pear*, while in its common room drinks and the long-awaited festival foods will be served. No one will allow Qonna to let her hair down either. Earlier, two maids braided and pinned it into submission before bolting down the linen structure she now wears on her head, with folded back corners building up like wings. Or ears, or whatever they were actually meant to look like. At least her mother chose a pale blue linen for the construction; it suits Qonna's skin tone and goes with the dress. A long time ago her mother settled on blue as the colour to dress her one and only daughter, and in her clothes chests are locked away so many shades of it she could mirror the skies in all times of the day and all seasons. Most of the other women wear paler colours, and this year a specific tone of light green seems to be the favourite, probably after one of the princesses wore it to a notable occasion. It doesn't go with all complexions though, and for once Qonna is relieved about her mother's fixation.

Most mothers flock together on the side of the hall, furthest away from the musicians to ensure they can hear each other talk without reverting to screeching. Their daughters stand about in smaller groups, friendship circles, and in that respect Qonna has always drawn the shortest straw.

Gia is not quite of the right class to be welcome at the Braid Makers and as Qonna has no sisters, who else could there be? If she'd been allowed to continue her studies or start any sort of apprenticeship, she might've been able to gather one of those circles around herself, women she knew well enough to talk to about slightly dangerous things, like are they really supposed to be attracted to this line of pasty, snickering boys? Enough to consider marrying one of them?

Qonna tries to throw a glance at her mother without being too obvious. She is being watched all the time. The woven belt stretching under her breasts is too tight, the shoes too flimsy, and she has at least five pins jabbing into her scalp. The most she's likely to get out of the evening is yet another torturous memory of hours feeling useless and wishing to all the gods of the Star Gia would just once be permitted to join her. Then they could make their own huddle and grapple with the important issue: is there any chance Gia could fall in love with the *Pear*'s new lodger?

The thought is so painful Qonna can't quite stifle a gasp. Gia will be the one watching over him now, and how could they not like each other? Gia is so damned easy to love. Qonna bites her lip. *You can't think about that, you soppy bitch. You'll make yourself bawl in front of all the town.*

The musicians come to the rescue. They play flutes, drums, a boxy string instrument, and a couple of small bagpipes. With the starting of the first tune, the whole room shifts around, the most courageous of the men pouncing on the women they've pre-selected.

Qonna steps back from the throng. This is not for her. Though she sees her mother's disappointed face across the hall, she won't court humiliation by pretending to be eager. If Gia was here, they could find so much to talk about, speculating over what truly lies in their future, far away from the Braid Maker apprentices with their first hint of upper-lip fluff who have the audacity to stare at these merchant daughters with proprietorial expectations. Growing up with three brothers, Qonna knows too well how their foot rags will smell after a night of dancing, and that alone is enough to put her off the refreshments available for anyone who prefers to sit out the dances.

Qonna watches pairs forming in front of her, hands finding each other, blushes and smiles rising. *Why do they all look as if they want to be here?* Few of the daughters stayed on her side of the room. One of them is clearly a bit too old for any of the men. She might be one of the younger mothers, but she wears fashionable green and her headdress resembles Qonna's own precarious arrangement. An older sister, perhaps, who serves as the chaperone.

Qonna takes a deep breath, then steps closer. The woman is slender and barely reaches Qonna's shoulder, her face narrow and lined around the mouth. "At least I'm not the only one not enjoying myself," Qonna notes.

The woman barks out a laugh, and the corners of her eyes crinkle up. Her eyes are hazel, her lashes pale. "It is a feat not to succumb to cynicism seeing them all bob about," she says in a cutting voice.

"Are any of them your sisters?"

"Two. Mother is feeling under the weather, so I've been dragged out to keep them under control." She points her chin to two dancing girls, one in soft blue, much lighter than Qonna's dress, and one in madder-red. Both are much younger. "They're my half-sisters by second marriage and usually they do their best not to spend more than half an hour in a room with me. Why do you wish to be anywhere but here, Qonnamaris na Qes?"

Everyone must know who Qonna is. She's always stuck out, and Seagard is too small to keep most secrets. "Because this feels like one of the deepest of all Eight Hells to me, and I'm forced to see the demons dance and play games I don't understand."

"Demons, huh?"

"I wish I was allowed to stay home. Apparently, this is something I need to do as a daughter of Seagard, though there's no way I could ever succeed. I need to let them assess me and judge me too foreign to pay attention to."

A spark of interest lights in her new companion's eyes. "Too foreign?"

Qonna shifts from one foot to the other. "They are aware of the fact that my grandfather came east from Birkland, a place all these men believe to be uncivilized, following customs the priests of the Star never get tired of condemning. All these clerks and apprentices believe me to be tainted by association, and their reputation would come under threat if they asked me to dance."

"I don't know, Qonnamaris."

"Call me Qonna please."

She gifts Qonna a quick curtsey. "I don't know, Qonna. Some of them might be tempted by something they perceive to be in need of taming."

"Those I especially can't stand."

"Fair enough." She inclines her head, and Qonna sees the complicated folds on the top of her headdress. "I for one am honoured to make your acquaintance. Eravis na Eloven."

Qonna has listened to enough of her mother's yammering about her family's station to know that at some point the na Elovens were quite closely related to them. She curtsies too. She must've seen Eravis' half-sisters at many similar events without realizing a blood tie existed between them, however watered down. "You're a cousin of mine."

"Of a sort. All the city's families have married into one another at least once. I defy you to find one among these candidates who hasn't a foot in our family tree. In a way, your heritage should make you a good choice. Get some fresh blood in, so to speak." As Eravis grins, her canines appear, sharp and pointed. "If I'd known I'd find someone this interesting to talk to, I might not have thrown such a tantrum when Mother pulled out."

A glow ignites inside Qonna. Can it be possible that in one day, after all those years of dreading the city dances, she's found a reason to attend?

While the couples sway and twirl, separating themselves only to find themselves again, Qonna feels something extremely unexpected: gratitude. When she glances once again towards her mother, Qonna sees her on the edge of her seat and seemingly perturbed. Qonna has found the one person among the attendees her mother doesn't want her to speak to.


"It took me years to put my foot down," Eravis says in a whisper loud enough for half the hall to hear. "I must admit I was not above using a little blackmail to get out of playing chaperone; it's the most soul-destroying thing I can think of. Getting crampy calves from standing around and waiting for the bagpiper to choke."

Qonna barely suppresses an undignified snort.

They wandered over to the refreshment table to nurse cups of apple juice-flavoured water. The servant would not be prevailed upon to let them have the wine. Qonna is glad of it—the room is getting stuffy.

The shutters are still open, but first lights have been brought in to counteract the darkness falling over the Westown streets outside.

Within the last hour the dances have become faster, the tunes bawdier, and the distance between dancing bodies ever smaller. They all gravitate towards each other in a way Qonna finds difficult to understand, but perhaps they feel a similar elation as when she realized Eravis was genuinely interested in what she thought. Eravis must be ten years older than Qonna and has had ample time to acquire her snark. Qonna appreciates it more than she should.

*Gia would never indulge herself like that. Gia is a much nicer person than I am, and I needed to find someone with a tongue as barbed as my thoughts.*

"He must've flattened her toes by now." Eravis buries a smile in her glazed clay cup. "She looks positively hobbled."

"But he is one of the more attractive ones," Qonna chimes in. "Maybe there's something to be said for dancing through the pain. Whatever can they have to talk about, though?"

"You'll soon find out it's not so much about the words with them. They're both reasonably pretty and that pulls most of the weight." Eravis' gaze swivels towards her sister in red. "I'll have to report back that we might expect a whole throng of apprentices to darken our doors within the next week, trying to out-compete each other for the privilege of submitting their proposals. Ah well—as long as it provides some sort of result, I should be happy. Two weddings to get through and then I can finally put up my feet."

"You never wanted to get married?" Qonna asks.

"Of course I wanted to. When they tell you it's the only thing you're good for, you can't help but dream. But every interaction I've had with my betrothed killed me a little inside. He never had anything to say that didn't concern his work, and there's only so much you can wring out of overseeing the stores at the guild."

"You were engaged?"

"Twice, but I managed to weasel out of both arrangements. Then father got married again and suitably distracted, and when the topic was raised once more, I'd made peace with spinsterhood." She nods towards the dancers again. "Neither of my sisters is prepared to be content with very little. They call me bitter, or tell me my heart has shrivelled to dust, but how often did I see this kind of attraction last? Not enough to be hopeful, and that's the truth of it. One of my dearest wishes is that one of them might surprise me and make a good choice of husband. What would you need to let yourself be persuaded?"

Qonna shrugs in response. She thinks of the young man with the swollen face and the dragonfly-blue eyes who sprawled at her feet today. *He should be what I want. He seems kind, thoughtful, and a bit shy. Awkward even. Of all the candidates in Seagard, Cisir da Fewell should be the most suitable. So why is the thought of him getting close to Gia so much more upsetting to me?*

# CISIR

## *heroics*

Cisir wakes in a strange room. His head pounds in a way that reminds him of the few hangovers he's had in his life. The warmth of the sun brushes the tip of his nose, growing more persistent, and through the open shutter wafts the smell of baking bread.

The room in the *Unicorn* was dingy and dark, while this one reminds him of his grandmother's in Windyhill. For a while he lies here, trying to piece the previous day together. He expected to be overwhelmed by his first day of service under the Sun, but today it seems as if Seagard has already chewed him up; he hadn't been nearly gracious enough in the face of such relentless helpfulness.

When he moves, trying to edge away from the sun spreading its fingers across his sore forehead, pain shoots into each and every limb.

"Do you need me to close the shutters?"

He jerks upright, or tries, anyway.

The young dark-skinned woman, Gia, stands in the doorframe, carrying a steaming bowl of—hopefully—tea. "It's getting quite late, if you're planning on getting to the Yellow House on time."

"I didn't … I didn't hear any bells."

"The eighth bell rang a while ago."

"Oh fuck. Sorry!"

She smiles at him and enters the room, setting the bowl on the clothes chest. "I'm accustomed to coarse language, no need to apologize. Would you like me to take a look at your face?"

He nods, extremely aware he's sitting on the edge of the bed and that his mother would have a conniption knowing her son is in an undeniable state of undress, staring up at a woman slowly drawing close, as if mindful not to scare him too much with her approach. Her hands are warm from the bowl, and he stifles a groan as her thumb brushes the swelling that strains his brow.

"Is it very painful to the touch?" she asks.

"It's fine." He swallows in a sudden flush of dismay. 'Fine' is the word he can't use much anymore. "It's bearable," he corrects. "Does it look bad?"

"As if someone kicked you in the head," Gia says bluntly. As the daughter of a Triangle innkeeper, she must know what she's talking about. "I can ask Dad to send word to the bridge," she offers.

"No. Thank you so much, but I can't not work on my first *two* days in Seagard."

To his astonishment and horror, she sits down next to him. Though an arm's length of space separates them, he can smell the rosemary clinging to her, and also something more corporeal. It's as if little flames are licking up his bones.

*Don't be stupid. She's just being kind.*

"Why?" she asks. "Do you need the coin so badly?"

"I have to pay for room and board at the *Hungry Unicorn*, so yes."

"I'm sure the Company of the Sun can come to an arrangement with them. I'm also sure Uncle Qes would rather have a healthy secretary than someone who's in danger of fainting over the inkhorns."

"Please forgive me, but I'll have to hear him say that. He's the master I've been given to."

She reaches out and briefly pats his knee, and suddenly the agony has yet another flavour. "I understand," Gia says. "There's enough water in the jug for washing, and the uniform seems clean enough. I'll send one of the boys to pick up your belongings from the *Unicorn* if you wish. Otherwise, they might want to charge you for an additional day."

"That's very thoughtful, thank you so much."

*Please touch me again. Oh, please don't.*

"I'll arrange it," she promises. "Drink your tea, and I'll have some bread ready for you when you come down. You need breakfast." She rises, pulling away from him, taking the rosemary scent with her.

He manages to make himself a bit more presentable, and too soon the stairs creak under his weight. He can't remember walking up them the day before; he's missing a chunk of memory, including the whole period the *Rotting Pear* was open for business. It's empty again; a broom made from birch twigs leans against one of the benches and Gia is crouched down, in the process of transferring dirt, crumbs, and old herbs into a bucket. It must be one of her daily chores before the house opens. Another bucket stands at the ready, smelling strongly of vinegar.

As Cisir approaches, she puts down the wooden shovel with the crumbs. "There you are." She sounds relieved, as if she hadn't believed him capable of making good on his decision.

She turns around and takes a packet from one of the tables, wrapped tightly in waxed cloth. It feels squishy and warm: a rolled-up bread, hopefully with some sort of filling.

"Thank you so much," he says again.

She smiles the soft, easy smile that sets his heart aflutter. "You're part of the family now," Gia says. "We protect our families with everything we have, don't we?"

*Part of the family*? "I suppose?"

"I hope you have a good day—and please don't bump your head again."

Cisir walks through a town eager to celebrate spring. Garlands are draped over doorways; a string of vendors is selling seasonal delicacies, and the air of excitement is at odds with the slowness of his steps. His head feels twice the size, as if it could tumble off his neck at any moment.

*This is stupid. You should've stayed in bed, being watched over by a kind, beautiful woman.*

But the other voice in his head belongs to his father. It speaks of duty and honour, of serving a family name that has always caused more problems than it could solve. Up in Windyhill there's worth attached to it, though also enough history to make people wary. In Seagard, all everyone seems to hear is the *da*, and he can wriggle all he likes.

The sun blazes on wet cobblestones, as if the gods of the Star wish to grace the day of the festival. It's already warm enough to make him sweat, and as the ninth bells begin to sound in the Westown he has almost reached the quay.

He's early enough to see the door of the House of the Sun swing open and the strange little doorstopper be pushed in place. The Sun unlocking the house stares at him. "Fuck me—I hope the other guy looks worse than you."

"I'm sorry?" Cisir asks, confused.

"I'll get you a cool cloth, mate. That needs some attention." The Sun stands aside to let him pass into the blessedly dark interior of the house, but Cisir manages to catch his heel on the sandstone dog and almost pitch in head-first.

"Careful, mate. No use to us if you smash yourself to bits."

Cisir thanks him because he always thanks everybody, then pushes on towards the First Sun's study. He had hoped his master would be late today, but there he is, sitting at the narrow desk in the middle of the room; behind him is the window Cisir spent so much time waiting at on his first day.

"I thought you might show up," Qes na Qarim says. "Most new Suns tend to be overeager. How do you feel?"

*Ready to cry.* "Fine, Master."

"You don't seem fine. Sit yourself down, boy." Qes stands and pushes his own chair towards Cisir, though there's a perfectly serviceable stool in the corner.

*It would be rude to refuse.*

His master manoeuvres him into place with a hand on his shoulder.

*Are all people from Birkland this confident to touch strangers?* What if he were to turn around and hug this man? Would he be pushed away?

The chair meets his backside, and he closes his eyes.

*Stop it. Stop it now. You made it to work. Just be happy you're here.*

"For his face." The voice of the Sun at the door rouses him.

"Thank you." Qes na Qarim takes the folded cloth, gives it another squeeze, then steps close to press the wet fabric onto Cisir's forehead. It's a surprisingly gentle pressure, as if he can perfectly gauge the pain radiating through Cisir's skull. "We need to keep an eye on you. Unnecessarily heroic, as Father would have said."

A drop of water dislodges from the cloth and trickles down Cisir's cheek. His master wipes it away as if it were a tear. He must've had reason to soothe his daughter when she was small.

"I'm sorry," Cisir says, his throat closing up.

"For what?"

"For being so useless. This isn't why you took me on."

Qes na Qarim grins at him. "You were injured in the service of the Sun. A warehouse accident. Happens more than you would think. All members of the Sun are entitled to full pay while recovering from work-related injuries."

"The Sun at the door thought I'd been in a fight."

"You might want to let him believe it. Could make things easier for you."

"In what way, Master?"

"In the don't-fuck-with-him way." Qes takes the cloth away, turns it over, and uses the colder side on him. "Don't worry, boy. We'll take care of you. Qonna would never forgive me if I let someone bully you. You should count yourself lucky. She's never shown much interest in a man before."

"Because she felt sorry for me."

"That can still be the start of something. Would make for a better story than how I met my wife."

At least the cloth hides some of Cisir's blush. "Your wife, Master?"

"Father was quite set against her, so our engagement came with trouble attached. I think he wanted to save my soul or something, and though I explained my position until I was blue in the face, he always believed I should've waited for love. Coming from Birkland, he might not have realized how little love would've helped secure our name in the city. My betrothal was a smart decision, but heart had nothing to do with it."

Cisir squirms. This is more information than he ever wanted to hear about his master's private life.

Qes sighs. "Sometimes I regret not having a cute story to tell, but you will have noted most things in the Cities are about money. We made it work in the end and three sons are preparing themselves to become part of the Company. You'll meet them soon."

*Qonna's brothers. Gods help me if they are as beautiful as she.* "I look forward to it."

"I think my father would've had a snarky remark for you. He wasn't always civil."

"It sounds as if you miss him, Master."

Qes na Qarim withdraws abruptly from his side. The cloth detaches from his face with a faint sucking noise, like a chaste kiss. "My father … he was infuriating but he brought his heart into the Company of the Sun, and I still feel it around me. Did you know this house, or at least the oldest part of it, belonged to him? Once it was the *Sprat and Crab*, a tavern he ran with my mother. I worked here since I could walk. Father rented it out to the Princes of Crooked Hill when the Company was founded, and they took us on and trained us. Can you imagine—a man from Birkland and his half-blood son in charge of a royal enterprise?" He chuckles. "It ruffled quite a few feathers back then and continues to do so. By becoming part of the Sun, you become part of its history and should be aware of it. Things might seem a bit unconventional from time to time. This is because of my father. He brought Birkland values to the Sun and despite what the priests of the Star would have you believe, Birklanders are the most family-oriented people there ever were."

"The Princes agree with the methods?"

"You can ask them yourself one day."

"Master?"

"They pop in from time to time, to let me catch them up on things. One of the ships we await is under the direct command of one of them, so it hopefully won't be long until you make your first acquaintance with our royal highnesses."

"Do they consider themselves part of the family too?"

"They should be." Qes na Qarim laughs. "Otherwise, the whole Company of the Sun is set to fall apart." He inclines his head. "Your eyes are clearer."

"I feel much better, thank you."

"Would you be up for a little light copying?" Qes retrieves a thick scroll from the shelf in the corner behind him. "You've seen my handwriting. Do you think you can decipher a few of the more important documents and get them into better shape? And later there are forms to set up and I'd rather have them in your hand than mine."

"Of course, Master."

"Excellent. We'll get you more parchment and an assortment of quills and reed pens you can cut to your specifications. You don't need to rush today. It might be wise to avoid another accident."

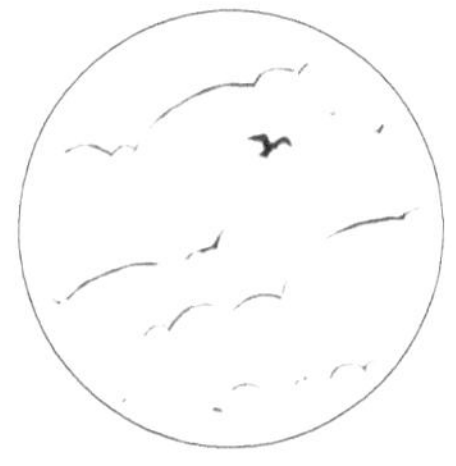

# QONNA

## *claimed to be ignorant*

He seems sweet."
Something curdles in Qonna's stomach. "I'm not saying he isn't, Gia."

Her best friend arches a brow at her. "What are you afraid of?"

*She knows me too well.* Qonna swallows. "You might end up liking him more than me."

"He's our lodger."

"And someone suitable to marry."

"Yes." Gia sighs. "For either of us."

"But I don't … I don't want to marry. I need more time before …."

"You're almost twenty. You should've been engaged by now. Your parents are doing you a favour, and you could make a worse choice than allowing yourself to be betrothed to someone shy and kind."

"Wouldn't that be a problem for you?"

Gia laughs. "I don't want to marry him either! I'm playing a long game."

Sour spit rises into Qonna's mouth. "Are you hoping for Pjer to change his mind? After all this time?"

Her best friend blushes. "I'm certainly still in love with him, if that's what you mean."

Pjer has darkened Qonna's future for years. The only good thing about him is that he isn't from Seagard but Applebeck, working for the Star's temple and delivering their consignments of cider and brandy. Ever since Gia mentioned the pretty boy rolling the casks through the narrow streets of the Triangle, Qonna has hated him, although they've never met. It's been a while since he appeared in their conversation and—if she's being completely honest with herself—she'd hoped he'd left his job for something more prestigious and married a fair maid from Applebeck to become someone else's problem.

Gia reaches out to touch her elbow. "I'm determined to marry for love," she says, as if that makes things any easier. "With no brothers around to take over the *Pear*, I'm a good prospect for Pjer. He's in the business and the *Pear*'s reputation has changed so much. We're taking in sons from distinguished families to lodge with us." She gives Qonna's arm a stronger pat. "Why won't you consider him? He'll make his way in the Sun, and he's young. If your father gives him his favour …."

*Because I want to marry for love too. Because I probably could do so in Birkland, but here at home there's no chance for me.*

Gia is even more of the old country than Qonna, but she appears happy to not waste time on regrets. Most of what Qonna knows about Birklandish customs is dangerous and has come to her via Uncle Lauron's stories, and though they've never openly talked about it, Gia must be aware of them too. Gia grew up with tales of women wielding swords, words, and political power, of opportunities to fight werebears, waterhorses, and other monsters.

When they were younger, they both were unsatisfied with the fate awaiting them in the Cities, and perhaps it rankles so much because Gia is the one who clearly has made her peace with Seagard, waiting for someone like the infernal Pjer to notice what kind of woman he once rejected, the weaselly little shit.

Qonna remembers the few months in which Gia was easily moved to tears and spent hours moping about until Qonna grew impatient and reluctant to be around her oldest friend.

*It was always rather one-sided,* the mean voice in her head reminds her. *Gia told you of all the Pjers she met, but have you ever been honest with her?*

How can Qonna be honest if she doesn't know how she feels herself? As wonderful as this opportunity is to see more of Gia, throwing Cisir's status in the mix is likely to cause strife between them. They both proclaim not to have designs upon her father's secretary, but Gia's heart might turn around one day and find something in those startling eyes to latch on to.

*Do they make him prettier than me?*

Gia's gaze has turned inward, as if she's considering similar prospects. Or dreaming of straddling Pjer and riding him into the sunset. Qonna stares into the dregs of her tea bowl.

*I should go. Leave her to dream.*

Gia lifts the teapot. "Want some more?"

"Yes, please." *Twat. That was your chance to escape.*

The tea has cooled since they'd sat down at the small table Uncle Lauron had shoved into the back corner for the *Pear*'s staff to use, but its fragrance has intensified. Gia's mother holds strong opinions on cleanliness and the quality of the beverages on offer. Gia sets down the pot again when a boy appears at the door, red in the face and breathing hard.

"Mistress Giannis?" He pulls a heavy leather bag from his back.

"Excellent!" Gia pushes herself up from the table. "Is that all or do you need to go back to the *Unicorn*?"

"That's all, mistress."

"Put it there, thank you. I'll get you a sweet bun for your troubles and you can seek out Mother."

He performs a quick bow and as soon as Gia's back is turned, shoots Qonna a grin, much at odds with the previous display of politeness. Whatever respect the boy holds for Gia, he obviously doesn't feel the same way about a woman who isn't supposed to give him orders. It's an attitude Qonna's quite familiar with, but it irks her. She bares her teeth at him in imitation of a wolf's snarl. He yips and pushes through to the kitchen, eager to claim his bun.

Qonna is left to watch the leather bag dumped on the bench closest to her. Her fingers itch to loosen the straps and delve in, though it might hold little more than spare foot rags, smallclothes, and a greasy comb.

Gia saves her by coming back from the kitchen.

"He could've brought it upstairs for you," Qonna says.

Gia lifts her shoulder. "But then we wouldn't have an opportunity to have a good look at it."

Blood rushes into Qonna's face. At least they think in similar ways.

Gia hooks a finger into the buckle, then rummages through without any show of guilt. "Spare shirt and trousers, foot rags—all reasonably clean—a brush and comb, two scarves for winter, and a thicker cloak with a family sigil stitched on it." She shakes out the fabric and reveals a round emblem, but it's one Qonna has never seen. She's familiar with the bull's head of the da Relians, the kestrels that are all that remains of the family that once built the house she was born in, and her mother's unicorn, but Cisir's family sigil is an owl with lowered wings, its round eyes staring accusingly at them.

"Huh," Gia says. "Quite a few bundles of letters too, and re-used parchment, wrapped in a faded silk braid."

"Put them back," Qonna squeals. "This is going too far."

"You don't want to know if they're love letters?"

"Fuck, no!"

It's been a long time since she's used this kind of language on her friend. Gia's smile falls and she drops the letters as if they're about to explode. The game has come to an abrupt end.

Gia stuffs the cloak back into the bag; a muscle tics in her dark cheek as she closes the straps again. "You're very defensive of his privacy."

"As you should be. He's your lodger, and he's already told me he has no sweetheart waiting for him at home. If these are love letters, they surely won't contain fond memories."

"He told you?" Gia sounds intrigued. "It appears your acquaintance has already progressed quite nicely."

"This is as far as it will go," Qonna says firmly.

Gia arches her left brow. "You say that now."

"I say that now and I promise you I will say it in a year's time. I need to go."

Qonna's mother does not ask any questions when Qonna enters *Pomegranates'* sitting room shortly after. The eternally present embroidery frame stands aside and her mother is taking her own tea. On the wooden stand next to her rests the Book of the Star. She likes to use her time away from the needle to read her favourite passages. It's the same copy Qonna was given to study and copy out whole sections from, and the mere sight of it makes the hairs on the back of her neck rise with resentment.

She crosses the room in four strides to reach her father's study where the rest of *Pomegranates'* library is housed. She knows she saw the book she needs only a few weeks before, and she finds it exactly where she hoped it would be. It's big and a bit ratty, as if her father once bought it as part of a whole shipment without being able to check it before his purchase. The ink is quite faded but it's more colourful than any other book she's ever been allowed to open.

Every page showcases a different family sigil with a short description underneath. The map bound into the frontmatter is long out of date; the boundaries between the Eight Kingdoms have long since shifted and Seagard itself isn't even marked, though if she squints and brings the page up close, she can see *The Hungry Unicorn* scrawled in, and a second notice that mentions the prince's house on the hill, with a curious assembly of lines next to it that seem to denote some sort of monument.

There's no logical order to the sigils and she has to thumb two-thirds through the book before she comes upon the owl with its spread-out wings. Drawn on parchment, it's a bit more elegant and less cross-eyed: DA FEWELL.

Compared to other families of the Hillakes and Southclere, there isn't much information on the da Fewells, but it still comes to several pages. Qonna quickly skims through, curious if any words snag, but the writer's hand is old-fashioned and rather imprecise, so she soon has to start again. For some reason, she imagined Windyhill to be a quaint little hamlet, but it turns out the settlement was quite substantial during the time the book was compiled, situated in the corner where three kingdoms meet: the Hillakes to the north, Rosevale to the west, and Greenclere above. It's described as overlooking wooded valleys and powerful rivers, and that the tower of Windyhill House was once believed to be the highest for many leagues around and home to owls of all descriptions.

Why does someone from Windyhill need to come so far south? The court of Crooked Hill is much closer and surely provides more opportunities. Cisir is old enough to carry a host of unpleasant memories, but travelling all this way to distract himself ….

*Your grandfather once did the same. Though Dad never talked about the specific reasons why he left Birkland in such a hurry. It must've been bad.*

The book lists a few illustrious ancestors, and he isn't the only da Fewell to bear his first name. She comes across it in every generation. *First son, then. Or the first to survive. If he's to inherit all that property, why gamble it away?*

Her own brothers are sure to take over *Pomegranates* before long; that's how it works in the Eight Kingdoms, though her own family's situation is unusual in some respects. Though her brothers will manage it, the house might not ever be owned by them. With her grandfather's death, the Yellow House has become theirs, as well as the quarterly rent paid by the Company of the Sun, but *Pomegranates* and the study she sits in at this very moment have always been Birklandish handouts shrouded in mysterious circumstances.

As the presumed heir of Windyhill, Cisir could have his pick of noblewomen. He would've been as much out of his element at the Braid Makers' dance as Gia, and the book revealed him to be far too ambitious a prospect for either of them. It feels like relief as it dawns on her. There are too many arguments against him promising his hand to a trader's daughter, much less to the *Rotting Pear.*

She snaps the book shut and turns around. She'll show her father all she found today, and he'll back off.

Qonna stills a step away from the door. She doesn't particularly want her mother to be part of yet another tricky conversation. She huffs to herself. Better give her mother a few days to cool off after

Qonna didn't dance to a single tune at the Braid Makers' and spent her whole evening laughing with an even older spinster.

She walks back to the table her father uses as a desk and pushes some of the clutter out of the way: the broken shell he liberated from the Yellow House, flushed pink and cool inside but spiky and gnarled on the outside, a rusty penknife and a flurry of quill shards, a bit of ink-stained sand.

Once again, she searches through the book for the owl sigil. The spine gives a damning crack as she opens the book before her father's empty chair. A lot of dust puffs from its pages, making her sneeze. She lifts her sleeve to wipe her face as her gaze falls on the last paragraph of the da Fewell entry.

She hadn't noticed it at first, added in another hand: *During the time of treaties, the da Fewells made a point of strengthening their Rosevalian ties, and it's widely believed they were about to betray the kingdom and push their own claim to the throne against their royal relatives. When the last treaty was signed and the new borders established, the whole family swore ignorance of such plans.*

The time of treaties lies far enough in the past to mean very little to her, but surely since then the kings and queens of Crooked Hill have done their best to keep their pesky cousins in line. She glares down at the book with its disintegrating spine and stained pages.

*Cousins.*

# CISIR

## *customs*

The ship the Sun has been waiting for reaches Seagard two days later. A shiver runs through the whole house and Cisir looks up from the section of the scroll he's been copying all morning to see the Sun on counter duty—Hevo?—burst into the room, startling his master enough for Qes na Qarim to drop the folder with the latest orders. Qes curses as they flutter around his feet like a swarm of stripy butterflies. "Eight fucking Hells!"

"A sighting!" Hevo pants, bright red in the face and beaming. "The *Buttercup* returns!"

His master steps over the mess of spilled order forms and runs from the study, leaving his befuddled secretary behind, until Hevo comes back and yells, "You too. Come and see!"

Cisir dries the quill, secures the scroll, and unfolds himself from his stool. Cheers echo through the House of the Sun as men stream from all its nooks to make their way into the front rooms and out onto the harbour bridge. Cisir easily looks over their heads and what he sees is quite a letdown: a tiny speck on the horizon.

He stands behind the other Suns, trying to make out how on earth anyone could see a particular ship in this smallest of blobs, but suddenly something winks at him, something yellow, like the flash of a golden coin. His jaw sinks as he realizes the whole ship is painted yellow and sailing under a brisk wind that carries it towards Seagard with more speed than he'd thought possible. A few breaths later he spies the monstrous sun painted on its main sail, straining against its sheets.

The *Buttercup* is smaller than the Bulls' vessel he's stared at each time he's walked from the main road towards the Yellow House, and it soon weaves closer to the port where it once started its long journey.

None of the Suns make an excuse to return to their work; every single one of the men dressed in the linen uniform gawks at the approaching ship, follows its swift manoeuvres. A fleet of smaller boats are made ready to meet the *Buttercup* and tow her into the harbour, the rowers taking their places on the benches with excitement. Some of them might have invested in the voyage a full year ago and are now seeing their dreams come true.

Cisir leans against the doorjamb, halfway in the house as he watches his master clap the backs of the Suns surrounding him, exchanging congratulations as if they themselves sailed into the west.

The closer the vessel comes, the clearer they see the state of her. The yellow paint hangs in strips, the sails are tattered, and the sun on the main sail carries the scars of many repairs. Two of her masts have been stabilized with ropes and splints. The *Buttercup* has been batted about and still makes a triumphant return. A soon as the rowboats reach her, men climb aboard, and Cisir spies wineskins making rounds among the crew. None of the sailors are in uniform, but some men are dressed in signature Sun yellow and bronzed by the elements. More cheers can be heard from the ship and Qes na Qarim slumps forward.

All signs point to a successful endeavour, a result likely to affect the rest of Cisir's first year in the Company. His master spins around to catch his secretary's eye. It's as if a great weight has been lifted off him. The lines in his face have miraculously filled in and there's a glow to his smile that reminds Cisir too much of his daughter. How would he have reacted if the *Buttercup* had been lost in the crossing?

Cisir has copied out too many notices of vessels presumed missing; he already knows that last year wasn't a good one for the Sun. Today will provide a welcome reprieve.

"The prince!"

The shout rises from the quay, from the crowd of onlookers that have come together to watch the latest joyful arrival. "The prince, the prince!"

Cisir cranes his neck.

In the first boat rowing ashore sits someone in a green cloak, hood pulled over their head. Qes shoulders Suns aside and snatches Cisir's sleeve before pulling him out of the house and onto the cobbles. The soles of their boots slap on the rounded stones as they hurry along, and finally Cisir gets caught up in the excitement.

His heart gives a painful jump as they slip into the crowd. People shove him from all sides, not only men working at the harbour, but women too. Some of them might be here to welcome back husbands sailing on the *Buttercup*, others may have speculated and now see their hopes restored after months of anxious waiting for news of disaster.

Many of them try to touch his master as they push through. Cisir finds himself acting as a shield for the man who took him on mere days ago. They finally come close to the quay side where the first passengers are climbing a rope ladder to dry land.

The prince in his green cloak comes first, round-faced and pale, much younger than Cisir expected him to be, with eyes as green as gooseberries and exhaustion etched into his face. Qes na Qarim surges forward to extricate the prince from the press of the crowd and Cisir shelters them both, or at least tries to—he has trouble keeping up. More Suns move towards them to form a corridor and let them pass. The noise falls away and they duck into the Yellow House, breathlessly waiting for the Prince of Crooked Hill to have the first word.

He's small and stocky under the richly dyed cloak, the backs of his hands and face freckled. He was probably the only clean-shaven one among the *Buttercup*'s passengers and perhaps this is what makes him appear so much younger than he should.

"Lilyis," Qes na Qarim says. "Welcome home."

Cisir can't help but stare at the person standing before them. Though his master called them by a woman's name, the prince who peels themself out of the hooded cloak has the beginning of evening stubble and despite wearing a long tunic that can be mistaken for a dress at first glance, the body beneath it sends a different signal. Lilyis wears their hair waist-long and intricately braided in a style no man in Seagard would get away with. Threads of grey are barely noticeable among the rings decorating it, the pins topped with golden snail shells. Though the prince's colouring is of the Cities, bright green eyes and chestnut-red hair, their clothes are so *other*, from the colours down to the cut.

"Don't mind my secretary," Qes na Qarim says with a side glance. "He's adjusting."

Beads of sweat break out along Cisir's hairline. "I'm sorry," he croaks.

The prince flashes a smile at him, but it's strained. "It'll take me a few days to acclimatize to this gods-forsaken place again." Lilyis' voice is deeper than Cisir expected. "Did you have any more problems with the Brothers, Qes?"

His master grunts. "They got a bit cocky last winter, trying to renegotiate contracts."

"Fucking priests," the prince bites out. "I'll ask Father to send a strongly worded letter, which will give them something to whine about. Is there tea?" Their eyes land on Cisir and he almost swallows his tongue.

"I'll get some for you, Your Highness."

"Good boy."

Before Cisir can escape their presence, his master catches his sleeve again. "Don't talk to anyone about the prince—not even your colleagues."

"Understood, Master."

"I'll answer any questions you might have later."


When Cisir comes back, balancing a tray with bowls, the teapot, and a plate of sesame biscuits, both his master and the prince have settled down behind the study's desk, flipping through a sheaf of blotchy scrolls. Qes na Qarim seems barely able to contain his glee.

"That is extraordinary—and there really is enough to fill a whole third tower at the Harp?"

"We might need a fourth soon." The prince seems equally smug. "I was able to get the administration centre to approve a fixed rent for twenty years. Also, before I forget, I brought a whole host of letters and presents for your family."

"Did you manage to spend much time with them?"

"You know Sloe. They can't keep their nose out of anything that sounds remotely interesting. I think they're stretching themself awfully thin and we had a talk about it." The prince groans in frustration before turning to Cisir. "The tea might get cold if you don't get your courage up to interrupt us, boy."

"Apologies, Your Highness." The bowls rattle when Cisir sets them down, then tries not to brush the prince's arm as he lays out the repast.

"I'm not going to bite you," the prince says.

"That's not …."

Qes snorts. "Stop fucking with him, Lilyis. He's already spooked, and I want to keep him for a while." His master takes Cisir's elbow when the tray is empty. "Sit with us. Lilyis was telling me that our storage space in Birkland is growing by the year. Excellent news. Oh, and that the *Buttercup* is crammed with casks of syrup, pelts, and silver from the eastern mountains."

Cisir watches in dismay as his master takes it upon himself to pour out the tea, fishing Cisir's used bowl from his desk space to serve him. "Master …."

"You strike me as a reasonable young man," Qes says. "You must've had some thoughts about coming to Seagard to work in a Company that specializes in trading with the far west. Have you done any research into what might await you here?"

"A bit."

"You must've made yourself familiar with Birklandish customs."

The prince balances their hot bowl on one knee, listening with a tilted head, as if there could be no finer entertainment than witnessing Cisir being schooled.

"I did," Cisir admits.

"Then you'll have prepared yourself to work with and for people who are attracted to the opportunities Birkland offers."

"It seems life is very different in the far west, Master." Cisir hates how squeaky his voice is, how his heart picks up.

"It is," the prince agrees. "Some of us prefer to spend as much time there as we possibly can."

Qes shoots them an irritated glance. "Be gentle," he warns.

"Fine." The prince takes an exaggerated sip of tea. "While in Birkland, I am known as Lilyis and reside in the House of Women. While on the Continent, I must resign myself to be Nian da Nileon, Prince of Crooked Hill, but my dear brother-in-law affords me the courtesy of calling me by the name I prefer."

"Your brother-in-law?" Cisir gasps.

Qes groans. "That might've been the straw that broke the donkey's back. It's a bit more complicated, and we'll have time to get into it later. Drink your tea, Cisir. It would be a shame to waste it."

"How … how should I address you then, Your Highness?" Cisir asks, lifting the bowl.

"Please call me Lilyis. Think of it as a nickname if that helps."

"And do you wish me to address you as a woman?"

A faint flush blooms on the prince's cheeks. "Amongst ourselves, please do. Amongst your colleagues … they must've heard some rumours, but it's safer to keep the truth from them."

"I understand, Your Highness."

Qes breathes out, relieved. "That's what I hoped for—someone sensible and kind. Well done, boy."

Cisir's head starts to spin. A few short weeks ago this situation would've been too fantastical to consider, but in the study he works in sits a real Prince of Crooked Hill, who actually is someone else and perhaps feels as pushed aside as Cisir himself most of the time. He gulps down the tea, though it's a bit too hot and burns the roof of his mouth. He can feel both his superiors studying his reactions. He might have fulfilled his master's hopes, but it's odd to be rewarded merely for being decent to someone who could have him sacked on the spot.

"Do you still have inventory to check?" Qes asks quietly. "Perhaps you could do that now. We might have to rearrange some things to make the incoming goods fit."

"Yes, of course." Cisir puts down the half-emptied bowl, bows, and flees the room.

As the door closes behind Cisir, he notices that he's shaking. Sending him out of the study was meant as a favour. The corridor is empty save for himself; he can hear the other Suns whooping and laughing somewhere in the building. None of them will do much work after toasting the Company's success. Should he press his ear to the door and continue to listen?

*Don't be stupid. They have plenty of private matters to discuss, and none of them are your business.*

Cisir puffs up his cheeks and slowly releases the breath, trying to calm himself.

It's true that he tried to find out why Birkland takes such pride of place in the warnings of the priests. Hearing Lilyis side against them confirms that the secret he just became a part of is very dangerous indeed.

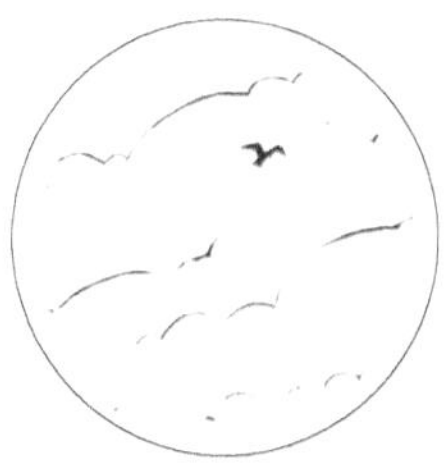

# QONNA

## *the wayward prince*

The news of the *Buttercup*'s safe return to Seagard spreads through town within hours. Qonna hears it from the cook as she seeks her out to discuss the next month's budget for breads, meats, and spices. The cook can barely keep her voice from squealing.

"… much more than anticipated, and almost all of them came home safely!"

"That's tremendous. My father is sure to arrange a celebratory dinner." If the *Buttercup* is back that likely means a visit from the wayward prince. Qonna forces herself to breathe deeply to contain her excitement. When the prince returns, there are always gifts involved. The last time he brought her a necklace made from polished shells, translucent and pearlescent, far too ostentatious for her to ever wear in public, and yet another reminder of what waits for her on the other side of the sea if she could only sneak out of this house, disguise herself, and … the excitement sours.

Princes are allowed to spend most of their lives abroad if they so wish, but a trader's daughter born in Seagard? This city won't change enough within her lifetime to ever allow her to pursue it. The pull of ancestral lands is for her brothers to explore, when they inevitably go on their first expeditions with the Sun.

The cook studies her face, as if waiting for her to say something to end their interaction. Qonna makes herself smile and retreats into the corridor.

*This is going to be your life, whatever you do. You either continue to help in* Pomegranates *or you'll run your own house one day. All that's left for you is to decide if you'll let yourself be married off. Fuck.*

As usual, her mother has installed herself behind her embroidery, her current project close to being finished; the small basket with loops of silken thread sits beside her.

"The *Buttercup* has made its way back to Seagard," Qonna says, entering the room.

Her mother's headdress wobbles. "Can we at least hope the prince has stayed behind in the west?" Her voice carries deep disapproval. The last thing she wants is to open *Pomegranates* to someone with that reputation. Too many rumours about Nian da Nileon have made the rounds.

"I'm not sure, Mother."

Qonna's mother turns around in her seat, her pale face a mask of displeasure. "When will your father learn that allowing him to visit is the worst thing he could do to his family?"

*The worst thing? Really?* "Why?"

Her mother draws in a sharp breath. It was a mistake to ask. Qonna earned herself a sermon. "Of all the men your father ever had the misfortune to be acquainted with, Nian da Nileon is the most unsavoury. The manner in which he treated his poor wife—banished her to the east to serve his sister. It was shameful, and he shows not a single scrap of remorse, gallivanting across the world to seek out depravity." This sounds as if her mother plucked it straight from the mouth of a priest. Brother Rago is prone to similar outbursts, and her mother surely visited the Westown temple more than once this week. No one could keep her from hearing the priest condemning the joyful atmosphere of the upcoming spring celebrations.

She's far from finished with Qonna. "You will do yourself a favour and plead a headache if your father conceives the idea to host another one of those infernal welcome meals. He should've had the good sense to keep you away from him and his damnable bribes." These are more passionate feelings than Qonna has heard her mother express in a long time. Usually, her words are as cold and sharp as her embroidery scissors.

Qonna can't help but fan the flames. "Bribes?"

"What would you call the heathenish monstrosity he had the audacity to present to you last time? So unsuitable, it begs belief. How would you ever be able to show yourself in such hideousness?"

"But you wear your pearls, Mother." Qonna nods towards the long string wrapped thrice about her neck. "How is that different from shells on a string?"

"Qonnamaris!" Her mother's voice is the crack of a whip. Qonna has gone too far. "What possesses you to compare my most precious heirloom to cheap, savage ornamentation? Go to your room. I do not want to see you again today."

"But …."

"Qonnamaris na Lorian na Qes—" Her full name, complete with both denotations of lineage, always means the game has come to an end.

Qonna withdraws.

When she passes through the first floor corridor, she peers down into the yard through its open shutters. *Pomegranates'* stables are small, so they only keep two donkeys for the servants to run their errands, though she sees the gleaming coats of three horses tied fast to the wall, brought over from one of Seagard's liveries, waiting for her brothers to go on an adventure. Qonna never properly learned to ride.

While her brothers occupy the bedrooms in the attic, Qonna's room lies adjacent to the dining room, with easy access in case she's needed by her mother. Through Qonna dearly loves the house, today it feels like a cell. There's no chance for her to sneak out and see Gia and Cisir, and given the big news, her father is likely to come home late. He won't realize she was put away to brood over her urge to provoke her mother.

The maids have tidied up after her. The bed is freshly made, all clothes packed away, her three books neatly repositioned on the shelf. The room is swept and dusted, so she has nothing to do but sit and stare out the window. If she strains her ears she can hear music drifting over the roofs. Someone is practicing the lute. It's a gentle pursuit. She might've learned to play, if her mother hadn't ruled it out. Brother Rago is suspicious of music, so she must be too.

Thin scraps of melody bring tears to her eyes. Seagard always felt unfair; it's nothing new to cry about. She had no reason to poke holes in her mother's arguments; she just has this need to point out a wrong and it won't leave her in peace.

Shouts and clattering from the yard wipe away the music. Her brothers are departing, probably meeting up with friends outside the city walls to go hunting or merely for a long, exhausting gallop.

*You stupid, stupid cow. This misery is all your fault.*

The knock rouses Qonna from fitful sleep. *Trust you to nod off when you're sulking.*

"Yes?" She hastily pulls her headdress straight.

"I hope I'm not interrupting. Your father sent me to fetch you."

She gawps at the Prince of Crooked Hill. The reason why she's condemned to her room has poked his head in. He appears paler than she remembers and wears a green cloak. How in all Eight Hells can her mother allow him so close to her door?

She blushes furiously. "No, I'm not … not doing anything."

"Afternoon nap?" he asks. His voice is raspier and the grin hitching up his mouth surprising.

"Where is my mother?"

"Took to her bed with a headache."

Qonna pushes out a deep breath and brushes her skirts. She's never been afraid of Nian da Nileon, not since she overtook him in height around her tenth birthday, and though he's stocky, she weighs more than enough to wrestle him to the ground if necessary.

He glances up at her. "I know you had some trouble over presents in the past." His gaze slides to the necklace draped over the side of her bookshelf.

"I love it, but Mother believes it's unseemly."

"Then don't let her see this." He shrugs a bag from his shoulder and digs around until he finds something small. It's a statuette, about the height of her forefinger, of a woman with ankle-length hair. She's carved from a single piece of amber, her round face serene. "Sister Sun—the most befitting of the Birkland Siblings for a woman associated with the Company of the Sun." He holds it out to her.

It feels warm in Qonna's palm, soft. Many hues of yellow, orange, and deep red mingle through the body of the goddess. Qonna's mouth goes dry. "Will you tell me how to pray to her?"

The prince flushes with pleasure as Qonna's reserved attitude is swept away. "No special protocol is needed, though you should probably address her as Sister Sun. Your auntle made it for you."

Another secret stashed away at the other end of the world: Qonna has family in Birkland. Her grandfather's first child. Usually, they don't talk about them. "Sloe Moon made this?"

"Took them ages."

"I wish they could come visit one day."

Something dark flickers in the prince's green eyes. "You and me both, Qonna. We should probably go join your father and brothers."

"They're back?"

"Yes, they greeted us as we approached the house." Nian's hand lands on the doorjamb, giving the wood a soft pat. One thing her mother doesn't want anyone else in town to know is that the person who owns *Pomegranates* is an elusive 'auntle', as the prince calls them—someone who casts a shadow from Birkland to fall on all their lives.

Qonna steps through the door. The dining room is empty, so they'll likely eat in the study, among the books and …. "Oh, shit."

The prince turns to face her. "What's wrong?"

She pictures the volume she found Cisir's family in, fallen open at the page where she cracked its spine. "I left something on Father's desk."


Qonna's three brothers favour their mother's side of the family, though they have their father's height and resemble each other so much in colouring and shape they could be mistaken for triplets, instead of a pair of twins and the youngest. Their hair is brown and wavy, their eyes a light brown, their skin much paler than Qonna's. They could be taken for Seagarders born and bred, and when they move as one there's something spooky to them. They all smile at their sister as she approaches in the company of the prince.

Her father seems flushed, as if he broke his resolution and had too much to drink. A folding table wobbles in the middle of the study, laden with platters of snacks. The desk is covered in wine cups. Qonna sees with relief that the book is closed and shoved aside with the rest of the flotsam. This won't be a conversation they have today.

As they make their way into the room, Qonna notices her brothers keep their distance from the prince. As future members of the Sun, the prince will soon become the one they serve, but some of their mother's attitude has rubbed off on them. Wherever Nian da Nileon goes, a bubble of space follows him. He surely is used to it and expects it as a member of the royal family, but it also must be a lonely experience.

Qonna pushes through the line of brothers and stands next to Nian, deliberately breaking the bubble. Her father hands her a cup filled with more apple brandy than she should have. "We need to celebrate," he declares. "It doesn't happen every day that we cover all the year's expenses in the first quarter."

Her brothers collect their own cups from the desk.

The prince pulls a grimace. "Well, don't get used to it. It could've easily gone wrong. I can't remember throwing up that much since my first crossing to Birkland. Sister Storm holds a grudge."

Her brothers shuffle uncomfortably, but her father smiles, wider than she has seen in a while. "Drink and be glad you made it home, Your Highness."

All of them take a sip. Qonna is careful to restrain herself. The brandy burns on her tongue; she barely stifles a cough. It must be the prince's doing that Qonna is part of the festivities. She never was before, and it feels strange to be included.

While her brothers fall upon the food, close to starving after their ride out, she watches her father and the prince interact. Now that she knows what to look for, she realizes her father does the same, keeping his distance, though a slightly smaller one; he seems to be worried about being touched by mistake. Given the way the prince is dressed—tunic longer than the ones worn in the Cities, his hair adorned with braids and trinkets—he appears so much more colourful, more adventurous, not at all concerned with city fashions.

As soon as the platters are plundered, her brothers retreat. The air clears immediately. If her father wonders why she lingers, he doesn't say. Instead, he offers her a refill and she accepts, though the cup is half-full.

The prince commandeers one of the chairs and picks through the remnants left by her brothers. "I suppose I must be grateful none of them went for the spinach pie."

"They don't like to eat green things," Qonna says.

"What—all three of them? How extraordinary." He lifts a piece and bites into the flaky crust.

Her father pulls a stool forward to perch on it. "Did you manage to bring the matter of the house up with Sloe?" he asks quietly, suddenly sober. "My wife has been on my back for years to gain clarity about the situation."

This isn't something Qonna should hear. She does her best to fade into the background.

The prince chews, taking his time. "I hope I can persuade them to come back one day. So no, I haven't brought it up. You can rent another house from what you make on your earnings in the Yellow House."

"Not such a big and prestigious one."

"I think your lovely wife is unaware of how unlikely it is for any of her sons to be named the official heirs—as far as I recall, Sloe's plans are much more focussed on your daughter." He glances at Qonna in her corner. "She is *Pomegranates'* named steward, after all."

# CISIR

## *delicate matters*

The day, though technically joyous, left Cisir drained, and he sees with terror that the common room of the *Pear* is heaving as he returns from work. It seems Lauron himself is among those who speculated on the future of the *Buttercup*. Though his wife and daughter have tried to spruce up the place for years, this evening sees a return to what the *Pear* must've been: a rowdy, bawdy tavern in the heart of the Triangle.

Cisir tries to squeeze past the benches and the counter at the back of the room, but his yellow tunic is too conspicuous for people to leave him be.

"To the Suns!" Someone makes a grab for his shoulder that Cisir barely dodges. "A happy day for the whole of Seagard!" Spit sprays his neck as he tries to wiggle sideways.

Gia pops in from the kitchen to extricate him. "Don't mind them. They're drunk."

"I'm sorry, I don't …."

"Not in the mood to celebrate?"

"This success is not of my making," he says.

"As a Sun you get to participate in it."

He grimaces. "It doesn't feel deserved."

She studies him through lowered lashes. "I'm going to make tea. Will you take a bowl with me?"

He exhales in relief. "Yes, please."

"We can have it in the kitchen, far away from the crowd." She steers him towards the fire, pushes a stool in place for him to sit on. "You must've met the prince today."

He can but nod.

"What was your first impression?"

It's the last thing Cisir wants to talk about, so he shrugs.

She smiles. "The prince always goes through a period of adjustment after his return, so maybe that shocked you?" She's clearly feeling him out.

He shrugs again. "He was nice to me."

She squints at Cisir, then smiles once more. "You should talk to my father. He can provide the best perspective on the old country. He was quite young when he left, but fully grown. He likes to talk about it too, though today he's a bit distracted."

"I'll ask him. Thank you, Gia."

The water starts to boil, and she removes the pot with a folded cloth. For a few moments she is blessedly busy with tea preparations. "You know some of the rumours are true?" She puts the bowls on the table and places the pot next to them. "The prince left his wife in Whiterivers twenty-odd years ago and has taken a sorcerer as his partner." Gia stirs the herbs in the steaming water, not looking at Cisir. "Of course, they can only be together in Birkland; that's why he's scarcely home before he returns west on the next available ship. Once he was meant to be First Sun in Seagard but promoted Qonna's father after it became clear how often he'd be away." She pours out the tea and hands Cisir a bowl. "When we were girls, Qonna and I often dreamt about what we'd get to do in Birkland. Visiting our families and so forth. Qonna belongs to the Badgers and the Moons and they're forest people, while Dad is of the Wolves, and the steppes lie much further in the east. It would've been a very long journey, so it's probably for the best that it'll never happen."

"Why can't it happen?" Cisir asks.

"Because we're both supposed to marry in the next year or so."

"Married women can travel." The tea is strong and sweet.

"Not without our husbands, and not with first babies on the way." She seems aware of how inappropriate it is for her to talk of babies to her parents' lodger. "You know how restricted we both are."

"My sisters travel."

"Your sisters must have money."

"Not an awful lot."

"But they have a different family background, and sometimes it's all about that."

He has nothing to add. It's true. How often has his name served to open doors so firmly locked for others? His sisters have some of the same privilege, and in fact, have never left the Continent. Birkland is at least six gruelling weeks away, and no one would've entertained the option of his sisters living on a ship with captain and crew, exposing themselves to dangers both corporeal and spiritual.

For a while they drink their tea in a silence that starts to become uncomfortable. "I can make you a tray to take back up if you'd prefer to eat in your room."

"That would be perfect, thank you."

Gia turns away and rifles through the kitchen shelves, pulling out bits and pieces while his back breaks out in goosebumps. Why is she so keen to talk about impending marriages? Is it a way to put him on his heels, in case he doesn't want to be considered? Or a warning not to get his hopes up?

Cisir hears the celebrations deep into the night, but at some point, he falls into exhausted sleep. He wakes early, and the sun is barely up as he peels his eyes open. Birds are singing in one of the few trees he's able to spot from the window when he lies curled up on his side, knees pulled to his chest. He will likely be the only Sun coming to work without a hangover today, but the air feels clammy; the blanket sticks to his naked legs and his hair clings to his neck. He can't remember his dreams, only that they were most certainly embarrassing. The empty tray he took into his room lies flung across the clothes chest like an accusation.

As a boy, his father punished him for taking credit for things he hadn't accomplished himself, but in the Company of the Sun it is expected that he participate in the festivities. The *Buttercup* left Seagard more than a year ago; he checked it in the lists at a time when he was crawling around Windyhill, trying desperately not to be a burden. The Sun's success was facilitated by the prince, the man who is not a man and wears two names with as much ease as other people don hats. Who lives what Cisir has somehow hoped for since the whole village of Windyhill changed their attitude towards him, the son of the manor who became an object of ridicule overnight.

He groans as he pushes himself off the bed, throws some water at himself, and gets dressed. He prays to all gods of the Star no one else is awake yet, that he won't have to speak to Lauron Wolf, his wife, or—gods beware—their daughter before he needs to be fully awake and human.

His steps make the stairs creak but for once he's lucky and escapes the *Pear*. The Triangle is deserted apart from a forlorn baker's boy pushing a cart through the narrow streets, bleary-eyed and barely able to greet Cisir with a nod. Smoke hangs low over the roofs; servants rekindle the fires for the morning meal. Even on the main road the atmosphere remains oppressive, and when it finally starts to drizzle it comes as a delightful relief, bathing Cisir's forehead with a soothing touch.

When he approaches the House of the Sun, the door is closed, and he hesitates before pushing it. It's locked, and for a breath panic makes his chest prickle before his head takes over. *You're here to work. You've done enough.*

He ducks underneath the roof and settles in to wait. He can see the ships lying at the quay from here, the small *Buttercup* wedged between the much bigger vessels of the Bulls. Its masts are flying sun banners, proclaiming her triumph for all the town to behold.

"Good morning."

He turns and sees the last person he'd thought to meet this early in the day: the prince, now wearing Seagard fashions of dark trousers and a tunic of a more acceptable length. Her hair is braided plainly and falls to her belt.

"Your Highness."

"You look as if you didn't celebrate enough last night."

"It didn't feel to be my place, Your Highness."

"What an honourable young man you are—and of such interesting lineage. A few centuries ago, we were quite closely related."

Something his father brought up whenever he needed to feel better about himself: *once we were kings.* "Is that what Master na Qarim said, Your Highness?"

"There was a book in his study, old but informative. Isn't it funny that but for a few twists of fate we might live each other's lives today?"

"I wouldn't have made a good prince, Your Highness."

"Why? Because you're a bit awkward? You can make it look like aloofness and no one will bat an eyelid. Or are you referring to an abhorrence against the thought of a life of idleness?"

"No one could accuse you of living an idle life, Your Highness."

Her eyes narrow. "And still they do. Do you have any questions for me?"

"Questions, Your Highness?"

"Yesterday you had a fair few and I can't imagine no new ones have sprung up overnight."

Cisir takes a deep breath. "Are you happy in Birkland, Your Highness?"

Lilyis folds her arms. "Happ*ier*, yes. In the last twenty years I've certainly felt more at home in the lands of the families than in my ancestral kingdom. In Birkland I'm given the opportunity to live as I want to live and to love whom I want to love, though not a day goes by when I don't wish to strangle them for their stubbornness." She smirks.

"Have you sworn off the Star?"

"What gave you that idea?" she asks cautiously.

Cisir stammers, "Be-because ...."

"Because you can't fathom how the Star could ever come to terms with *this*?" She gestures at herself.

Cisir nods unhappily.

"You'd be right," she says. "The Star has been preaching against me for decades. I'm still here, though. I might not be First Sun in Seagard anymore, but I am First Sun at the Stoneharp and the person in charge of all our Birkland concerns. Have you been tempted to leave the Star behind?"

It's the question Cisir's been dreading for years, and if it had been put to him by anyone else, he would've flailed about in his haste to deny any such thoughts. But because it's this extraordinary person, who radiates strength and a kind of assertiveness that makes him feel safe, he swallows and confesses. "I don't know what else there is. It seems a frightful prospect to go through our lives without divine aid. I've studied the teachings of the Star, the sacred scriptures and some of the more obscure ones, but none of them speak to what I fight with." *What I'm so ashamed of.* He isn't able to meet the prince's eyes as he speaks. "The idea of being despised by all the gods residing in the Heavens is too much to bear."

"I know." The prince's voice sounds rough. "I must warn you that Birkland cannot provide all the answers you need. Whatever you wrestle with, none of the Siblings will save you. What happened to you? Why have you left your family and come this far south?"

Cisir tries to steady his breath. Does he dare to confess? "I was made to give up my fiancée."

The prince presses on. "Why?"

The memory hurts Cisir so much biting his lip as hard as he can comes as a relief. "Because I fell in love with someone else. With many someone elses."

"Did you do anything about it?"

Cisir gasps. "No, of course not."

"You didn't even kiss some of them?"

"No!"

"And you still confessed to her?"

It comes out in one big surge, as if a dam has finally broken. "I wanted to be honest. I wanted to be open with her. I thought we'd come far enough for that, but she broke off the engagement straight away. Ever since then, Windyhill has proven itself the worst place to be. Too small to live down a scandal of such size. My father took some time to come around to the truth that he would never be able to clear my name. He changed his will in the end, naming my brother as his heir, and it was strongly suggested that I leave."

"You believe your fiancée spread the word around?"

"Yes, Your Highness." He swallows. "In fact, she boasted to my sister about it. I was lucky her influence is limited to Windyhill, otherwise I might never have been hired by the Sun."

"Your master might surprise you there, although Qes wasn't always so amenable. He's had his own struggles trying to fit in, otherwise he would never have agreed to the marriage he made so early in life. It took a lot of hurtful experiences for him to come around but I'm grateful for it." Lilyis studies his face, watches how he reacts to her words. "There aren't many men in Seagard who can be trusted with such delicate matters, but he undoubtedly is one of them, as well as bound to me by family ties."

She notices Cisir's confusion. "I'm all but married to his half-sibling. Unfortunately, my wife seems quite set on surviving all of us, so we've given up hope on being officially wed, though a few years back we held a little ceremony at the Golden Lake to celebrate the many years we've put up with each other." Her eyes shine as a smile creeps up her face. "In the eyes of the Star, our relationship has been an unnatural aberration from the start, and twenty years of devotion and making it work against all odds is declared as not meaning anything apart from our proclivity for depravity, while the Siblings, the Tall Gods of Birkland, have given us their blessing on the shores of the holy lake—and many times before." Her smile falters. "My choice was an easy one in the end, though I need to keep it secret. You should speak to Lauron Wolf one day. He can give you a whole new perspective on what it means to live a life in Birkland."

A life in Birkland … as if he would ever have the chance to experience that for himself.

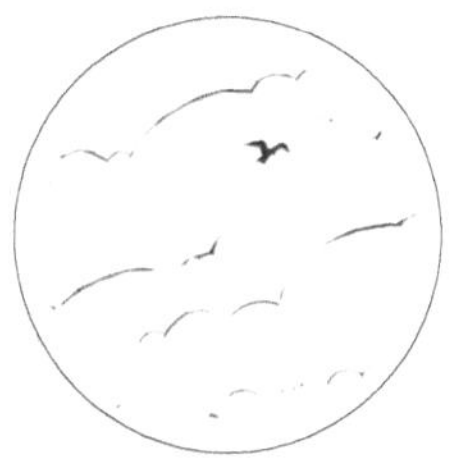

# QONNA

## *a shrewd investment*

Her father's eyes are swollen, and from time to time a low hum escapes his mouth. "Never again."

He lingers much longer than usual over breakfast, taking his time working through toasted bread, slices of ham, and the saltiest of cheeses in their kitchen, chewing slowly as if every movement causes him pain, while drinking endless bowls of strong, bitter tea.

"Cisir is sure to wait for you, Dad."

"I trust he can keep himself entertained," Qes says sourly, "if he really thinks anyone will show up on time today."

"He appears to be a dedicated young man," Qonna remarks.

"Does he now." For the first time this morning, a glint of the familiar astuteness returns to his eyes. "How refreshing to see you take such an interest in someone. Enough to research his family history."

*Shit. Of course he noticed. Whatever Mother says about him, he was never stupid.* She hides her face behind a bowl of tepid tea. "Can't I look up someone if they have an interesting name and sigil?"

"You can, but I know you're far from careless. Why did you want me to know about it?"

She suppresses an irritated grimace. "I wanted to test whether you were aware of the baggage attached to your new secretary."

"To mark the fact that you care about him or to ensure I don't consider him to be more than a dancing partner?"

*Be honest.* "I'm not sure myself."

"In the few days Cisir has been with us, he's proven himself restrained, sensitive, and kind. These are qualities hard to come by in the Cities. It pains me to admit, but your brothers don't show much thought for other people's lives. You don't need to worry, though. I simply like to see you preoccupied with someone besides Gia."

"Gia isn't the only one."

"But she was for a long time. You both were obsessed with each other as girls. Your mother was quite alarmed for a while—she's always listened too closely to Brother Rago's hateful ramblings."

*I don't want to talk about that.* "Does Mother know about the arrangement regarding this house?"

He groans. "You want to do this now?"

*Best to press on. Push him off course.* "We don't often find ourselves with no witnesses. Not nowadays. Dad, I don't understand. What will becoming *Pomegranates'* steward mean for me when it's time?"

He huffs. "I'm not quite dead yet."

"That's not what it's about." An icy hand settles on her heart. Why will she only gain her new position after suffering a terrible loss? "Does Mother know?"

"No. She never had reason to study the paperwork. She never asked to see any of it."

"She assumes, like I did, that my brothers will take it on?"

"How it usually goes in the Cities."

"Would any of them fight me for *Pomegranates*? They're always out and about these days and soon they'll join the Sun, one after another."

"I don't know, Qonna. None of them have expressed a wish to be involved with the management of the house and it makes sense to appoint someone as steward who's aware of what it means to run it." He steeples his fingers. "Unless you object to the arrangement?"

"No! It will be the one chance I have to live a different life. How could you keep it a secret?"

"Because I wasn't sure about my sibling's plan. I haven't spoken to Sloe for more than twenty years. Lilyis has acted as our messenger, and sometimes it's safer to take her words with a pinch of salt."

Qonna blinks. "Lilyis?"

"Oh fuck. I meant Nian."

"Dad?" *Lilyis is a woman's name.*

He rises so hastily he nearly topples his chair. "I need to get to work."

She stares after him, not sure what exactly has just happened. What he is so keen for her not to question.

A short message arrives for Qonna at the house while she checks over the finalized accounts for the last months. It feels good to know all the work she does to keep *Pomegranates* running is noticed. Once she feared the only reason she was allowed to learn to read and write was to be useful to her mother; today she knows it was a shrewd investment in her capabilities, just in case.

The kitchen maid pokes her head into the room. "This came for you, Mistress Qonnamaris."

It's a square of the finest grass paper that can be had in the Cities, sealed with sweetly scented beeswax and the sigil of a three-stemmed lily. Her name on the outside of the missive is formed with care, each stroke of the quill with exquisite deliberation. She knows exactly who has written to her. A prickle of anticipation races down her back.

She carefully peels off the seal. It's an elegant sigil, much more refined than the da Fewell's awkward owl.

"Very suitable." Despite her words, Qonna's mother sounds vaguely disappointed, as if she can't find a good enough reason to forbid her daughter to go. She hands back the paper between the tips of her thumb and forefinger, as if Eravis na Eloven's invitation is likely to burst into flames. "You will not stay more than an hour. There are other matters that need to be seen to around the house."

"Yes, Mother." Qonna can't quite hide her smugness. Drinking tea in one of the biggest houses of Seagard would've filled her with pure dread if she hadn't spent so much time talking to Eravis at the Braid

Makers' dance. She'll have a few hours to prepare, agonize over dress and shoes, and come to the conclusion that it isn't very important in the end.

She ducks out of her mother's presence into the quietness of her room. More has happened in the last five days than she'd ever thought possible. Something has finally shaken loose, and she needs to keep her excitement in check. If a friendship with Eravis na Eloven is achievable, she'll have gained a friend she can't be kept away from. The na Elovens' money makes them too important to snub, and chances are high Eravis keeps many more books in her house, more poetry than Qonna would ever know what to do with. Qonna will bring her own volume of Rosegardian offerings along, though it's tattered from years of hard use, flecked with ink and tears, and often is the only thing to soothe her when incandescent with rage.

Qonna has passed the house of the na Elovens many times. Ironically, it's situated opposite from the Red House, the headquarters of the Honourable Company of the Bull, and almost as gaudily painted. There isn't a single piece of wood on its front that hasn't been carved into fantastic shapes and all its shutters are stencilled with white lilies, as if the fat blooms bulge from the rooms into the street. They appear faintly indecent to Qonna, but there's no accounting for taste. The Eastown, *Pomegranates'* immediate neighbourhood, is much less colourful, and, Qonna thinks to herself, much less vulgar.

It might've been a mistake to walk, to turn up on the doorstep slightly out of breath, her headdress a bit squashed by the freshening wind. The servant who opens the wide front door certainly sneers eloquently enough, but before Qonna can gather herself, he melts away into the darkness of the house.

"Qonna!" Eravis appears like a saving spirit from one of the rooms, reaching out with both hands. "I'm so glad you could come. It's one of those rare days when all my sisters have gone out and I find myself in need of company—and there is tea and cake."

She pulls Qonna with her. They walk past many closed doors and finally reach a throughway to a square of ornamental garden. The house is dizzyingly large, much deeper than the front facing the main road suggests. The little garden is filled with budding rosebushes and sprouting herbs. A half-moon-shaped seat has been placed under a bower laden with star-eyed, pink-tinged blossoms. The smell caught by the surrounding walls is powerfully sweet, heavy and spicy—a garden perfect for a gaggle of young women preparing themselves to be married off, and neither Eravis nor Qonna fit in well. Qonna's headdress almost gets tangled in the creeper as she is bid to sit down at a table strewn with tiny tea bowls and cakes cut into disappointingly small pieces.

"I hope you don't mind sitting outside," Eravis says, "but I don't especially care for the servants listening in on every mean thing I have to say about my sisters."

"I don't mind, no. I never knew this was here."

The back of the house is peppered with more windows than the front, though these have been painted plain white and there are no carvings apart from a spray of lilies over the lintel of the door they came through.

"I know what you think," Eravis says, "and I confirm the first impression is correct. The na Elovens, like our house, are all about the front. Few people will ever be permitted to regard us from this angle." She gestures towards the shutters. "Perhaps the Red House is to blame. Everyone has to keep up and spend a fortune on paint so nothing is left for the other sides." She pours out tea with a sour expression. "None of these flowers were planted for my particular enjoyment, but I make the best of what I was given. Soon my sisters will leave the house and then the garden will finally be mine to use as I see fit."

The territorial sentiment shouldn't astound Qonna as much as it does. She harbours similar feelings about *Pomegranates*, and now she finally knows that one day her devotion might pay off, due to the mysterious benefactor who likes to fuck with the city's customs. A few days ago, Eravis' feelings made perfect sense to her. Much of their lives will be similar, depending on how well Qonna's mother handles the news that all three of her precious sons might have to find new homes when the reins are passed to Qonna. At least Qonna is aware that she resents their privilege, not them as people. She doesn't know them well enough for that.

"I wanted to ask you about your plans for the season." Eravis pushes the plate with the tiny cakes towards Qonna. "Do you expect to attend many more dances?"

"Not if I have a say in the matter." The cake is soaked in honey. It starts to crumble seductively as she picks it up and tries to manoeuvre it into her mouth.

Eravis looks on with a smile. "It might be too soon to make any promises, but most summers the manor on the hill fills up with relatives of the royal family, and with Nian da Nileon returned from the far west, there are sure to be more of them than in other years. You might not be aware of it, but the da Nileons have made it a habit to bolster the ranks of their daughters' companions from the most prominent merchant families in Seagard. There could be a place for you, if you play your cards right."

"How?" Qonna is much too intrigued to beat around the bush. "Why should they ask me? After all these years of father working with the royals?"

"Let's just say I have heard some rumours about a certain Princess of Crooked Hill expressing curiosity towards the less wealthy families of the city."

"Which princess?"

"Nivael da Nileon's youngest daughter Noa. Noalis da Ozanil da Nileon, to give her full name. She might be a year or so younger than you, but she's grown up rather headstrong."

"You know her so intimately?"

"I've been called to serve in her household since she was very young and have been in correspondence with her since. I might've mentioned our interaction at the dance."

"Is that the only reason you invited me today?" Qonna can't help but feel disappointed.

"No, though she mentioned having knowledge of you and your family situation." Curiosity glints in Eravis' hazel eyes. "To be a princess's companion can open a lot of doors in the city. I think you know that."

"My family has had many dealings with the royals; there's no reason why they couldn't make a direct request. As the First Sun of Seagard my father has been paid by the da Nileons since the Company was founded."

"It's a personal request, Qonna. Not only from the princess, but also from me." Her benign smile makes Qonna's stomach twist. "The manor can be a boring place to spend the summer, especially if you're not the most proficient embroiderer and don't give a toss about who gets married to whom at court. You don't need to tell anyone yet, but I'd be grateful if you entertained the idea of joining me at the manor."

*A whole summer away from home? Count me in.*

# CISIR

*no one ever wants trouble*

Gia must've said something to her father, because Lauron Wolf waits for Cisir when he returns from work in the evening. The Birklander has prepared a jug of the second-best ale and beckons Cisir in.

"Ask away," Lauron says with a grin. "There must be so many questions burning a hole in your tongue by now."

Cisir plops down in front of him. *There's no use pretending anymore. You may as well get on with it.* "How can she live like this?"

Lauron chuckles and pushes a cup of ale over the table. The *Pear* is not busy; after yesterday's excesses, its regular patrons have listened to reason and stayed home. "You mean Lilyis? Belonging to the royal family has always had its advantages. More people are prepared to keep your secrets. It's not a new thing, boy, though it may be shocking to you. Twenty years ago, she started to build a life for herself that plays to its own strict rules. Most of us are grateful and like her enough to accommodate her. Qes might have gambled high on your integrity, but it seems to have paid off. Or are you tempted to run straight into the Westown temple and spill your guts to the priests?"

"Of course not!" Cisir could as well put his own neck on the executioner's block.

"Then be honoured he placed so much trust in you. You haven't been with the Sun for a week and are one of the few people in the know. Drink. The ale doesn't get any fresher."

Cisir obeys. The ale is bitter on his tongue and slams into him like a fist. He hasn't eaten much today.

Lauron chuckles again. "You probably need a few quick lessons to appreciate what operation you've become a part of, and what heritage we brought across the sea. For years Qes' father and I were joined at the hip, and I mourn his loss every single day. Qarim Badger built a new life in Seagard under the direst of circumstances and he left us an incredible legacy." Pain digs lines in Lauron's dark face. "The Company of the Sun has long been a refuge for people who find themselves longing for freedoms the Cities are not prepared to offer. While the Star and its priests have never trusted any of us, the Sun is still there, and as you have seen, it prospers."

"Do you belong to the Sun too?" Cisir asks.

"Not officially, though quite a few contracts hidden away in Qes' study would suggest otherwise. Qarim Badger and I tried out a fair few ventures and the idea to lodge Suns in need of a bed is merely the latest of them. It might stick this time."

Cisir takes another gulp of ale and a warm fuzziness settles in his belly, before it releases an angry growl.

"You must be famished, boy. I'll see if the pea stew is ready." Lauron pushes himself up from the table. "Don't move. I'll be back before you know it."

The pea stew is thick and has chunks of spiced sausage floating in it. Cisir wolfs it down while Lauron continues.

"The next months will show if Qes' streak of luck holds out. He expects three more ships to return before winter to finally best the Bulls' end of year profits. Speaking of which, did you have any problems yet?"

"Of what kind?"

"Of the 'getting-surrounded-by-Bulls-and-threatened' kind."

"No." *Should I have?*

"Wearing the Sun uniform can have unfortunate consequences. You might consider wrapping yourself in a cloak until you find a group of friends among your colleagues."

"I don't want any trouble."

"No one ever wants trouble and still it finds them. Bulls tend not to be the sharpest knives on the rack, and most of them are related. If something happens, you tell me." Lauron's hand, covered in decades of scars from tending the cooking fires and pots of the *Pear*, grabs Cisir's. The muscles bulge along Lauron's forearm. "Listen to me, boy—you come and tell me. You don't try to hide it because you can't bear to be humiliated, understood?"

Cisir stares into Lauron Wolf's face. This man has survived living in the Triangle for longer than Cisir's been alive. "Understood."

"Good boy."

Cisir glances down at Lauron's fingers. He shouldn't be this excited to be touched. It feels as if his skin is about to walk off on its own. When Gia's father gives him a last pat and withdraws, Cisir is ready to burst into tears. It's already been a hard day without dealing with new complications. He wants Lauron to stay. To make him feel better. "I have a question," he croaks.

"Let's hear it."

"How do you deal with the Star?"

Lauron barks out a laugh. "That's a big pot of maggots. Are you sure you want to know?"

"Please."

Lauron leans in. "The secret is that I'm more afraid of the Siblings than the priests."

"Afraid?" It's the right word, Cisir realizes. He's always been afraid of them.

"The Tall and Small Gods of the old country might seem more relaxed to you, but delivering yourself into their care is a risk. They might not give a fuck about whom you love or marry, but they're jealous and demanding. Ask Lilyis Sun and she'll tell you how much. Thankfully, I married a woman who's happy to go to temple every week, so we're left alone, but when I was unattached, Qarim and I ran into quite a few difficulties. There weren't any other Birklanders in

Seagard at the time and there still aren't many, for this exact reason. Anyone who doesn't have close connections to the royal family finds themselves pressured and persecuted. Why are you thinking about the Star and the Siblings?" Lauron's brown eyes hold so much fatherly warmth. He must know, or at least suspect, what Cisir's battling with. Gia might've told him what Cisir confessed.

"Because … because the doctrines of the Star are difficult to live with."

"Hate to break it to you, boy, but I think that's sort of the point. The gods of the Star might not be half as greedy as their servants and there's no way of knowing whether the priests interpret them accurately. With the Siblings, the connection can be immediate."

Lauron pours out more ale, but Cisir dreads his tongue loosening and doesn't drink. "Immediate? You mean—magic?"

"It doesn't happen often, but over the last decades there's been a new awakening in the old country, so we know our faith is based on something tangible, not the guesswork of old men who hate to see anyone enjoying themself. I know Sister Sun is with me, because there are people who wield her power. Which is an assurance and a reminder not to stray."

Cisir shudders. "What are Sister Sun's rules?"

Lauron laughs again, but this time much less bitterly. "They were never written down, so I'll go with what our wizard taught me when I grew up in the steppes: give thanks for every good thing that happens, but don't expect her to run your life for you."

"Have you found that helpful?"

"It certainly served to manage my expectations." Lauron drinks deeply. "Though after years of struggle, things are starting to come together, and I've expressed my gratitude a lot lately. It's been a road of many steps. I never planned to take on the *Pear*. Like everyone who comes to the Cities, I had different dreams and preconceptions. But it happened, and after many years I finally had enough saved to marry. Gia's mother … I can't count the ways I've given thanks for meeting her, for being allowed to wed her. Raising our daughter in a house that we own, after decades of paying off the loans …." Lauron's voice breaks. "It's almost too much. Sister Sun has given me more than I thought I would ever have when I milked a hundred goats each morning, staring at the bleakness of the steppes." He wipes his face with his palm and smiles shakily. "So you see, I'm not in a position to consider the Star. I'm utterly bound and grateful for it."

Cisir has been trying to drop off to sleep but he can't tonight. Staring at the ceiling for hours is better than having nightmares about the last months of his life in Windyhill, the shame that was reflected at him from every face he saw.

*For what*? For something that existed more in his head than anywhere else. If Lauron Wolf, a goat herd of the Birkland steppes, could build something he's so thankful for, why can't Cisir do the same?

It might involve crossing the sea in the other direction, but somehow he's managed to get into a position in which he has access to more than one ship. As the First Sun's secretary he might not be expected to travel, but one day he could ask to serve the Company of the Sun in a different way—accompany the prince on one of her yearly returns to see her partner—and then his life could begin.

Seagard has finally shaken off its festival hangover. As Cisir makes his way through the city, bleary-eyed and with the hasty breakfast trying to settle in his stomach, he wonders if he should be more apprehensive about the day ahead.

He breathes out in relief when he sees the yellow banners flying on the bridge and the door propped open. He's becoming more familiar with the smell that permeates the public section of the house. Hevo is busy rearranging the baskets in front of the counter, making everything as appealing as possible to the customers who come by in person. He acknowledges Cisir with a small wave and goes back to shuffling little packets of tea.

Cisir takes a moment to notice that Birklandish goods take pride of place in his display: the small leather bottles of birch syrup, the heaps of silvery pelts, the containers made from boiled bark and rolls of colourful woven binding, the goat hair cloth and strings of amber pearls, the necklaces of nearly translucent shells. Is it really Birkland represented or the prince's idea of it?

Based on what Cisir sees here, he might be in danger of setting too much hope on the existence of a foreign continent. Stepping through to the First Sun's study, Cisir is astonished to find Qes na Qarim already seated, a frown of concentration etched on his forehead.

"Good morning, Master."

"Ah, excellent. I hoped you make it early. There's something I would like you to do for me." He waves a folded, sealed piece of paper. "Would you mind terribly going up to *Pomegranates* and delivering this to my daughter? I would ask the boys but none of them have come in yet and it's rather urgent."

"Of course, Master."

"Have you been to the Eastown before?"

"I'm sorry, but I don't think I have."

"Everyone there will be able to direct you to the house; it's difficult to miss. If you walk towards the Northgate and take the thoroughfare at the *Sneezing Hedgehog,* you should come straight to it."

Cisir remembers the *Hedgehog's* sign. "Thank you, Master." He's grateful to be given a task; more walking might finally wake him up. He bows and retreats, but not before he notices the self-satisfied smile on Qes na Qarim's face.


The sign in question has the teardrop form of battle shields but was clearly never meant as such. It hangs on creaking chains above Cisir's head and is painted with said hedgehog wiping its nose with a handkerchief. Many taverns in Seagard bear slightly silly names, but at least that makes them memorable enough to be used for directions.

The thoroughfare is narrow, not built for carts or carriages, but it brings him to a much wider road, which he follows eastwards until *Pomegranates* looms above him. His jaw drops.

Hidden in the Eastown is a house more in keeping with the buildings on the main road, covered in carvings of pomegranates, with a band of kestrels in flight beneath the top floor windows. The front hasn't been painted in a while and the colours have mellowed. Its windows are square and have two shutters; new ones made of wooden slats hide the older, unpainted set. The house has two entrances, one wide enough for two horses to pass through, and a smaller door facing the road. That's the one Cisir knocks on.

He waits, gazing up at his master's house and its silvered straw roof. It's almost as big as Windyhill Manor's main building, though clearly much newer. The carvings are of a more modern style, flatter and more abstract than the ornamentations lining the larger road.

When a servant opens the door, Cisir sees a wooden staircase leading to the upper floors. His heart gallops like a horse that's snapped its reins. The servant glances at the sun stitched into Cisir's tunic and ushers him up the steps.

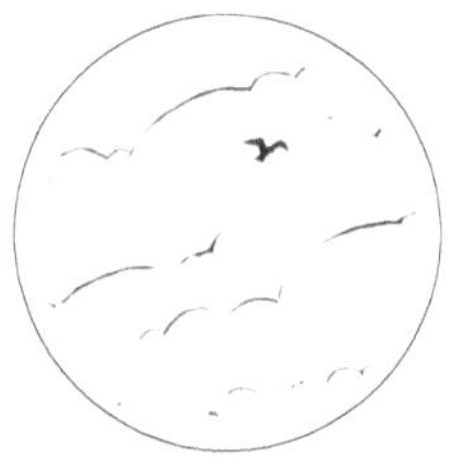

# QONNA

## *out of line*

Why didn't he send one of the boys?" Qonna takes her father's letter from Cisir's hand. It feels weird seeing him in the sitting room, a few steps from her bed. He seems aware of the implications— when has she ever seen him not flushed and uncomfortable? As if he longed to jump out of his skin? "Never mind. I'm sure my father had his reasons."

*Annoying reasons. Interfering reasons.*

"Would you like some tea before you head back?"

He squirms but nods. "That would be nice, thank you."

Qonna directs him towards the small table close to the window, overlooking the narrow road beneath. "Did you have problems finding the house?"

"No, your father's directions were very helpful." As soon as he's folded himself on the high-backed chair usually preferred by her mother, he relaxes, as if slipping into a well-rehearsed role. "I hope your morning's been pleasant?"

Qonna suppresses a snort. "It's not over yet, is it? But thank you, so far I have nothing to complain about. In fact, I'm awaiting news from a friend of mine and—depending on what she writes—it might turn out to be an exciting day."

His bright blue eyes widen. *Does he think I'm talking about a proposal of marriage?* "Exciting?"

"With the prince returned from Birkland, it won't take long for more members of the royal family to descend on Seagard for the summer. Did you come from the Northgate when you first arrived in the city?"

"Yes," he says.

"Then you'll have passed the grounds of Gard Manor, the seat of Nivael da Nileon. He spends most summers there away from court, though I'm sure it would be more comfortable for him to remain at Crooked Hill. It can get hot here, and the smell wafting up from the harbour … you'll know soon enough what I mean."

A servant appears in the doorway, a young girl in a grey frock and severe headdress, who grins as she discovers her mistress sitting across from a young man without any chaperone in sight.

*She'll blab to the cook.* Qonna's hackles rise. *Dad will think he won when he hears about it.*

Qonna waits stony-faced until the bowls, teapot, and a small plate of caraway biscuits have been laid out, trying to avoid showing any sign of feeling rumbled.

Cisir stares down at the table, acting guilty enough for two. As soon as the door closes, he speaks up. "I'm sorry if this left the wrong impression. It's difficult to …." He puffs up his cheeks. "Gia must have told you about my engagement."

Qonna feels a jolt deep in her bones. "She didn't."

*He spoke of such intimate things with her? And she kept his secret?*

"Oh. I'm not in a position to be considered by anyone, whatever my name might suggest. I was removed from my father's will a few weeks ago."

"I'm sure no one would think …." She swallows the rest of the sentence. *Of course they would, stupid cow.* "I'm sorry to hear that. It must've been a difficult experience for you."

He fiddles with one of the biscuits, scattering crumbs all over the table. "It was. It still is."

"You can't be the only one trying to build a new life in the Cities. Why …? I'm sorry, I shouldn't be nosy."

"No, it's fine." He finally manages to break the biscuit. "You should know about it in case your father gets ideas of asking you to dance with me again." As he tells her of his engagement, his voice is much firmer than expected. While he speaks, Qonna's jaw drops further and further.

"It was a misunderstanding," she can't help but exclaim.

"Not really. It was stupid to assume she wouldn't take it as an affront against her person, and she was very offended indeed."

"She still shouldn't have bad-mouthed you." Of all the things Qonna anticipated, the confused glow of empathy wasn't one of them. "No one can help falling in love sometimes. Or with whom." The blood pounds in her ears. He hadn't been quite specific about what was so damning in his confession to his fiancée, but she knows what he means, has always known it. She watches her own hand reach over the table and squeeze his wrist reassuringly. "Have you spoken to Gia's father yet?"

"Yes."

"Uncle Lauron must've told you most marriages in the old country serve to bind the families closer together, and that many of them exist between two men."

His mouth falls open and he pulls away so violently he upsets his tea bowl. The tea splashes across the table, soaks into his sleeves. "I'm sorry, I …."

"I'll get a cloth." She glances around the room.

*You've touched the thorn stuck in his paw*, comments the mean little voice. *Did you see how he jumped?*

She snatches up the nearest piece of fabric and begins to mop the spill. He sits there, breathing heavily, as if battling the urge to run, but his muscles tremble too much to let him come to his feet.

As she hands him the cloth so he can dry his forearm, he blinks rapidly. "Lauron Wolf didn't tell me any of that."

"Oh. I didn't want to shock you."

"No, it's … that's useful information." He's as red as a boiled crab. "But I can assure you I never …."

"That's none of my business." She refills his bowl, feeling strangely elated. "I wanted to let you know there are solutions for many situations, and it also means falling in love with another man is considered quite unremarkable in other parts of the world."

"It's not just men though. It's absolutely everyone."

"Why are you so worried then?" *Look who's talking.*

"Because that's not how it's supposed to work. You fall in love, you marry, you love your wife forever."

This time she doesn't stifle the snort. "Have you ever seen a living example of that? What about your own parents?"

"They didn't fall in love. There were … dynastic concerns. I always wanted to do it properly and I believed I loved my fiancée. I sent her poetry. Bad poetry."

"We all have that urge from time to time," she admits.

"I cannot stress enough how awful it was. But after the first three months, my attention started to wander again, and … and this is what I cannot forgive myself for. She had every right to break our understanding."

"You were infatuated with her."

"I genuinely believed it to be true love."

How had she managed to end up in a situation where her father's secretary unburdened his heart to her?

"Did you choose her yourself?" Qonna asks.

"No, my father introduced us."

"Perhaps you wanted to follow the protocol so badly that you convinced yourself for a while?"

He gulps down his tea, maybe to play for time. "Perhaps," he echoes. "That would be a generous interpretation. Can I ask you not to tell your father about any of that?"

"None of it will leave this room. Do you know what happened to your fiancée?"

"She married my second-eldest brother soon after."

"No wonder you felt like you had to leave. Listen, Cisir, whenever you need someone to talk to, you know where to find me. I'm glad you felt safe enough to tell me all of it and I won't betray your trust."

He looks as if he wants to cry but nods and rises. "Thank you. I hope it serves to avoid more misunderstandings."

After he leaves, Qonna stares at the broken biscuits for a long while, until she remembers the missive he delivered. Some of the tea has reached the paper and made the ink run, but she knows her father's atrocious hand well enough to read the words.

*"The prince asked us to join him for a meal at the* Unicorn *today. Meet us at the sound of the midday bells. Be nice to the messenger."*

She sighs, anticipation descending over her. As the *Hungry Unicorn* is the most prestigious inn in the whole of Seagard, she needs to consider what she'll wear and if it will make sense to take one of the maids along. Turning up at the *Unicorn* unaccompanied might send the wrong signal. Or perhaps there's someone else she can ask.

It's a small detour to go via the Triangle. She finds Gia and her mother engrossed in the task of scrubbing tables and benches with vinegar and salt; both wear aprons, their hair covered in scraps of water-stained linen. When Qonna appears in her blue dress, both stop and ask her to join them for a bowl of tea.

"I'm sorry, I'm on a mission. Gia, would you like to eat with the prince today?"

She smiles. "May I, Ma?"

Garalis wipes her hands. "We're almost finished here, anyway. Your green frock should be dry enough to wear."

While Gia bounds upstairs, her mother turns to Qonna. "I'm sure she's grateful for the opportunity, but please be careful not to …." She crosses her arms. "I know Qes can be stubborn and sometimes doesn't consider how inappropriate his decisions are for a young woman growing up in this town."

"It wasn't Father's idea, and we're going to the *Unicorn*, not further up the hill."

"That's good to know. I'm worried Gia might forget she belongs down the hill with us."

It always struck Qonna as strange how people talk in the city she was born in: up the hill is everything past the Triangle, some parts of the West- and Eastown, and technically *Pomegranates* is also considered 'up the hill', though it's never spoken of as such. The larger houses belonging to the richest of trading families are 'up the hill', and at the very top sits Gard Manor, the seat of the prince's father, surrounded by ancient trees, an artificial lake, and more space than anyone needs to live on.

While Lauron is generally relaxed about these categories, Garalis has always seen them as unbending barriers dividing her city, a question of class and rightful ownership. Qonna's father achieved his goal and escaped, but Lauron's family identifies with the space that gives them safety. The feeling of belonging must be wonderful. Based on what Cisir told her today, he doesn't have it either. Life is precarious up the hill.

Qonna avoids looking at Gia's mother, desperate for her friend to return. Gia emerges in the aforementioned green dress. Its sage tone makes her appear strangely pale, as if her mother managed to leach out most of her colour with a simple directive, and though Gia smiles, the set of her soft shoulders portrays a hint of uneasiness. "I'll be back before you know it," she promises, giving her mother a kiss on the cheek.

Qonna can't remember when she last kissed her own mother. Certainly not in the last three years. In fact, ever since her blood started, there's been no physical contact.

Gia takes Qonna's elbow and leads her into the street.

"Thank the Star," she whispers. "Ma had lots of plans for us today. I tell her again and again, it's not possible to get every speck of grime out of the *Pear*. Before she married him, Dad was never concerned with cleanliness, and decades of rotting rushes leave their mark on a place. You look thoughtful, Qonna. Wasn't this supposed to be an adventure? Meeting a prince at the *Unicorn*?"

Qonna's thoughts are still busy with jealousy. "Would you say that you love your ma, Gia?"

"Of course I love her. She might have ambitious standards, but she's still ...." Gia breaks off.

They stand in the middle of the Triangle in its first daily rush, with taverns preparing to open at the midday bells, tables and benches being dragged outdoors and stairs being swept, window shutters thrown open with energetic *thwacks*.

"I'm sorry," Gia says. "I didn't think. Let me give you a kiss too. Will that help?" Gia embraces her and presses her mouth to Qonna's.

It's the shortest of kisses, but the first Qonna has received in years. Her stomach cramps, and suddenly she feels beyond uncomfortable. *Isn't that what you wanted?* It should feel like kindling held too close to a flame, but Qonna steps back, disturbed. "It always helps," she lies.

Gia's hand slips into the crook of her elbow. She seems satisfied, and in a way she's achieved what she must've set out to do: she thoroughly distracted Qonna from the fact that her own mother had long drawn away from her. In the blink of an eye, the surrounding houses seem oppressive, their colours garish. A blackbird swoops from one of the neighbouring roofs, trailing a disjointed fragment of song, as if the whole world has stepped out of line.

# CISIR

## *call to prayer*

Cisir has deliberately avoided the Westown for this very reason: he can see the copper star on top of the temple from every street. It towers over roofs and the small squares among houses, vibrating slightly on the breeze rushing in from the sea. It turned green long ago but that doesn't make it less threatening. This Star is much larger than the one affixed to his family's chapel and sits on a square bell tower. Cisir watches the Brother tasked with ringing the midday bells trudging up many flights of stairs, his form like a black fabric cut-out whenever he passes one of the tower's many windows. The tower is one of the few buildings in Seagard built completely from stone and its style doesn't quite match the surrounding quarter.

Cisir waits until the Brother has his breath back. The green-grey shape of the bell starts to swing, first slowly, then with more confidence. The first ring is incredibly loud; anyone trying to take a nap after breakfast is surely wide awake now. Cisir is not the only one who uses the bells as a call to prayer today; a handful of people come rushing across the square towards the temple, most of them likely stopping off before they buy a bite to eat and return to work. Cisir pulls his coat closed to make sure no one sees the yellow uniform. He joins the throng pushing in.

From the square, the Westown temple appears stern and unadorned, but inside its walls are covered with dark blue paint, even the columns holding up the ceiling, so they melt into the room. Above him, stylized golden stars wink by the light of the thick beeswax candles on the altar stone. In contrast to his family chapel, there are no benches. Everyone who wants to pray needs to do so on their knees. The floor seems freshly swept but is also covered in large, uneven flagstones. Nothing about being in the presence of his gods is supposed to be easy.

Cisir keeps to the back of the group. The other citizens press forward and one by one, they sink down. Some of them prostrate themselves with their foreheads pressed to the ground, but Cisir stares at the golden stars above their heads and wonders how much it must've cost the Star to build this house of the gods, how many cartloads of stone must've been brought from the quarries further inland, and how high the ladders were for the artist to reach the ceiling and paint it.

Its effect is utterly captivating, but it shows the human hand. One of the Brothers decided not to allow benches, to make the citizens of Seagard grovel, everyone, even the old man on his crutches who will need help getting up again. Every single thing around Cisir is the result of a human choice. For the first time in his life, he feels resentment in the presence of the Star. It tastes bitter in his throat. He backs against one of the columns, watches the others pray.

A few Brothers in their cream-white robes mill about, keeping an eye on things, though the only bits anyone could steal would be the candles. Otherwise, there's only emptiness. Why does the temple feel so at odds with the city it dominates?

*Because you've become closer to people who are in a different position. None of the Birklanders belong here.*

The Star is the organization that wants to keep them out, that is deeply afraid of their influence. The temple shouldn't feel strange to him. It's what he grew up with, the stern gods with the stars in the Heavens following his life with their judgmental gazes, the threat of Eight Hells below, pits of beckoning demons trying to tempt him and feed on his soul. Every prayer spoken between the blue columns is uttered in fear of the unknowable, the un-evidenced, but ultimately, the temple is exactly what it appears to be: empty.

Cisir has dawdled long enough. He'll probably have to come up with a good excuse for his master as to why he felt compelled to divert via Westown. He tucks in his chin and quickens his steps. Never during his first week has Qes na Qarim mentioned taking a break to accommodate his own prayers, so that might not count for much. Above Cisir, the last ring of the midday bells dissipates with a lingering echo; the main road funnels the wind, forms it into a rough, shoving hand as he rounds the corner of the fork leading down the hill.

"Fucking watch it!"

The wind transforms into an actual push that staggers him sideways in surprise. He didn't notice the five young men standing in the middle of the road.

They sport short, dark red cloaks and are all tall and muscular with strong jaws, each wearing their hair in a long braid falling down their back. All five of them have the same colouring: faces glowing from healthful outdoor pursuits, narrow blue eyes, and hair the hue of wet sand. It doesn't impress them that he is in fact taller than all of them; it serves as the main reason for why they take an interest in him at all. They must be Bulls. The Red House lies mere steps away on the same road. They might be on their way to get food or waiting for someone else to join them, and the whiff of entitlement rolling off them is so palpable Cisir knows Lauron Wolf did not exaggerate. These young Bulls are dangerous, especially in groups, and gods protect him, their eyes sparkle with glee. Before, they were bored, now they've found someone to pass the time with.

The closest jumps at Cisir and pushes him again. "This is our road," he says, and when a clasp on his sleeve hooks Cisir's cloak by mistake and pulls it open, revealing the yellow tunic beneath, all five close on him.

"Such a pretty flower," the smallest of them scoffs. He breaks into a nasty smile, and it reveals to Cisir that he's the one Cisir will have to watch out for, the one who definitely won't play fair. He has more to prove than the others.

"You're far from where you belong." One of them has a deep, gravelly voice. "No place for the likes of you up the hill, flower."

Cisir backs off, but one of them steps around and as soon as Cisir corrects his path, the small one moves forward. They're about to surround him.

"I'm on my way down," Cisir's voice vibrates like the stilling bell. "If you let me past ...."

The small one pokes Cisir's shoulder blade. It's far from ideal to have *him* at his back, though the other four could easily beat him to a pulp. If he's lucky, they'll be cowardly enough to let him go before the situation escalates.

Plenty of passersby see, but no one interferes. When the Bulls said the road belonged to them, this is what they meant. No one will willingly provoke their wrath.

Cisir lifts his empty hands. "It was a mistake. I want no trouble."

"Different things, flower, what you want and what you get."

He is poked again, and this is the sign for the four bigger ones to rush him.

Cisir dodges the first fist, pulling up his cloak and throwing it over the face of the small one. He pulls the seam closed until it cuts into the Bull's throat, who bellows and lashes out, but now Cisir is behind him, and the Bull can't see a thing through the tightly woven fabric.

"My cloak is thick enough to choke your friend." Cisir's arm trembles, but the years of relentless training he was subjected to have taken over. He flips his eating knife and jabs its tip through the cloth. The blinded Bull howls as it pricks his temple.

"You can leave me alone," Cisir says. "No blood needs to be spilled."

The four other Bulls goggle at him while their leader continues to struggle in Cisir's grip. His movements grow sluggish as no more air comes through to him. "Don't take too long to decide. In a matter of moments he'll lose consciousness."

The Bulls hold up their palms and step away.

Cisir rotates until he stands next to the fork in the road, and as the bundled man slumps in his arms, he pushes him down upon the cobbles. He starts to run.

Cisir can hear at least two of them following him, their shouts and the clap of leather soles. When he darts into the first thoroughfare towards the Triangle, they're hard on his heels. He's only been in Seagard for a week, and they've likely grown up on these streets, but there's something that pulls him forward, an instinct to burrow into the city.

He swerves through yards and gaps between outbuildings. Whatever has taken him over allows him to squeeze through openings that should be much too narrow. He comes upon the back wall of the *Pear*, runs into the open door of the laundry shed, and pulls it closed behind him.

He has no idea if the Bulls are hunting him this far downhill, but he crams himself between the half-barrels and crouches down, his breath rasping violently. He feels strangely elated, though if they corner him here, his only hope will be Lauron Wolf coming to his aid, or Gia with the largest pan they have.

*I got out*, Cisir thinks as sweat runs down his face. He folds his hands under his chin to keep it off the clay floor. *All those years of torture at Father's behest, and today they saved me.*

He was never the most talented with a blade; his brothers showed much more aptitude. Today was the first day his limbs didn't get in the way and that his body knew without a doubt where it needed to go. That of all places in the city, the *Rotting Pear* in the Triangle was the safest place to be.

Cisir waits a long time, and then a bit longer, before extracting himself from the laundry shed, but at some point he needs to show up at work. His future depends on him holding on to his position. He dusts himself off and tries to walk as confidently as possible, taking the shortcuts he discovered on his first few mornings.

It helps that the main road has filled up significantly. He can join the crowd of servants running errands, messenger boys, and traders out on business if he walks with a stoop and keeps his head down. The harbour bridge is full of people standing around and there's a queue outside the Yellow House waiting to buy tea, spices, and other necessities Hevo keeps stacked behind the counter. The customers move aside as he comes through.

Hevo and the two other Suns working glance up with odd expressions—half apprehensive, half pitying.

*Can I get in trouble for staying out so long? Best get the bollocking over with.*

Cisir pushes on towards his master's study. Neither Qes na Qarim nor the prince are waiting to berate him, but his pile of documents to be copied has grown in his absence and is in danger of toppling. Cisir takes a deep breath. He knows what to do about that. It'll take a long time to make his way through, but nothing about the task is scary or new.

He lays out his tools and has begun to refill the inks when Hevo bursts into the room. "It's utter chaos in the front—are you all right?" He comes closer and checks Cisir over. "We've all been through something like that. I managed to get away with a split lip but there's not a scratch on you." Hevo peers at him; he has a narrow face and lank black hair, and as he grabs the top of Cisir's arm to turn him around, he's surprisingly strong.

"How do you know?" Cisir asks, perplexed. "It only just happened."

"Any sort of rumour turns to wildfire in the city, and there have been enough run-ins between Suns and Bulls that the whole of Seagard is attuned to it. Not a scratch!" he repeats admiringly before he releases Cisir. "You must've run like a demon to get away from five of them."

"What did they do to you?" Cisir asks.

Hevo winces. "They jumped me and Yoren when we walked across Temple Square. It was dark and we didn't notice them coming until it was too late. I couldn't see straight for a week."

"Why did they do it?"

Hevo shrugs. "No one can quite remember how it started. Probably one of those things that happen if you have two rival Companies employing men of similar age and don't give them enough to do.

I suspect the Bulls started it—the da Relians are so inbred, there's always one of them who's too confident to keep himself alive."

*That might be true of my family too*, Cisir thinks.

Hevo continues. "We were all worried when you didn't return from your errand. The First Sun told me to watch out for you."

"Where is he?"

"He's gone to meet the prince at the *Unicorn*. How are you feeling? Do you need tea?"

"Tea would be nice."

Hevo smiles. He has sharp teeth that make him appear a bit shifty, but Cisir smiles back even so. It's his first interaction with his fellow Suns that makes him feel as if he's part of something bigger. "Thank you."

"We might have some sesame biscuits left." Hevo turns away. "Don't worry. The First Sun knows how it goes, and he'll have heard by now what you were involved in. You wouldn't think we Suns are underdogs in Seagard, but the Bulls have always made the bigger profits, and that counts in the Cities. Though this year might change everything if our other ships come in. Did they give you a nickname?" he asks before stepping into the corridor.

"They kept calling me 'flower'."

"Yes, that's one of their favourites. It's usually that or 'princess'."

"Why would they do that?"

"I guess because they need to make themselves feel more manly. I'll get the tea sorted for you."

As he disappears, Cisir stares after him. *What does 'more manly' even mean?*

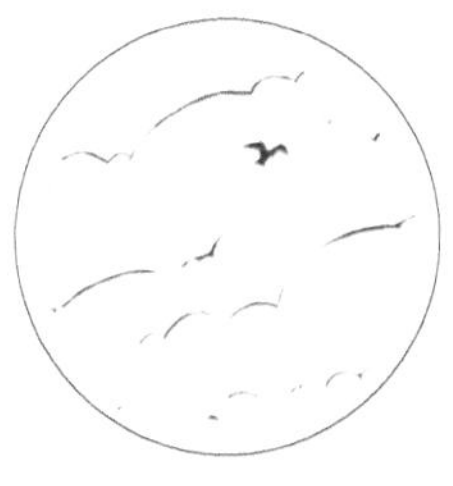

# QONNA

## *separate worlds*

Is that something you need to take care of?" the prince asks.

Qonna's father closes his eyes. "Later," he says with a sigh. "As if I didn't have enough shit to deal with. It was merely a question of time until the Bulls got on my back again. The last time, I had to trot up to the Red House and demand a statement."

"But this time I'm in town." The prince pushes the wine cup away. "And soon my father will arrive. We can help you rein them in."

Qonna's father pulls a face and Qonna knows he's struggling to hold back. "Don't take it the wrong way, Your Highness, but these incidents occur with regularity. It's best if I don't need you at my side every time I complain to the Bulls. We have to sort it out among the Companies, otherwise they'll never quieten down. I bet they've started a new cohort of apprentices; that usually means it's time for another round of clarifications. The da Relians have always had a never-ending list of cousins waiting to leave their country houses and throw themselves into the fray. I dread the time when my own sons start their careers in the Yellow House and I need to protect them from the Bulls. Sometimes I worry they don't understand that many of the young men they count among their friends will end up on the opposing side. If we can't get both Companies to conform to a code of civility, there'll come a point when the prosperity of the whole city will take a hit."

The prince glances at Qonna and Gia on their bench under the window, raptly listening. "Have you thought about drawing up something official? You could get my father to sign and seal it—what is a royal family for if not to force everyone to play nice? Both Companies have been around for decades. The Bulls need to accept they won't ever be the only ones competing for investments. It makes sense to hold them to some sort of codex, and the Suns too." The prince turns to the two young women. "What do you think?"

Qonna's mind goes blank as soon as she's addressed directly.

Gia answers, "It sounds like a most sensible proposition, Your Highness. Growing up in the Triangle, I've witnessed enough destruction at the hands of idle young men to last me a lifetime. To give a significant portion of them firm rules to adhere to will serve to instil a greater sense of community throughout the city."

"There you go," the prince says, leaning against the high back of his chair with an air of satisfaction. "The voice of reason."

Qonna's father arches his brow. "Fair enough. I'll mention the idea to the First Bull when I pester him about the latest incident. Can't you ever not get involved, Nian?" he grunts as he signals the serving boy to remove the remnants of their meal.

The prince, resplendent in a rust-coloured tunic trimmed with fox fur around the collar, grins. The corners of his eyes crinkle up, and there's a slight gap between his front teeth that makes him seem much younger than he is. "You know me well enough by now to answer your own question. Will you head back?"

"I need to check on my poor, harassed secretary and make sure he hasn't been spooked too much. Will you walk Qonna and Gia back, Your Highness?"

It's an odd request, given they all met up at the *Unicorn*.

"Yes," the prince says. "I wanted to pop by the *Pear* this week before Father commandeers all my attention." He smiles at Gia and Qonna. "Unless you would like to walk alone?"

"No," Qonna says hastily. "No, I think that would be fine."

How can they just walk with Nian da Nileon, the wayward prince himself, through Seagard? Though dressed finely, he's restricted himself to the city's customs, but his hair spills loose across his shoulders, braided back from his temples with wire, and he wears a gigantic pin in the shape of a golden sun entwined with a silver moon. The way he moves along the roads, he seems oddly out of place. Qonna thinks about the name her father called him—the name she's not supposed to know. *Could it have been a mere nickname?*

Nian sees Qonna staring at his pin. "It was a non-wedding present," he says. "I try to wear it as often as I can. It reminds me I don't need to get too worried about anything that happens in the Cities, because I'll soon board another ship to the west."

"You must miss your partner very much," Gia says.

"The Siblings have granted me more than I ever thought possible," Nian says with an unmistakable wobble in his voice. "Perhaps being here and missing them so much is what's kept us together for so long."

"Aren't you ever tempted to stay in the old country?" Gia asks.

Qonna shoots her friend a warning look but is ignored.

"Every single time," Nian admits, "but all my blessings come with conditions, and I accepted them long ago. What about you, Gia? Your father said there was someone you were interested in? Someone working for the Applebeck Temple?"

"I'm flattered you remember, Your Highness, but I have no understanding with him." Gia sounds the tiniest bit bitter.

"It's a mere crush?"

*What the fuck is happening?* Qonna's heartbeat picks up. How can someone like Nian da Nileon be interested in the life of a tavern owner's daughter? The *Pear* is no place for princes, wayward or otherwise. She feels the urge to insert herself between her walking companions, to quell the conversation before it strays into painful territory.

"Not just a crush, Your Highness, but things do not always work out." Gia sounds older than she should. "My father's house will guarantee that I'm in the position to make a good marriage one day."

"It certainly has come up in the world," Nian admits. "Your mother has worked wonders, and I hear Qes is considering making it into official accommodations for Suns who need somewhere to stay?"

At last, a chance for Qonna to step in. "Most apprentices are recruited in the city, but some come from further away and all beds on the premises have been filled."

"Cisir seems quite content to live with us," Gia says, "and that might be only the beginning."

As they reach the Triangle, all its taverns have opened their doors, and the streets are filled with people drinking ale in the afternoon sunshine. It's a strangely peaceful scene, as if the quarter won't transform into its nightly chaos later. The *Pear* is already busy; all shutters and doors are thrown wide and the serving boys run around with trays of bowls and jugs. The smell of stew and toasted bread wafts out to them.

"I'll let my father know you're here." Gia disappears inside.

The prince turns to Qonna. "It was a pleasure to share a meal with you both," he says courteously.

She curtseys and feels like an idiot. "Thank you, Your Highness. Neither of us has much opportunity to visit the *Unicorn* or the Westown."

"Why is that?"

"Because we are both very much involved in the running of our parents' houses."

"You don't go to the temple for prayers?"

"If I have to." It comes out so blunt that he laughs. "Apologies," Qonna says. "My mother certainly attends weekly congregations, but I usually find something more useful to do."

"Lilyis fucking Sun!" Uncle Lauron appears on the steps leading into the *Pear*, his arms wide. He rushes at the prince and pulls him into his arms. "So good to see you."

Gia stands behind her father, looking thoughtful. It must've hurt to talk of her hopes for the *Pear*. As Gia's father sways the prince back and forth, Qonna realizes Uncle Lauron is weeping. "If anyone doubts the Siblings look upon you with love, they don't know how you've cheated the sea so many times!" Qonna sees Gia rolling her eyes behind Lauron's back before she waves to her friend and vanishes inside the *Pear*.

Qonna withdraws slowly. She knows Uncle Lauron can be unbecomingly demonstrative when he's a few cups of ale in, and that it's precisely what her father is afraid of. She also knows 'Lilyis Sun' sounds like a name from the old country.

When Qonna comes home, one of her father's scrawled notes is waiting for her.

*I found him at the Yellow House, unscathed.*

That's all the message says, but she knows what it means. Relief fizzes along her limbs. Since when is she so concerned for someone she just met?

*Since he allowed himself to be vulnerable. Since you found out you worry about many of the same things.*

Her mother is absent too, which is unexpected. Qonna uses the opportunity to settle down in the sitting room's window seat and watch the street running past *Pomegranates* for a while. It's the time of day when citizens are returning home, perhaps picking up bits and pieces on their way across town before rejoining their families. On an eventful day she doesn't expect her father to come back early, and only the Star knows what kind of engagement her mother is honouring. She has some girlhood friends among the ladies of the Cities, and it's likely that an afternoon visit has overrun.

As far as Qonna is aware, there are no dances coming up in the next two weeks. She can't expect to be invited to a meal in the *Unicorn* every day; it felt as if the prince was making a deliberate point by including her. Perhaps it'll remind her father that she should be part of more decisions discussed among the men, that both she and Gia have something to contribute, though neither of the two Companies are prepared to consider female apprentices.

*But you couldn't even say anything when you were asked. You clammed up and Gia stepped in to cover your arse.*

Qonna's brothers return to the house in a tight huddle, the spatters of mud covering their cloaks and boots speaking to how they spent the day. They seem flushed and happy and must've dropped off their horses at the livery. She pushes herself up to check the kitchen.

The cook glances at her, astonished. "But your mother left no instructions, mistress."

"Where is my mother?" Qonna earns a wide-eyed stare and sighs. "Is there some soup at least that is ready for them before our evening meal? Some bread or cheese?"

It happens all the time that her brothers demand to be fed during the day, and a few scraps need to be found to offer to them. Qonna brings the tray back up and finds them installed at the big table. The oldest twin, Qatt, is building up the fire in the brazier, while Qov and Qitli are lounging on the chairs. They haven't scraped their boots.

Qonna is tempted to launch the bread and cheese at their heads, but they would probably laugh, and she would feel too guilty to let the servants clean it up. She grips the tray so hard her knuckles pop. "You're home early."

"Is Dad still on the bridge?" Qatt cleans his sooty hands on his trouser seat. He'll sit down on their mother's embroidered chair covers next. Qonna's brothers have always been thoughtless like that—and so was she, until she was forcibly involved in the consequences.

"You haven't heard about the incident?" she asks. As soon as she sets down the tray, all three descend on the food. She blinks once, and the table is strewn with crumbs.

"We were far outside the city walls all day," Qov says, his mouth stuffed. "What happened?"

"Father's new secretary was accosted by the Bulls."

"The one he had earmarked for you?" Qitli asks. He's the youngest and has the sharpest tongue.

"Don't be daft," Qov jumps in. "Qonna won't be sold off to someone of such low rank. Mother would have a fit. Is there more cheese?"

Qonna blushes despite herself. The time will come when they too will marry to further their family's position. "Yes," she grits out. "It's in the kitchen."

"Oh dear." Qatt gives her a look of pity that's worse than all the teasing she could possibly imagine. "I hope he made it out alive."

"He's fine, but obviously there are talks to be had."

"Shit," Qov says. "Dad won't be in a good mood for weeks. He hates creeping to the Bulls and complaining—and the grey gelding threw a shoe today. I need him seen to by the end of the week."

Qonna finds it difficult to take her brother's concerns seriously, and in turn they don't care about the mud on the floors. All four of them were born in *Pomegranates*, but they live in separate worlds. Whenever Qonna interacts with them without the buffer of either parent, she leaves disillusioned and exasperated. She retrieves the plundered tray, pushes a palm along the table to brush the crumbs onto it, and empties them into the brazier where the bits of bread burn to fragrant ash. Her brothers are drawing up a contingency plan in case the grey gelding doesn't make it to the farrier in time.

Before she leaves the room, Qonna stares back at them. So often they appear as three parts of the same person, but each of them must have his own fears and dreams for the future. They can't possibly be as self-consumed and unbothered as they seem. Even with all the schooling they received, the number of tutors they went through to be adequately prepared for their entry into the Company of the Sun, they must experience the same sense of dread when they lie in bed unable to sleep, the same helpless rage.

# CISIR

## *you won't be walking alone*

When Cisir arrives at the Yellow House in the morning, he helps Hevo open the front and watches him push the little stone dog into place. How strange that Cisir's run-in with the Bulls was so helpful in befriending the other Suns. Perhaps they see it as some sort of initiation.

While they work, water boils on the small brazier and they sit down to a quick bowl before Cisir moves on to the study. Hevo likes his tea so strong that it strips teeth, and though it tastes much too bitter, it definitely wakes Cisir up quicker than his walk through town.

"Thank you for your help opening up the counter," Hevo says. "Even if no one was waiting in line for once, it's always good to have the baskets set up and ready."

"It was no bother. The only thing waiting for me in the study is a mountain of scrolls to copy."

"At least you don't have to deal with the customers." Hevo snorts. "Though I suppose that gives me enough stories to be stood a drink or two. What made you choose the Sun, anyway?"

"I don't know. I saw the advertisements posted in the village square and it sounded promising." *It was far away from home.*

"I didn't know we sent them that far north. You're from somewhere up there, right?"

"Windyhill," Cisir confirms. "Near the Rosevalian border. You?"

"Greysteele, originally."

"Where's Greysteele?"

"All the way up in Northwood, but my Pa moved us down to Southclere when I was a few summers old. After Ma died he needed to be a bit inventive, and a few of his former friends were out for his hide. Wasn't easy for him to find work in Seagard; not everyone wants to employ Northwood people. Pa said I should try the Sun because they have actual Birklanders, so they can't be too choosy about that. Turned out he was right. It's a good position, really, and next year I should have enough saved to search for someone to marry and finally move out. Can't wait to get away from my step-ma." He offers up all this information seemingly without drawing a single breath, but he doesn't look worried about Cisir ever using it against him. "Fact is, most of us Suns have our reasons for ending up in the Yellow House. They must have no shortage of applications, seeing that the royals are bound up in it all, but Pa says twenty years are not enough to make people less wary, not for something so fickle as shipping spices halfway around the world, so maybe we only think they can take their pick." Cisir tenses in discomfort at hearing his father's opinion expressed, and Hevo clears his throat. "How is the First Sun close up? I only see him from time to time; I've never shared an office with him."

"He's fine," Cisir says. "Quite patient."

"That's good." Hevo pushes against his legs and rises to his feet to check the situation behind the counter, but the morning is slow. He sits back down with a relieved grunt. "How are you finding it? Must be a bit confusing when you're used to a village."

"It's …." *You can't say 'fine' again.* "It's not too bad." *How is that better?*

"Is it true you choked out one of the Bulls? With your bare hands?"

"The smallest one," Cisir admits. "I used my cloak to restrict his breathing."

Hevo seems impressed, which makes Cisir squirm. This is not who he wants to be—the Sun who nearly strangled a Bull. "It's a trick, nothing more. I learned it a long time ago, when our sword master …." He bites his tongue.

"Sword master?" Hevo squeals. "You had a fucking sword master?"

"A long time ago." *Not true.* "I was never any good." *Too true.*

"You managed to get away from five Bulls, so I'd say you're good enough. I'd get my ears boxed for saying it, but that's the sort of skill we need around here. Most of us are city boys. Yoren is quite good with daggers, but he gets carried away and stabs himself by mistake." Hevo grins. "The Bulls have all grown up being tutored with fighting lessons on their rota. I swear, some of them can't even write. But you can't get into the Bulls if you're not related to one of them. You're probably the only one who can hold your own against them."

"The next time they won't let me get away so easily," Cisir mutters.

"The next time you won't be walking alone."

A glow radiates through Cisir's chest. "I hope you're right."

Someone approaches the counter and Hevo rises to serve them, but not before giving Cisir a friendly pat on the shoulder.

It seems Qes na Qarim has taken special care to dress today. His beard is freshly trimmed and his curly hair pulled away from his face in a short braid. With so many of his features on display, he appears older and grim-faced. "You should probably take the pens and ink with you. We'd better ensure there's a record of the conversation."

"Master?" Cisir had prepared himself for a day at the desk.

"We're dropping in on the Bulls today."

"Really?" All the moisture vanishes from Cisir's mouth.

"Lilyis thought it was warranted, and you usually ignore her at your peril. If I won't follow up, she'll find a way to insert herself into the situation, and then we'll have a much bigger problem. Trust me, that's how it always goes." Qes takes up a folder with strips of paper and a wax tablet and stuffs them into the bag he hands to his secretary. "I'd hoped to spare you this kind of inconvenience for a few months, but perhaps it's better to push you into deep water straight away."

"Is that a good idea, given that the conflict originated with me?"

His master snorts. "Don't flatter yourself. Apologies, that sounded meaner than intended, but we've had twenty years of smouldering grievances. It might also help you understand exactly what we're up against."

"Hevo tried to explain."

Qes na Qarim shrugs one shoulder as he pins his cloak in place. "Hevo is a good lad and useful to have at your back. Be a bit more careful with Yoren; he has a sneaky streak. Both have a skewed view of what's going on. I offer you the chance to judge the chief players face to face."

"I'm sorry, Master. I should be grateful for the opportunity."

"Yes, you should, but don't worry about it. Not everyone is suited to taking the bull by the horns. Unfortunately, when dealing with the da Relians, there's no other way. They once were the rulers of Southclere and feel beholden to their heritage, which has always made them a thorn in the thumb of the princes. The sooner you learn to handle a house full of arrogant young noblemen, the better." He touches Cisir's shoulder briefly, merely to get him to step out of the study, but it jolts like a spark igniting. Cisir pulls back with a squeak.

"Fuck." Qes shakes out his hand. "What was that? Did it hurt you as much as me?"

Cisir rubs his shoulder. "It was almost like a bite." *What did I do?*

His master's eyes narrow. "Let's walk up to the Red House and try not to touch while we do." Qes follows his words up with a chuckle, but Cisir still cringes.

The morning is mild, the skies light blue and covered in thin strips of cloud that stripe the streets with disjointed shadows. It doesn't take long for Qes to pull open his cloak as sweat darkens his temples. Cisir's master is bound to be nervous about what's to come, although he tries to hide it with a stern face, his mouth set in a flat line.

For once, Cisir is not concerned with keeping his yellow tunic hidden. Qes na Qarim is known as the First Sun and it would be strange for his secretary to shy away from displaying the Company colours. People stare at them while they walk, stepping aside to let them pass as if there's an invisible barrier around his master that commands space, which also means Cisir isn't forced to brush against anyone. The patch on his shoulder smarts as if he'd been burned. *It's never felt like that.*

As they pass the first thoroughfares into the Triangle, a strange longing bubbles up. Cisir is about to walk so far out of his depth the thought of running away and hiding in the *Pear*'s laundry again is horribly tempting. The hairs on the back of his neck rise when the colourful facade of the Red House comes into view. It's surrounded by the largest houses on the main road, all painted and ornamented to an absurd degree, and red banners fly along its front, the bull's head on them like a warning to keep away.

*We shouldn't be here.*

Coming so close to it feels like a horrible idea, and his master shifts his broad shoulders before sending Cisir to knock at the blood-red door. The man who opens it is surprisingly old but square-jawed and muscular like his younger relatives. He takes one look at them and groans. "There I was thinking my day couldn't get any worse."

Qes nods. "Rinald, it's been a while."

"Not long enough," the Bull grumbles, "but I should've expected trouble when the gods thought it necessary for me to get up four times in the night to piss—never a good sign. Come in, boy."

'Boy' isn't directed at him, but at his master. "Good to see you too," Qes says as he pushes in.

"I'll announce you," Rinald says. "Stay put, for fuck's sake."

As Rinald limps away from them, Cisir notices that one of his legs has been replaced with a wooden peg. Despite the old man's instruction, Qes walks after him until they reach the middle of the yard. It's a wide, cobbled space with a long stable at one side and stone troughs lining the others. They are planted with seedlings that will grow into blooms and soften the edges in summer. The surrounding walls are painted red, and the effect is disturbing. Stone stairs lead to a door covered in square iron nails, which sports the biggest lock Cisir has ever seen. Someone in the Red House is deeply afraid.

It only takes a few moments for Rinald to appear again. He huffs as he props open the heavy door. "He's expecting you."

"Thank you." Qes gives the old man a quick bow before leading Cisir into the Red House. It's surprisingly cold and the corridor they walk through is festooned with shields, battered enough to suggest they were once worn on the battlefield. Faded banners drape the walls, showing variations of the bull motif. Whereas the Yellow House cannot deny its humble origins, the Red House comes with a rich history of triumph and bitter defeat. The wooden floors creak under every step, as if the building itself has absorbed centuries of passionate hatred. While its facade is modern, its inside appears much older, gnarled and twisted. It smells of leather and beeswax, and the door lintels are carved into battle scenes. Cisir's master clearly knows his way around. He knocks on a specific door.

"Come in!"

The door opens with an ominous creak. The study of the First Bull is enormous and dark with almost every shutter closed. A brazier filled with embers provides a reddish light. The man sitting at the gigantic desk at the back of the room looks up. At first glance he seems white-haired, but upon closer inspection he's merely very blond and quite young too, perhaps the same age as the five Bulls who attacked Cisir.

"Is that him?" The Bull's voice is deep. "He doesn't seem that scary. From what my boys told me, I pictured him as somewhat more impressive." His eyes are dark, the silvery lashes an unearthly contrast, and as the Bull pushes up from his desk, Cisir notes that he wears leather armour. His gaze is intrusive enough for Cisir to take an instinctive step back. Strangely, the First Bull is a type he has more than enough experience with. "I appreciate you taking this matter as seriously as it should be," the Bull says to Qes. "My cousin could've been killed."

"He wasn't." Qes' voice sounds flat.

"Not for lack of trying. Of all the incidents we've handled over the years, this is one of the most distressing." With every step the man draws closer, Cisir's hackles rise. He spent a whole childhood among entitled noblemen; this one believes himself to be the one who rules them all. Embossed on the armour's breastplate is the shape of the Star. He carries the gods before him into every fight, and something about his confidence is utterly abhorrent.

Qes sighs. "Let us look at the facts, Bjell. Five Bulls tried to corner a Sun. One Bull was threatened. No one was seriously hurt, and the more your boys protest, the more pathetic they make themselves. Cisir happens to be my personal secretary, so I am partial to him being treated fairly. He managed to take five Bulls by surprise, which should be lauded and used as an opportunity to learn. Neither the Bulls nor the Suns gain anything by continuing these embarrassing spats. It makes more sense for us to come to an agreement."

Bjell scowls, but the firelight smoothes out his face. This close to him his age is more apparent. "An *agreement*? With the Suns? My dear late uncle would descend from the Heavens to smite me if the Bulls ever stooped that low."

"Your dear late uncle was a delusional bully. You don't need to run the Red House as he would've. I'm trying to extend a helping hand here."

The Fist Bull scoffs. "We've never needed your help—and we never will." He bares white teeth at Cisir. "Your boy must prepare himself to reap his just rewards."

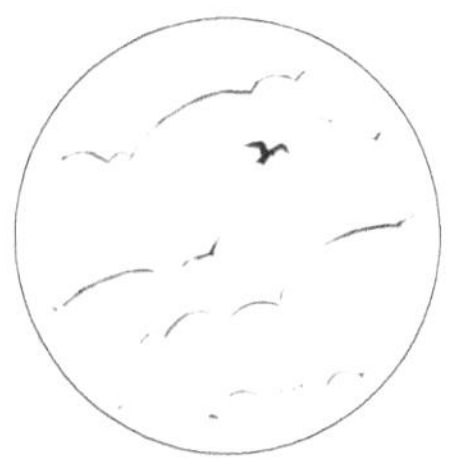

# QONNA

## *without claim*

The next time Eravis invites Qonna into the rose garden, the first blooms have opened, soft yellow and not especially fragrant, dotting the bower like the lightest stars. "The older princes are due to arrive at the manor in a matter of days, and it sounds as if I might be granted my wish to bring you along. Has your mother said anything?"

Qonna folds her hands. "I didn't have the chance to speak to her."

"Why are you avoiding her? Did something happen?"

"There's something she doesn't know. Something she's likely to blame me for, though I'm not the one in control of the situation."

Her new friend's hazel eyes widen in alarm. "It sounds worrisome."

"It is, in a way. It grants me more freedom than she would be happy with. It might nullify the problem of finding someone to marry me."

"Have you told your brothers?" Eravis asks.

"Hells no."

"I assume it will affect their future?"

"Very much so, including their own prospects for marriage. I would never have known about it if the prince hadn't let it slip. It seems there's an unusual arrangement in place." Qonna shudders as she thinks back to the moment she understood what her future could look like.

"An unusual arrangement how? Regarding your father's house?"

"I don't know if I should talk about it. My mother would rip my head off if the particulars became known before she herself was aware." *Rip my head off and kick it all the way down to the harbour.*

"That's a good point. Though any agreement that grants a woman more agency than her mother is comfortable with sounds extremely intriguing. When did you speak to Nian da Nileon?"

"The prince is a friend of my father's. It's not a mere business connection; there are family ties that keep us close to the Company of the Sun. He also gave me something when he visited, something I want to show to you, because I can't possibly show my mother."

The amber glows against Qonna's skin. In the soft light beneath the sprawling rose, every feature of the goddess appears animated.

Eravis reaches out to touch it. "Who is she?"

"One of the gods of the old country—a gift from the prince."

"May I hold her?"

"Of course, please do." As soon as the coveted piece of amber leaves Qonna's hand, she feels deprived of its warmth. "She's called Sister Sun. In Birkland there are two classes of gods, the Tall Gods and the Small Gods, the Siblings and the Cousins—eight Siblings in total and innumerable Cousins. Many families have a preferred Sibling, depending on which terrain they inhabit. Though, according to Uncle Lauron, everyone is free to pledge allegiance to a personal god as well."

Eravis turns the statuette in her hands, admiring it from every angle. "Would Sister Sun be your personal choice?"

"I don't know if the rules concern gods who are *given*. Based on everything I know about her she seems a good fit. Actually, the prince didn't choose her for me—his partner did, and they should know, being a wizard and all."

Eravis' eyes widen. "Have you ever met this wizard?"

"No, but they're related to me via my grandfather. Families in the old country can be complicated." *Not that families in the Cities are less complicated, mind.*

"You've never seen them perform magic?"

"I haven't, but my father certainly has."

Eravis is obviously ready to scoff, but manages to rein it in. She gives Sister Sun back. "As a young girl I loved the old stories about powerful sorcerers pledging themselves to impulsive kings."

"And queens," Qonna adds without thinking. "All those legends about the Queens of the Lakes."

Eravis tilts her head. "What would you do with a wizard at your disposal? What would you change?"

Qonna leans back in her seat and studies the wall of Eravis' home, so imposingly high and stern on its undecorated side. A contrast to the wealth of colour in the small garden around her. "I would probably try and exact some pressure to get myself taken seriously."

"Would you want to rule?" Eravis asks.

"Not a kingdom, no."

"What if the wizard could teach you?" Eravis digs her heels in. "If the magic was your own?"

"I think you need to be talented in some way, though Dad says his half-sibling didn't know about their own gifts for a long time and had to catch up rather quickly. Whenever he speaks about magic it sounds like something destructive—no twinkling lights, but something that hurts."

"All the more suited to make your point." A strange expression appears on Eravis' pale face. "If I had such powers, I would never have to bow to my half-sisters' idiotic whims again, nor cajole my stepmother to grant me the smallest requests. No more standing around at dances, no more being sneered at for having missed my chance to get married. I'd throw the door closed on my way out of this hellhole." The last word vibrates with hate. "I would kill to be rid of it."

Qonna frowns. *Is she serious?* "Would you rather live like my friend Gia? Working in her parents' tavern, spending her days cleaning up after the cook and the patrons?"

Eravis pulls a grimace. "We're related to the da Relians on my mother's side, and knowing who's been admitted into the Red House over the years, I'd be ten times as qualified to join the Bulls' ranks. We should have the same opportunities as our brothers, don't you think?"

"Of course."

"We should sail across the known world into undiscovered territories, explore lands we've never heard of before. In a way you're lucky. Your connections to Birkland give you a glimpse of what's possible. Don't they have queens in Birkland? Isn't it what the Star is so riled up about? What if the Eight Kingdoms afforded us the same options?" Eravis' gaze burns into the amber goddess in Qonna's hand and Qonna fights the instinct to flinch away from her, from the violence that has so suddenly broken forth. "That is what I would use magic for. To make the whole continent sit up and listen."

"The princes have arrived," Qonna's father says with a deep sigh, staring at the small pile of correspondence sitting next to his plate. "As always, they come bearing demands." He tears off a piece of bread to soak it in his broth and watches it disintegrate. There's something unusually resigned about him today. Qonna's mother takes her morning meal in her room, but her brothers are present for once, slightly creased and tired as if they drank too much last night.

Qonna smothers her slice of fruit bread in butter; the salt corns embedded in it scrape against her small eating knife. "Will you have to visit them at the manor?"

"I don't have a good excuse not to. I wish they wouldn't always show up in full force. I can take one of them easily, but they're turning into a royal infestation."

"I don't remember it being that bad," Qonna says, taking a bite.

"Because your mother had the foresight to shield you from them for most of your life, and the last time you were ill and we thought it better to …."

"… to continue keeping me away? Dad, do you remember Eravis, the friend I've been visiting? She asked me if I'd be willing to accompany her when she serves as companion to Princess Noalis."

"Dammit, Qonna." He sets down his spoon with a *clank*. "That's exactly what we've been trying to avoid."

"Why? Isn't that what we should do? Use our connections in the city?"

Qatt emits a low groan.

Qonna shoots her brother an irritated glance. "It would be so much easier if you'd explain things to me! I might not be about to join the Sun, but I need to know what the fuck is going on!"

All three brothers gasp.

Her father narrows his dark eyes. "There are princes and there are *princes*. While your mother wholeheartedly approves of the old king and his wife as well as some of their offspring, you must be aware the da Nileons associated with the Company have rather spotty reputations. Nian is only marginally more objectionable than the crown prince or his own father, after Nivael chose to take the most unsuitable woman as his third wife."

Qonna scowls at him. "Why are you always two different people? How can we know what to do if the First Sun operates within such different rules than our father? You asked me to join you and Nian at the *Unicorn*—why would you oppose me spending time at the manor? I don't understand."

Her father blows up his cheeks and slowly releases the air. "You're right. I have to be two different men and sometimes I get muddled." He looks around the table at each of his four children. "As the First Sun of Seagard, my loyalty has to lie with the Company, and I've laid my services at the feet of all princes involved in it. As the current steward of *Pomegranates* who needs to keep the interests of his closest family in mind, I must be extremely careful not to be taken advantage of. This house came to our family in unorthodox ways and with various conditions attached, and I find it incredibly difficult not to resent the princes for the restrictions placed upon us. Their presence is a constant reminder that it could be taken away in an instant. *Pomegranates* was never bestowed upon me personally, and we will only ever have *use* of it, never own it."

Her brothers utter another collective gasp.

Qov clenches his fists. "Does Mother know?"

"Not as such. But her father was aware when the marriage contract was drawn up. He decided his daughter should not be told before the wedding and since then … I haven't had the heart to confess that all we have is merely borrowed. It's as good as our own, as my sibling won't be back to claim it, but the legal situation is clear."

Qitli snarls at his sister. "You knew?"

"Only for a few days."

"You should've told us!" Qov wails. "What will our friends say if it becomes common knowledge?"

"It doesn't need to become common knowledge," their father cautions. "We've kept it under wraps for decades."

Qatt interjects, "But what are we, if not the family in possession of the finest house in the Eastown? What do we have to show for ourselves?"

Qes na Qarim takes a deep breath. "You will become part of the Sun. You've had more than enough opportunity to run free and spend your time as you please, but what awaits you is a life of service. I had hoped to spare at least your sister, but it seems the princes will get their claws into her even so."

Qonna watches her brothers storm out of the room, muttering in outrage. "I'm sorry. I didn't realize what you were trying to do."

Pained lines show around his eyes. "I should've been clearer with you. I should've included you earlier."

Qonna touches her father's wrist. He flinches, then takes her hand. "Apologies. I didn't mean to pull away. Something happened with Cisir the other day and I'm still not sure what."

It's been half a week since the secretary has come up in conversation. "What happened?"

"I touched his shoulder and there was a strange *zap*—as if I'd tried to catch a lightning bolt. It really hurt, both of us."

"That sometimes happens to me if I shuffle my feet too much on the rug."

"It was nothing like that. It was violent. I'll be sure not to touch him in the future. As if the poor boy didn't have enough problems to deal with."

"What are you afraid of?" she asks softly.

"I can't say. Perhaps it'll be of help to keep the Bulls away from him. I fear his unfortunate run-in has painted a target on his back." Qes squeezes her hand. "I regret I ever tried to push him on you. I should've known better."

"He's actually a very nice man, and though I won't consider marrying him anytime soon, we had some interesting talks. I'd like him to stick around."

He smiles, exhausted. "That is as glowing an endorsement as I'd hoped to receive for his character. I'm glad you're making new friends, though Eravis na Eloven sounds like an intense person."

"She is. Did you know the na Elovens are related to the da Relians? She believes she could've become a Bull if she'd been a boy."

"As far as I'm aware, all Bulls are of noble blood, and carrying a *da* in your name is one of their basic requirements. All families in Seagard have crossed lineages at some point or another."

"Apart from us," Qonna grumbles.

"You forget that your mother is very well connected." He sounds stern.

"Right. That's why you married her—for her connections."

He sniffs. "I was not that callous back then. We disappointed each other so much over the years I forget about it sometimes. I wish I could give you more hope, but the Cities require certain conventions."

"Have you never thought about going back to the old country?" *To find a place where you could be truly free?*

"I was born in Seagard. I might not fit in as much as I want, but it's where I belong. This city is in my bones, and it calls to me every single day, even if—technically—I own nothing in it."

"Maybe ownership isn't the most useful concept for us," Qonna says. "Have you ever thought of that? Perhaps making a life without claim is the true aim to aspire to?"

He laughs, surprised. "You sound like your auntle."

# CISIR

## *make a point*

They give Cisir no warning this time. There is no buildup, no swagger; they attack him as he walks home after work, ambush him at the thoroughfare he always uses to get to the *Pear*. After a few quiet days he had become complacent, and it feels earned as the first blow lands and arms wrap around his neck.

Someone tries to get a bag on him, to retaliate with the same method he used to such effect, but none of them are tall enough. He cries out, less in surprise than in frustration, and is rushed by at least a dozen Bulls. The blows rain down while he curls up until he's down on the cobbles. They take turns kicking him. Cisir yowls as a boot lands in his kidneys and a fist crashes into his face.

*So that's how you die.*

The pain flares brightly and is so overwhelming it takes a while to realize that as quick as they came upon him, they've retreated, leaving him sprawled in the narrow alley.

*Dying would probably hurt less.*

Cisir had worked until late; their anger must've been fuelled by the hours they waited for him to emerge. How stupid of him to believe they wouldn't invade the Triangle. He saw no faces he could point out later. The only option left is to bleed and feel his face swell up, the pain intensifying until he finally loses consciousness.

Cisir comes to in the *Pear*, stretched out on one of its tables with its regulars standing around and staring down at him. Gia and her father are at his side, Gia with a large flat bowl and a blood-soaked towel over her left shoulder like a barber.

"Qes is on his way," Lauron Wolf says. "I'm sorry, boy."

Cisir's left eye is swollen completely shut and every breath makes a strange piping noise.

"He was lucky," Gia says. "They didn't break any ribs."

"He wasn't lucky," her father spits. "He was hurt with full intent— just enough to make a point."

The patrons around the table shuffle aside to let his master through. From what Cisir can see through his right eye, Qes na Qarim is flushed and extremely angry. "Ah fuck. That's the last thing we need. Can you understand me, boy?"

Cisir manages a faint nod.

"Gia and Lauron will take care of you while I sort this mess out." Qes shushes the onlookers into the other part of the room. "You weren't able to *zap* them away?"

"To *zap* … no, I'm sorry, I …." *What does he think the* zap *is?*

"Shit, son." Qes hesitates, then lays his palm across Cisir's brow. No flash of pain follows. As if what happened before was a weird singular occurrence. His master's hand is warm and calming.

Tears run out of Cisir's working eye. "I'm sorry," he whispers again, distorted through his broken mouth.

"None of it is your fault, son." It's the second time Qes has called him *son.* It should feel wrong, but it doesn't. It dims some of the hurt to know Qes na Qarim doesn't mock him for giving in, for blubbering in front of the whole *Pear*.

Lauron Wolf stands beside Cisir's master. "This needs to be addressed," he says through clenched teeth. "It was a precise act of aggression towards the Sun."

Qes clears his throat. "I need to be clever about it. The last thing the Sun can afford is an all-out war with the Bulls. We don't have nearly as many young men in our service. Bjell might be able to make sacrifices, but I can't risk any of my other Suns getting underfoot."

"You know what you have to do."

"I've prayed hard to not need it."

Lauron gives a grim chuckle. "You have to unleash the princes—with full force."

It takes three days until Cisir can swallow more than thin soup and it feels as if everyone is scared to leave him alone. Lauron's whole family takes turns watching over him, making sure his bed is kept clean, his face cooled, salve spread on his bruises. When he wakes, he often finds Gia reading at his bedside, trimming the wick of the single tallow candle every other hour. The Wolves are huddling around him as if they fear the Bulls will burst into the bedroom. How can the whole family be this accepting when his own father had so deliberately removed him from the will and his whole life in Windyhill? As if his father had never given him the name of his illustrious ancestors in the hope of continuing the da Fewell legacy? Now the small space above the common room of the *Pear* has become his sanctuary—so much that it might become a problem to leave it soon.

The first Sun who comes to visit is Hevo.

"They said you were doing better. Good day, Mistress Wolf." He inclines his head at Lauron's wife, who is currently on duty, and holds out a small packet wrapped in printed linen. "With compliments from the First Sun—some of our best tea on offer."

Gia's mother takes the present with a warm smile. "Much appreciated. I'll prepare a sample for you both." She leaves them and Hevo claims the chair she vacated. "I wish I was looked after by someone half as charming. I only have Pa sending up the dog when it's time to leave for work." He grins, but it's strained. "How are you feeling?"

"Both my eyes are open, and I can use the chamber pot by myself, which is a big improvement. Have things changed at the Yellow House since it happened?"

"We're not allowed to leave alone on errands, and when we walk home there are two armed guards with us, so it takes ages until everyone's been delivered safely. Yoren says that's totally unnecessary, but at least we know the First Sun and the princes watch over us while things quieten down. The crown prince had a fit when he was told. Apparently he's been searching for a reason to fuck up the da Relians good and proper for a long time, and he might've found the perfect excuse." Hevo glances around as if worried that the mistress of the *Pear* could hear his foul words. "Wouldn't surprise me if we're in for a tense summer."

Gia comes with Cisir as he hobbles across the threshold for the first time since the attack. She watches him take the crucial step onto the street, witnesses his rapid, shallow breaths. He can't hide out in the *Pear* any longer. His bruises are fading fast. He might've wished his recovery to be less speedy, but he's always healed rather quickly and knows putting off his return for much longer will let his anxiety fester.

If they want to jump him again, they'll have an armed guard to deal with. His master has sent a man to fetch him. As he stomps across the street to the steps leading into the *Pear*, Gia straightens up next to Cisir.

His guard wears leather armour, similar to the First Bull, but on his chest blazes a golden sun, marking him as a royal guard paid for by the princes. The helmet has cheek plates and a neck piece made from gleaming mail, though his smile shines still brighter.

"How is the invalid?" the guard asks in a booming voice, and both Gia and Cisir blush.

"Getting there," Cisir grits out.

"Mistress," the guard says, bowing slightly and removing his helmet with fluid grace. "Guardsman Jark, at your service." Above the dazzling smile he has long-lashed dark eyes and thick auburn hair combed back into a braid. If Gia doesn't fall head over heels in love with him, Cisir would be only too happy to do it for her.

"Giannis, daughter of this house," she says, beaming at him. "And Cisir da Fewell, the invalid in question."

Neither of them seems to mind how utterly ridiculous it is to perform a round of formal introductions out in the street. Only a week ago, Cisir lay upon the cobbles, beaten nearly to mush, and now he's been given a royal guard to herd him to the harbour bridge.

"Ready?" Guardsman Jark asks him. "Do you need a strong arm?"

Cisir would love nothing more than to cling to the man, but he is all too aware of Gia watching them. "I should be able to manage."

"As you wish, but I've been sent to be of assistance, and I take my designations seriously."

*Does he have to be so bloody charming?* Jark might've stepped from one of the legends in his polished headgear; all that's missing is his noble steed. "Let's see how it goes." Cisir's voice has gone gruff, as if he needs to impress.

"Don't forget your bag." Gia hands it over but Jark intercepts it.

"I'll carry that."

Gia curtsies. "Until later, then. I hope you have a good first day back at work."

Cisir pulls a grimace. *It can only get better.*

"How could one possibly exchange the beauteous vistas of the north for this?" Jark asks as they make their way through the Triangle.

*Beauteous vistas?* "The need to earn a living will do that for you." Cisir is already sweating and debating with himself how he can get Jark to offer his arm again.

Guardsman Jark strolls next to him, the leather bag slung across his broad back. At his belt he wears not one, but two swords, the sheaths buckled on top of each other. He probably has other blades hidden about his person, in his boots or in his smallclothes ....

"You look in pain, if you don't mind me saying." The charm has bled from Jark's voice and left only concern. "They roughed you up pretty thoroughly."

"It could've been worse," Cisir says.

Jark's gaze sweeps over him from top to bottom. "Could it? I didn't want to say anything in front of Mistress Giannis, but you should probably give it another two weeks before properly returning to the Yellow House. The First Sun has quite a good grip on the situation without you getting in the way."

"As I said, I need the money. I haven't received my first salary yet and I'm already forced to stop working and incur more costs. All these days in bed will end up on my bill."

Jark reaches out to steady him, but Cisir takes a step back. He's incensed enough that he might zap the man without wanting to. *If it really works like that.*

An expression of anguish darkens the handsome guardsman's face. "I've been called to assist at the Yellow House from time to time, and I've never had the impression that the First Sun was tight-fisted enough to deny someone who was hurt for belonging to the Sun. He's always struck me as someone who cares about the men he employs. Don't be too disappointed if he sends you home again. I mean, to the *Rotting Pear*, not the northern reaches," he adds helpfully. "I am at your disposal, should you decide you want to continue crawling to the bridge."

"I need to."

"Don't rush on my account." Jark holds out his arm.

Cisir swallows what's left of his pride. "Thank you." He grips the leather arm plate and thankfully, nothing happens. Perhaps he can finally allow himself to forget about the weird zap.

Limping along on Jark's arm, he draws many glances, and every man, woman, and boy who passes by stares at his bruised and deformed face before rushing on.

"Don't mind them," Jark says quietly. "They don't know anything about what you went through."

*Why must he be so kind to me?* Cisir doesn't know what to say in return, so he thanks Jark again. They walk in silence for a while, then Cisir asks, "Do you miss the north?"

"I was stationed in Crooked Hill for years and it's not a landscape you forget easily," Jark replies. "Whenever I'm back in Southclere, I can hardly wait to see the mountains again, the pure majesty and ravishing bleakness of the Hillakes."

"I don't think I've ever been so passionate about a view," Cisir says, breathless from the exertion of hauling his body along. "Is that where you come from? The Hillakes?"

"Oh no, I'm from Applebeck."

Cisir feels a laugh bubbling up. Of course he's from Applebeck, a few miles along the south coast. No northerner would get excited about the mountains they were born among. "I've never been to Applebeck, but it sounds like a nice, quiet little village."

His guardsman snorts. "If you like being bullied by the Brothers! All of Applebeck bows to the temple. I couldn't wait to get out and cut my teeth on more exciting endeavours. All my brothers are working in the temple orchard and its breweries, but when the royal recruiter came to the village, I was the only one who passed the trials." He winces, then amends his statement. "I was the only one who *signed up* for the trials, so it's not quite so remarkable."

Jark's expression brightens as they pass onto the main road and the masts of the sailing ships become visible above the rooftops. "Almost there," he says with a wide smile, pulling Cisir's hand into the crook of his elbow. "Just in time for a heroic return."

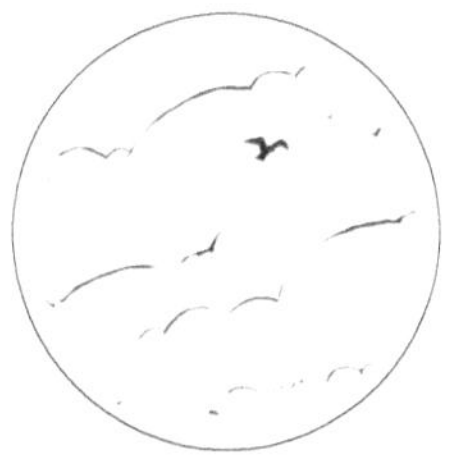

# QONNA

## *close to ruin*

The princes sent a carriage into town, and Qonna is the last of the young women it collects on its sweep. The narrow interior is stuffed with rustling fabrics and slightly squashed linen headdresses. Qonna turns around to see her mother standing in the door. For once she's abandoned the sitting room to witness her only daughter enter a new life. She might not approve of Eravis na Eloven, but the fact that she brought Qonna into the position to accompany a princess counts for something. Qonna prepared herself for an argument and can't help but feel slightly disappointed her mother acquiesced so quickly to the royal invitation. Perhaps because it came on nice parchment with a seal the size of an apple.

Qonna isn't the only one making the journey further up the hill. Though the other passengers seem to be her age, they are infinitely gigglier, and all know each other. Qonna squeezes into her corner of the carriage, listening to their strange little conversations as they remark upon the smallness of the houses they pass in the Eastown. Soon Qonna is sure she hasn't met any of her companions before, and they've obviously never set foot in the quarter where she was born. The only explanation that makes sense is Qonna *na* Qes has somehow landed in a carriage full of *da*s, who would never in a thousand years attend the Braid Makers' dance.

Qonna fusses with her blue dress. She already sticks out among them. She's twice as tall and though dressed in her finest, it's plain compared to the others' fashions. Some of them wear jewel brooches pinned to their headdresses, while the only ornament Qonna carries is the amber statuette concealed in the deep pocket beneath her skirts. When she presses a palm to her leg she can feel its form. She forces herself to breathe more slowly. There's no reason to panic. She might be the only trader's daughter present, but she received the same invitation.

Her companions squeal in delight as the horses pick up the pace, tackling the last steep incline before the gates to the long, winding manor drive. Qonna has passed these gates only a few times in her life, so now it's her turn to stare in excitement at the view unfurling beneath the path. The swell of the hill frames rows of houses at its feet; the sun sparkles on the placid sea all the way to the horizon. It's been a long time since she was able to see the beauty of her city. As encased in the Eastown as *Pomegranates* is, its roofs and walls surrounded by other buildings, it doesn't allow her a view. The royal family settled on the ridge for a reason.

When Gard Manor appears after the next curve of the drive, she's the only one who gasps. The others gawp at her. They must've visited the princess many times, so nothing about it is unfamiliar to them. A squat tower covered with early flowering roses sits amidst a complex of stone buildings and though its walls seem old, Qonna sees many signs of recent improvements. The roofs are not straw-thatched but tiled, their red-ochre glaze shiny. Generous stabling stretches along one side of the yard, and the gardens behind the main house are surrounded by tightly clipped hedges. The trees lining the road and grounds are old, but many younger trees have been planted in pretty clumps; meandering paths lead through them to a lake so regular in form it must've been placed by human hands. Eravis' small garden is beautiful, but it pales against the effort the princes have put into their surroundings, turning something that was once close to ruin into such splendour.

Qonna strains her neck, wanting to take it all in, which earns her pitiful glances from most of the women. They happily mocked the houses in the Eastown, but Qonna's reaction to the royal manor embarrasses them.

Their arrival is greeted by a throng of servants assisting the ladies with their dresses, and closer to the door, no one but Eravis herself, nearly unrecognizable in a voluminous creation of spring-green linen, worn much tighter around the chest than she'd dared at the Braid Makers' dance. She appears to have been stitched into it, and the headdress is built up with so many folds and pins it must weigh as much as a basket crammed with laundry.

Eravis holds herself more proudly than at home, and by age alone she's sure to take a special place among the women. She comes at Qonna with outstretched arms, favouring her among the noble companions. "Thank the gods you're here."

They're swept inside in a wave of pale colours and excited laughter, stepping through the broad door directly into the largest room Qonna has ever seen. It takes up the whole of the main house, with a long stone-clad fire pit running almost the full length of it. Braziers stand in the corners, and high windows illuminate the brilliant white walls, painted in a pattern of ochre-red flowers and ochre-yellow suns between the windows with a gigantic tapestry above the dais at the west wall. It depicts a hunting party in a landscape of rolling hills covered in tiny blue flowers, with many lords and ladies present. At the front of the party ride a red-haired man and someone in a long robe swarming with spirals, carrying a staff. A royal prince and the sorcerer in his service.

Qonna can't suppress the shudder running along her back. That's quite a statement to make in a city with a new temple of the Star.

"You're here!" Yet another woman joins them.

"Excuse my friend," Eravis says with an incline of the head. "Qonna, this is Noalis da Nileon."

The princess reaches out and takes Qonna's hand as if to shake it. "Noa to my friends." It's a gesture Qonna didn't expect, so she complies. Two women shaking hands is unprecedented in her experience. "I've heard so much about you," Noa says. She is neither tall nor specifically small, and nothing in the way she's dressed singles her out from the other women in the carriage, who keep to themselves despite the princess standing apart from them.

Noa notices her glance. "Don't mind them. They're not here for me; they want my aunt. She has a few positions open, as three of her ladies got married last year and have inconveniently entered their confinements at the same time."

"They've come to jostle for a place at court?" Qonna asks.

"Half of them will be disappointed," the princess says with a hint of malice. "Can't say I don't look forward to it if it teaches them to be a bit less obvious when shunning me." She makes a noise against the back of her teeth. "I'm delighted to have you here, Qonna. I believe my father has tried to bring about our meeting for quite some time."

"Your father?" Qonna has never met Nivael da Nileon. Of course, she knows of him—you can't be the daughter of the First Sun of Seagard and not know *about* him—but he has no reason to favour her.

Noa lifts her shoulder. "He is of the opinion I should be acquainted with the future steward of *Pomegranates*."

Eravis makes a weird, strangled sound. The cat has been yanked out of the bag.

No one seems particularly interested in what Noalis da Nileon has to say in her father's hall. The young townswomen who came with Qonna wait in a tight cluster close to the smaller side door that must lead into the private quarters of the manor, and when it finally opens and a servant appears to announce the various Royal Highnesses about to grace the hall with their presence, they emit an excited hum.

Qonna finds it strange that Noa is here among the onlookers and not part of the stripped-down version of a courtly procession, but she stands with Qonna, calm and composed. From the side, Noa's eyes appear almost yellow; when her long dark lashes shade them, they're light brown, the same colour as the statuette of Sister Sun. Qonna finds it hard not to stare at her, and the arriving princes are a welcome distraction.

The first man to stride into the hall must be the crown prince, with a narrow face and short dark beard. She's seen approximations of his face on satirical woodcuts: the ever-waiting heir, praying each night for the death of the old king.

Next to him walks his wife, the one in the market for new companions. She's younger than him, his second wife, and something about her makes Qonna restless. As if the future Queen of the Hillakes and Southclere is so tightly coiled in impatience that she's become volatile.

The second couple must be Noa's parents, the youngest son of the king and his third wife, the one he wasn't supposed to marry. Both are dressed more simply to allow the crown prince and his wife to shine, and Noa's mother is far from the irresistible beauty Qonna expected her to be—in fact, she's middle-aged, much closer in years to her husband than scandalous third wives are likely to be, and followed by the wayward prince himself, who spots Qonna instantly and sends her a crooked grin.

All the young women in the room notice and turn to watch her sweat with discomfort. Do they begrudge her the attention, or have they concluded she's about to become the most ill-suited mistress in the history of the kingdom? Before she can recover, Noa takes her by the wrist and pulls her forward.

"Mother, Father, I need you to meet Qonna, the First Sun's daughter."

Something flickers across Nivael da Nileon's face: pain, mixed with something more intangible. "There certainly is a family resemblance," he says. He has the same eyes as his daughter, and his long red hair fades into gold. He resembles the prince in the tapestry too much for it to be a coincidence.

"It is very nice to meet you," his wife says with a genuine smile. "I hoped to see you this time. Noa is looking forward to deepening the connection between our families." She pulls her stepson into their group.

The wayward prince makes a face. "Ow, careful with the sleeve, Hilvis. I can't rip it on its first outing."

"Don't whine. Nobody cares about your new frock." Both employ a playfulness in their tone that suggests they're used to each other, as well a warmth that feels out of place in such a grand house, with all those haughty faces woven into the tapestry above them.

Qonna curtsies, the least objectionable reaction to any of these people. Noa keeps an eye on her; Qonna can sense her gaze. Much more might depend on the introduction than her being entertained during her stay on the hill.

"We heard about your father's current problem with the Bulls," Noa's mother says. "I am sorry to say some things never change. They've been bullies ever since I can remember, and though the new First Bull has been in power for a couple of years since the death of his uncle, he seems intent on keeping to his principles." She talks as if she expects to be permitted her own opinion about Company politics. She turns to Eravis. "Our cousins have never had a propensity for restraint."

Suddenly the whole scenario makes sense. If Eravis is related to Nivael's third wife, she would've had a foot in the door early on. And though it seems strange that Noa herself isn't given her own throng of friends to travel with, she's still in need of an experienced chaperone. She might be the last in a long line of royal children, but this meeting between them should be everything her mother wishes for Qonna.

*Theoretically.*

Servants carrying cups of wine make the rounds as Noa's young aunt settles on one of the high-backed chairs on the dais, her bored-looking husband next to her. The man who spent so much of his life waiting to step up and take the crown doesn't strike Qonna as the embodiment of a kind and generous king. He's the type of man who appears haggard after a few days on horseback, his nose sharp and his mouth hard.

*You shouldn't be allowed in the same room as him*, says the mean voice Qonna knows so well. *No wine for you. You need to keep your wits about you today.*

With so many people around, Gard Manor doesn't feel like a safe place, and though her glance is pulled to the side of the hall, where long tables are erected and piles of glazed bowls appear to be laid out for the guests, everyone around her displays various degrees of discomfort. Noa and her mother talk quickly about the option of Qonna staying overnight, the wayward prince is already halfway through his next cup of wine, and the nervous laughter of the carriage companions sets Qonna's teeth on edge.

It takes a while to realize that Noa's father has asked her a question. "Has your father's secretary recovered?"

# CISIR

## *advance and retreat*

Y ou don't wish you could be like him?" Hevo asks admiringly.

Yoren, the designated troublemaker among Cisir's younger colleagues, sniffs. "He talks too much—and not even about interesting stuff! That's what happens if you read too much poetry. It rots your brain away." He snaps his fingers. "No thank you. The only way he gets the girl is by boring her into submission."

There seems to be a secret arrangement between them to distract Cisir on this endless day. Every other moment they bring tea to the study, and after the midday bells, a whole meal for them to share over the scrolls. As if he needs constant supervision. The truth is that his writing hand works fine, but his back hurts too much to sit still for long. Despite the salves and tasty broth he was treated with at the *Pear*, he knows it'll take some time to get over the punishment for having his wits about him. It feels as if ants are crawling over his spine, and not only because he's deeply uncomfortable with Hevo and Yoren discussing the man who will be his personal guard for the foreseeable future.

Hevo sighs dreamily. "You don't need much personality when you look like that. He'll have women tumbling over their own feet to chase him." He turns to Cisir. "That's your chance, by the way—with him around, there'll be plenty left over for you."

"I'm no prize for anyone to be consoled with," Cisir mutters. "I can barely walk and all the bruises …."

"Yeah, like a green grape," Yoren counters with a smirk. "Some like men to be pitiful, though. There's always a way to spin it."

"I didn't come to Seagard to find a girlfriend," Cisir snaps.

"You didn't?" Yoren sounds genuinely surprised.

Hevo pours out more tea for them. "You don't have a girlfriend either. None of us has."

Yoren sniffs again. "Yes, because I can't afford one yet. Wooing takes coin and I can barely keep myself in clean shirts and foot rags. What chance do we have if the bloody Bulls throw their wealth around and our raise isn't due until next year?" He nudges Cisir, conveniently ignoring his pained wince. "Even in Seagard, pretty girls are a finite resource."

"A *finite* resource?" Hevo scoffs. "Listen to yourself. The last time I saw you try to flirt with someone, you didn't get out a single intelligent word—you're as useless as the rest of us."

The rest of *us*. Cisir smiles to himself. Whatever the Bulls intended, it surely wasn't for him to find his feet among the Suns.

"What about the girl at the *Rotting Pear*?" Yoren asks, clearly trying to deflect. "Any joy there?"

Hevo slaps him on the back of the head, just hard enough. "Don't be such a dick. His landlord's daughter is strictly off limits!"

*And halfway in love with my guard.*

"Hevo's right." Cisir hates the slight resistance in his voice. "Gia deserves much more than …. " *Me. You. She deserves better than us.*

"You have the name," Yoren protests.

"The name doesn't mean anything. I'm the First Sun's secretary and *my* next raise is due in two years. If the Bulls haven't flattened me by then. I'm sure a royal guard is paid much better, and he has that face."

"Right?" Hevo agrees with an enthusiastic nod. "We could ask him to show us some sword tricks."

"Have you ever held an actual sword?" Yoren mocks.

Hevo shrugs. "No, but I'm a quick learner. We should beg the First Sun if we can't have a few lessons to prepare ourselves for summer.

There's going to be another ambush at some point—and now I need to get back to my counter. Can't have anyone waiting for their cloves and nutmeg. Are you finished with that?"

Cisir barely has a chance to nod before the tea bowls are removed from the desk and the rest of the bread packed away. Hevo and Yoren leave the study with encouraging grins. Cisir waits until their steps fade away before he allows himself to sag.

It's late afternoon when Cisir's master returns, closely followed by a carriage. Out of it spill Qes' daughter, Lilyis, and a man who can be no one but the youngest son of the old king. Two princes make their way through the stores of the Yellow House, led by Qes na Qarim, while Qonna takes possession of her father's chair.

"You don't seem well enough to be back at work," she admonishes.

"And you are too dressed up to visit your father."

She smiles. "It looked like rain, and the princes offered me a lift."

He cleans his quill. "You were at the manor today?"

"Yes, to meet the princess and give her the chance to decide against me before I decamp for weeks on end up the hill." She fusses with the sleeve of her blue dress.

"What about you? Have you decided on her?"

She gives him a calculating look. "Even if I had any say in the matter, for some reason my mother is quite keen for me to become closer acquainted with Noalis da Nileon. Despite her mother. And her father. And her half-brother. Though my mother might be disappointed to hear there are no unmarried noblemen in attendance at the manor. It's all skirts and headdresses."

"It could also be a relief to her."

The line between Qonna's dark brows deepens. "I don't think her objective is for me to make friends. She's dragged me to every guild dance in the city in the hope *someone* takes an interest."

"You don't want to marry?" His heart tries to claw up his throat.

"Someday, maybe," she says with a shrug. "Certainly no Braid Makers' or Sign Painters' apprentice. Maybe there's more husband material at the Goldsmiths' but their dance isn't until harvest time, and they tend to foist their apprentices on the young widows among their ranks to keep control of the workshops. Probably not much joy over there." To hear her use the same words as Yoren chills him.

*You're a prude. A prude with a filthy imagination.* He bites down on his tongue.

"I'm sorry." She must've picked up on his uneasiness. "I shouldn't distract you from your work."

"Has your father asked you to keep me company?"

"No, but after a tense meal at the manor I'm in no mood to hear three grown men talk about syrup as if it's the most important thing in the Eight Kingdoms."

"It *is* one of our most profitable goods."

She smiles in delight. "I like to eat it; I don't need to be informed in great detail about the best transport methods and the latest storage fees in Coldharbour."

The name she mentions so casually is marked in the centre of the map nailed across the study wall. His eyes are drawn to the lake covering so much of Birkland, the little decorative waves drawn onto it.

She follows his gaze. "Is this where you plan to go? To try and get a place on one of the prince's Birkland voyages and stay?"

"Is that what *you* want?" he asks.

She squirms. "I think about it from time to time. How it might be, being in the old country. If half of Uncle Lauron's stories are true, I could make myself heard in Birkland. I could claim a position with the Badgers and ...." Her voice trails off. "It's a stupid dream. Who says the Badgers want anything to do with me? I'm part Badger, part Bleakheath, and two parts Southclere—I'm everything and nothing." Her humour has sloughed off. "I don't know enough about the old country to make it work. All I have are contorted impressions fed by legends and Uncle Lauron's nostalgia for a place he left voluntarily a long, long time ago. It makes more sense for me to discover my Bleakheath roots; at least here I know how basic interactions work."

Something must've happened at the manor that left her with a taste of mild despair. She notices him studying her face and throws up her hands. "I know I don't have anything to complain about, born in the Eastown and with so many connections at my disposal. I'm going to stay with a princess, for fuck's sake!"

"I didn't say anything."

"No, you didn't need to." She crosses her arms. "You're a polite, kind young man who had his whole life taken away, yet listens to me rant on about feeling not appreciated enough."

*Am I polite? Kind, even?* "Your frustration is as real as mine, Qonna."

"Don't fucking patronize me."

A tense silence descends. They sit at her father's desk, staring at the Birkland map, the artfully placed names of villages they will never visit in person. They both start apologizing, talking over each other.

"I didn't mean—"

"I'm so sorry—"

"For fuck's sake," she says. "Look at us, so pathetic. No wonder we'd make such good friends." He gasps, as much in delight as terror, and she pulls a face. "At least that's how I feel."

He clears his throat. "I would like that."

"I didn't want to ambush you ...." She snorts. "Apologies again. Poor choice of words."

When he smiles it hurts. "It's fine. I never had many friends."

"Me neither. What do you think about this? Before I join the princess's household, we'll have tea with Gia at the *Pear*—three friends sitting down and talking."

He feels a soft warmth. "That sounds good."

"A word of warning, though. I saw your royal guard standing outside. Gia won't shut up about him for months to come." Qonna rolls her eyes. "Believe me, I've been there with her before."


"Who was the young woman talking to you earlier?" Jark waited until they left the harbour bridge to ask the question that must've bothered him for hours. Clouds gather above the city and there's a hint of mugginess to the air that sticks Cisir's hair to his neck as he makes his way over the dull cobbles to the main road.

"She's the First Sun's daughter."

"It seems like you're getting on well."

Cisir nods. "Yes. It happened quite fast, but we've had many opportunities to speak."

"She's certainly stunning," Jark says and for once, Cisir doesn't feel a stab of unbridled jealousy. Qonna is counting on Jark paying attention to Gia; it didn't sound as if she herself were interested. *She told you she doesn't want to marry. Believe her.*

"She is," he agrees.

"Wouldn't that be something—winning the hand of your master's daughter? Every apprentice in Seagard must dream of it."

Cisir stops, annoyed. "What are you implying?"

"Nothing, I'm just saying …."

"Do you have designs on any of the princesses?"

Guardsman Jark seems truly embarrassed. "No, of course not. It's just a good match." He's decked out in blades but shifts from one foot to the other, like a boy who nicked a jar of pickled apples. How strange that a single day changed how Cisir talks to this man who's been ogled at and admired all day.

*Because Qonna made you her friend. Because you know she cares about you.*

"I must apologize," Jark says eventually. "It's none of my business. Do you need a hand?"

"Yes please." As Cisir grabs the guard's arm, Jark covers his hand with his own. "I'm too nosy for my own good. It's not often we're dispensed on such personal duties."

"It's nice to take an interest, but you haven't been in town long." Cisir waits for him to let go, but Jark squeezes his fingers.

"Shall we walk?"

Jark is silent for the rest of the way, holding on to Cisir the whole time.

Cisir's evening meal is bread, cheese, and a bowl of the *Pear's* vegetable stew served at the small table the family uses, while Jark drinks the cup of ale Lauron persuaded him to accept for his services.

Gia is supposed to help her mother finish off the week's laundry, but she keeps darting in and out of the kitchen to ask her father questions of no great urgency. Every time she comes close to Jark, she lowers her eyes, and as soon as she's sure he isn't looking, she stares openly, a game of advance and retreat.

Either Jark isn't aware of the effect he has on people, or he's too used to it to care. While Cisir fishes the first fresh peas of the season from the bottom of the stew, he realizes Lauron Wolf, by comparison, is very much in the know about what's going on with his daughter and the dazzlingly handsome guard who materialized this morning to disrupt all their lives.

*Qonna was right. She'll swoon over him for months, if not years. I might come to do the same.*

When Jark takes his leave from the *Pear*, rejoining his division at the manor for the night, Gia misses his departure. "Oh, he's gone?"

"It's getting late," her father says with a barely suppressed grin. "He'll have a long walk up the hill and must come all the way down again to collect Cisir in the morning."

Her face lights up. "Yes, of course." She turns to Cisir. "How was the first day back? You're clearly exhausted."

He smiles, relieved to be on safe ground. "I'm exhausted, but it was a good day."

She slides onto the stool opposite him. "So, did your guard talk about how long he's staying in town?"

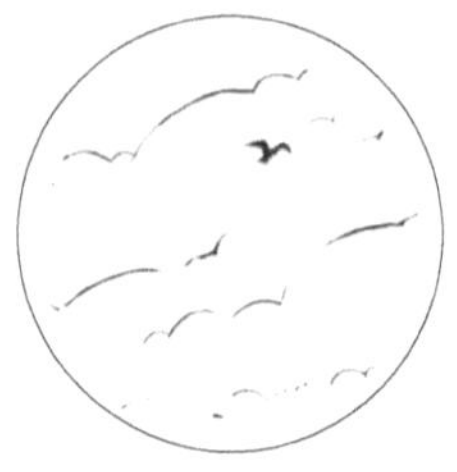

# QONNA

## *the need to ask*

It would've made more sense to meet up at the *Pear*, but Gia insisted on coming out of the Triangle.

"Your parents are right, you know," she says to Qonna. "You really shouldn't wander about the Triangle on your own. It might not be as dangerous during the day as it was, but it's not appropriate." Gia has these flare-ups of righteousness from time to time and the best strategy to handle them is to nod along. Gia seemed happy to walk up to the Eastown, where she discovered Qonna about to freak out in front of her open clothes chest. Ordering tea and cake from the kitchen was the perfect distraction.

"He'll know where to find you, right?" Gia's fingertips drum on the empty chair next to her.

"Yes, Cisir's been here before." Qonna takes the tray from the maid and lays out the bowl and small plates for her visitors. Her mother had withdrawn into her own chamber but insisted on Qonna using the dining room to meet her friends. Her mother never felt easy having Gia around, someone who so clearly belonged downhill, as she put it, and who knew what she would've said if Qonna had trusted her enough to disclose that the third person they're waiting for is her father's secretary. The best way to handle her mother is to let her only know what she absolutely needs, though sometimes Qonna feels guilty that her father and brothers operate on the same principle. The world her mother lives in is not the world of her children, and she has no idea that the two young women shuffling tea bowls on *Pomegranates'* big table are waiting for someone she most likely wouldn't approve of, now Qonna is moving up into better company.

When the front door finally opens to admit Cisir, Qonna and Gia straighten up, but Gia deflates when it becomes apparent there's no armed guard at his side.

"Didn't he want to come?" Gia asks.

Cisir shrugs. "I'm sorry. He had other orders for the afternoon and had to go up the hill." He holds himself differently since Qonna last spoke to him. Perhaps it's the result of the injuries, but he seems broader in the shoulder and quieter, as if the initial nervousness and constant blushing are fading as he finds his place in town. Walking about with one of the most beautiful men on the Continent might've changed him too, as if Jark's glow gilded him.

Cisir chooses the chair closest to the door and keeps his distance, as if too aware there's a mother without a shred of humour close by.

The maid returns with a tray of ginger cake, caraway biscuits, and the last of the honeyed figs, cut into dainty pieces. The spark in her eyes lets Qonna know the cook will be informed about this get-together as soon as she returns downstairs. Countless times Qonna has profited from the gossip making its rounds through *Pomegranates*; she knows whatever secrets she keeps are not truly secret at all.

Gia goes straight for the figs.

"They were really good last year," Qonna says. "Cisir?"

"I'm not really hungry."

"Horseshit. You've surely not had time to eat."

He smiles. "My colleagues keep me in bread and biscuits since the incident. It gives them an excuse to check in on me every other moment."

"Suit yourself, but this is the last of them. We wait until they're in full season before they're cheap enough to jar."

"If you say so." He lifts his eating knife and picks up a halved fruit on its tip. Just how he turns the knife on its way to his mouth tells more about his background than he can know. Cisir da Fewell has certainly been schooled to eat with as much decorum as any of the princess's companions. He chews thoughtfully, then smiles again. "You're right—they're really good."

Qonna pours out the tea, feeling a tiny bit smug. "There you go—one point for me. And this takes me to why I thought it might be a good idea." She makes a circling motion with the teapot in her hands. "Bringing us all together, I mean."

Gia arches a brow. "This should be interesting."

"I'm not going to make a whole speech, but it's nice to know there are friends around, especially when I'm set to spend my summer so far up the hill I might as well be out of town. To know there are people who understand me while I'm battling it out with courtiers."

Gia takes a very deliberate sip of tea. "You're not leaving me in the dust because you found better friends?" She grins but Qonna detects a hitch in her voice.

"I could never leave you, and if you ever feel that way, please tell me." Qonna swallows painfully. "Things are changing a lot, and now that I know how many people are aware of *Pomegranates'* circumstances, it gets ever more complicated." Her eyes well up. "Please write to me, Gia. I'll ask Dad to take care of the message delivery. Give them to Cisir in the mornings."

Gia nods. "I will. It seems you've thought it through."

"Because I'm terrified of being stranded in Gard Manor. It's an opportunity I can't refuse, but I'll miss you—both of you." She makes herself look directly at her father's secretary. "I know I can't ask you to write without instigating speculation, but you need to know I'm grateful for the talks we've had over the last weeks. I dare say it's rare to find someone you have so much in common with." He sits very straight and tries to keep his face under control, but she can tell he's pleased. "My father already holds you in high esteem, and he tends to be an excellent judge of character. I feel we need to keep an eye on each other, if that makes sense."

Gia and Cisir share a glance. "It does," Gia says. "If you mean that we're all in strange situations."

Qonna breathes out in relief. "Yes. I think that's what I wanted to say. All three of us are forced to tip toe through life and it would be so much easier to do it together." She lays her hands on her family's table, palms up.

Gia doesn't hesitate to grab her left. Cisir has to heave himself up to touch her right, and though getting up appears painful, he does it. All three flinch as a spark runs from his skin through Qonna to reach Gia.

"Ow!" Gia slaps at him. "What was that?"

"I'm not sure." He rubs his left hand, troubled. "It happens from time to time. I don't know why. I didn't want to hurt either of you."

"We know that." Qonna hears voices coming up from the yard, boots on the stairs, and stiffens. Her brothers aren't supposed to be home this early; it feels like an intrusion.

Qitli is the first to reach the door. "Oh. You have cake?" He leans over Cisir's shoulder and snatches the biggest slice, upends the dish with the figs upon it, and eats everything in one big bite, aware his older brothers are hard on his heels.

"Weren't you meant to be on yet another hunt?" Qonna asks sourly.

"Would have been, but one of the da Relians got into a ghastly accident. Bones poking through skin and all."

Qov is the next one in the room and to plunder the plates. "Felt in poor taste to keep going after that, so we dropped off the horses."

Qatt enters and is the only one to hesitate, staring at Cisir's uniform. "Why do you need Dad's secretary?"

Cisir pushes himself up and all her brothers' eyes go wide. "A private matter," he says, "but I'm happy to deliver a message to the House of the Sun."

"Don't leave on our account," Qatt says. "You haven't finished your tea."

"I'm expected back on the bridge. Qonna, thank you so much for everything. I'm sure we'll see each other soon."

"I'll walk you down." Gia jumps up, but Cisir waves her off.

"I'm feeling a lot better, and Jark won't be back yet."

She blinks but remains standing next to her chair while Qonna's brothers descend in earnest on the remnants of the meal. Cisir tucks in his chin and leaves.

Qonna clenches her jaw, frustration bubbling up. "Congratu-fucking-lations for ruining my afternoon."

Qatt throws up his hands. "I said he needn't go but he didn't listen."

"You scared him off," Gia accuses, "and he had just relaxed enough for us to get some proper sentences out of him!"

"He's only Dad's secretary," Qov says with a shrug. "He's no one special."

"It's been so long since I've been in here." Gia sits on the edge of Qonna's bed, the only bit not covered in dresses, cloths, scrunched-up underskirts, and unspooled braids. "The last time must've been six years ago, maybe more. I think you smuggled me in and got in big trouble over it." She tests the ropes underneath the mattress with a bounce. "Will you have your own room at the manor?"

"Probably not. There are a lot of people crammed in. I imagine I'll end up sharing with Eravis. It might be nice to have someone close by who can explain what's going on."

Gia bounces again. "I wish you weren't scared. It's just another house."

"With powerful people in it. What if I make some grievous mistake that ruins all my chances?" *It would be so easy to slip up, to tell the wrong person how I really feel.*

"Chances to do what?" Gia's voice drops to a whisper. "I thought you didn't want to marry yet."

"I don't mean marry, I mean … to be well thought of and retain the princess's favour. They're going out on a limb to include someone like me in Noa's household, however temporary."

"It'll be all right," Gia says. "Probably for the best you don't have your eye on someone specific." She makes a face and Qonna is relieved to realize Gia wants to change the topic.

"I'm sure Jark will be back tomorrow morning to supervise your lodger."

Gia beams at her. "You're right. It's just—you know, when you see someone and you know instantly he's the one you want?"

"Oh—like Pjer?"

They both burst out laughing.

"Exactly like that." Gia smirks.

"Listen, even I can see this guard is stunning, and you're welcome to him."

"If I can get his attention." Gia groans. "His walking through the Triangle twice a day has drawn a lot of glances. There'd be a queue for him reaching all the way to the harbour bridge if he were more … aware."

"Gia, what have you done?" Qonna forces a little laugh.

"Nothing much. Just tried to talk to him. He always has somewhere to be. I couldn't discover if he has someone waiting for him up in Crooked Hill. He might already be engaged and half of Seagard is barking up the wrong tree." She sighs. "Why do I always do that to myself? Why do I always go for the men everyone else wants? Why do they always need to be *extraordinary*; why can't they be nice, sensible people like Cisir?" She bounces a third time. "Are you sure he wouldn't make a good husband for you? Maybe not now, but in a few years?"

"I don't want to marry anyone—maybe you, if that were an option." Qonna grins at Gia, while her stomach turns a slow somersault. "But the thought of continuing the current situation with my brothers, plus some extra duties thrown in … no."

"Cisir wouldn't behave like your brothers."

"He might if it's his house."

Gia blinks. "Why would you want to marry *me*?"

Qonna shrugs. "It feels like the most logical and intuitive thing. We know each other and we've had fights and times when we didn't see each other much—and still we found our way back to our friendship. We know the worst and the best of each other. These things take time. Anyone I'd be allowed to marry wouldn't have that. I'm scared I'd lose patience a week into the marriage." Qonna's best friend draws her brows together. "Don't worry, I know that isn't what you'd want. I've listened to enough pretty-man-related rants to have no doubts on that score. There'll always be Pjers and Jarks, but that doesn't change the fact that I would lay down my life for you. All you have to do is ask."

"Come here." Gia pulls Qonna to the edge of the bed. "These are dangerous things to talk about. You can't shout them across the room." Her hand folds into Qonna's. "Wouldn't that be something, if two girls could wed each other and be allowed to live in the Cities with their own possessions, their own friends, their own lives? You'd need to go to the old country for that."

"I know." The heat of Gia's palm seeps into hers. *I wish I never had to let her go.* "But *Pomegranates* is here and that means I must stay—and you're here too, and I could never leave you behind."

Gia squeezes her hand. "I bet Jark has a fiancée sitting in every village between here and Crooked Hill. There's no way he'd be swayed by a tavern keeper's daughter in the Triangle."

Qonna squeezes back. "He might surprise you." Her eyes itch, a sure sign she's about to bawl. "How will I ever be packed and ready to collect by tomorrow morning?"

Gia smiles at her. "I'll help. How many chemises do you need?"

# CISIR

## *guarded*

Cisir sees Qonna's oldest twin brother again when Qatt na Qes walks into his father's study four days later. Qes stands up. "You're early, but we're about finished here. Cisir, have you met my son Qattir?"

"Briefly." Cisir, elbow-deep in dusty scrolls, gives the younger man a quick, shallow bow.

"Today he's less green and splotchy," Qatt confirms. "Seems having him followed by an armed guard has put the da Relians on the backfoot."

"Things have quietened down for now," his father says, "but we'll keep some guards here as long as the princes are in town, just in case." He turns to his secretary. "I'll be back by five bells, and there's only the revised inventory to sign off. Could you prepare it for me?"

"Certainly, Master." Cisir watches Qatt na Qes scoff, hearing his father addressed as such. Qatt and his brothers carry a similar entitlement to the Bulls. Perhaps it's what the Sun needs, an influx of boys oblivious to the space they take up, but Cisir knows it will be a period of adjustment for father and sons both, and that he'll end up between the lines at some point. He's in the perfect position to be used as their go-between.

He waits until both have left the study and the door has safely snicked shut behind them to permit himself to exhale. He'll have peace until five bells at least. Best if he prepares the inventory straight away, to have it ready whatever comes his way.

He's located his notes to write out the approval form when someone knocks at the door. "Have they gone?" Hevo pushes in with his shoulder, carrying the inevitable tea tray. "So that was one of them, huh? What do you think? Will he make trouble for us? He doesn't look like someone who takes kindly to instructions." He sets down the tray. "These types never do."

Cisir puts the scrawled notes aside, grateful for the timely interruption.

Hevo continues, "Must be weird for you, having all of Qes' sons flood in. At least I can hide behind my counter. Yoren will hate them infesting the stores; you know how possessive he is about his sorting system."

The tea is strong and bitter, but over the last weeks Cisir has become used to it, and it plays a crucial part in keeping the whole Yellow House going.

"Sorry there are no biscuits today, but I haven't had the chance to run out and buy some." Hevo settles on one of the stools dotted around the room. "I always dread knowing things will start to change soon, when we don't have a say in them. I mean, having Qes' brood at the House was in the cards from the beginning of the whole venture, so unless they stage a rebellion—are you listening to me?"

"Yes." Cisir takes another sip of tea. It's so astringent the inside of his mouth tingles. "I'm listening."

"You don't think it weird his sons spend so much of their free time frolicking about with the da Relians, but as soon as they enter the Companies they become enemies?"

"Perhaps they'll try to keep the peace." It sounds stupid as he says it. *It never works like that.*

"Huh. Sure. Speaking of which, have you spotted anyone lurking in the shadows lately? Watching you?"

Cisir shudders. "You mean Bulls?"

"It seems strange they would back off completely."

"I'm happy to heal while they strategize."

Hevo gnaws on his fingernails. "Maybe they'll do it to someone else next, though. The royals can't stay on the hill forever, can they?"

"I have no idea. I'm trying to distract myself."

"Things are starting to feel oppressive. The last time that happened, we got news of the loss of our biggest ship. Two years ago that was, and we never established whether the Bulls had a hand in it."

Cisir frowns. "Raiding a Sun ship?"

"And sinking it," Hevo adds gravely. "Sitting here in Seagard we only ever have half the story. The true fights are fought out there, on the seas, in Birkland and around the Spice Isles. There's no question the Bulls have the upper hand in the far east and we need to catch up. We're much better set up in the west, but there aren't a lot of spices grown in Birkland. At some point the princes must make up their minds, but as long as Nian da Nileon insists on traveling back and forth each year, I expect we'll be stuck with that. Shame, really—have you seen how much nutmeg costs these days? Thankfully, I never developed a taste for it, but even the price of raisins has shot up."

Hevo is happy to prattle on about price fluctuations all day. As one of the Suns behind the public counter, that's what he's most familiar with.

*That's going to be your life. Soon you'll have nothing to talk about but raisins, dried fish, and birch syrup. You could've been married already. You could've spent a lazy morning in bed, looking out over Windyhill village and tangling your fingers in your wife's hair.*

For a moment the loss is so painful Cisir struggles to breathe.

*I would never've heard Qonna say she wants to be friends, though. I would never be the one Hevo comes to with tea when the day is slow.*

As Cisir's master returns to check over the forms and the official copy of the inventory, the House of the Sun has gone quiet, as it often does during the later part of the day. Most customers run their errands in the mornings, eager to spend their afternoon in one of the taverns.

Qes na Qarim's business is quickly concluded. He puts quill to scrolls and scratches his signature, then seals the documents with the sun emblem. He slumps into his chair and rakes both hands through his hair. "I'll take them up to the manor and see how Qonna is getting on. Has Gia said anything to you yet?"

"No, she hasn't. Could … would it be too much hassle to come with you, Master?"

Qes seems surprised. "Are you sure? It might be a long evening. You never know with the crown prince."

"I'd like to see Qonna again too."

A smile spreads over Qes' face. "That's nice to hear, and to be honest, having someone with me might be a good idea. Keeps me grounded when I want to gnash my teeth at them."

"Do you expect much teeth gnashing, Master?" Cisir asks nervously.

"That depends on his mood. With every year he has to wait for his throne, he gets crankier, and I haven't seen him for some time. I'll ask one of the boys to reserve a carriage for us. After the day I've had, I'm not prepared to torture myself climbing the hill."

As the crow flies, Gard Manor isn't that far away from the harbour, but considering the position of the roads and the twists along the drive, Cisir is deeply relieved to make the trip on a flat leather cushion in a small carriage, despite the hard bench beneath it and the ridge that sticks into what is left of the bruise covering his kidneys.

"Is that a tower?" he asks as the house finally appears.

"It used to be a proper stronghold, but that was a long time ago. It's all been modernized and made habitable again. It wasn't always this glamourous. When the king bestowed it upon his youngest son, the spiders were as big as rats and the whole tower roof filled with bats. At least that's what my sibling said."

"Your sibling, Master?" Cisir asks to keep Qes talking.

"Half-sibling, actually, but most people forget about that. Technically, Sloe is still the first Royal Sorcerer in service of the crown prince, though they haven't come back to the Continent for twenty years. Unfortunately, this means Nurin da Nileon sees me as an extension of his wizard, though I couldn't so much as list all eight Tall Gods. I'll try to get us out of there as soon as I can." Qes reaches as if to pat Cisir's arm, then retracts his hand. "You should probably keep to the background." He pushes the door of the carriage open.

They're intercepted by two royal guards in the same get-up as Jark, leather armour with their broad shoulders protected by mail. As soon as they recognize the First Sun, they retreat and open the door behind them. Cisir's master leads him into the hall of Gard Manor.

The lintel is deceptively low. Behind the door, the room opens into something that reminds Cisir so strongly of home his breath stutters. It's a larger version of the house he grew up in: an old hall that has been repainted and in part refurnished, but retains the open roof, big fire pit, and the high, narrow windows that need to be shuttered with the help of a long-handled crook. The hall is being prepared for the evening meal and is filled with servants. One of them is dispatched to inform the princes.

Qes retreats to a row of stools lined up against the south wall, out of the way of the tables being arranged. An astonishing number of cups and flat bowls appear while Cisir settles down, pressing the leather bag with the documents against his side.

"Of course, you pop up when everyone is dressing for dinner." Lilyis greets them first, in a freshly pressed linen tunic slightly too long for current fashions, but with her hair unadorned and loosely braided to comply with Seagard's style. All the wildness Cisir associates with the prince is dimmed, and she appears disappointingly ordinary, someone short and middle-aged, in very good riding boots. "You brought reinforcements." She glances from Qes to Cisir. "You've healed up well."

"Only a few twinges left," Qes answers for Cisir and he's grateful that, this once, he doesn't have to lie.

"You were lucky," Lilyis says gravely. "I've had enough dealings with the Bulls to appreciate how quickly these things can escalate."

"Have you spoken to Qonna?" Qes asks the prince.

"Not today, but I saw her walking in the gardens around noon. She and my sister seem to have hit it off. Are you worried Father won't look after her?"

"I'm more worried about your uncle."

Lilyis laughs. "Nurin has his hands full with his wife. She keeps him on his toes."

"He still has a reputation."

"Your daughter could break him with a well-placed kick."

Qes scowls. "Qonna is inexperienced and often too kind for her own good."

Lilyis' smile slips. "My stepmother has an eye on her and all the young women under this roof. She would never allow any of them to come to harm, even if Uncle Nurin's teeth hadn't been pulled since he chose his second wife. There he is."

The crown prince is disgruntled enough to make Cisir fight a wish to slink back against the wall. He's much thinner than the depictions Cisir has seen, with hollows beneath his cheekbones and an air of exhaustion. "Qes," the crown prince greets the First Sun. "Finally. I thought I'd have to storm down the hill and prise the inventories out of your hands. Have you brought the invoices too?"

"Yes." Qes holds out his hand; Cisir places in it the scrolls he's guarded since they left the Yellow House. "You look tired, Your Highness."

"I am fucking tired. You try and keep up with someone who enjoys competitive dancing. I thought I could catch a break once we roped in a few fresh companions, but I hoped in vain. I should've listened to my dear brother and picked someone my own age. The last thing I need are more mouths to feed—the succession is complicated enough as it is. Are you coming, Qes?"

Lilyis interrupts, "I'll take your secretary on a tour of the grounds in the meantime. He deserves to see some flowers and nice views after what the Bulls put him through. You go ahead. Maybe we can find Noa and her friends."

As soon as Qes and the crown prince leave, Lilyis slumps. "Let's get out while we can; a quick turn before dinner will be just the thing."

"I thought everyone was dressing?"

"You really don't want to stick around when my uncle is in one of his querulent moods." Lilyis steers him out the door, into the soft breeze coming up from the sea. "Have you found your feet at the Yellow House yet? It seems Qes is quite happy with you. Happy enough to give you a nursemaid anyway."

"A nursemaid?"

"The dreadfully handsome guard. I've seen him around the place. Jalf? Jor?"

"Jark."

"That's it."

"I don't really need him anymore," Cisir admits. "The limp is almost gone, and the Bulls have kept their distance." *I wish I could keep him. See his face every day.*

Lilyis walks across the gravel covering the yard, towards the path to the lake stretching out beneath the manor. To the right grows a small clump of birches. Among the trees rests a group of stones similar to the ancient circle on the slope across from Windyhill. "Did you know these monuments are remnants of a time when we shared the same beliefs as the families in Birkland?" The prince nods at the rocks. "Father keeps this information close to his chest, otherwise we'd have a whole gaggle of priests stomping up the hill, trying to smash what little is left. I always found it rather ironic that you can best see the belltower of the temple from this very point."

They turn to the city beneath them and the squat tower Cisir has avoided since the day he was attacked. To his feet lies a meadow awash with buttercups, and the wind rustles in the crowns of silver-barked birches guarding the stones. For this moment, everything feels suspended in a brittle sheet of translucent ice, a perfect picture of the place he's always wanted Seagard to be.

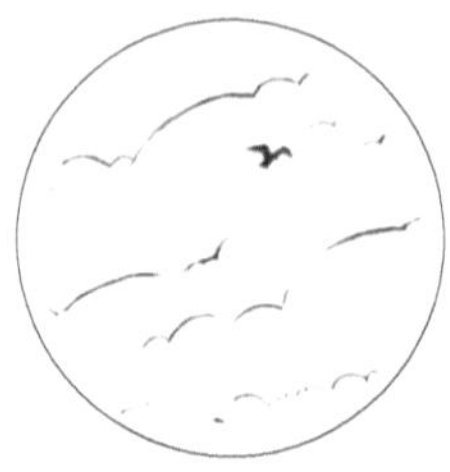

# QONNA

## *how this works*

Qonna beams at her father. "What are you doing here?"

"Just business." He leans in to kiss her cheek. "How are you finding the manor? And the company?"

"Weird." She pulls him to the window seat of the small solar she shares with the other women. "You never told me half the things going on with the princes."

He smiles tiredly. "I didn't want you to have a bad opinion of them."

"Suffice to say that Noa is much more open and not terribly discreet, given that it's her own family she slags off."

"Is that how you spend your days? Gossiping about everything that happens at court?"

"There's also an awful lot of embroidery. Mother would be proud. At least Noa was allowed to learn the lute; she's rather good. Everyone here is interested in poetry and learning as much about the history of the Eight Kingdoms as they can, so one of us is usually reading aloud. Noa brought a whole chest of books, can you imagine? My mouth gets dry quickly though, so we take turns. Have you heard about the temple in Westheath dedicated to producing copies of books the Star disapproves of, so they can send them to all their dependencies to warn off their Brothers? Pretty clever, to fan the interest by burning them, becoming the only ones who have them at their fingertips!"

"Qonna, are you happy here?" her father asks. "I can get you out, if that's what you wish."

"It's an adjustment, I won't lie. Though I appreciate the need to cultivate the connection, if I'm the one following in your footsteps against the tide of tradition. I'd never believed Nian's sister should be treated as less than her half-sisters, only because of her mother. Did you know that eighteen people have to tragically die for her to get within sniffing distance of the crown, though she's a direct descendant of the old king?"

Her father frowns. "Do you believe she would like to become Queen of the Hillakes and Southclere?"

"She's certainly clever enough, but so are most women here. Even the crown prince's new wife has a certain shrewdness to her, which apparently drives him up the wall."

"Yes, he said something to that effect." Her father lowers his voice. "You only need to send a message to the Yellow House if you want to be rescued. I hope you know that."

"I know, Dad. Thank you. Are you staying for the meal? Dinners are a big thing here and the food is wonderful."

"It depends on whether I can extract my secretary from the prince's clutches."

Her face lights up. "You brought Cisir?"

"He asked to come along. He seems worried about you. Is there something you're not telling me?" There's a grey tinge to his face.

"No," Qonna says.

"You seem to have become familiar with each other."

"He's my friend." *But there's more.* "There's something about him I recognize in myself."

Her father winces. "He sees himself as an outsider."

"That could be it," Qonna admits. "Or that he was so clearly searching for someone to connect with, after the awful shit that happened to him at home."

The lines dig in around his mouth. "Your mother does the best she can."

She blushes. "That's not what I meant at all."

"Are you sure? I know you always had to go against her ideas about the direction of your life. If I had forbidden Lauron from ever speaking about the old country, would you have known what you were missing?"

Qonna gazes out the window. In the yard, royal guards arrive from their duties in the city, a whole flock of armed men, dusty and tired. The noise the bits of mail make on their bodies echoes up to her. "There are plenty of women here who know exactly what they're missing," she says eventually. "It's not that hard to see. Noa should be much more involved in her family's decisions. If she was a boy, they'd have to find something for her to do, something meaningful that doesn't bore her to tears. We're all pushed aside in one way or another, and that might be what Cisir picks up on. Has he told you what happened with his father?"

"No. I'm his master. I shouldn't be aware of such personal details. He's a diligent and conscientious worker and will make his way in the Sun; that's all I should concern myself with, now there's no chance of him becoming my son-in-law."

"Dad ...." *Please don't*, she thinks, biting down on her lip.

"Which is fine. It will probably come back to bite you in the arse, but it's your choice."

"I think I hear them going downstairs," she says pointedly. "You should get at least a cup of wine out of coming all the way up the hill."

Dinner is by far the most formal meal at the manor. Each group has its own section of the tables and everyone with royal blood is placed on the dais under the resplendent tapestry. A goblet carved from crystal is placed next to the crown prince's plate, something Qonna had never seen before coming here; she'd only read about it. Baskets stuffed with various sorts of bread are lined up as well as bowls with fruit preserved in honey. She'd never have felt so resentful over the last figs if she'd known what was waiting for her. The only thing she misses is cheese. For some reason, it's the one food the royals don't believe in; instead they serve whole platters heaped with cold cuts, cured sausages, and artfully arranged pickles, including the green fruit Uncle Lauron loves so much that are imported from Birkland by the barrel.

The servants placed her father next to Noa's mother, who never sits with her husband on the dais, though she could probably find good reason to, but today she seems delighted to pick the First Sun's brain over roasted lamb dusted with cumin seeds and braised pork in a thick apple sauce. Many of the dishes are tastier versions of food Qonna has eaten all her life, though her mother would never have allowed so many varieties of shellfish on her table. Oysters are too cheap for someone born in Seagard, but must be a rarity at Crooked Hill, so far from the coast. No wonder the princes eat their fill here.

They sit next to each other, looming above their household and guests: the crown prince, haughty and starved-looking; Nivael da Nileon, severe with his long copper-golden curls and yellow eyes; and his wayward son, dressed simply with a round freckled face and soft mouth that belies the miles he has travelled across the sea to be close to his partner. The three princes have the same eyebrows and the same nose, as well as the reddish tinge to their colouring, even the dark-haired crown prince.

It takes Qonna a while to spot Cisir. He's been seated at the end of the table, the furthest he could sit from the dais. He's trying to make himself smaller, to disappear. No one's allowed to get up and walk around during formal occasions, so the only thing she can do is to lift her cup and wait until he glances over, which he doesn't for half an eternity, but when he finally notices her gesture, he smiles across the hall. Gard Manor must remind him of home, though back then he was one of the family drinking from the best goblets and eating from the costliest plates.

When Qonna puts her cup down, Noa is studying her.

"Tell me about the secretary," Noa says as they return to the solar after Qonna's father and Cisir head down the hill. "He's the one who was hurt?"

"Yes."

"He seems to have recovered well."

"He moves differently than before."

Noa tilts her head. "You are in love with him?"

Qonna sputters. "No!"

"Why not?" Eravis leans in, needles and silken thread pushed aside. "He seems friendly."

"He is friendly, that isn't the problem." *The problem is that all of you have decided we would pair so well.*

Noa grins. "You know my aunt's companions will start to talk about you two? If you're not about to get yourself engaged to a man, don't try to catch his eye so publicly."

"They can talk about us to their heart's content. They don't know either of us."

"Doesn't matter," Noa says drily. "They'll make up stories to suit themselves. Believe me, I've spent enough time at court to know how it works. They've been waiting for something juicy to get their teeth into, and they see my small group of friends as the least important. I mean, we're literally only three people. My aunt has a whole clutch of personable maidens at her disposal."

"Perhaps I should be flattered that they find me interesting," Qonna mutters.

Noa huffs. "It'll start out sweet, but then they'll start bitching. That's how it always plays out. You need to be careful." Her voice is tense.

"What happened?" Qonna asks. "What did they say about you?"

"That my parents had to marry because Mother fell pregnant. That she was much too old and it was a great shock, an ill-advised affair that became a royal marriage by mistake." Noa's voice wavers. "They'd never dare mention it to Father's face, but Mother has been confronted many times. It's true—she should've been too old to conceive."

Eravis takes her hand. "That doesn't mean you aren't loved."

Noa's eyes are suddenly very shiny. "I want to believe that, but then there are all the other things: the fact that neither of my royal grandparents have ever spoken to me, for instance."

"I'm so sorry," Qonna blurts out.

Eravis squirms. "They were likely …."

"… just busy?" Noa barks out. "They're the fucking rulers of the kingdom. They can make the time." A tear spills out, streaking over her cheek. "They don't want to know me. They see me as an inconvenient complication. If they took any interest in me at all, I'd already be married off to one of the other kingdoms. Bleakheath, probably. I don't know you well, Qonna, but no one should have to deal with the whispers and poorly hidden sneers. I know they're bored and don't realize these things hurt as much as they do."

In the last days, Noa has never shown herself as vulnerable, and she seems like a new person. Someone who needs to be comforted. Qonna tries to take her hand, but Noa withdraws. "I'm sorry," Qonna says again.

Noa dashes away the rest of her tears with the back of her forearm. "I hadn't planned on crying." She sounds angry at herself. "Usually, I look forward to spending the summer at the manor and seeing the sea every time I open the shutters, but the last few times I had no new aunt to contend with, someone who's barely two years older than me. At least Uncle Nurin knows he made a rash decision."

"Did he marry her for her coin?" Qonna dares to ask.

Noa shrugs. "If you need to know, he married her for her face. The coin was a nice coincidence. They try to keep me from those rumours too, but my uncle has more illegitimate children than any other prince in the history of the Hillakes. That's a fact. He never could resist a pretty maid and as the crown prince he never had to learn how to. I can't say I feel sorry for him, but I guess that's exactly how everyone else feels about our future queen. I hate that everything changed, and Grandfather still refuses to die." Her words are harsh, sharp-edged. "I don't expect my life to get significantly better when he does," she admits after a moment of silence. "Only the gods know how Grandmother will react, though she sure as Eight Hells won't die of a broken heart."

Noa snatches up Qonna's hand, the same hand she drew away from before, and kisses her knuckles. "I shouldn't have said all that. It makes me just as vile as any other rumourmonger. Please forget my words."

Qonna blushes. With one sentence, Noa has reestablished distance between them. "Of course, Your Highness."

"On some days it's hard to bear. I know what Mother would say, that all the companions are intimidated and don't know how to sort me. I'm allowed to sit at the top of the hall, but I don't have much going for me." She keeps hold of Qonna. "It would be easier if I had brothers."

"No," Qonna and Eravis say simultaneously, before all three laugh out loud.

"I can't let them spoil the summer for us," Noa decides. "I'll put up with them and hope the weather holds so we can spend more time away from them, strolling through the gardens and visiting the stones."

Qonna perks up. "You mean the group of boulders near the lake?" Her hands get sweatier.

"It's not any group of boulders," Noa says. "They once were placed here for people to come and see. Father's theory is that the first house standing in the manor's place was a shelter for the pilgrims, back when the Star hadn't arrived to take over the Continent." She finally releases Qonna's hand to point out of the window towards the birches. "Other stories exist, of course. I've heard claims that the stones were once a portal to the land of the dead, or a magical place where everyone is immortally beautiful. When I was little, I found an offering of flowers, nuts, and bread among them. I've always wondered what it meant."

Qonna frowns. *An offering? To whom?*

# CISIR

## *just this once*

It's the first day since the incident Cisir doesn't get his private guard but collects his package of cheese and bread from the kitchen and walks alone. The mugginess of the last days has dispersed into a fine drizzle glazing the cobblestones of the main road, dropping from the eaves of the straw roofs lining it at both sides.

He knows what's waiting for him at the Yellow House. He's becoming used to the daily routines his colleagues stick to to make their lives easier, like the order in which Hevo sets out the baskets and packets of tea.

When Cisir arrives, the doorstopper is in place and a new banner has been fixed to the left of the front door, made from a broad stripe of yellow cloth stamped with the announcement, New Stock Now Available.

Everything that came over from Birkland on the *Buttercup* was logged in the accounts and passed the last quality checks before being added to the goods on sale, as soon as outstanding back orders were fulfilled. After days of carts lining up on the harbour bridge, today's the day when the first pedestrian customers are allowed to flood the house to get their hands on the new arrivals. Though it's early, Hevo is already dealing with a queue of citizens seeking syrup, grass paper, and pickles. Some have come for furs, bark cloth, or amber. Most of those are sold to businesses directly, but there must be apprentices among the crowd, swooping in after the guild buyers have had their fill.

Cisir squeezes past while Hevo and Yoren dash around the front room. They both fizz with excitement. The whole house has a different scent; the herbs are fresher, the teas stronger, the rolled-up pelts less musty.

Cisir stills as he hears voices behind the door. He fears Qonna's eldest brother is back to claim his place at his father's side, but someone laughs. Cisir knocks softly and the door to the study swings open.

The room is warm and smells of drying woollen clothes. Next to the brazier stands the woman Cisir saw sitting next to his master at Gard Manor, and at the desk is Lilyis herself, thumbing through a sheaf of rough paper—a collection of order slips.

"Good morning," his master says, "and what an excellent morning it is. The stores will be empty by end of the week if demand keeps up."

Lilyis smiles. "Two more ships expected, might I remind you— hopefully in time to fan the flames. I think we can safely predict our most successful quarter to date. Your boys up front are being run off their feet."

"Should I go help?" Cisir asks.

"You'd only get in the way," his master says. "This won't take long and then we'll get out of your hair."

Lilyis resumes checking the order forms before concluding, "We need to get our hands on more syrup next year. It flies out the door. Even with all the Sun towers at the Stoneharp crammed with caskets, it won't be enough if we can't find more families in Birkland to keep up the supply. Sloe said there are families beyond the steppes who cultivate specific roots to boil up for sweetness in years when there isn't much honey to be had. Not all of Birkland is covered in birches, so people have to be inventive. Perhaps that's something we should look into. Their growing conditions are not so different from parts of the Continent. If we could get our hands on some of those roots, we could plant them ourselves, cut down on transport costs …."

"Lilyis," the older woman says warningly. "We can talk about it later."

Lilyis jumps up, flattening the papers in front of her. "I'm getting hungry anyway."

Cisir clears his throat. "Before I forget, I was given some letters for Qonna today." He extracts the sealed papers and hands them over to the prince. "If you wouldn't mind handing them to her, Your Highness."

"Of course not." Lilyis beams. "Since when are you writing to each other?" She glances at Qonna's father.

"They're not my letters," Cisir clarifies.

"Oh. I'd hoped for a sweet little story."

Cisir bites his lip. He can feel the pitying stare from Lilyis' stepmother. He shouldn't have asked to come to the manor to see Qonna. Everyone has clearly jumped to the wrong conclusion.

Qes takes his cloak from the back of a chair. "Is it still raining?"

"Yes," Cisir confirms. "Shall I send one of the boys to fetch a carriage?"

"We won't melt," Lilyis says. "It's only a few steps."

"I'll be back in an hour or so." His master leaves him with a desk strewn with papers and scrolls that need to be filed, three empty tea bowls, and lots of crumbs, but Cisir exhales in relief when he's finally alone.

He should feel more involved in the continuing successes; this time he had a hand in them, even if he merely provided the inevitable paperwork, but he's too tired. After the first attempt at tidying up, he spends a long time staring into the backyard, where crates are stacked up as donkey carts arrive: more orders being moved into town.

Although he hasn't been given particular instructions, he knows what's expected of him in order to keep the ball rolling. Whatever his master has planned for later, Cisir has more than enough to keep himself busy.

*This will be your life. Doesn't help anyone to fret about getting bored. You knew what you were signing up for.*

Did he? Why is he tempted to taunt the gods and sneak into the Westown to see whether he can get a reaction out of the Bulls?

*Do you want to get killed? Why?*

He recoils from his own answer.

"Can you take my place? Only for a short while? Please." Hevo jumps from one foot to the other. "I need to take a piss but Yoren has to have a second pair of hands up front. People are getting impatient, so I can't just fuck off."

"Sure." Cisir puts down the quill and wipes his hands. "What do you need me to do?"

"You're tall; you can get at the upper baskets. Yoren will direct you. I'm about to burst." He runs from the room and Cisir hurries to be of assistance.

The queue has tripled. Customers are shifting about and will soon start to grumble. Yoren shoots him a grateful grin. "Wonderful. Can you get the box there and start refilling packets? We prepared so many, but we're almost out. How many of you good people are here for tea?"

A flurry of hands fly up.

"And syrup," someone shouts. "Don't tell me you're about to run out!"

"Plenty of syrup left, good sir." Yoren is practiced in wrangling the crowds.

Cisir is armpit-deep in fragrant tea when Hevo reappears. Neither of them suggests Cisir go back to the study, and it feels good to be helpful, to distract himself from the questions he's started to pose to himself.

The First Sun doesn't return after one hour, nor after three. When the midday bells ring, the queue finally disperses and Yoren is able to close the door for the first time since opening this morning. "Let's eat quickly. It's bound to get busy again as soon as our own teapot comes to the boil." He rolls his shoulders, and a series of cracks runs through his body. "Ow, fucking ow."

Hevo volunteers to make tea and Cisir fetches his food package to share the provisions he brought from the *Pear*. They fall upon the flatbreads like a pack of wolves.

"What kind of cheese is that?" Hevo asks, his mouth full.

"Something they make at the *Rotting Pear*, an approximation of a Birklandish type."

Yoren chews thoughtfully. "The girl at the *Pear*, the round, pretty one—she's half-Birklandish then?"

"Yes."

"Have you noticed them do anything funny?"

Yoren's tone sets Cisir's teeth on edge. "Funny how?"

"I don't know. They have weird gods in the west, right? Different rules they live by. Much less *clenched* in their attitude."

Hevo rolls his eyes. "For fuck's sake, mate."

"I'm only saying!" Yoren holds up his palms. "If they feed him, they might also be happy to fulfil other needs."

Cisir bristles. "I'm surprised you hold such opinions when the Yellow House is so dependent on our relationship to Birkland. Our First Sun is half-Birklandish too."

"Yeah, but he tries to fit in. He doesn't make weird cheese and bread to suit his outlandish tastes," Yoren states with a shrug.

"The Brothers talk constantly about how we can't let ourselves be blinded by the promises of the west," Hevo says quietly.

"And still they ask us to fund them with the profits made off our trade with it," Cisir replies. He found the payment request this morning among the First Sun's correspondence.

Yoren blinks. "They built a big temple for the city—they need to make the most of it."

"They can only be paid if Birkland provides the goods for the Sun," Cisir reminds him, terse and sharp. Of all the people in the city, it was the Birklanders who made him feel at home. "Forget it, Yoren. I never asked them to pack me food for the day and still they give it to me every morning, because they're kind."

"Gods," Yoren says, taken aback. "I've never seen you so fired up. Are you sure you haven't gone soft for her? Or the opposite, mate? Nobody would blame you, honestly, but no need to bite my head off."

Cisir glares at Hevo to get him to comment, but he merely seems uncomfortable. "I need some air," Cisir pronounces. "Can you please let me know when the First Sun comes back? I'll walk around in the yard for a while."

The rain has picked up, so Cisir can't actually walk without getting drenched. The next best thing is to go into the overflow storage where the empty containers are kept and pace up and down between piles of baskets, racks and wooden boxes, cobwebs, and a bundle of birch twig brooms shoved into a corner.

What does it mean that he feels so protective of the Wolves? They took care of him during his recovery, that must be it, and Gia is so gentle and warm—to everyone, not just him. No one deserves to be talked about that way; he's fairly sure they're plain wrong, in addition to not making sense. The House of the Sun only exists because of Birkland—all the smells, feels, and tastes of it, the sweetness of syrup and the sourness of pickled fruit, the softness of the pelts and cloths, and the bright colours of the woven ribbons stored in large, patterned coils on the highest shelves.

"I was looking for you!" Jark dashes across the yard, his cloak pulled up to cover his auburn curls in the pelting rain. "They sent me out to find you—the First Sun has arrived."

As soon as Jark ducks inside the storage shed, the rain intensifies. He shakes out his cloak. "It felt wrong not seeing you this morning. Instead, I had to babysit the princess's companions on their walks in the park."

Cisir crosses his arms to keep himself from reaching out. "That must be a more enjoyable task than waiting for me to limp out of the Triangle."

"None of the companions walk faster than you." Jark grins, giving the wet cloak a last snap. "What are you doing back here?"

"I don't know. I needed to find somewhere to think." *Say it.* "It felt weird for me too. Not seeing you today, I mean. Strange, how quickly one becomes used to things."

"Things like what?" In the gloom of the shed Jark's teeth are sharp and white.

"Having someone at one's side." Cisir strains to talk over the rain drumming on the roof.

"You've gone all formal." Jark takes a step back. The smile falters. "Apologies, I didn't want to spook you. It must be frightening, having me say that I missed you."

"No … that was what I was trying to say. I missed … I missed you too." Cisir's face feels on fire. *Please. Please grant me this, just this once.*

Jark smells of leather and rain as he touches Cisir's cheek. Cisir's whole body begins to itch as if he'd sunk into an anthill, right up to his neck. The rain becomes louder and still not loud enough to mask

Cisir's rasping breath. He wants to lean in, but his arms are in the way. He wants to say something, but all words are meaningless under Jark's touch.

Jark's thumb is on his lower lip. Cisir waits for him to do *something*. His gaze flicks up and down, eager not to miss a sign.

"I'm sorry," Cisir blurts out. "I've never been kissed before."

Jark's eyes narrow. "Do you want to be kissed?"

"Desperately."

Jark rises to the tips of his heavy boots, and then his mouth is on Cisir's, impossibly soft and careful, his hand curling around the back of Cisir's neck before he releases him. "So … was that what you imagined?"

Cisir can barely hear Jark over the rain and the thundering of his heart, but he nods.

"You're shaking, though," Jark remarks.

"Can you do it again?"

Jark gently pulls Cisir's forearms apart, uncrosses them to fit himself between Cisir's hands. The leather breastplate scrapes against Cisir's chest; cold emanates off the wet mail, feathering against the underside of his jaw.

Their second kiss is still slow as they figure out the best angle for their noses. Cisir has to sink down further, and Jark has to stretch a bit, but finally he's wrapped in Cisir's arms. Cisir's knees start to give out as Jark's tongue touches his. *I can't believe it's finally happening.*

"Fuck," the royal guard says against his mouth. "Can you smell smoke?"

They melt apart. The rain hasn't let up, but there's most definitely the acrid taste of fire creeping into the shed.

"You need to go," Jark says mournfully.

"What?" *Did I do something wrong?*

"The First Sun, remember?"

Cisir gawps at him, at this most beautiful of men, his wide dark eyes. "Oh. I forgot about him." He grabs an empty box and puts it over his head to keep off the rain as he peels away from the one he wants to cling to as long as his breath holds out.

Puddles form in the yard, but the air is hazy as he runs towards his master.

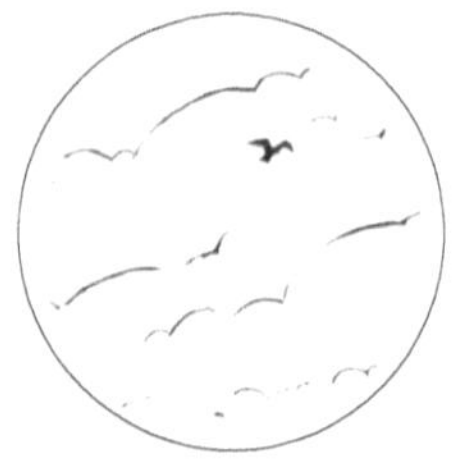

# QONNA

## *starting to turn*

Have you ever seen so much rain?" Noa grumbles, lowering the volume she'd read from for the last two hours. She'd chosen a romance to lift everyone's spirits after the morning strolls were cut short and they decided to wait out the bad weather inside the solar.

The warmth of late spring had fled the house, and the princess had wrapped herself in a soft goat hair shawl that framed her pale face and dark lashes, distracting Qonna from her embroidery when she read to them about knights with strong jaws and sighing ladies who tried to avoid falling in love. Of the three of them, Noa had the best voice, and she took care to mimic different people when reading the characters, so her impressions of the best knight of the realm and his sassy young squire became too vivid for Qonna to not follow with her mouth hanging open.

Eravis glances up, annoyed. "That's the best passage. Can you please continue?"

Noa scowls at her. "What's the point? It won't stop raining today. We might as well go to bed and sleep until dinner."

"I can take over," Eravis offers. "Since you've gotten yourself into a mood."

Noa flings the book away. It catches on the edge of the small table and *thumps* to the floor. "Oh shit." She flushes and retrieves it, dusting off its leather binding. "I've dented the edge," she cries in dismay. "Can this day get any worse?"

"It can't be only the rain," Eravis says.

"The rain is enough to spoil everything," Noa huffs. "What other reason do I need to feel sad, apart from seeing myself in this very room in ten years' time, still waiting for it to stop? What could possibly happen between now and then?"

Eravis smiles thinly. "You'd be married, for one."

Noa glances at Qonna and rolls her eyes. "Yeah. That. Married to a reedy prince of Bleakheath, so thin-blooded he's huddled up to his nose in furs in the height of summer."

"Why Bleakheath?" Qonna asks. *Why so far away?*

"Because it sounds miserable—like the least appealing of the Eight Kingdoms."

"And you might go live there." The words taste faintly metallic on Qonna's tongue.

"It'll be another room to stare out of," Noa says sourly. "I'll probably spend most of my days with no one else to read to, because no one wants to live in Bleakheath anyway."

Qonna sighs. "Could be an interesting place—rugged and romantic. When the heather flowers, the whole kingdom will be awash with purple blossoms."

Noa's frown lifts. "Purple blossoms?"

"And the most delicate of scents."

"Ooooh, now that's starting to sound nice."

At the hint of her grin, Qonna continues the fantasy. "So far away from Crooked Hill your grandfather can't keep you from jumping on a horse and exploring."

"A horse?" Noa encourages her.

"A gentle-hearted mare, as white as milk, with a silver tail and the most comfortable canter you could wish for."

"You sound like the book," Eravis interjects.

"Shh—go on, Qonna." Noa folds her hands in front of her chest. "What will I see?"

Qonna takes a deep breath as the picture unfurls before her inner eye. "An ocean of heather spilling up to the hills, with tiny flowers growing along the edges of the path in pinks and yellows. There'll likely be sheep and the odd pretty shepherd boy."

"Can't have those if I'm married," Noa says thoughtfully. "Unless I go about it in a cleverer way than the queens of old."

Eravis' mouth thins into a disapproving line, but she holds her tongue.

Qonna tries to comfort Noa. "I'm sure you can make it work if you want to. There'll be so many valleys to visit and pine forests to traverse."

Eravis scoffs. "Have you ever spoken to anyone from Bleakheath?" Her words carry a worrisome bite.

"No," Qonna says, "but I read some books. My grandmother came from there."

"Oh." Noa crumples. "I didn't want to bad mouth it."

"I don't know anything about her family. She disappeared one day and never told Dad anything—or at least nothing he wants to share with me and my brothers. She probably spent most of her childhood herding sheep."

Eravis shifts on her seat. "You shouldn't admit that out loud."

Qonna can't help but feel annoyed at someone she didn't even know being pushed down like that. "It must be close to the truth."

Noa's eyes light with curiosity. "Once upon a time, all our ancestors herded sheep or something similar. Especially around the Hillakes— impossible to not get close to sheep, I'd say."

"I've never been as far north as the Hillakes," Qonna muses.

"Then you need to come to Crooked Hill with me!" Noa jumps up, dislodging the book again. It tumbles to the floor and lands on its pages, bending at least two. "*Fuck.*" Noa swallows as she tries to smooth out the parchment. "Father will be so disappointed. He always tells me to take care of books."

"We'll put something on top to press out the creases," Eravis promises. She turns to Qonna. "Would you like to spend time at court?"

"It's basically the same as here," Noa warns, "only with mountains." Her face brightens again. "In autumn, the woods around Crooked Hill turn the most amazing colours, from deepest red to sunniest yellow, and in the gardens, rosehips ripen to thick clusters and the birds swoop in to eat their fill. If you can't go to Bleakheath to search for the missing part of your family history, you should at least be allowed to travel *somewhere*." She sighs. "Lots of rain in the mountains. You can't bloody escape it." She holds out the damaged book to Eravis. "Are you still happy to switch?"

Someone knocks on the door to the solar. "Noa, are you there?"

"Mother?" Noa flies across the room to let her in.

Hilvis da Nileon shivers in visible relief. "Thank the gods. I'd feared you'd chosen this day of all days to venture into town."

"Why? What happened?"

Her mother takes her by the wrists. "Seagard is burning."

From the hill all that's visible is white smoke, clothing the whole city beneath them, obscuring the temple's belltower. The inhabitants of the manor stand at their windows to stare out. The rain pulls the smoke here and there, like a sheet shaken out by thousands of hands.

*It can't be real. It must be some kind of joke.*

Qonna turns away from the horror. Noa cries in the arms of her mother; the princes have huddled together and whisper among themselves.

"The rain must be a good thing," the crown prince says. "Most of the roofs will be thoroughly soaked and it will make it easier to control the flames."

His nephew glances around, close to panic. "We need to get down there to help."

"We'll send the guard," Noa's father says.

"I'm going to take them," his son declares.

Qonna shoulders her way into their circle. "I want to come with you."

Both older princes seem shocked, but Nian da Nileon takes her arm. "We don't know what we'll find there, so I need you to keep your head—can you do that?"

"Yes," Qonna promises.

"Nian ...," the crown prince starts, but his nephew cuts him off with a gesture.

"Her whole family is in the midst of it. She has a right to help."

"We can't let the First Sun's daughter endanger herself," Nurin da Nileon exclaims.

Nian's father steps in. "Nian is right. She knows the city much better than any of us. Shortcuts, hidden yards—" He turns to his son. "Go now. We can't leave the citizens in doubt of our intentions."

Qonna's mouth goes dry. Who knew she wouldn't meet with more resistance? She must follow up on her words; she needs to be brave.

"Can you ride?" the wayward prince asks her, his green eyes alight with purpose.

Qonna takes a deep breath. "I'll figure it out."

While Nian gives orders to the head of the royal guards, the stables explode in a flurry of preparations. Boys run to the stalls with saddles and bridles; the noise of leather thwacking against leather reverberates from the ceiling.

Qonna's hands shake as she removes the pins from her top headdress and rips it off. Before her mother found out, she'd had the opportunity to sit on a horse, one of the ponies her brothers learned on. At that time Qatt and Qov were young enough not to understand why their sister should be denied a place in the saddle. The horse that is brought forward is one of the heavy-set carriage horses, gigantic and dappled with slate-grey splotches. She takes the edges of her overskirts and knots them around her waist while the stable boy blushes furiously but can't quite bring himself to avert his gaze. He holds the stirrup for her and Qonna clambers up, her heart hammering so hard it hurts.

*It's going to be all right. I can do it.*

All around her guards climb onto their own mounts, though Jark doesn't seem to be among them. There are about twenty men on horseback, one of them the prince, ashy pale beneath his freckles, seated on a horse that matches hers. Nian gives her a nod. "Try to keep close to me."

They cut through the grounds of the manor. The paths Qonna meandered down so sedately fly by as the horses walk downhill in formation. The guardsmen drag their linen scarves up to cover noses and mouths as smoke billows up to meet them.

Qonna shoves the reins under her left knee and pulls up the cloth that composed her upper headdress. She tries to fasten the folded fabric as high as possible at the back of her head, only to expose some of her hair that's now hidden by a single layer. Since she had started to bleed, she'd never been in public without her hair covered. It feels deeply wrong.

*It's not important right now. Concentrate, for fuck's sake.*

Her eyes water almost immediately. They haven't passed the gate in the lower wall of the manor grounds yet, but some of the men behind her start coughing and the horses shake their manes in irritation. The main branch of the road sweeping past the gate is a tunnel filled with smoke, though none of the houses seem to be on fire. Windows are open and voices sound out, servants and family members deciding what to move if the flames come too close.

*The same could be happening at* Pomegranates.

The rain has lessened but not quite stopped. Sweat rolls down Qonna's face and she lowers her eyelids, while the horse shifts uneasily beneath her. Carriage horses are trained to remain calm, but hers can't be the only eyes stinging.

The prince jumps from his saddle and catches a boy who comes running towards them. Qonna can't hear what he says, but around his eyes, nose, and mouth, the boy's face is streaked with ash. He doesn't seem too disturbed and Qonna grits her teeth. Her hand creeps onto the horse's neck to give it a calming stroke.

The royal guards push up behind her and when the prince spins around to them, she can hear the armed men straightening in their saddles.

The prince vaults back onto his horse. Sweat sticks his hair to his temples as he briefs the guards. "The fire started in the lower Westown and is making its way up. Water is being brought up from the harbour, so that's where you go. Qonna, do you want to check on *Pomegranates* before we join them?"

She nods, already struggling for breath.

*He doesn't plan to dump you there. You need to prove yourself.*

Ashes and rain become a dark grey paste on the cobbles and their horses slip, but Nian was right, the smoke clears more and more as they make their way towards the Eastown. By comparison, this quarter is quiet, the fire not close enough to worry anyone yet. In a town of straw-thatched houses, fires are something all citizens expect.

Qonna sees with relief that rain still drips from the roofs, the windows are closed to keep the smoke from ruining the furnishings, and that the Eastown seems prepared to sit it out. *Pomegranates* itself rises from the hazy street, its shutters giving a hostile impression, but it stands unharmed—kestrels, pomegranates, and all.

*It stands—you're allowed to breathe.*

For the first time in her life, Qonna rides into the yard like her brothers, and amidst the joy of it she barely notices ripping her underskirt on the pommel of the saddle when she dismounts.

The prince takes the reins from her and she runs into the house, leaping over two steps at once to reach the door to the sitting room where the inhabitants of the house have congregated.

"Qonna!" Qov jumps to his feet. "You shouldn't be here." As he grabs her arm, she sees her mother, the cook, and two maids on their knees, praying, clutching the Stars around their necks. The younger maid is crying.

"We thought you'd be safe up the hill!"

Qatt and Qitli surround their mother. Qonna dodges her middle brother to address her eldest. "Have you heard anything from Dad?"

"He sent a message about an hour ago," Qatt says with a strange hint of self-satisfaction. "He ordered us to stay here and be at hand in case we need to evacuate."

Qonna notices that before her mother sits the wooden box she stores her jewels in, and she's rolled up a few of her choicest embroideries in case they have to abandon the house her children were born in. The house that is supposed to be Qonna's future.

"I needed to make sure you were well," Qonna rasps, her throat raw from smoke. "I've come with help from the manor, and we'll ride on to the bridge."

Her mother struggles upright, her face distorted, and Qonna prepares to be sent to her room, but her mother embraces her so tightly all the air is squeezed from her. "Be careful," her mother says. "The favour of the gods can only do so much."

"Qonna," the prince yells up from the yard.

"I need to go." She kisses her mother and leaves her scandalized brothers in charge, wheeling around and descending the stairs so quickly she almost trips and falls on the last steps. The prince throws the reins of her horse at her.

"We need to hurry." He drags his neckerchief back up. "The wind is starting to turn."

# BOOK TWO

# CISIR

## *everything is lost*

Cisir finds his master slumped against the side of a stone-hewn trough, and though he's unmistakably breathing, Qes na Qarim must've keeled over from exhaustion. Like the rest of the Suns he's covered in filth, and most of his eyebrows have been singed off, while his hair is protected with a knotted scarf.

Cisir tries to crouch next to him but every muscle in his legs screams, so he merely leans over. "Master. The princes want to receive a report." He can barely speak himself. The smoke has crept deep and dried him from the inside out. Whenever he brings his hand to his face, he comes away with accumulations of dirt, ash, soot, and grime. As if the fire built a crust around him.

Qes' reddened eyelids flutter. All his lashes are gone. "What?"

"The princes. They've come down the hill to check on us."

For a heartbeat it seems as if his master will tell him and the princes to fuck themselves, but then Qes groans and scrabbles about. A broad strip of skin on his left forearm has heat blisters and he is marked, as all Suns are, by days of desperately trying to control the fire.

"They need to look around," he grunts as Cisir offers his arm. "What else can we say but that everything is lost?" He reaches up, then pulls away, as if remembering the last time it hurt so much.

Cisir rips the soaked woollen cloth off his back and wraps it around his arm to provide more of a barrier. When Qes grabs hold of him, he can still feel the pain of the peculiar zap, but dimmed, more like an aggressive attempt at tickling.

"Fuck," his master says from the bottom of his heart. "Why must we haul ourselves across this .... " His voice breaks and he winces as he shifts his weight onto his right foot. When Cisir straightens up fully, he's the tallest thing amidst the remnants of smouldering beams and pieces of stone, half-burned tables, chairs, and fabrics, reminders that the fire has not only razed half the city to the ground, but also taken the lives of its inhabitants. There must be barely a family in Seagard that hadn't lost something during the last three days that saw so many quarters reduced to wasteland. Some cobblestones on the harbour bridge cracked under the flames and the quay is deserted, all boats and sailing vessels brought further out to sea to avoid sparks jumping over.

None of the houses on the waterfront survived the blaze. The desperation on his master's face is mirrored in the world surrounding them. The skies are blue, the last slow columns of smoke discolouring it, but no clouds dot the horizon. There won't be any more rain to help with the hidden embers. Early summer set in when it was least wanted.

More people emerge from the rubble around them, sifting through the heaps in search of anything that isn't burned beyond usefulness, for trinkets lost in the haste to save a life. Looking over his shoulder at the site of the Yellow House, Cisir's stomach twists.

This was supposed to be the start of a new life, and like everything he's attempted, it has fallen into ruin. The only surprise is how quickly retribution came for him. As soon as the wind swerved three days ago, any doubt was wiped from his mind.

*You kiss one man and the gods descend to deal out punishment. Don't be stupid.*

It was the exact moment he knew something had gone wrong and smoke flavoured the air. There's nothing left to do but slog through what once was the city he hoped to make his home, at the side of his master whom he cannot touch anymore without causing pain to them both.

The riches unloaded from the *Buttercup* and not yet sold were destroyed; there's nothing left of the stores or the basket shed, despite their desperate attempt to drench as much in seawater as possible. Turning towards the Westown, some buildings withstood the fire. The bell tower of the temple oversees the destruction, its stones barely scorched, and many people have fled to it, seeking refuge when their homes were destroyed.

One of the most wondrous survivors stands among collapsed houses and outbuildings, its moss-covered roof only slightly crisped. The *Hungry Unicorn.* Horses are tethered at its front and royal guards stand around, helplessly staring into the distance.

When the First Sun and his secretary approach, someone in blackened skirts pushes the men aside. Cisir's master makes the most extraordinary noise—a violent sob, as he recognizes his daughter shoving through to him.

Cisir tries to avert his gaze as they fall into each other's arms, but the guards can't help but stare at the First Sun breaking down in the square. They're both crying.

Qonna kisses her father's cheek. "*Pomegranates* remains safe," she says, half-strangled by tears. "I've been back to check on it this morning."

Lilyis steps out from the *Unicorn* wearing a similar head covering to his master, her face grey and strained. She nods at Cisir. "Well done. Come inside; there's ale and bread for you."

Seeing the inside of the *Unicorn* so pristine and seemingly untouched by the catastrophe at its door feels distasteful, and most of the people gathered therein are painfully clean. The only one covered in ash, with eyes raw from smoke, is Lilyis herself. Her tunic is strewn with singed spots, her skin as well, but she sits among the nobles who chose the *Unicorn* as their headquarters. Strange that the only houses in this part of town that refused to burn were the oldest inn and one of the newest—the temple. Now both serve as the gathering places of survivors, and the royals send a clear message, snubbing the Brothers.

The two older princes look drawn but collected, as if they've left the rage behind them. Nivael da Nileon comes to his feet and leads the First Sun to a cushioned bench. "Is anything left?"

Qes na Qarim rubs a hand through his face, but only smudges the filth further. "No. All houses on the bridge have been destroyed. We can only thank the gods that so much of the *Buttercup*'s load had already been sold and transported off. We don't have too many customers waiting for deliveries, and the *Buttercup* itself is anchored out at sea. People are starting to search through the rubble, but the danger of reignition …." He clears his throat. "I don't want to lose any more Suns."

"How many *did* you lose?" the crown prince asks.

Qes' gaze flickers to his secretary. "Some are unaccounted for, but the ones we're sure about … two of the messenger boys and three other staff." He bites down on his mouth. "We brought them out to the quay, where the bodies have been …."

Someone takes Cisir's hand, with a slight snap against his fingers as the zap is smothered. Qonna stands next to him. He closes his eyes in an attempt to hold it together as he wonders how many of the dead remain undiscovered. He couldn't cry if he wanted to. His eyes feel as if they're filled with sour sand. Qonna's grip is strong, painful, but exactly what he wants. Perhaps she's the only person in the world he can allow himself to crumple for.

Nivael hands the First Sun a clay cup of ale and he clasps it to his chest before taking his first shaky sips. Qonna's father spent three days amidst the destruction, barely coming up for air between pulling people out into the streets, and loading their most prized possessions into little boats, while everything he helped build for the last twenty years turned to ash. The crowd outside the *Unicorn* is silent with anticipation.

"There might be Suns we only find when we start to clear the bridge," the First Sun says eventually, because while Yoren lies in a row with the other bodies at the harbour, no one has seen Hevo since the House of the Sun was officially given up, when the wind fanned the flames over its back walls and the whole complex came down with a deafening crash and the smell of burning syrup.

Cisir swallows. While the success of the Sun had nothing to do with him, its fall must have its causes in something he did. There must be a reason why Yoren was struck by a falling beam.

*Because you were angry with him for what he said about Gia? Come on.*

Though there can't be an excuse for Hevo falling victim to the wrath of the Heavens. Hevo who had been nothing but kind. A lump forms in Cisir's throat. He needs to be grateful for having survived. He needs to banish all thoughts of angry gods. Hevo is sure to be hiding somewhere safe—but where in the city could that be?

Qonna gives him a cup too. He doesn't want to let her other hand go but he's shaking too much; he needs both to hold on to the cup. Exhaustion blurs his vision and drags on his bones, and all the little blisters on the back of his neck itch. The ale is impossibly cool against his mouth, strong and bitter, the most delicious thing he's ever tasted.

"We took all available rooms," the crown prince says to the First Sun. "You will stay and rest."

"*Pomegranates* stands," Qes replies. "I have somewhere to go and will take Cisir with me. Give those beds to people who have nowhere to sleep."

"There are too many," Nivael says. "Most of the Triangle has gone by now and they're still evacuating to the Eastown."

The First Sun nods. "We'll never know what would've happened without the rain."

Cisir turns to Qonna, who smiles at him. "The Wolves have decamped to *Pomegranates*. Mother is busy finding space for everyone, and Gia is staying in my room until we know what's going to happen. We have to get your burns seen to."

"I need to get back to the bridge before that. The first scavengers are descending and we haven't found Hevo yet." *I haven't searched the whole city for him.*

"No," Lilyis interrupts. "You will go to *Pomegranates* and sleep. I'll drag you by the ear if I have to."


It's inconceivable that three days ago Seagard was such a bustling, happy place. The main street, having served as the firebreak to save most of the Eastown, is strewn with broken furniture, discarded pieces of charred cloth, and dropped bits and pieces marking desperate flights. Caskets line the street. Someone has saved their wine.

The whole town is a heap of discarded or damaged possessions, the cobbles covered in splinters and accumulating ash. Cisir's boots leave prints in it as he's shepherded towards *Pomegranates*, where a cluster of streets remains unharmed. Everything once described as 'down the hill' has been destroyed.

Walking up the hill, the devastation is laid bare. The fire chewed through at least two-thirds of the city and spewed out the closest the Eight Kingdoms has ever come to the Eight Hells: a town of grim-faced people raking through the filth, clutching the few things they were able to save. Many wear a whole collection of bags strapped to their person.

From somewhere inside the smoking ruins Cisir hears screams rising, but his master trudges on, pulling him along the narrow Eastown streets. If the fire had jumped the main road, all these houses would've been lost. If the roofs hadn't been drenched with rain, if the road had been a few steps narrower …. He can't keep thinking like this.

His legs and feet ache so much, he can barely walk behind his master to the front of his house. Suddenly *Pomegranates* has gone from one of the youngest buildings in town to one of the oldest. Its colours no longer seem cheerful but triumphant. The double-sided door leading into its yard stands open. Inside everything that the Wolves managed to rescue from the *Pear* is piled high and protected by cloth to keep the floating ashes off it, as well as water, should it start to rain again. There are benches and whole crates—clearly they had enough time to pack and flee.

Qonna puts a hand on his back and gently pushes him to the smaller side door, leading to the backstairs. The corridor houses more crates, rolls of fabric, and from the first floor comes the noise of heavy things being moved about. The last time Cisir was in *Pomegranates*, the house was incredibly well-ordered; now it's a chaos of flotsam. This can't only be stuff from the *Pear*. *Pomegranates* stores other families' goods too, and many people sit in the dining room, commenting on the position of chairs, two other tables, and a whole wall of clothes chests.

Cisir spots his own at the bottom of the pile and swallows smoky spit. His first reaction to finding some of his possessions preserved is not relief but disappointment. He'll be one of the few who hasn't lost everything to the fire. He'll still have the letters he couldn't bring himself to burn, remnants of Windyhill buried in the chest.

Lauron Wolf bursts into the room. "Thank the Siblings," he bellows. He's sweating, his sleeves turned up. "Come, Qes. We've prepared a battery of salves and potions. Gia!"

His daughter appears behind him in a blood-spattered apron. "Bring them in, Dad. I'll get cots ready."

The sitting room is littered with blankets and people in various stages of being cared for. Some are sleeping, some fiddling with bandages, and among them are more women than Cisir has ever seen in one place since coming to Seagard, all in aprons and simple head coverings. In the midst of them stands Noalis da Nileon, Princess of Crooked Hill, wearing the same clothes.

It seems the whole of the kingdom has agreed to assist.

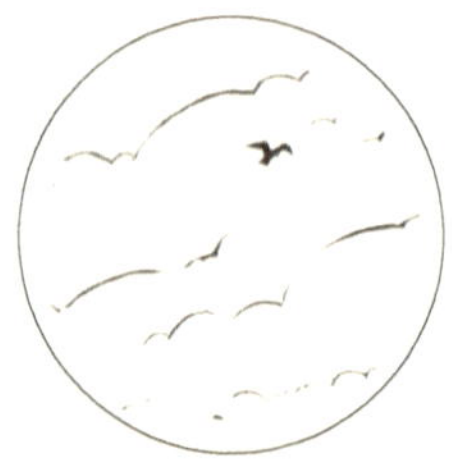

# QONNA

## *all the help*

In a few days Qonna has seen more men in a state of undress than in her entire life. What was a slow trickle of injured helpers during the first two days became a long queue on the third and while Noa, Eravis, and Gia threw themselves into their mission with enthusiasm, Qonna found herself reluctant to stay around.

She took every opportunity to accompany the wayward prince around town, organize transport for cartloads of possessions, and find space for them. She learned more about the city she was born in than she had in the rest of her life. In the same moment that most of Seagard seemed lost forever, buried under a flood of rubbish and ash, Qonna discovered its hidden corners, rode further into the Westown than ever. She listened to uncounted tearful outbursts of citizens overwhelmed by the burden of building a new future on so much destruction, and though Nian tried to keep her away from the harbour front, she saw glimpses of long lines of the dead, of priests walking among them deep in prayer.

But those sights did not touch her as much as Gia peeling the shirt from Cisir's back, revealing the mass of burned spots underneath it. His neck looks cooked. Gia gives her a jar of greenish salve to hold and digs out a handful.

"This will cool your skin. I'll be as careful as possible, but it will hurt."

"That's fine," Cisir says quietly, gripping the edge of the cot.

Gia checks over every last bit of his back. Qonna stares at Gia's hands—one cleaning, the other spreading the salve. Sometimes she stops, dips a pair of Qonna's tweezers in apple brandy, and extracts a splinter. When she comes to a big one that requires some digging, he draws in a sharp breath.

Qonna kneels next to him and again they clasp hands. He leans his forehead against her shoulder as Gia delves in with the tweezers and the tip of a penknife dipped in more brandy. His teeth grind together, breaths erratic.

"Just one more moment," Qonna says. "You can do another moment."

"Got it." Gia holds the splinter up in triumph. "That's the last one. Do you need to take your trousers off?"

Qonna nearly swallows her tongue.

"No, I don't think so," he says.

Gia nods. "Perfect. I'll get you a fresh shirt."

Cisir straightens. His face seems raw, his eyes bloodshot. "I shouldn't have made such a fuss," he whispers. "I haven't broken a single bone."

"Without treatment you'll become a walking blister," Qonna says sternly. "You've done enough. You're allowed to rest and heal. We have many people to help."

"But Hevo's still out there."

She cups his cheek. "My father has other people searching for him." *That might be a lie. Whoever isn't found by now is dead.* "You need to lie on your front and sleep."

"If I lie down, I'll never get up again." Sweat beads along the ridge where the rag he knotted over his hair presses into this brow.

"Get down," she growls.

"I need to take off my boots."

"Fuck the boots. Go to sleep." As she crouches to adjust the folded blanket that serves as a pillow, he asks, so quietly no one else can hear, "Have you seen Jark?" She can sense the fear in his voice.

"Not since yesterday."

He deflates with relief. "He was alive yesterday?"

"Yes. He came with us to check on the situation in the temple and stayed behind with some of the other guards."

"Thank you." His eyes close as he relaxes onto his stomach, his feet hanging so far over the edge of the cot he reminds her of a cricket on a slanted leaf.

Gia catches Qonna's eye as she comes up, her brows arching in unspoken comment. Qonna ignores it and walks to where her mother stands wrist-deep in bloody water. "How is Father doing?"

Her mother seems beyond tired, but she smiles. "The hair will grow back, and he was incredibly lucky. Have you seen the boys outside?"

"They must be in the attic, trying to cram the corners. Or maybe they've returned to the temple."

Her mother inclines her chin towards her husband's secretary. "How is he?"

"He'll live," Qonna says, clamming up. Her mother's voice held too much insinuation. *Gia must have told her.* But her mother isn't blind. She must've seen how easily her daughter comforted a man she hasn't known for long—a man who is not her brother.

Since the fire started, Qonna has only had a handful of hours of sleep, and exhaustion tugs at her with every step as she returns to her room from the last round of checks. Gia will take first watch, so she's dressed again in preparation.

"Is he still asleep?" her best friend asks.

"Out like a light." Qonna begins to dissemble the knot of her apron strings. "Only the gods know what he's been through. Any news about the missing Suns?"

"No. Do you need help?"

Qonna lets her aching arms fall. "Please. I'm knackered."

Gia steps behind her and opens the knot with a single movement. One moment her breath brushes Qonna's neck, the next she steps away. Qonna turns around and draws Gia into her arms. Gia squeals in surprise, then folds her hands behind Qonna's back. "You must've been frightened today," Gia says gently. Her palms are warm against Qonna's pained muscles. "But he could've been hurt much more."

"This isn't about him," Qonna murmurs into Gia's headdress. "This is about us. We could both have died, Gia. If the roofs hadn't been soaked, the fire could've overwhelmed the Triangle so fast no one could've gotten out alive." *We could so easily have lost each other.*

"Dad says it's a miracle so few died."

"Many of them Suns, though. Losing five men and boys, and potentially more."

"We don't know what will happen, Qonna. We need to focus on what we can do. Everyone resting in *Pomegranates* tonight has been saved, and more have found refuge in the temple. Cisir's friend could well be there."

"He won't be," Qonna prophesies.

"You can't take his hope away from him. He needs to heal again, and your father—what would've happened if your father had been the one struck down by the bearing beam?"

"I don't want to think about it." Qonna releases her hesitantly. The apron lies at her feet and she bends down to pick it up. The floor is strewn with a thin layer of dirt and the ever-present ash. *Pomegranates* went from scrubbed raw to sticky and filthy in no time at all and it'll take weeks to sort it out again.

Qonna's nightshirt hangs on a nail behind the door; she sheds the rest of her clothes while Gia fetches tea from the kitchen. She returns as Qonna crawls into the bed they take turns sleeping in and struggles upright to take a bowl from her.

"This one is camomile," Gia says. "I put a lot of honey in it. Will you be all right on your own for a while?"

"Of course." Qonna takes a sip of tea. It's thick with sweetness. "But please wake me if you need a break."

"I will." Gia bends over and kisses Qonna's brow before she leaves, clutching her own steaming bowl.

Tears rise to Qonna's eyes, but don't quite spill.

Qonna dreams of being trapped in the smallest of rooms while smoke rolls towards her. The door is locked and there is no window. She's in *Pomegranates*, but *not* in *Pomegranates*; the room is both familiar and foreign. She wakes up when she starts to scream, like the noises she heard echo through the streets for days.

She's no longer alone in her bed. Gia has her back to Qonna and sleeps with her knees pulled up, the swell of her body calmingly solid beneath the blankets. Qonna settles close to her. *I wish I could put my arms around her without making it weird.*

"You had a bad dream?" Gia asks softly.

"Yes. I've been dreaming of fire, like everyone else in Seagard." Qonna rolls around to glance towards the small amber statuette on her narrow shelf. In the darkness, Sister Sun shrinks into the shadows. "I prayed so often for my life to become less restricted, but I didn't want *this*." *To be guilty of so much destruction.*

"It's not your fault," Gia says with a deep sigh.

"People are bound to blame someone. Why not the ones they wanted to kick out in the first place?"

"The Triangle was one of the worst affected quarters. It makes no sense for us to burn down our own houses."

"There will be unrest," Qonna says, feeling the bite of truth. "After a few days people will tire of being helpful, as soon as it's apparent there isn't enough room for everyone who survived. Even if the princes persuade more families to open their houses. Even if they allow them to stay on the grounds of the manor. Too much has been lost."

"I can't speak to that. I haven't left this house since we arrived on that first night. You were the one riding with the princes. You saw the dead at the harbour."

"Barely. Nian is very protective."

"It must've been horrible." Gia's hand stretches out over her side.

Qonna takes it, swallowing. "The only thing that makes it bearable is to think about it like an event in the past. It might be a cowardly thing to do, but …."

"If it helps you, I can't see harm in it," Gia says. "It's an extraordinary situation. Gods willing, it'll be the only time in our lives we experience the like."

For the first time in her life, the phrase strikes her as much too insufficient. "Which gods, Gia—the gods of the Star or the gods of the old country?"

"All of them," she says softly. "We need all the help we can get."

"If you had to choose one of the Birkland Siblings, who would it be?"

Gia sighs again. "The Wolves have always been at the beck and call of Sister Sun, so I might not have a choice. Ma isn't keen on me talking about her, as you can imagine." Gia looks at Qonna's face in the moonlight, the direction of her gaze. "I saw the gift from the prince," she admits. "Though there's no amber in the steppes itself, it's traded widely among the families."

"Can I still choose Sister Sun?" Qonna asks, her voice squealing on the last word. "Quarter-Badger that I am?"

"There are no restrictions that I know of."

"Do you pray to her?"

"Sometimes. When I think the gods of the Star might not be inclined to help. Nonetheless, Sister Sun didn't make Pjer come back and choose me. And now that the *Pear* is gone, he has no reason to make the trip from Applebeck. I should be careful not to turn too far from the Star. It might not be worth the trouble."

"Magic might be worth it, though."

"Magic?" Gia chuckles. "Once the Wolves were famously favoured, so many of them born with the talents Sister Sun needed to gift her blessing. But magic is never a guaranteed result. You can't abandon the Star in hope of that."

"What about my auntle Sloe?" Qonna asks. "They seemed destined to receive it."

"From all that I've heard, they are not an ordinary person."

"We share the same blood."

"No one has the *same* blood, Qonna. Their abilities might've come from their mother's side. They're definitely an outlier."

"Don't you wish you could see them throw blue light just once? Like in the song?"

"What song?"

Qonna clears her throat. "Dad says *Blue River* is about Auntle Sloe."

Gia grunts. "It's a very old song."

*All about Sloe being beset by temple guards and killing the lot of them, while filling a whole river with blue fire.* "Apparently not. Dad says they've only been singing it here for twenty years or so."

Gia fidgets in her blankets. "We should probably be grateful the Brothers took in so many people," she says. "Not searching for new gods who are more exciting."

"That sounds like something your mother would say," Qonna scoffs.

"She did say it, years ago. She also said that if we want to be accepted in Seagard, we can't go on about how much more convenient the old country was. Ever since the Westown temple was built, the Star has claimed the city."

*And has strong opinions about me moving around in it.* "There's a monument on the grounds of Gard Manor, so old the prince says it was there long before the town, even before the *Hungry Unicorn*."

Gia sits up abruptly. "What are you saying?"

"That it looks like the Siblings were here before the Star. That once Birkland and the continent of the Eight Kingdoms called on the same gods." *We would've had more freedom once.*

"For fuck's sake, Qonna." It's been a long time since Gia used such strong language. "It's the middle of the night and who knows how many injured people will claw at the doors of *Pomegranates* in the morning. Why do you want to talk about *religion* of all things?"

"I don't know." Qonna shudders. It's painful to admit, but if she can't be honest with Gia, who else? "Because I'm scared."

"We're all scared. If you're convinced people will become uneasy about future shortages, we have much reason to be. You need to sleep."

"I can't." *I can't lie still for a moment longer.* "I'll get a cup of water, maybe that'll help." She pulls at the blankets covering her, smothering her. "Do you need something? Are you hungry?"

"No. Won't you need a light?"

"I know this house. You could come with me?"

"Qonna …."

"I'm sorry. Go back to sleep. I'll try to be quiet."

# CISIR

## *bitter with ash*

O h fuck!"

Cisir is up before he can think. "Qonna?"

"Who put a pile of chests there of all places? I think I broke my toe." She touches her foot and squeals in pain.

He grabs the single oil light in its protective wrap of dried hide and stumbles to the corridor. "What are you doing?"

"I wanted to get to the kitchen for some water." She hops on one leg. "The whole of *Pomegranates* has turned into an obstacle course. Can you bring over the light?"

She's in her nightshift, her dark braids loose and about to unravel, but the energy to blush has gone out of him. After all that happened to them, it's unlikely she has a single thought to spare on how inappropriate the situation is. He's his trousers, his mauled back exposed, and she barefoot and bareheaded. He takes her elbow to help her balance, and the zap goes through them, softly. Why would the gods create such a connection between two people who barely know each other?

"I don't think I'll ever get used to that," she groans. "Can you help me down the stairs?"

It's a good thing he brought the light, because the steps are littered with piles: boxes, small tea chests, books. Every empty spot is used to house other people's belongings, although the kitchen was kept reasonably clear. The scarred table is strewn with used tea bowls, but the water barrel is half full when Cisir lowers the light into it.

Qonna takes two clean cups from the shelves and holds them out. The water is blessedly cool against his hand as it washes over the rim of the first cup. Usually, this is the realm of *Pomegranates'* servants, but the maids are fast asleep.

They find two stools to perch on and Qonna miserably rubs the little toe she bashed against the chests. "How are you holding up?" she asks. "Were you there when Yoren died?"

His heart shrivels. "Sort of. We were trying to pull out as many pelts as possible, and the syrup, because your father said it would burn and set everything else aflame, and all the oil stored on site …." He glances over at their small light. "Something exploded before we could get to it, and Yoren was too deep inside the stores. We got him out by his ankles before anything else fell on him and for a while he lived. I wonder … I wonder if the gods really meant for it to happen."

She barks out a joyless laugh. "I'm glad to hear I'm not the only one turning philosophical. Poor Gia had to deal with me yammering on about the Star and the Siblings, while she only wanted to sleep."

"You think it might have been a punishment?" The words taste sour in his mouth.

"How could the gods want to kill a whole town? There must be innocent people in Seagard, children who can't even speak yet. How could they be a target for such wrath? And if it turns out to be a punishment, that's me done."

"Done with the Star?" he asks quietly.

"Precisely. Everyone already believes me barely civilized; I might give them something proper to talk about. What about you?"

He swallows. *If anyone in this town can understand, it's her.* "I'm afraid I did something … something that warranted a violent reaction." His heart picks up its pace.

She gives a quiet snort. "You? You must be the sweetest man I've ever met."

*I need to make her understand.* "I kissed Jark, though."

She stares at him as if he's grown a second head. "*You* kissed *him*?"

"Twice. It wasn't an accident. I decided to do it." He straightens his spine, ready to plummet. "I *wanted* to do it." As soon as he says it, he folds up again.

"You can't be the only man in Seagard kissing another man." She leans in, her toe forgotten. "How was it?"

"Wonderful. Too wonderful not to make me nervous." His stomach flips thinking about it.

"Whose idea was it?" she presses. "His?"

He nods.

"Congratulations." She seems in earnest.

"I haven't spoken to him since," he admits. "I don't know how he feels about it after the fire."

"Grateful that it happened," she exclaims. "And if he isn't, you let me know and I'll kick his fine arse from here all the way to Crooked Hill!"

It feels good to hear her so impassioned on his behalf. Despite everything he saw, heard, and smelled in the last three days, he notices the bubble of delight floating up within him. "That would be much appreciated."

"I'm jealous," she says, beaming at him. "Not because of Jark—because of the experience. To be kissed by someone you truly want to be kissed by. I don't know if I'll ever be able to do something that simple."

"Nothing about it is simple," he says.

"Exactly."

"And Gia—Gia doesn't want to?" As soon as it's out of his mouth, he wants to slap himself. *That was an idiotic presumption.*

In the faint light between them, Qonna's mouth sets. "She doesn't, and I don't know if I really want to. You heard her go on about Jark. She shouldn't want to, either—that's not a burden I wish to place on anyone's shoulders."

*She knows. She knows exactly how you felt all these years.*

It took a city burning down around his ears to find someone in a similar situation. "I understand completely," he mutters. "I would never have pressed my attention on anyone for fear of steering them towards such a painful conundrum."

She tilts her head. "What will you do when you see him again?" She slowly draws her fingertip around the unglazed cup.

*Try very hard not to panic.* "Be lost for words, most likely. It might come to nothing. He might declare it a moment of wretched weakness, a stupid mistake that doesn't count for much, given the seriousness of our situation."

"Why?"

A shiver races down his naked back. He must express it, even if it hurts like nothing else. "Because I'm not worth the risk?"

Her pale eyes latch on to his face. Her expression flickers between heartbreak, pity, and something feral, an anger for him that is almost as delicious as her defence. "You're so used to selling yourself short. I thought nobles were supposed to be arrogant and entitled."

"I'm sorry to disappoint you. There must be plenty of others who do, though we don't tend to push ourselves forward. I bet half of the da Relians are sensible young men at heart, but running in a pack of cunts makes them unbearable."

Her eyes widen. "That might be the only time I've heard you curse."

"I'm sorry," he says, but something is starting to come loose, something he's wanted to shed since he can remember. "Being around your father is starting to rub off on me."

"It's hard to rein myself in too," she says. "Dad must've had plenty of opportunity for foul words when you were trying to save as much from the House of the Sun as you could."

Hearing her speak the name of it hurts like a punch to the throat. Such a promising name, and now all is ash, the whole harbour bridge nothing more than split cobblestones and charred splinters, the glorious Birkland map devoured, the little treasures the First Sun had collected in his study lost. Twenty years of it. "It feels impossible."

"Did you know that before it became the House of the Sun, it was the tavern my grandfather ran with his wife? Uncle Lauron helped them set it up and Dad worked there for years. I wonder whether he sometimes secretly hoped to see it gone. Not like this, but in theory."

"If he has, he must feel the guilt for it too." Which perhaps explained the desperation with which he tried to extricate as much as possible from the stores, the order books, and most of the amber to prevent it from going up in flames. "Will he rebuild?"

"That's for the princes to decide," Qonna says. "Though the Company of the Sun has lost its home, there are still ships set to return." She yawns. "What will you do tomorrow?"

"Search for Hevo again. I have a mind to walk past the temple to rule out that possibility."

"You could send someone over."

"I need to see it with my own eyes. "No one can just vanish, can they? What about you?"

"Gia and Mother will find many things for me to assist them with. Hobbled as I am, I might confine myself to *Pomegranates*." She tries to wiggle her toe and winces. "I think it's starting to go purple."

"Let me see." He slides off the stool to his knees. Her skin is cool under his hands, all but the toe in question, which seems to glow. He rips the hem from his left trouser leg.

"What in all Eight Hells are you doing?" she asks with a laugh.

"You should stabilize it against the bigger ones." A little zap runs between them, but she manages to hold still as he wraps the fabric tightly.

She leans forward; their heads are very close. He smells a hint of sweat and smoke on her and it's all too obvious that only her nightshirt is between them.

"Let me try something," she says, and as he glances up, her mouth is on his.

It is not a wanting kiss, but something much more settled, a confirmation they both welcome.

Cisir breathes her in but doesn't catch fire. He closes his eyes in relief. If that was her drawing a line under the possibilities, it did precisely what he needed.

"Friends then," he says as she retreats.

She smiles. For one more breath her hand lingers on his cheek. "Friends."


After helping Qonna back up the stairs, Cisir grabs a blanket from his empty cot and leaves the house, knowing there's no way he'll be able to sleep. Not after having been kissed again.

His boots are too loud as he steps into the yard and he has trouble squeezing himself past the crates piled up at the door, but after shoving against them he can finally breathe. Though the air outside is uncomfortably warm and bitter with ash, the light is returning, reminding him that Shortest Night is less than a month away. The skies show a strange lilac as dawn creeps up on the coast. He knots the blanket around his shoulders, hissing as the rough weave grazes his tender back, and makes his way to the smaller side of the door leading out into the street. The hinges creak a tiny bit.

It's reckless, but so is staying put, not knowing what awaits him once he's officially allowed to embark on the search. He's far from the only one walking through the fields of blackened beams and bedsteads. In the rising light more scavengers are about, rooting around for people, treasure, opportunities to make their fortune. He's not the dirtiest either. Some of them are women with their skirts hitched up and soaked rags bound around their feet to protect them against glowing embers.

For a while he stands at the fork leading towards the Westown, and there it is, in all its blood-red glory: the House of the Bulls prevails. He's unable to ward off the resentment. He heard the flames slowed when the wind turned, but how is that fair? If there wasn't so much smoke around, he could see all the way to the *Hungry Unicorn*, and then to the bridge, but where once were narrow streets and thoroughfares, all has been transformed into one spread-out heap of rubble.

He resigns himself to following the remnants of the main road, and—to his astonishment—finds a line of carts stretching towards the harbour, where vendors are giving out tea and all kinds of food to sustain the citizens who volunteered to watch the fire die down and ensure there are no new flares.

Cisir shudders at the row of bodies. Thankfully it hasn't extended much since he last saw it. At the site of the Yellow House, three of Cisir's colleagues huddle together, clutching pieces of bread from the carts. As he approaches, they jump up.

"Thought you were gone," one of the messenger boys cries. "What about …?"

"The First Sun will be fine," Cisir says. Of course Qes na Qarim didn't leave the rubble unsupervised. There's a chance of something hidden waiting to be liberated. Why did he expect to poke about undisturbed? They'll watch every movement like hawks, and what will happen if he does find evidence of Hevo? Find him crushed nearly into meal? Still, Cisir stalks across the bridge lifting bits, hesitantly at first, then ever quicker, hurting to get it over with: the shock, the disbelief, perhaps the tears.

Not all of the house burned. There are squashed caskets and chairs, split boxes with matted furs under them, singed but perhaps useful for something. He detects no sign of bodies underneath the spoils. Could Hevo have turned to powder, mingled with the ash floating in the air? Could he just disintegrate without leaving so much as a shard of bone?

Cisir rubs the back of his hand against his mouth.

Up to his knees in debris, he knows he'll have to endure at least a few more hours until he can make himself stop searching.

His heart stutters as he hears a soft whimper. So quiet that at first he believes his mind is playing a trick on him, but then it comes again: a *mewl*.

He's on the ground, ripping at broken chairs and more flattened caskets, and at the end of the stores, some are still whole—unfilled but surely too small for Hevo to crawl into and wait out the Hells descending? Cisir dives into the first ones, but they're as empty as the day they were stacked back here.

Tears rise to his eyes.

*You're going mad. The pain has burned up your mind.*

There it is again.

In the last surviving casket crouches something small. Not a person, not a child, but something round-bellied and the colour of red sandstone, scrabbling at the wood with broad flat paws.

Cisir stares down at the plump little dog. It whines and tries to get at his hands with a shockingly pink tongue. As he bends down to lift it out of the casket, he knows exactly what he holds, wiggling and yipping with excitement. It's the doorstopper he saw Hevo push into place so many times, come to life.

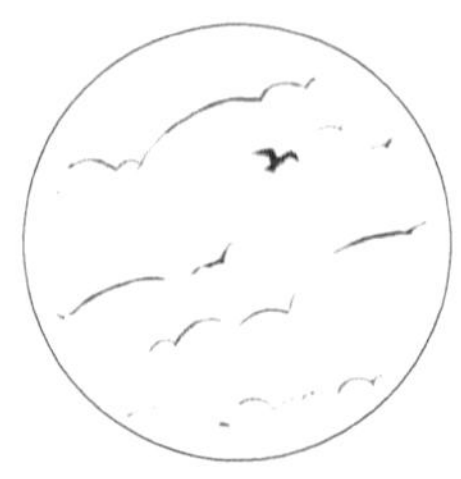

# QONNA

## *ruthless practicality*

Gia freezes; her apron strings fall to her side. "You did *what*?"

"I kissed him and then we both decided we didn't need to take it any further."

Gia laughs. "You've gone mad. How can you think about such risks? With *Pomegranates* stuffed to the rafters, how did you manage to be unsupervised?"

Qonna shrugs. She had looked forward to confessing for hours. She never had a kiss to brag about before. "As I said, we both knew it would lead nowhere. It's a relief, really. We don't need to ever think about it again."

"Are you sure that's how he feels?" Gia's eyes narrow at her.

"Yes," Qonna says.

"You kissed him and you got a sensible word out of him afterwards?"

"Yes."

"Maybe you're right," Gia concedes. "It's a bit sad, actually. You seemed to be so suited to each other."

*Apart from the fact that he kissed the most beautiful man in Seagard before me and that I don't feel inclined to do the same.*

Qonna yawns and steps to the window. It's quite early, and cold air rolling in from the sea mingles with the heated atmosphere in the city. Mist swirls in the streets and dilutes the smoke. The skies are already bright and blue, a mockery of the sights both must face today. Qonna is so tired that her bones are made of stone, pulling her limbs to the ground. She pats the deep pocket beneath her skirts, locating the amber statuette she slipped in under Gia's sceptical gaze. Her room smells like fire and medicinal herbs, and it's likely this disturbing whiff will remain for months—who knows how long *Pomegranates* will receive citizens with scrapes and burns? Outside of her room, people move about.

*Will they ever leave me alone to sort out my life? Or will my house be overrun from now on?*

Gia catches her eye before shouldering the door open. "Are you ready?"

Qonna yawns again. "I will be."

The first one she sees as she goes down to the kitchen is her mother, sorting through the stores of salve and herbal teas, and Qonna stills. She has never seen her mother in this room. To think that mere hours before, Qonna had the audacity to kiss her father's secretary where her mother now pushes clay jars and bundles of herbage around. It feels like a fist wringing out her stomach. Her mother wears a sensible headdress and the same style of apron as all the helpers; one corner of her skirt is secured underneath her belt. Never before has Qonna seen her dressed with such ruthless practicality.

"Mother," she croaks.

"Qonna, very good. Can you please put all of those in the basket and bring them up for me? And then you need to go to the temple and inquire after their situation. We should offer help if we can. Some of the people there would be more comfortable in *Pomegranates*. Your father promised to organize shelter for anyone who is not too badly hurt and can be moved."

Qonna's jaw drops. How is it that the woman who was such a hindrance for years is so forceful and decisive in matters that benefit not only her family but the whole population of the city? *Extraordinary situation, indeed.* "Yes, Mother."

She's rewarded with a tight smile. As her mother turns away, the star-shaped amulet on her chest gleams. How likely is it she's waited all her life for the chance to prove herself? To be charitable when disaster strikes the town?

Somone knocks on the window shutter. Outside of the kitchen stands someone in a blood-spattered dress, pale and distraught.

"Come in, come in!" Qonna's mother calls as she heaps jars into the basket. Qonna can barely lift it when she hauls it off the table. She sets it onto her hip and makes the trek upstairs, her breath strained as she reaches the living room.

"Perfect." Gia dives into the basket before Qonna can so much as put it down.

Cisir's cot has another man in it and more have been spaced out on the floor. Most of the people who found refuge in *Pomegranates* are older women, but some young men are around, the ones with critical injuries drugged into rest.

Qonna wants to moan about the task she was given, but compared to emptying chamber pots and cleaning wounds she has nothing to complain about. She leaves the basket against the wall. She should want to stay and help, to sacrifice her time for the benefit of all who were hurt, but the smell of the room nearly makes her gag. Her mission will get her out of the house at least. Into a town that's barely a town anymore.

As she closes the door behind her, she stops to listen. No horses coming towards her, no wayward prince to relieve her of her duty, so she walks away. After these last days the surroundings are still strange to her. Only a week ago it would've taken her quite a while to reach the open; now the destruction has spread so far up the hill that she strides through the square within heartbeats. Initial clearing efforts exposed most of the roads. Piles of rubbish line them, but most come barely to Qonna's hip and don't restrict her view as the houses did before.

Groups of men are moving everything that hasn't been burned, perhaps discovering bodies to add to the pit. No one pays her any attention. She isn't dressed as the woman she is, but like a servant, and there are many of them in the streets today. Every item that can be sold will be found at some point. Every citizen who survived the fire seems possessed by the wish to bring order as soon as possible, to make sense of the new landscape created by rubble, cracked cobbles, and scorch marks. That is exactly what her mother's doing too. Distracting herself by serving the town.

Qonna reaches the big fork in the main road, and after only a few steps the Red House appears to her right, like the hull of a ship emerging from fog. The bright facade is muted, ash clinging to every small ledge. In front of the throughway leading into its yard stands a cart laden with caskets, accompanied by a few exhausted-looking Bulls. It seems the Red House has also come around to the idea of helping.

It's the first time Qonna's been this far west since the fire. Based on the devastation she lives with in the Eastown, the Westown astonishes her. As if she'd stepped through a door into a different land, a reality utterly strange. Smoke invades her mouth, ash adheres to her skin. She drags her thin shawl up to cover her face. In the Eastown the roads have been cleared, but here she only has a footpath snaking through the rubbish leading to the temple's belltower, in which a small, contained fire burns to guide the people to their gods.

The walls of the temple are nearly black at the base and halfway swallowed by what's left of the houses that stood closest to it. Qonna spits out a curse as she scrapes her ankle on a slate shard. It will take weeks, maybe months to make the Westown truly passable again, truly inhabitable.

Beyond what she saw around the *Hungry Unicorn*, this is how the Eight Hells must feel to walk through, limping, half-blinded and half-choked. When she finally reaches the temple door, she can't help sinking against it in relief, pounding her fist above her head. A small section of it opens and suspicious eyes peek out.

"We're full."

"I'm coming from *Pomegranates* to ask if you have wounded to bring over."

The priest gasps. "Wait."

It takes him a while to confer with his Brothers, and finally the door is unlatched and pulled back to let her in. A sharp smell wafts towards her. They must've burned some incense not long ago to clear the air. The temple of Seagard is dark and indeed crammed. Every single spot among the soaring columns is covered in human life. Children cry in their mothers' laps, old men huddle around the columns, while the Brothers have chosen to guard the altar, probably to ensure none of the citizens defile it with their grubby hands. The women gathered in the space that once felt so cavernous and almost indecently empty are clothed like Qonna, smell like her too, and beneath the crisp citrus scent of incense lingers the stench of displacement: sweat, dried blood, and piss.

"Come with me." The priest returns to guide her over ash-caked limbs and ripped shirts to the corner of the temple with the most light, where they've stashed the people they need assistance with.

"Qonna!" Guardsman Jark is barely recognizable, his head swaddled in a dirty bandage, with deep smudges under his eyes. He no longer wears most of his armour, but the traces left on his padded undershirt are reminder enough of what he is. Jark's hand folds around her wrist, his eyes wide.

"Cisir is well," she says, before he can even wonder how to ask. *You're right*, Qonna thinks smugly. *I am already ten steps ahead.* "He spent most of the night at *Pomegranates*."

Jark smiles in relief. "What are you doing here?"

"My mother sent me to offer our services."

"You're a godsend," Jark exclaims, which makes the priest flinch. "We need to get him out of here." He gestures towards the man whose head is propped up on Jark's leather breastplate. His face is hidden under blood-encrusted linen, but the sleeve poking from the grimy blanket is yellow.

"Hevo! My father and Cisir are desperately searching for him—how did he end up here?"

"His father lives in the Westown. He must've run off to check on him. We found him only this morning and he's in bad shape."

"Is he conscious?"

"No."

"He should be brought to *Pomegranates*." She turns to the priest. "Who else needs help?"

He flushes, perhaps not used to being spoken to in such a demanding way by a woman in a dirty headdress. As Jark squares his shoulders in silent threat, the Brother ducks and complies.

She helps fashion stretchers out of bits of refuse from the square. By the end she barely notices the splinters making their way into her skin. Sixteen of the worst-afflicted citizens are hoisted from the flagstones and rolled onto the scorched tarpaulin, and so the slow caravan towards the east begins.

No carts can come close to the temple yet, so the only option is to make the way on foot. When Jark picks up the front end of one of the first stretchers, Qonna takes the back. He doesn't protest, merely nods and files them into the queue. Some of the others are carried by younger priests, who are likely relieved to get rid of these patients, to lessen the pressure on the temple to keep them all safe.

Qonna's arms hurt after a few steps, her breath hitches, and sweat runs down her face, and though Jark slows down, he doesn't ask her to give up. Stumbling across a field of rubble isn't what any of them are used to, but she least of all. She grips the stakes hard, though her skin starts to blister.

Hevo lies eerily still and fresh blood appears on the bandages. Jark's leather armour is stuffed beneath him, but the guard is wearing his weapons again as well as his mail. He's used to that, but it irks her that he isn't out of breath. As she comes to a halt, almost slipping on more slate, his expression holds no pity.

"I need … need a moment," she pants.

Qonna can't see the Red House yet. She looks down at her flaming palms. Nothing in her life has prepared her for this, but the man on the stretcher belongs to the Sun and therefore is part of her life. Hevo deserves the best care, for her mother to make a fuss about him.

Qonna grunts as she bends down. She made the decision to carry him, and so she needs to carry. There's nothing left but to grind her teeth and see it through, if only to show the priests behind her that she's not to be underestimated.

Her ankle starts to play up as they finally reach the Red House, but from here on the streets are clear. Her eyes burn as sweat drops from her brows, and when her nose starts to run and soak the shawl around her neck she leans into the pain of her shoulders and palms, the feeling that her ankle could snap anytime.

The queue of stretchers winds around the carts in the Eastown, some of its inhabitants staring at them without understanding, but others join the priests. Qonna is ready to cry as her eldest brother comes towards her.

"Let me," Qatt says before shoving her out of the way. "Oh, this is one of ours!"

"Yes, I found Hevo." Her hands leave skin on the stakes as her weeping blisters rip open.

*Gia will have salve for them; don't be so whiny.*

"Father will be relieved," Qatt says. "Run and let him know."

She is far too winded to run, but she swerves around the queue and limps faster, until she reaches the street she was born on.

A cart blocks half of it. She's seen the horse before—it's the same that stood in front of the Red House earlier. Excitement flickers through her, and fear numbs the tips of her fingers. The Bulls have come to *Pomegranates*.

# CISIR

*a new leaf*

Cisir feels the puppy's heartbeat in every fibre of his muscles. He should release it, let it run, but he's unable to set it down. He can only crouch in the rubble and breathe in its smell, slightly musty and of course smoky, but without doubt, alive.

It holds quite still after trying to lick his face a few times, though it must thirst and hunger after who knows how many days in the casket. Its ears are soft against his arms as it leans against Cisir's chest and he cradles this astonishing proof of grace.

He wants to cry, but he can't; he can only sit and wait until he's able to move. He barely notices that the sun has come out to burn his blanketed back, sweat rising on his mangled skin. The puppy in his arms is falling asleep.

"What the fuck are you doing here?" One of the boys moves in behind him. "You're really peaky, mate—everything all right?" His gaze drops to the bundle in Cisir's arms. "That's quite a miracle, that is, finding the little guy. Will you keep him?"

"I just picked him up a moment ago." Cisir's voice sounds rusty.

The boy shrugs. "Never too early to make your mind up about important stuff. Would be another miracle if you found out who he belongs to."

*He belongs to us—don't you see?*

The boy would likely react with panic if Cisir explained how he knew, so he merely nods and tries to stand. His knees crack and the boy's brows arch. "I've come to tell you the master's daughter found Hevo with the Brothers. They're putting him up in *Pomegranates*."

Cisir clutches the puppy tightly. "I knew it. I knew he was alive."

"Barely, it seems. But at least we know what happened to him."

"I need to see him." *To make sure he isn't angry at me for bringing this on him.*

The boy studies his twisted face. "You probably should, mate."

The puppy is still asleep when Cisir reaches the Eastown, the blanket wrapped around his hips to free his scabby back. It feels as if he's carrying a baby along the ruined streets, someone vulnerable and helpless. The dog gives a soft, wet snort as Cisir enters the yard where Qonna's brothers are trying to establish order among the heaps and piles.

The three boys stare at him, his bare shoulders and the bundle. Qitli na Qes is the first to run over to him. "By the Heavens … where did you find him? Should I see what we have for him in the kitchen?"

"Yes please, that would be most helpful."

The other two stand beside him. "He looks like a hunting dog," Qov says. "A really expensive one."

"You should leave him here with us." Qatt strokes the soft ears. "Mother won't like having a dog among the wounded. We got a delivery from the temple and none of them are in good condition. They have their hands full up there; he would only get underfoot."

"Thank you," Cisir says again. "Just for a bit. I need to check on Hevo."

"Is that the boy they brought up? Yeah, he's in a bad way."

It wrenches his heart out to hand the puppy to Qatt. Cisir delivers the blanket with him. "It won't take long," he warns but none of the brothers heed him. He makes his way up the stairs. Compared to last night the room is fuller, but he spots Qonna immediately. She kneels next to Hevo's cot, his body lifeless, his naked feet drooping over the sides.

"Cisir!" Qonna smiles at him, but it's a cautious smile. He can see the prospects aren't good, as Qatt said. He should feel self-conscious, standing half-naked in a room predominantly filled with women, but the whole situation is so unreal there's no space left to get worked up about details.

"What happened to him?" he asks quietly as he crouches down.

"He must've been in his father's house when it collapsed. Gia cleaned the wound and proposed stitching him up as best as she can. He hasn't come to yet, though."

"Thank you so much for finding him." He touches Hevo's arm. There's no zap with him. Should he take it as a bad sign?

"I came across him by coincidence," Qonna says. "It was Jark who's been taking care of him."

Cisir looks up, blood rushing into the tips of his ears with a *whoosh.* "Where is he?"

"With my father in his study. They're conferring with the Bulls."

Another hot wave runs through him. "The Bulls?"

"They turned up without warning."

"I should … I should see what's going on."

Qonna grabs a shawl from one of the chests next to the wall. "Put this on first," she advises. "No need to insult *everyone's* sensitivities."


Qes na Qarim's study is light and quite small, filled with books and a narrow table serving as a desk. There's barely room for the brazier and the few men sitting around it. The First Bull brought two others with him, in their blood-red tunics and with the scowls Cisir has come to expect from these young men, though neither of them belongs to the group that attacked him.

His master heaves a sigh. "I tried to find you."

"I was searching around the bridge, Master."

Bjell da Relian studies the get-up of his rival's secretary, the fringed shawl wrapped around him, the ash-caked boots, and scorched trousers. Cisir is the only one there who looks like the people of the city nowadays, dressed in anything that survived the flames, with the stamp of reckless necessity. The First Bull wears impeccable leather armour, his silvery-blond hair plaited into a long, shiny braid, not a speck of dust on him or his attendants, while Qes na Qarim might have donned clean clothes, but his brows and lashes are singed, as well as one side of his cropped beard. He wears the traces of the flames like his secretary does, hidden under the soft goat hair fringe.

"Let me catch you up." His master shoots a glance towards the corner of the room where a man stands, one whom Cisir has studiously avoided acknowledging. Jark is battered, bruised, but he stands upright in his royal guard armour, sheathed weapons on display. "The Honourable Company of the Bull came to us with a proposal. A most unexpected proposal at that."

Bjell da Relian shifts on his seat. "These are extraordinary times and whatever happens in our future, I would like some aspect of my legacy to be a generosity of spirit that suppresses our petty squabbles. We're in similar straits. The Red House might have withstood but our storage facilities fell victim to the fire. The main offices close to the harbour are no more. We lost staff and space, and it seems to me that the smart thing to do is find a way to remedy this situation together, not fight each other over limited resources."

Cisir blinks, unsure if he's supposed to comment. He didn't expect the First Bull to be so reasonable.

His master takes up the tale. "Which is beyond laudable, given the situation in question could easily benefit the Bulls so much more than the Sun."

Bjell inclines his head. "I came with an invitation. We can make room at the Red House until new facilities are up and running at the harbour bridge. The da Relians will hold out our hands to help."

"And the Suns are most grateful." Qes gestures at Jark. "Though before any contracts can be drawn up, the princes need to be informed. I'm sure they'll appreciate the selflessness and noble intentions of the Bulls, but due to the Sun's dependence on the royal family, we shouldn't make further progress into detailed plans without affording them the courtesy of giving their consent."

Cisir braces himself for the First Bull's reaction. Surely, this is the moment when he sheds the mask?

Bjell da Relian's pale face remains unmoved. "This is acceptable. Further negotiations should take place at their leisure."

"What do you think?" his master asks as soon as the Bulls take their leave. "Should we trust them?" He offers the seat the First Bull has vacated to his secretary and Cisir only hesitates for a heartbeat before sitting down.

"He might talk about noble intent, but that can't be the true reason."

Qes pushes out a deep breath. "My feelings precisely."

"What do you suspect, Master?"

"You tell me—what makes more sense?"

Both Jark and Qes are waiting for Cisir to speak his mind—his master and the man he wants to kiss again before this day is done. His head pounds almost as much as his heart. "It feels like preemptive action," he says eventually. "As if they fear being sanctioned if they don't assist us."

A slow grin spreads on his master's scorched face. "Exactly."

Jark clears his throat. "They might well anticipate the princes' refusal to tolerate their attitude in these circumstances. Would they strip the Bulls of their assets?"

"Happily," Qes confirms. "This house once belonged to a family that ended up on their bad side. In times of great need, the royals could certainly justify ruthlessness towards anyone they believe to be a threat. I'm astonished the Bulls came to that realization so quickly. Usually, they need to go through a few humiliating experiences before they learn to rein it in."

"Under their old regime that definitely was true," Jark interjects, "but you've heard him. He's trying to turn over a new leaf. Not all da Relians are bull-headed brats. While he waited to replace his late uncle, he must've seen him make many mistakes."

"You might be right," Qes says. "Let me write to the manor. Cisir, are some of the boys close?"

"I can find one of them to take your message up the hill, Master."

"I'll go myself," Jark volunteers. "I am long due to return and report."

"That would indeed be best." Qes draws a piece of paper to him, and as he bends over it, Jark smiles at Cisir with so much warmth that Cisir shudders. It hurts to stay still, to not vault the desk and go in for a hug, to assure himself nothing about it is a dream, that they both lived through the fire. He flinches as the smell of the honey-coloured sealing wax wafts.

Qes holds out the folded missive to the guard, who takes it with a small bow and retreats.

When the door closes, his master narrows his eyes. "What was that?"

His throat constricts in fear. "What, Master?"

"Who walked in on who naked?"

Cisir gasps. "That's … that's not what happened."

"But there was something?" Qes smiles again, with a hint of self-satisfaction that's hard to bear. "It's none of my business. The only thing that matters is that this whole disaster might turn out to be good for us in unexpected ways." He inspects the ink stains on his hands. "If only to see Bjell prostrate himself in his desire to be helpful to the Sun."

"Yoren died, Master." *He will never make inappropriate comments again when we all drink tea together.* "As have many others. Your house is full of suffering people who would rather not have lost their houses and most of their belongings."

"I always feared you'd be a spoilsport—though you're obviously right," Qes adds quickly. "And I won't take my smirk outside this room. I would never hear the end of it." He rises from his seat. "Does my daughter know about your thing with lovely Jark?"

Cisir grinds his teeth. "Yes, she does."

"She wasn't too disappointed, I hope." Qes leaves an expectant pause for him to fill.

"Master …."

"Calm yourself. Of whatever nature your 'something' is, I'm not about to shout or object. Try to be discreet—otherwise you might have whole squadrons of young women baying for your blood."


"I hope you haven't given him a name already." Qitli kisses the puppy's brow before giving him back to Cisir. "Qov thought 'Spark' would work well."

"He certainly has the right colouring," Cisir mutters, taken aback. The three brothers have a hard time letting go of the little dog. It feels heavy in his arms. "Did he sleep the whole time?"

"Not the whole time. We played with him. He likes this." Qatt holds up a curious item fashioned from knotted cloth. "Qitli made it for him, from one of his foot rags." He offers it to Cisir.

"No, thank you," Cisir says with a shudder. "I'm sure I can find him a new toy."

"He ate a whole bowl full of scraps," Qov says, "and took a big shit next to the flower pot over there. Where will you take him?"

"I'm not sure. It depends on whether we can get the princes to agree to move the whole Company of the Sun to the Red House."

"Yeah," Qatt says. "The big man came grovelling, we saw. Tell Dad not to milk it; he might spoil it before long. If Spark stays here, can we … can we take turns with him?"

Only a few years ago, these three would've been small boys desperate for a pet, as much caged by their parents' expectations as their sister. "I'm sure we can," he says, careful not to make an actual promise. "You named him, after all."

All three beam at him, and Spark the puppy sputters out the most adorable snore before he curls up against the soft goat hair shawl. Cisir's back unlocks; something he held tight for four whole days melts away. There might be a future after all.

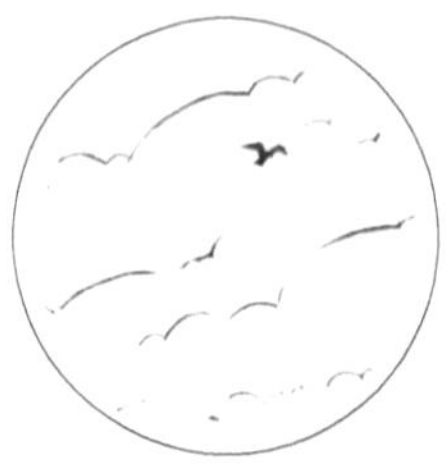

# QONNA

## *the same side*

Qonna had never seen skin sewn up like cloth. Gia cropped the side of Hevo's head as close as possible first. The cut runs from his right jaw onto his crown and is bleeding so much Gia can't keep up with blotting it. As the needle's sharp point pierces the flap, Qonna's retch takes her by surprise, but she clamps a hand over her mouth as her mother makes good use of her embroidery skills. It helps that Hevo remains unconscious. The stitches are incredibly even, the living flesh neatly tucked in, and while she works there isn't a single flicker of disgust on her mother's face. She's collected, and her breath flows calmly; she doesn't get distracted by her daughter watching on with horrified fascination.

"It will make a dashing scar one day." Her mother snips off the ends with the tiny scissors that usually rest in her basket with her silken threads. "It would've been much more difficult with him thrashing about."

The door behind Qonna swings open and Noa and Eravis appear on the threshold.

"What did we miss?" The princess appears excited at the prospect of watching another fiddly operation, which makes Qonna admire her even more.

"New people came from the temple this morning." Qonna's mother cleans her hands on a cloth. "There's plenty to do. Qonna, can you help?"

Noa points a thumb over her shoulder. "Nian is here for you, Qonna—he's down in the yard, getting thoroughly acquainted with the puppy."

"What puppy?" Qonna asks. *Did I miss something?*

"There's a puppy down there with the First Sun's secretary." Noa wears an apron and hair covering, as well as an impatient expression. She likely longed to reach *Pomegranates* and get busy once again. "I asked Father to ready some of our own rooms for refugees from the city. As soon as this house gets overwhelmed, we can transport some of them up the hill, as well as open the grounds for temporary accommodation. Nian has taken the organization in hand. He's here to tell you everything you ever needed to know about tents and field kitchens."

*I'd rather stay here with you.*

"Isn't he sweet?" The wayward prince holds out a young dog with paws so big it will surely grow into a monster. "Apparently, he wandered about on the bridge, all alone and lost, waiting for your father's right-hand man to rescue him." Nian kisses the puppy and shoves it into Qonna's arms. Even at such a tender age it weighs more than she anticipates, and she exhales a soft *ooof* as it tries to lick the tip of her nose.

"Very sweet," she agrees, though her muscles protest, remembering yesterday's ordeal. Her palms barely had time to recover, the edges of the popped blisters getting snagged in the dog's soft coat. "But he must belong somewhere. Someone must miss him."

Cisir steps from behind the tarpaulin-draped piles. "I'll ask around," he promises, smiling as she hands over the young animal, its tail wagging excitedly as it recognizes the man who brought it to *Pomegranates.*

Horses are waiting for them, and this time Qonna feels much more confident as she pulls herself into the saddle. She gives Cisir a little wave as she departs the yard. How can it be that the fire, the catastrophe that devastated the city, has finally allowed her to do as her brothers have always done—though under supervision of the prince, she rides again.

As soon as the road is broad and clear enough, the prince lets his own horse fall back. "What do you think about the Bulls' sudden discovery of concern for the greater good? I can't quite believe that there isn't some secret intent."

"Is that what my father suspects?" she asks.

"He must be—after twenty years of being treated like an interloper by the Red House, to be sought out and asked for cooperation? The da Relians have never been courteous to your family." The wayward prince pulls a face. This morning his cheeks are blotchy, his green eyes reddened by lack of sleep, and he's dressed simply, his hair twisted into an unruly knot. "We can't paint them all with the same brush, I suppose, but it comes as a surprise to find the current First Bull this amenable after his uncle terrorized us for so long. Can you do me a favour and keep an eye on the Bulls in the background?"

Qonna gasps. "You're bringing me to a meeting with the Bulls?" *How is he getting away with stuff like this?*

He smirks. "There are many ways to put someone on their backfoot and I thought I might give this one a try."

"Nian ...." *Would he heed me more if I called him Lilyis?*

"Ah, there they are."

They've reached the fork in the main road. Amidst the rubble shoved to the side wait a dozen royal guards on horseback, a formidable delegation. Nian signals their leader before turning back to Qonna. "Of course we come with the full force of my family behind us, in case they dare question your right to be present."

A whole contingent of riders pulling into the yard of the Red House certainly sends a message. Qonna has walked past the building more times than she can remember and often wondered about the host of predominantly blond young men stationed inside, but never anticipated that one day she'd be admitted as far as this.

Around them, window shutters open as Bulls of various stations gawp down at the two people backed up by a mass of stony-faced guards kitted out in mail and leather. Qonna has a sudden urge to check her headdress but forces her hand back down. She might be intimidated but they don't need to know it. She takes care to dismount with as much grace as possible.

"Your Highness." An old man with a peg leg makes his way across to Nian. "What an unexpected pleasure."

His voice drips with sarcasm, but the wayward prince smiles back at him. "Were you expecting my father to attend? He is busy preparing the manor for the citizens of Seagard and my stepmother can't spare him."

A crease appears between the old man's brows. "Just be careful, Your Highness. He's in a right mood."

"Thank you, Rinald. Can you announce us, please?"

Rinald's bright eyes dart over to Qonna. "Mistress na Qes, I presume?" He heaves a deep sigh. "Ah, well. At least it will be entertaining."

The iron-shod end of his wooden leg creates a distinct noise on the cobbles as he makes his way to the main entrance of the Red House. He must navigate the stairs a dozen times a day, but Qonna sees hesitation in the old Bull's stride. He's not really what she thought to find in this most ostentatious of decorated houses.

Nian holds out his elbow to her. She towers over him at this distance, but she appreciates the gallant gesture. The Red House is new territory for her and being able to clutch at him while they walk into their enemy's lair most welcome.

The interior smells expensive; it has more doors in one corridor than Qonna has ever seen in a single house. Someone has gone to great lengths to beautify every single doorframe with carvings, but they are unpainted and have something slightly unnatural about them, as if the lintels had sprouted a tumour for every year the da Relians lived there. They reach the First Bull's study as young Bulls poke their heads into the corridor. Some seem merely curious, others scandalized that two most unlikely people have come to put the thumb screws to their leader.

Rinald grimaces as he pounds on the door. "Visitors," he bellows, "and not the kind you enjoy."

Nian chuckles, but bites down on his grin as Rinald pushes the door open.

The First Bull clearly didn't expect anyone to disturb him. Qonna recalls catching a previous glimpse of him in leather armour, but today he's wrapped in a blood-red robe. As he hastily pulls it closed over his chest, Qonna realizes Bjell na Relian isn't actually dressed but must've snuck down early to get some work done before the servants woke. He wears leather slippers and his robe barely covers the hem of his nightshirt.

"Your Highness," he says icily. "Welcome to the Honourable Company of the Bull. I was under the impression we already had a meeting scheduled with your uncle to go over the details of our venture. I remember receiving the urgent missive from the manor late last evening."

"Bjell, may I introduce you to Qonnamaris na Qes, firstborn of Qes na Qarim and named future steward of *Pomegranates?*"

Bjell's eyes widen. He seems too stunned for words, and Nian continues. "I thought it made sense to introduce you both properly, given that future interactions are unavoidable. Qonna, this is Bjell da Relian, First Bull of Seagard and self-proclaimed heir to the lost throne of Southclere."

Bjell's pale face shows open dismay. "I never …." He catches himself. "That was the title my late uncle chose to be addressed by. It is certainly not how I see myself."

"Oh good," Nian says. "Because we don't want my own uncle to get the wrong impression regarding your ambitions. As the crown prince of the Hillakes and Southclere he has his own interests to protect and can get awfully snippy if he feels threatened."

Bjell starts to sweat. "Have you come to ascertain my loyalty, Your Highness?"

"I certainly thought it a good idea to check in as to where we stand—and don't forget that *you* came to the Sun. It seems only fair to reassure us that the true agenda of the Bulls can withstand such a violent turn."

Qonna has never heard the prince speak like that. There's so much insinuation lurking behind his words, so much iron resolve. This short, stocky prince seems to have donned a robe of his own, another personality.

*Is this what Lilyis is like?*

Qonna suddenly understands how Nian da Nileon might come to be considered dangerous.

"I promise you our only intent is to put the good of the city first and foremost in our endeavours." Bjell's face, so drained of colour before, now has red blotches on the cheekbones. "The gods have chosen to spare the House of the Bulls in their infinite mercy and so it behooves us to share our good fortune with all citizens who haven't had such luck."

Nian smiles at him. "I'd hoped you'd see it like that—it is also the principle Qonna's father is working under. *Pomegranates* is crammed with wounded Seagarders in dire need of assistance and my family is most devoted to freeing up more resources. The Red House would be such a resource for us, so don't be surprised if my uncle makes demands."

Bjell pulls himself up. "You came to warn me?"

"Not so much warn as to prepare you. Having the Company of the Sun move into the House of the Bulls is an ambitious idea, and you might not have foreseen that the Suns will come with a lot of scrutiny. My family has been closely involved with the Sun since its inception, but my uncle reserves the right to offer his opinion whenever he can. Qonna has spent some time at the manor recently and can attest to it."

As Bjell's attention is drawn to her, his left hand slides up to hold his red robe closed. Qonna finds herself moved by the gesture—without intent, the First Bull of Seagard has shown himself vulnerable in some respects, and as concerned with his modesty as any well-bred maiden. "Consider your warning received," Bjell says flatly. "This could've been a letter."

"It wouldn't have been half as much fun—and given the general dearth of amusement in the last days, I so loved seeing you squirm."

A shocked laugh escapes. "You also brought someone along to witness my discomfort." Bjell's eyes land on Qonna.

She grins back at him. "It served to make me much more sympathetic to the Bulls," she says. "After all, we find ourselves in the same situation. My father is working himself to the bone to keep the

Suns together, and it's good to know he will receive all the help you can give him."

Bjell shrugs his pale braid behind his shoulder. "I will do what I can, Mistress na Qes, to assist the First Sun. My young cousins are already furnishing part of the house to accommodate their colleagues from the Yellow House—the ones who survived and are able to work. We don't have much storage on the premises but should the expected ships arrive from the far west, we will figure out something."

Nian clears his throat. "We can all agree the clean up of the harbour quarter and the Westown must take precedence. We need space to rebuild and to get as many citizens under new roofs as we possibly can. You'll find my uncle keen to facilitate the rebirth of the city, and should you find yourself in trouble handling his demands, please let me know. I'd be happy to help."

Bjell blinks, as if the offer confuses him. "Happy to help?"

"You wouldn't be the first da Relian I've worked with. My prejudices against your family have long softened. Stepping into your uncle's position, with all the schemes he had put into motion, can't have been easy. I'm well aware the kind of cooperation you proposed would've been impossible under his regime. I'm beyond grateful."

"You show it in strange ways."

Nian shrugs. "There's a good reason they call me 'wayward' but I'm glad we finally find ourselves on the same side."

# CISIR

## *back into place*

Cisir expected his master to react with disgust or indifference to the dog accompanying him to the study, but Qes na Qarim goes down on his knees and talks to Spark; the morning's pressing tasks seem forgotten. It takes a long time for him to come up again, dashing the back of his hand against his scorched cheek.

"He's going to grow big," Qes prophesies. "We'll have to make him a huge bed."

His smile reminds Cisir of Qes' sons' enthusiasm; Cisir had anticipated Qes to take on the role of his own father, who always preferred to keep his hunting dogs shut away.

While Qes na Qarim searches for a basket to designate as the official domain of his secretary's puppy, Cisir notices the pile of letters on the desk, some of them in a scrawl nearly as illegible as his master's own, the signature bold and sweeping. It seems the royal family has many opinions to impress on the First Sun.

"I should give you more days to recover." Qes stuffs a cushion embroidered with a grumpy-looking unicorn into the firewood basket and lifts Spark to test the fit. "How was Hevo this morning?"

The guilt gnaws at him. "Unchanged. Gia says he's starting to move about more though, and she hopes he'll wake soon."

Qes watches the puppy curl up on the cushion. "May all the gods hear her," he mutters. "We need to fight for every Sun if we want to hold our own against the Bulls."

Cisir crosses his arms. "You want to go ahead and relocate into the Red House, Master?"

"I think we won't have any other option. The princes are enthused by the idea of cooperation and it would make many things easier." He shifts his broad shoulders. "I know it's petty, but the fucking high-handedness of it bothers me. If the wind hadn't turned at the last moment, we would have the Bulls crawling into *Pomegranates*, and that would feel so much safer."

"I think I know what you mean."

"Lilyis is prepared to be generous but agrees that we need to go into the situation without bowing our necks. She took Qonna along yesterday."

"Into the Red House?" Goosebumps break out on his raw neck.

"I know why she did it. The Red House is stuffed with young men desperate for female company, and not that long ago the First Bull was one of them. Throwing a woman into the mix has been effective."

"How did Qonna feel about it?" Cisir asks.

His master arches what is left of his brows. "She took it in her stride, it seems. She and the prince are starting to get quite close, and I must admit it worries me. Lilyis can be mischievous. Having her so closely linked to my daughter might have unforeseen consequences for both."

"Such as?" *What does he think Qonna will do? Become even more reckless and outspoken?*

Qes winces. "I know Qonna doesn't care much about it, but her reputation … at some point Seagard will rise from the ashes and then the old rules will slot back into place. I can't begrudge her the new freedom, but it's only a question of time until everyone becomes concerned about her riding about town with the one member of the royal family whose name has been spoken in hushed tones for decades. Aw, he's falling asleep." A slow smile spreads on his master's face as he gazes into the refashioned firewood basket. "Have you noticed he looks a bit like the little doorstopper we used for the

Yellow House?" His eyes go wide. "Oh fuck. I know it sounds daft, laughable, but … *could* he be?"

Cisir clears his throat, both wishing it to be true and too fantastic at the same time. "He might well be, Master."

"I never knew where the doorstopper came from. I always assumed my father had bought it. He had odd taste sometimes and would bring bits and pieces in to decorate the front room, probably to make him feel as if the house still was his to decide over, in small ways at least." He rubs his face again. "It will be a pain to make do without the quarterly rents for the Yellow House. They kept my wife in embroidery silks for many years. I never questioned my father's choices, but maybe I should have. Qarim Badger was a man with a singular history."

Cisir can't help but nod along encouragingly, and his master continues. "He was a wizard once, so it makes sense to assume he bought the doorstopper for reasons best not speculated on."

"A wizard, Master?" *Wielding actual magic?*

"In the old country, wizards are like priests, but they also serve as governmental advisors. Their connection with the Tall Gods …." He presses his lips together. "As far as I'm aware, Father never displayed as dangerous a talent as my half-sibling, but it all has to come from somewhere, hasn't it? Now we have a would-be magical dog sleeping on my favourite cushion."

"Could the fire have brought him to life?" Cisir remembers the puppy's heartbeat against the underside of his jaw.

"Could have—Brother Flame certainly is one of the more capricious gods. What did you say his name was?"

"Your sons named him Spark."

"Huh," Qes says with a low chuckle. "Imagine that."


Reading Nivael da Nileon's letters makes Cisir's head hurt. His handwriting is bad in a wholly different way than Qes'. It belongs to someone who was taught calligraphy and then deviated from its forms with no shred of consideration for his correspondent. And Nivael indeed harbours strong opinions about the de Relians and their underlying ambitions. While Cisir drafts the replies, he hears noises from the yard and the sick rooms, people shuffling things around or calling out in pain. From time to time his master leaves his study to dispense orders to servants or look in on his wife and the wounded, while Spark sleeps through the commotion.

Sometimes Cisir imagines Qonna's voice on the other side of the wall, and he feels a pull towards it. Not exactly unwelcome, but still disconcerting. His scalp starts to itch, all the small cuts and scabs Gia dug the biggest splinters out of, and a film of sweat rises on his brow.

He should be resting, gathering his strength, but knowing that a mere few feet away lies Hevo, stretched out and unable to wake, helpless and vulnerable to any treatment mistakes, makes it impossible.

Cisir stares at the trembling quill in his hand and puts it down before he can ruin any of the letters spread before him. He needs to close his eyes and breathe.

"Should I get you some tea?"

It's not his master checking up on him but Jark, the filthiest Cisir has ever seen him, though Cisir can tell he tried to clean himself up before entering the house.

Cisir is overwhelmed by the wish to touch his grimy face, to wipe off the dirt himself. He swallows. "Why are you here? Sorry, that came out wrong. I'm glad you're here, but I think Qes knows."

"Knows what?" Jark smiles at him. "Can't I offer tea to the man I've guarded with my life for many mornings? I've a proven interest in keeping you with us. Now that I've seen you sitting up and ready to argue, I'm much relieved."

"I don't want to argue. I thought you'd be busy clearing up the Westown."

"Oh, I was. I'm on a supply run and thought I could drop by."

"It won't get you into difficulties?"

"It might at some point. Please breathe, Cisir. I'm not here to put pressure on you."

But breathing is nearly impossible. "I wanted to see you too," Cisir admits.

Jark stands at the door, clearly fighting the impulse to come closer, but he must know as well as Cisir that indulging in any kind of closeness is too much of a risk with *Pomegranates* full of people. Cisir puts his hands on the table, ink-stained and covered in tiny, crusted cuts. "How is it outside? Did you find more bodies?"

"No. Thankfully, most people are accounted for. I see your friend hasn't woken up yet."

"I don't know if he ever will. Gia and Qonna try to be optimistic, but …." His breath stutters.

"Hey, hey, hey." Jark rushes in to comfort him. His arms find their way around Cisir's shoulders and Cisir's face is squashed against the scratched and sooty leather of Jark's breastplate. He shouldn't allow himself to cut loose, but a sob works itself up his chest and is out before he can wrestle it down again.

Jark's right hand strokes his back firmly, like he would do with a horse that needed soothing. "You can cry. We've all cried a lot in the last few days."

Cisir doesn't want to cry. He'd much rather kiss. He claws at Jark's sleeve to keep himself from suffocating.

"Cisir, have you seen my mother anywhere?" Gia halts in the doorframe. "What—what's going on?"

Jark pats Cisir's head but doesn't release him. "A slight wobble."

"Oh," Gia breathes. "I can make some camomile tea."

Jark's chin touches Cisir's head as he nods. "That would be greatly appreciated."

"That was mean," Cisir protests as her footsteps are leading away.

"No, it wasn't. Nothing about me comforting you needs to look suspicious if you only keep calm enough."

"Is that truly what you're doing—comforting me?" *Have I got it so totally wrong?*

"You seemed to need it." Jark pulls the First Sun's chair back and sits himself down, soot and all. "Friends do that for each other, and I would like to see us as friends."

"I'd like that too." The desk hides their hands from anyone else bursting in, so Cisir takes Jark's in his. While the callouses Cisir developed from a childhood of incessant weapon training have been replaced by ink stains and a pale ridge on his middle finger from holding quills and reed pens all day, Jark's palm is rough against his. It's also warm and steady.

"Have you had many of these friendships?" Jark asks.

"No. I'm relieved one of us knows what to do."

Jark grins. "That's nice of you to say."

"I can't well begrudge you following through on what I was always too scared to," Cisir notes. "I've lost my heart more times than I can count."

"Oh."

Cisir entwines his fingers with Jark's. "Somehow that feels worse."

Jark presses back. "Don't worry on my account. I have no claim on you because we kissed."

"I would like to offer you a claim," Cisir whispers with a racing heart. "If you wish."

"Camomile tea!" Gia materializes in front of the desk again, and the slight panic in her voice tells him she probably heard too much.

"Thank you." Jark keeps his posture relaxed. "You brought two bowls, how lovely."

She stares down at their clasped hands. "Are you feeling calmer?" she asks Cisir.

"In a way," he says, fighting a blush.

*This was badly done. You should've talked to her before confronting her without so much as a warning. You're such a self-serving cunt.* He grinds his teeth to interrupt his spiralling thoughts. "It was helpful to have him here."

"So I see." Another young woman, someone not brought up around Birklandish ideas of how families work, might not have understood what she saw, but Gia isn't merely clever, she's also Lauron Wolf's daughter, and there's no way she hasn't perfectly grasped the situation. "Would you like to stay and drink tea with us?"

Gia winces. "I'd love to, but I need to find Mother. Your friend Hevo woke up, but he's in a bad way."

Hevo lies on his side, knees tucked underneath his chin. His eyes are open, and his lashes flutter, but he stares at the empty cot next to him. It hurts to see him wrapped around himself, protecting his body from something invisible to everyone else.

"We've tried to get him to unclench," Noa says quietly. "But as soon as we touch him, he lashes out. He won't take any calming draughts, either. I don't know what else we can do."

Hevo's whole body shivers from time to time, like he's waiting out a wave crashing over him, and then he starts to whimper.

"The blow to his head must've done something to him," Jark says.

"Others with similar injuries are much quieter," Gia admits.

"You need to give him time," the eldest one of Qonna's friends says pragmatically. "Leave him be and he'll soon start to eat and drink the draughts."

"What if he doesn't?" Noa sounds scared. "What if he wastes away in front of us?"

Gia takes her elbow. "We won't let it happen. We'll ask everyone we know for help. Perhaps the Brothers have wounded in similar condition at the temple. We could ask them for assistance?"

Cisir bites his lip. The man trembling in front of them doesn't look like his friend anymore. His eyes are wide, yet unseeing. Something brushes against Cisir's calves and he nearly swallows his tongue.

Spark pushes through the ring of people around the shivering Sun, his glossy tail wagging slowly, warily. He sniffs Hevo, licks the hands clamped around his shins.

Hevo calms.

Cisir watches in astonishment as the puppy sits up against his friend, striking a protective pose, his tiny teeth bared in a growl.

Gia narrows her eyes at the puppy. "I'll get my dad," she says. "There might not be a proper wizard in all the Eight Kingdoms, but I'm sure he can help somehow."

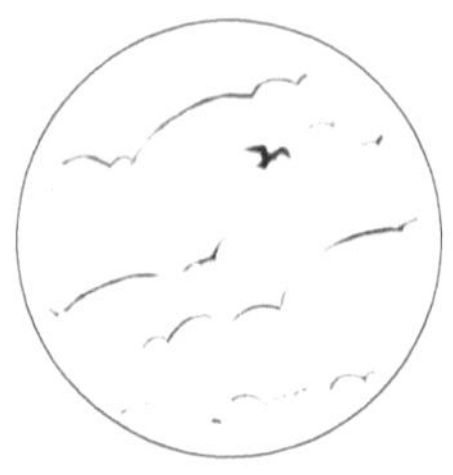

# QONNA

## *their own plans*

Qonna comes upon a circle of people sitting in the room next to hers. Uncle Lauron is there, as well as her own father, Gia, Cisir, Jark, and Noa.

"Who died?" she asks as her heart tries to climb out of her throat.

"No one—yet." Uncle Lauron's face is grey with exhaustion. "We need a professional. I can't stand in for a trained wizard." His eyes swerve in Qonna's direction. "I wish Qarim Badger was here—he would've known exactly what this is."

Jark clears his throat. "Do we need to panic? All we have to go on is a dog and a man who isn't properly awake."

"Spark isn't just a dog," Qonna's father says quietly. "Or at least that's what I suspect. Something strange is going on with Hevo, something that stinks of manipulation." He bites his top lip. "As much as I would like to focus all our efforts on his recovery, we have other things to worry about. Moving into the Red House, for example." He shoots a glance at his secretary. "It pains me to leave a Sun behind, but the Company needs to press forward, and we can't allow ourselves to become too distracted. If you can't help him, Lauron, we need to let it run its course."

Qonna takes a deep breath. "What do you mean by 'manipulation'?"

"We shouldn't talk about it." He rubs his face.

Uncle Lauron grabs his wrist. "What do you suspect, Qes?"

"I fear magic must be involved in some way."

Her heart misses a beat.

Jark laughs with a hint of hysteria. "Magic? Weird things happen with people who are clomped on the head."

"No one disputes it. But the way the puppy behaves around him, that is the strange bit. One thing my half-sibling taught me is that sometimes the gods of the old country like to experiment with different forms. Cats, birds, foxes …."

Qonna holds her breath.

Uncle Lauron gulps, as if trying not to throw up. "You're right. We shouldn't think about it."

"Magic, or what we've come to mean by this word, is strictly bound to the Tall Gods," her father says. "I know that from personal experience—the Siblings *always* work to their own plans. Whatever happens, we must keep the priests away from this house. None of them will have a sense of humour about a manifestation of gods the Star has worked so tirelessly to banish from the Continent."

"Heresy," Jark says. "You're talking about heresy." He looks at Cisir, clearly scared.

The secretary sighs. "We don't know what any of it means."

Her father nods in agreement. "Yes, we need help. We have to ask the prince to weigh in."

"Which one of them?" Qonna asks.

"The one who spends most of his time in Birkland," Uncle Lauron says. "The one who stood closer to the Siblings and their powers than any of us."

"I thought you'd be busy moving the Suns into the Westown," Nian da Nileon says as he arrives in *Pomegranates*.

"Before we do so, we need your opinion on something." Qes turns to Qonna. He's sweating.

Noa takes her brother's hand. "Listen to them, please. A man's life is in danger."

"How so?" His sister's presence seems to make Nian more inclined to patience. He settles into the chair that is offered to him.

"You've experienced what it feels like to stand beside a wizard. Ideally, we'd have someone with an even closer connection here, but this burden must fall to you," Qonna's father declares.

*He's trying to stall,* Qonna realizes.

"My father was in the habit of bringing trinkets into the House of the Sun …."

"Yes," Nian says with a snort. "I remember having a word with him about it."

"I believe some of these objects spoke to him because they felt connected to the Siblings. I never … he never brought me into the faith of the old country, and I must admit I haven't paid too much attention to the gods of Birkland, apart from feeling slightly embarrassed by a father who couldn't leave them behind. It might've changed when Sloe came to Seagard. We both saw them unleash all Eight Hells on the men who came to attack us then. I couldn't deny the blood splattering up to the ceiling of the Yellow House. You've seen Sloe in full flow many times. You must know what we're dealing with here."

Qonna looks from one to the other, waiting for the prince to fly into some sort of denial.

Nian frowns, crossing his arms. "What actually happened?"

"Cisir?" Qonna's father turns to his secretary, who carries the puppy.

Spark tries to wiggle from his grip, clearly determined to return to Hevo's side and resume his watch.

Nian blanches beneath his freckles. "Is this a joke?"

Qes' hand touches his elbow. "Lilyis, please."

Qonna had never heard her father address the prince directly with that name. It carries with it the sound of legends, of powerful queens of the past. It is, for all intents and purposes, a woman's name, and yet the prince's face softens. Her father used the name strategically, not because he wants to rile him.

Nian stands up to pet the dog. "He does indeed look like it. I recall Qarim saying he had found a guard dog for us, and that I'd like it because it was cheap and wouldn't have to be fed. He had a strange sense of humour sometimes and I always had to pick my battles with him. Too often I spoke out against something he had set his heart on and, coming back from Birkland, found he had done it anyway." A small smile plays around his mouth. "I didn't begrudge him the doorstopper. I always rather liked it, and he didn't have to insist." His fingers scratch the puppy's chin, and Spark calms for him. "I have indeed witnessed some of the Siblings taking animal form. I'd say you're right to be alarmed, though I don't understand why it puts a man's life at risk."

"Come with me," Qes says.

The whole company moves to the door of the sick room.

Cisir puts Spark down and immediately he's back in front of Hevo, licking him, soothing him.

The prince turns to Cisir. "This is how he always reacts?"

Cisir shivers under the attention. "Ever since Hevo woke up, yes." The secretary's voice is rough.

"You call this 'waking up'?"

Qonna's father pushes through. "Have you ever seen someone afflicted in the same way?"

The prince seems helpless standing among the cots. Small, as unsure as any of them. "I can't be certain. Sloe never took me to see any of their clients, and these days they're more concerned with politics than healing. But they've spoken of people getting stuck between the land of the dead and the land of the living, and that it always constitutes a big problem for the wizard in charge."

It sounds so very removed from the teachings of the Star. "The land of the dead?" Qonna asks. "Is that the Birkland Heavens or the Birkland Hells?"

The prince grimaces. "There is no Heaven in Birklandish beliefs and none of the priests would welcome me talking about it, Qonna. I could get into a lot of trouble."

"I didn't know they have no Heavens," Cisir says quietly.

Lauron groans. "You can still be rewarded for a life well-lived, though the Siblings' rules are much more fluid around the idea."

"Do you truly believe in it?" Qonna asks him.

He twitches. "It's how I was brought up in the steppes. It's a private thing, Qonna."

"I'm sorry, Uncle Lauron." *I want to know.*

"It's fine. Our wizards taught us that the Wolves have always considered themselves favoured by the gods, though I've never seen evidence of it. It meant that we strictly observed the rituals around sending someone to the land of the dead. There was so much singing. We burned a great many treasures with them to ensure they were well equipped for the next life. I recall my mother being insistent upon a golden clasp my aunt had her eye on. She didn't want to part with it and always said she needed it in the land of the dead."

Qonna's palm presses against the amber figurine hidden in her pocket. It feels heavier now she knows what's bound up with the presence of Sister Sun. "Can wizards go into the land of the dead?"

The prince frowns. "I've never heard of anyone able to do it."

Cisir interjects, "But if we think that's where some part of Hevo is trapped, how can we get him back?"

Qonna opens her mouth to protest, but the desperate expression on Cisir's face stops her.

"I don't know," Nian says. "Unless someone hid a properly trained wizard on this continent …. I'm due to leave for Birkland in a few weeks, and I'll put this case to Sloe, but it could take at least six months for them to join us here. Not that I haven't been searching for a good excuse to drag them back to the east, but by then it would surely be too late for your friend. I don't know what we can do to help him today. We can't rely on a dog to keep him alive, whatever Sibling we're dealing with in this form." He looks at Lauron. "What do you think?"

Gia's father shifts from one foot to the other. "It makes sense to assume he's Brother Flame, right?"

"Right," Nian says. "Brother Flame is one of Sloe's closest Siblings, so they might indeed be able to sort the situation."

"Hevo is a Sun," Qonna's father interrupts, "and we have a responsibility to him. If we assume he is unable to return to us, we need to care for him the best we can."

Noa clears her throat. "If I may?"

The men around her fall silent. The prince smiles at his sister, his green eyes alight. "Noa?"

"What about the stones?" she asks. Qonna bites down a proud smile at her friend.

Lauron scowls. "What stones?"

"The small monument in Father's garden." Noa sends a nod towards Qonna before she continues. "He always said they were the oldest part of Seagard, and why there's a city here in the first place—because in ancient times people came to visit the stones and pray to the old gods. I remember him saying something about a belief that the monument once signified a place where the boundaries between realms are at their thinnest. We could bring Hevo to the stones and see what happens."

It's a revelation to see them all so utterly stunned; the prince opens his mouth a couple of times, like a carp out of water, then he blinks and shuts it again.

Lauron nods slowly. "Before we rely on bringing in a wizard all the way from Birkland, we should at least try it."

"It's an excellent idea," Qes admits. "It might serve to clarify the circumstances very quickly."

Noa blushes with pleasure and the sight makes Qonna want to clap her hands in delight. "I thought it might."

The prince takes her shoulder. "In a few days we'll start to receive citizens on the hill, so we should do it before they arrive. Otherwise, we'll have more priests howling at our door than we can shake a stick at." He studies the faces of everyone in their circle. "So that we are clear: it is imperative the Star does not get wind of our plan. The fact that the Westown is still in chaos might work to our advantage; it will certainly keep them distracted for another week or two. Qes, should we try to transport him tomorrow morning? Will he be well enough?"

Qonna's father shrugs and turns to his daughter. "The women should know."

"I'll ask Gia."

Nian smiles at her. "In three weeks, we'll celebrate Shortest Night and as far as I'm aware, the boundaries are supposed to thin even more then, which might help us."

Qes squirms. "You make it sound like a conspiracy, Lilyis."

"The Star would call it 'conspiracy', I suppose, though the only thing we aim to do is prove or disprove a theory. I don't know what to expect when we bring him into contact with the stones. He might fall back into full unconsciousness. We need to be prepared for that."

"As I said before, Hevo is a Sun. If we can't get him to come back, we'll care for him nonetheless." Qes' face is deadly serious. "We will not fail him, whatever happens. Cisir, did Jark say anything about his father? Has he been found?"

"Not that I know of, Master."

"I'll send out more boys. We can at least find out if he's among the dead uncovered in the last few days." Qes beckons to his daughter. "I'm sorry, but I don't think we should involve your mother yet. She never agreed to you and the boys becoming close to the Siblings and I know she'd struggle with keeping it from the Star."

"I understand, Dad." *I truly do.*

"I'll tell her as soon as we know what's going on, I promise. For now, tell her we're moving Hevo closer to the prince's physicians."

A series of secretive nods makes the round and Qonna's heart clamours. It's like being part of a plot, involved in saving, if not the kingdom, at least something important in it. Noa stands beaming between her half-brother and Qes' secretary. A deeply troubled expression mars Cisir's face.

# CISIR

## *plausible deniability*

The sun is barely up. The litter Hevo's strapped into hangs between two of the prince's carthorses and is ringed by royal guards. The puppy snuggles in next to Hevo, covered by the blanket and keeping him calm, but Cisir walks next to them feeling swamped by the riders around him.

He slept little. It shouldn't have surprised him to be so close to events—he brought Spark to *Pomegranates*, so he's bound up in the proceedings, and probably would be even if he didn't consider Hevo his friend.

He had hoped Jark would be part of the guard accompanying them up the hill but Jark was given different tasks this morning, and other members of what Cisir has come to consider 'the conspiracy' plan to meet them at the manor. Lauron Wolf will walk up with Qonna and his daughter, while the First Sun will join them after his business with the Bulls has been concluded for the day. It seems neither his wife nor his three sons will be brought into the fold.

They soon reach the upper part of the city, the area spared by the flames. Here and there Cisir spots window shutters that are nailed shut and speak to the inhabitants' fear of being robbed. The sight wakes his unease. So far, things have kept quiet, but at some point public squabbles are sure to break out between the families who lost their houses and the ones who were passed by.

A thin drizzle coats the cobbles with a smear of ashes, and he needs to be careful not to slip and fall. This part of the upper hill has a hostile atmosphere, the few servants who are around so early staring at the guards with mistrust. Who is the mysterious man afforded such protection? They might well suspect one of the princes in the litter Cisir has trouble keeping up with, and soon rumours are likely to spread about a royal being unwell, perhaps even the crown prince himself.

The road following the walls of the manor grounds is muddy, the ditch in front of the walls filled with matted grasses and rain-flattened wildflowers. Cisir should be grateful. Whatever smoulders in hidden corners of the city will soon be extinguished if the night rains keep falling. The dead will have to be disposed of too, and the thought of standing in the drizzle around a yawning pit, being preached at by the Brothers of the Star, makes him shudder. The dead must've been transported uphill in similar fashion, though carts carried many of them piled up in their shrouds, and the burial ground serving the city will take the last ones in the next days.

Hevo's face is grey and has developed a waxy sheen, with discoloured hollows underneath his cheekbones. He stares up at the rain, barely blinking, his lips bitten to shreds, while the little lump of dog twitches next to him under the blanket. When they pass the gate at the top of the hill and turn into the drive, Cisir's breath rasps and he's tempted to cut across the grass to reach the house. The drive leading gently downwards is long enough; he'll be able to calm himself before their arrival. Around the artificial lake below the house, many tents have already been erected in preparation for the first citizens.

As soon as they're spotted, people step into the yard fronting the tower. Noa and her older companion, as well as her mother, wait for them. Until Gia comes to the manor, they'll be in charge of Hevo's health. Lilyis and her father join them, both grim-faced and pale.

"Let's get him inside and settled." Nivael de Nileon gestures to the guards extricating the litter from the horses. Cisir grasps one of the back handles, wincing as the wood rests on the scrapes on his shoulder. Hevo seems so small under the blanket but the whole contraption is weighty enough for Cisir's knees to tremble. The puppy wriggles free as they walk through the hall into the guest quarters of the house. A room has been prepared for them, with a proper bed.

Noa is right behind him, and she pushes Cisir resolutely out of the way. She picked up linen towels and a bowl of steaming hot water on her way in.

"Go wait with the rest of them," she says. "You can leave the dog to me."

The next group arrives shortly after.

Qonna and Gia wear woollen shawls protecting their headdresses against the rain and both are slightly out of breath after their ascent.

"Did you manage to bring them over in one piece?" Gia asks gravely, as if she has more respect for the one who got his hands on Jark first.

"Safely delivered. Noa's already with him."

"What's the plan then?" Again, it's Gia who speaks. "Wait until dusk to sneak him to the monument?"

"That would probably be safest." Lilyis steps close, her face twisted in a grimace of worry. She looks up at Cisir. "How are you doing?"

"I'm fine," Cisir says. "Not really, though." *They'll understand. They won't laugh at me or sneer.*

"None of us will be fine for a while," Lilyis says, "but you certainly have a bit more colour than the last time I saw you. I assume you'll come with him?"

"It would be nice for him to see someone he knows when he wakes up, and as Yoren is dead …. I don't want to imagine how scared he must be if he is where we think he is."

Gia smiles sadly. "The land of the dead is not like the Eight Hells. Not a place imagined for punishment." She glances at her father.

Lauron Wolf is the last one making his way towards the manor house. He wears a dark cloak with a felted hood drawn over his hair, which sports quite a few moth-eaten holes. "No," he snaps, already tense. "The land of the dead is not bathed in flames." He shifts in his heavy boots. "No one gets poked with pitchforks. Though I agree that Hevo must be scared." He scowls at the front of the manor house stretching out before him. "So that's it? Not quite as glamorous as I expected." He stares over his shoulder to take in the view. "Nice lake, though. I wouldn't mind camping out here."

"You've never been so far up?" Qonna asks.

"They do a good job of keeping the citizens out of the gardens," Lauron says. "I always use the eastern rather than the northern gate whenever I have reason to leave the city."

Lilyis makes a noise against the back of her teeth. "It hasn't always been this nice. The manor used to be a pile of rubble, full of rats and spiders."

Lauron's gaze spins to her. "I'm sure it was. Just lucky it's too far up the hill to catch alight."

The prince bristles at his words. "I'm sorry for your loss, Lauron."

"Of course you are. But then you won't stick around for long, right? When you come back the next time, much of the harbour will probably be rebuilt."

Lilyis clenches her jaw but doesn't deny the accusation.

Lauron brings his attitude to everything he sees on the hill and Cisir quickly loses patience. Compared to the comforts the Wolves experience at *Pomegranates*, the manor is not much of a step up. With Qonna and the other women busy in the sick room, Cisir waits out the day with the princes, sitting on a low stool and waiting for his master to arrive. Even without throwing Lauron into the mix, the atmosphere is terse, with not a whisker to be seen of the crown prince, his wife, or their entourage. It appears these high guests have taken to eating in their chambers. Cisir flinches as Noa's mother carries a tray into the manor hall, laden with tea bowls and slices of raisin-studded cake.

"You've been waiting a long time," she remarks, her grey eyes grazing over the scratches visible beneath his collar.

"I thought my master would conclude his business with the Bulls much quicker. He wanted to be up here by ten bells."

"Nothing with the Bulls goes smoothly," Hilvis da Nileon says with a sour twist to her lips. "Though Bjell is one of my few cousins who possesses a longer attention span than a gnat, he knows how to use bureaucracy to get his points across. Qes will be longing for death by now. Be glad he was so good as to spare you."

"The First Bull is your cousin?" *Is it always this complicated in the south?*

"Yes, but we both tried to deny it at times." Hilvis smirks.

"When you married into the royal family, was his uncle still at the helm of the Bulls?"

"Indeed, he was."

*That can't have been fun.* "How did he take to the marriage?"

"About as well as could be expected. But then, the king hasn't forgiven him, either." She pours out tea, then firmly pushes a pin back into her headdress before handing him one of the bowls. "A lot hinged on my husband's previous marriage. When both his wife and their son died in childbed, someone had to pick up the pieces."

The tea is strong, but of excellent quality. With a pang Cisir remembers the many times he sat with Hevo and Yoren, sharing tea before they had to go back to work. The bitterness of that particular brew. Somehow Hevo always managed to make it sting enough to strip the roof of his mouth. It's strange to imagine that the last time Cisir sat in this hall, it was filled with noble folk and no one knew of the catastrophe to come. Today the hall is dusty and appears neglected, with old water stains lurking beneath the fresh chalk paint above the empty dais.

Noa's mother watches his face. "Are you trying to find fault with your own behaviour these last days?"

A weight settles in his stomach. "Doesn't everyone?"

"No." She reaches out to touch his elbow, and he prepares himself for the zap, but again, nothing. *Why are the only people this sometimes happens with his master and his daughter?* "Not everyone searches out guilt as relentlessly. I can tell you're the type to overthink."

"If we had found him sooner …."

"He ran off. He wasn't supposed to be in the Westown, if I understand correctly."

"No, but we should've thought of him having family to protect. We could have put the clues together quickly; maybe we wouldn't be in the situation to risk everything on the hope that Lilyis' partner has the right idea about gods we've never dealt with."

Her face is serious enough to stoke his worry. "You know about her."

"It was almost the first thing my master told me. To test the waters, maybe." Cisir knits his brow.

"Anyone in the know must bear in mind that some secrets are more dangerous than others. None of the royals in residence concern themself much with piety, but there are always servants present."

He gasps. "I didn't mean …."

"Be more careful next time, and don't assume to know people's hearts, simply because you wish them to be nice." It is a stern rebuke, though she softens it immediately. "I'll excuse it once, but not twice. I'm aware you fret too much about your friend to think straight. Regarding the prince's partner, they can't weigh in on a situation thousands of miles away. Noa's idea might have merit, but I already told her she needs to prepare herself for disappointment. If her theory should be proven right, no one can anticipate the consequences."

"What's wrong?" Cisir's master asks as he pulls off the wet hood of his cloak.

Cisir sniffs. "The prince's wife gave me a lecture."

"Yeah, she does feel the urge sometimes. Don't worry. She does it to her husband too. Have you already given it a try?"

"It was decided that we should wait until dusk to limit the risk of discovery. They brought him to one of the guest rooms and are keeping everyone out."

"Very sensible. Best that you weren't involved in our Red House dealings today. As grateful as I am to the Bulls extending a helping hand, we nearly came to blows about their ideas of appropriate accommodation." He scratches at the back of his neck. "They can't expect us to run our offices out of their old stables. The whiff of horseshit will creep into absolutely everything. It took a lot of bickering, but we won at least a few rooms in the main house. Not too close to the First Bull's study, mind, but at least in the same building."

"How did you manage that, Master?"

"A lot of moaning and strategic bribery."

"Bribery?" Cisir whispers.

"Don't look so shocked, son. We might have to share some of the cargo from the west, but we'll have facilities to get it off the ship, sell it, and cart it around what's left of the town. Did you sleep?"

"No. I waited for you."

"You could've had a sniff around."

"I didn't think it to be a good idea—to stick my nose in, I mean. The crown prince hasn't come down all day, though."

"Interesting." Qes na Qarim rubs his palms together to warm them. "He always was a shrewd one. The less he knows about what's going on, the better. I wonder whether Nivael forbade him to leave his rooms."

The crown prince hadn't struck Cisir as someone who took well to instructions. "Can he do that?"

"It's his house and one day his brother might need plausible deniability." Qes sighs. "Well, whatever happens, we should prepare ourselves for a wet and uncomfortable night."

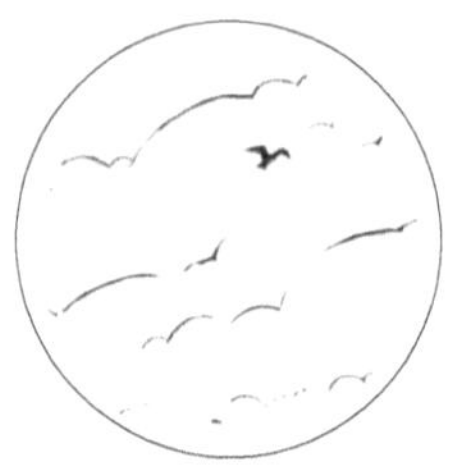

# QONNA

## *in the dark skies*

As darkness falls, Spark leaves Hevo's side for the first time in hours, drinks from the water bowl pushed into the corner of the room, and proceeds to claw at the door. Not whining, but growling, deeper than he should be able to.

"I think it must be time." Gia's shoulders tense. "I'll let the men know."

During the last hours, only four women have been allowed in the sick room: Gia, Qonna, and Noa, as well as Noa's mother. Even Eravis was sent away to join the crown princess's companions for the day, her face like thunder.

As soon as Gia opens the door, Spark barks at her, and Hevo sits up in the bed like a puppet manipulated by its strings. Noa grabs Qonna's hand as they watch the young man who had been motionless for hours swing his legs out of the bed and put first the left, then the right foot on the ground. His face is blank, his eyes closed, and his mouth hangs open.

"Do we need to restrain him?" Noa whispers.

"Let's wait and see what he does," Qonna decides, holding on to the princess's fingers. They are firm and warm in hers. "That might be it."

A heartbeat later, Hevo pushes himself up, his thin stained shirt falling over his bruised ribs, exposing half a shoulder criss-crossed with scabs.

"Oh fuck." Gia is back with Nian and his father in tow. Behind them appear the concerned faces of Uncle Lauron and her own father.

Gia ushers the four men aside and holds the door open to let the wounded man step through.

"Is he sleepwalking?" Nivael da Nileon asks, fascinated.

"He follows the dog," Qonna says.

"At least we won't have to carry him down the hill." Nian beckons to the women and few moments later, they all follow the dog.

Cisir opens the latch of the hall entrance and lets their weird little procession pass. As Noa pulls Qonna past him, she stretches out her other hand and catches him. The three of them make a chain as they come out into the manor's yard.

The rain has almost stopped and there's movement in the dark skies: clouds flitting aside to finally unveil a full, red-ringed moon, its face pitted and painted with silver, much closer than any of them suspected. Its light flickers on the long grass; every blade bears a lick of moonshine. The only bit of the puppy visible is its tail as it makes its way through the park with its sodden flowers. Spark leaves a dew trail for Hevo to walk on, and both head straight for the stones.

"Fuck, fuck, fuck." Her father mumbles under his breath until Lauron punches him in the arm to shut him up.

Cisir tenses in her grip, and the strange sensation she always has when they touch intensifies, like a swarm of ants invading the underside of her skin. It becomes almost too much to bear. She clings on as they watch the other man and Gia stumble forwards.

Qonna's heart gallops. The princess pulls at her, loath to miss anything, while Cisir side-steps like a skittish colt. Whatever rituals were once held in this place to honour the stones, they can't have been stranger than what Qonna and her companions see tonight.

The wind tears through the crowns of the birch trees, kneading them back and forth loud enough to hurt. Noa starts to run. In the same moment, Hevo's white shirt vanishes into the shadow of the trees, as if the circle is swallowing him, boots and all. The three of them catch up as the others form a loose ring amidst the fallen and standing stones, staring at the wet dog cowering on the biggest rock, the one that has half-collapsed on top of the others to form a hollow too small for anything but a squirrel to squeeze through.

"What now?" Lauron hisses.

"Shh, Dad. Just wait." Gia covers her mouth with both hands to suppress any noise, and Qonna would like to do the same, but Noa and Cisir hold on to her, Noa gripping her left hand hard.

Hevo stands in the middle of the stones, utterly still, neck bent, dark hair flopped into his face and hiding any expression.

Nothing happens.

The whole circle, humans and stones and dog alike, wait.

Noa pants next to Qonna as the wind picks up more and more. Above them the moon is once more wrapped in thin strips of clouds, its light dimming. Disappointment settles on Qonna's heart.

"That can't be it," Nian wails, giving sound to all their hopes being crushed. "Why? Fucking *why*?"

"Because of this." Qonna's father says it quietly yet is heard beneath the tumult of branches snagging against each other. Everyone shifts slightly: the princes, Gia, Uncle Lauron. Even Noa releases her. With a shudder Qonna sees Hevo turn towards her, his eyes still closed, but the empty face tilted.

Cisir lifts his left hand, the one wrapped in hers. A faint glow hovers between their fingers. Qonna shrieks and lets him go. The light dies with their touch. She stares at her hand. *How? How on earth?*

Lauron starts to laugh, shrill and unhinged.

"For fuck's sake," Nian barks. "As if we didn't have enough of that."

"What do you think it means?" Nivael da Nileon asks.

"I have absolutely no idea." His son puffs up his cheeks and lets the air out slowly. "Just because I sleep with a wizard? I'm far from the expert."

"Let me try something." Qonna's father walks around the stones to reach his secretary's side. "Cisir, can you take my hand next?"

The zap is loud enough to make them all flinch, and the glow appears in a violent flash.

"Exactly as I thought." Qes shakes out his hurting hand. "Lauron, come and touch him."

"I don't want to. It looks painful."

"Come on, before it starts to rain again and we all catch our death."

Lauron sidles over, followed by his daughter. He screws his eyes shut as he holds out his hand and folds it around Cisir's wrist.

Nothing.

Qonna feels Cisir start to shake. Gia is the next to step forward and test him but again, nothing happens.

"Thank all the Tall Gods," Lauron mumbles.

"Do we all have to touch him?" Noa asks.

"No, I think that has proven quite enough," Nivael snaps. "If Qes can't stand to hold his hand for longer than that, but Qonna can, that probably means the effect has to do with whatever Qarim Badger passed down to you both. And likely your sons too, Qes. If you please." He makes a strange gesture, as if asking them to open their mouths and break into song.

Qonna tenses up; something in her wants to reject his authority.

Cisir faces Qonna, his palm held up.

Qonna shivers. *You can't be selfish. You need to try and help.*

She presses her own hand into his skin. The glow is reddish, like fire, a golden winter sunrise. It washes over Cisir's cheeks. His eyes widen as he observes the same effect on her.

The dog yips at them.

Nivael da Nileon makes another gesture, this time as if trying to lure them over. "You need to touch the stone."

Qonna feels Cisir's warmth; she sees the fear in his eyes and that he wants nothing so much as to run, but they both remain in the circle, moving towards the stone Spark guards. She gives Cisir a nod, urging him on. He bites down on his lip as they slowly step over another fallen stone to get closer, as if they perform a sacred dance.

Hevo's body steps aside to give them access.

Nian calls out to them, "Keep those hands together and use the others on the stone."

They bend their knees. Their empty palms make a slapping noise against the rock.

The shadow underneath it cracks into light—not large enough to let a person through, much less them both, but spacious enough for a wiggling puppy. Spark's fur is bathed in golden light as he pushes in, and Qonna's vision fractures at the edges as her throat constricts.

"Qonna, don't!" Cisir's voice holds a hint of panic. "You can't—come on, breathe!"

He's right. Who knows what will happen if they stop touching the stone? His grip on her intensifies; the shine streaming off them bathes the whole circle in its light, while Hevo's body stands next to them as though the spectacle doesn't really concern him.

"That's right," Cisir blathers on. "Keep at it, Qonna. We can hold on until he comes back. Look at me, Qonna—everything's going to be fine."

*Fine. The word he likes to use too much. It's a prayer, she realizes. Not so much a description of a state but a desperate wish.*

"Yes," she grits out. "We'll be fine."

A howl splits the silence, reverberating over the whole hillside.

"Should we try to help?" Qonna can barely get the words out. "There's not enough room to go after him, there isn't—"

The clasp starts to hurt so much that it sears into their skin. Qonna's palm sweats as she clings to him.

Another howl, then a high-pitched whine that seems to break from the earth itself. The puppy's bottom is the first thing that pokes from the stones as it squirms back into the land of the living, almost barrelling into Qonna's chest.

Nian is there, pushing in from the side. "Here, boy, here …."

Spark is covered in long scratches; blood seeps into his coat like ink spreading across a page.

"Poor little boy—give it here, give it …."

Spark is holding something clamped between his teeth, something he isn't prepared to give to the prince.

Nian growls in frustration. "Cisir, can you try?"

Cisir takes his palm off the stone, pulling Qonna with him. The crack in the stone closes with a last glare of light, leaving behind the smell of singed hair and skin. Qonna is left standing alone and trembling before both Gia and Noa rush towards her, their strong arms propping her up.

"We've got you," Gia says, kissing her temple.

"Everything will be fine," Qonna mutters as she watches Cisir kneel to catch the wounded dog.

Spark appears more grown up than when he went through the stone, as if he was gone for weeks. He retches, coughs, and something small lands in Cisir's hands.

"What is it?" Both princes jostle for space.

Cisir holds up the beslobbered prize. "A hazelnut."

"What?" Qonna asks, stunned. *All this pain for something so small?*

"Or some sort of similar nut, anyway." It looks insignificant between Cisir's ink-stained fingers.

Lauron steps forward. "I think he needs to eat it."

"He'll break his teeth!" Cisir protests as Spark weaves around his legs.

"Then we'll have to crack it open on the stones first," Nian says impatiently, searching for something.

"Why does he need to eat it?" Qonna's father asks his old friend.

Lauron's voice is rough as he answers. "Because it's what nuts are for. They didn't feature much in the legends of the Wolves, but your father's family hails from the forests, where nuts are one of the most important foods. There's no time to find a collection of old country fairy tales to check, but it makes sense."

"Nothing about it makes sense," Cisir says under his breath, trying to find a surface on the stones that will serve to split the shell.

"Which actually tracks when dealing with the Siblings. Hah!" Nian straightens up, clutching a small piece of stone. "Watch your fingers, Cisir. No need for more bloodshed today."

"Qonna should do it," Cisir protests. He chose her, in front of all these others.

Nian holds out the rock to her.

When Qonna grasps it and brings it down, the sound of stones connecting with the nut is a thunderclap. Spark whines and lies down in front of Hevo's bare feet. Noa's breath hitch as the nut breaks fully open. The glow is back.

When the shell falls away, Hevo's eyes snap open. Cisir bellows out in surprise as the body of his friend falls upon him to wrestle the tiny kernel off him.

"Hey!" Qonna tries to step in but is violently pushed aside.

The nut crunches between Hevo's teeth and he falls to his knees, spasming against the sloping rock.

Noa's father rips his own cloak off his back and covers Hevo, trying to still the convulsions. "Is that how it always works?" he asks his son.

Qonna can make out Nian's shrug in the sudden darkness. "It's not the weirdest thing I've seen, being almost married to a wizard."

Qes huffs. "Is he awake?"

"Seems like it," the older prince confirms. "Boy?"

"Hevo." Qonna's father kneels, pushing back the Sun's dark hair. "Hevo, can you hear us?"

A sob breaks from the young man. "I can hear you, Master. I can hear you!"

# CISIR

## *gold falling*

Cisir awakes hours later curled into a ball against the wall of the solar that's usually kept for the women but infinitely more comfortable than the drafty expanse of the great hall, feeling as if all the strength has been sucked from his marrow.

He's not alone; his master sleeps on one of the chairs with Lauron Wolf slumped against his shoulder, while the low table in front of them displays a battery of empty cups and bowls. They needed a strong drink after last night's events.

Blinking in the grey light, Cisir tries to remember the details, but bedded on rosemary-sprinkled rushes and amidst the furnishings of Gard Manor, everything receives the taint of dreams. Did Qonna really crack a nut to extract its fiery kernel? Did he truly hold her for such a long time, did they clasp each other, watch each other realize that nothing could ever be the same again?

All eight people circling Hevo and the stones will have to carry a secret through the rest of their lives, a secret that causes his heart to pound at the thought of it. The Star would hound them all if word ever got out, would put them on trial for worshipping false gods and true magic.

Cisir draws his legs in. The wall is icy under his fingers as he guides himself towards the door.

Spark lies stretched out before him, looking up and wearily wagging his tail. His coat is streaked with blood and in the morning light there's no doubt he aged in one night. When Cisir pushes past him, Spark follows, as if he can't permit himself to let Cisir out of his sight. As if it's no longer Hevo's body that needs protecting but the man who helped bring back his soul.

"Good boy," Cisir mumbles, making his way down the low stairs to the guest quarters on the ground floor.

Hevo was allowed to keep the room to recover. Gia sits at his side, sleeping with her chin buried in her folded arms, but Hevo's gaze flicks upwards as Cisir enters. He still has a grey tinge to him. Perhaps it's the sweep of stitches around his temple that makes him seem so different from the gentle young Sun Cisir has come to like.

"Shh." Hevo gestures towards his guardian. "She finally nodded off."

Cisir whispers, "How are you feeling?"

"How am I supposed to feel?" Hevo sneers. "After being used in an unholy ritual?"

"That's not what happened." Hevo's accusatory tone takes him by surprise. He did his best to make things right at great cost to everyone involved. He expected to be thanked, not be berated.

"What else could it have been? Those stones are a seat of evil. Have you forgotten the teachings?" Hevo asks sternly.

"We brought you back!" Cisir crouches in front of the sickbed next to Gia's skirts. "You were hurt in the fire."

"I don't remember getting hurt. I remember waking up in deepest night, brought far from the city for the princes to play with."

"What?" *How can he skew the truth like that?*

Gia stirs as Cisir loses control of his voice. "You don't recall being in the temple?"

Suddenly Hevo seems unsure. "No."

"Or that Qonna brought you into *Pomegranates* to let her mother patch you up?"

"No."

"Many people have done their utmost to help you. You were lost to us."

Spark lets out another little whine, drawing Hevo's gaze to him. "Get him out!" Hevo yells, almost causing Gia to fall off her chair. "Get him away from me!"

"But he says he doesn't remember." Lilyis massages her temples, her eyes red-rimmed.

"Why would he have such a reaction to a dog if he doesn't know him?" Cisir's voice becomes shrill again. *I need to calm down. I can't help Hevo being unappreciative by screeching.*

"It sounds as if he's scared." Qonna breaks into a massive yawn. "I can't imagine how it must feel, coming to under the moon, with new wounds, barefoot. We need to make all possible allowances for him."

"I don't condemn him," Qes na Qarim says. "I'm merely surprised at how he's handling it. He always struck me as more rational than that."

"Yes," Lilyis agrees. "But fear can do strange things to us; he wouldn't be the first eastern man to come into contact with the Tall Gods and double-down on the Star's teachings. I've seen it many times in Birkland. Some people are ill equipped to deal with doubt."

*Am I one of those people? I can't be. I've doubted myself all my life.*

Qonna interrupts him. "What if he recalls the land of the dead? What if he's justifiably terrified to speak of it, to make it real?"

Lilyis sighs. "Usually, people who suffer a near-death experience can't shut up about it."

They've gathered around the long fire pit stretching through the hall, with Spark lounging to Cisir's left, his head on his big soft paws.

"We need to give him time," his master says. "He might start to talk at some point, to get it off his chest." He gives Lauron a nudge, who still seems unhappy to be at the manor at all.

"Not everyone can be relied upon to be grateful," the Birklander says flatly. "He might come to see what he was given—preferably without cursing the gods of the old country. They don't take kindly to not getting the credit they deserve."

A shudder runs through Spark's body, drawing all eyes to the young dog. *As if something is about to burst forth from him.*

Lilyis shifts her shoulders. "I'll speak to my father and sister when they come down. I think it might be better to spare Noa the pain of being confronted by him yet."

"That's a good plan," Qes agrees. "Given it was her idea to bring him to the stones."

Cisir trails his fingertips through the soft coat of the dog. Scabs have formed over the gouges in his back. "Good boy."

Qonna squints at them both. She wears a faded blue dress that surely was never meant for the likes of the manor, and a simple cloth knotted over her hair. None of the conspirators have the energy to do more than absolutely necessary to be presentable. Lilyis called for tea as they wait in a tight circle of five. Gia remains with Hevo, and it seems that he at least doesn't directly blame her.

Cisir wishes he could pull Qonna aside and talk to her, ask her what she thinks about opening the stones with him. *How can we have done what we did?*

His master yawns and sets off his daughter once more, who covers her mouth with the back of her hand. "I should ready myself to face the Bulls," Qes groans. "At least whatever shit Bjell pulls today won't impress me much. Unless he can conjure up another Sibling." His gaze flicks to his secretary. "You'll take the day off," he orders. "Walk Qonna back into town and let her give you a place to sleep in *Pomegranates*. We need you well rested. Something tells me this isn't the last time we'll come to rely on both of your talents."

The rain starts again as Qonna and Cisir set out from the manor after a quick breakfast of sweet rolls filled with almond paste. "There's a shortcut through the grounds," Qonna says, "and a gate at the bottom." She pulls her shawl up to cover her hair with another layer. "I know I should be grateful for every drop to drench the city, but it must be the wettest spring we've ever had."

Compared to the brilliance of the night skies, the day after is resolutely grey and gloomy, and as if to make up for the miracle that happened among them, the birches around the stones appear bedraggled and strangely resentful.

"Can we have a look?" Qonna asks.

"Of course."

The only one who hesitates to draw close to the stones is the dog. Spark sits at the foot of a birch and watches them inspect the site.

The ground has been churned up by their boots, the long grass and flowers trampled flat. Qonna pushes her hands against the slanting stone they touched last night, then bends down to retrieve something from the ground.

She comes back to him with her hand outstretched, and on her palm lie two halves of a golden shell. "Do you see," she says, beaming, before handing him one half. "I thought I saw a glint of gold falling in the dark."

*I didn't even think about that.*

"Should we give them back to Hevo?" As soon as the shell touches his skin, it's the last thing he wants to do.

"They'll remind us of what we did," she proclaims. "I intend to keep mine." Her fingers close around the gold. "What should we do now we know what we're capable of?"

*I don't know. I don't want to know.* "I'm afraid to think about it," he confesses. "Whatever it means, it must be a dangerous power to have."

She bites her lip. "Last night I thought about something. The morning you found Spark in the rubble was after we had kissed in the kitchen."

His heart stutters. "What?"

"If this is what we can do together—influence stone in some way—is it too far-fetched to believe we could have done the same thing to him? We might not have to be close to an object to do it." She thoughtfully rubs a finger across her chin.

"What are you saying, Qonna?" His voice is going screechy again.

"That we should kiss again and see what happens."

*She will kill me with her kisses.* "Qonna …." *Please take that back.*

"No one needs to know. You don't have to tell Jark. It's just another experiment."

"It'll have consequences." *Horrible consequences. My heart will knot itself into an even bigger mess.*

"I won't fall in love with you, if that's what you're worried about."

"I'm not presuming you'd want to!" he cries, stunned that's where her head went. "I thought we'd decided we wouldn't do it again."

"That was before, though. Why aren't you more excited about whatever this is? It might be magic, after all. Not like it's portrayed in the stories, but actual magic."

"Which is not supposed to be real," he whispers. *It shouldn't be real. Not anymore.*

She scoffs, pressing the fist clenched around her half of the golden shell to her chest. "What's in your hand is hard, shiny proof that there is something beyond this world. Somewhere that has soul nuts."

An ill-advised laugh bubbles up. "*Soul nuts?*"

"What else would you call it?" She burrows into her skirts with her other hand and pulls forth something else, big enough to stretch across her palm but small enough to be easily concealed.

He saw a lot of good quality amber in the Yellow House before it burned away, but this is an especially fine piece, in many different hues ranging from a light honey-gold to dark orange. "The prince gave it to me. Go on, you can touch it."

The amber feels warm, almost soft. He studies the smooth face of the deity. "Who is she?"

"Sister Sun. My auntie sent her from Birkland."

He opens his mouth to ask, confused about everything she said and thinks better of it. "You believe the statue was some kind of joke?"

"I think it might have been a warning. From one wizard to another." She grins.

"Wizard?" *She can't mean that.*

"What else would you call it?"

"I don't know—a mistake? I can understand why you've been graced with the Siblings' favour, but my family has never been near Birkland."

"You forget that this land once belonged to the Siblings too, and who can say what role your ancestors once played?" Her voice trembles with excitement. "For all we know, you could descend from someone important and powerful. Can you at least try to be a bit more curious?" Her light eyes hold a gleam of annoyance.

"You always knew you had a sorcerer in your family—this is all news to me!" he protests. "I never heard a peep about such talents."

"Because anyone displaying them would've been rounded up by the priests and killed. I'm not proposing to yell about it through the whole of town. I only want to explore it a tiny bit further. We might be able to help so many people. I know that in the stories magic is most often used by people desperate for power, but we could do it differently."

"Qonna," he warns again. *Everyone we try to help will react like Hevo. As if we tainted them.*

"Just think about it for now." She gestures towards the dog. "I'm sure Spark would agree."

"Please leave him out of it."

"I'm aware things have happened in your life that made you scared of stepping into the light, but it doesn't always have to end in disaster."

*But it always has. It would be stupid to expect to get away with it.* "I wish I had so much hope." He swallows thickly.

"Will you let me kiss you?" She steps closer, staring at his mouth. "To check if I was right."

"Do we really have to?" he whispers.

"Please."

"Fine. But let's make sure nobody can see us." He walks back towards the stones to hide among the dripping birch branches, and as soon as they stand in the circle, Qonna takes his face between her hands. Her mouth moulds to his. She's warm and soft and her folded fingers clutching at the golden shell lie against his neck. He can't help a quiet moan as she leans in, and he can feel her tongue against his own. He's back in the basket shed and Jark clutches at him, his hands sure and strong.

He utters a soft plea, "I'm sorry, Qonna, I'm sorry—"

She lets go of him.

Someone claps, slow and sarcastic. "Marvellous. Really good show." The voice is gravelly, as if it hasn't been used in a long time.

They both spin around.

Cisir gawps at the man sitting in the long grass, naked and freckled, with rust-coloured hair falling to his waist. Qonna's gaze drops down to his crotch, and she starts to laugh.

# QONNA

## *protect him*

He doesn't look like a god. For one, his feet are dirty and his calves bruised.

"Brother Flame?" Qonna asks as soon as she has enough breath.

He grins at her. "No. You can call me Teasel—and so you are warned: it absolutely describes my personality."

Cisir's face, bless him, is red as a beet. "Did we do that? Did we free you?"

"Oh, dear boy, no. Not this time, anyway." He stands up and yes, he is indeed naked. Which answers most of Qonna's questions about male anatomy. He also seems young, barely older than herself, and when Teasel turns to him, Qonna can see the scabs that were hidden under Spark's thick fur. On his near-translucent skin they look like tooth marks, disturbingly fresh and red around the edges.

"But we did something the first time?" she persists.

Teasel pulls a face. "I admit, I was beginning to give up, but then—here we are. You are both very cute, fumbling about like that."

Qonna can't suppress another laugh. "What are you?"

"Someone who made a mistake—several mistakes—many years ago. Someone trying to redeem himself by lending a hand." He shrugs, which makes his anatomy give a little jump, and while Cisir turns an interesting shade of purple, Qonna rips off her rain-spattered shawl. "Put this on. You're embarrassing us."

"As you wish." When he takes the piece of goat hair cloth, she notices old scars on his forearms. He wears them like broad bracelets, taut and shiny, as if he spent many years in his human form shackled to a wall, his skin rubbed raw and healed many times over.

He knots the blue shawl over his waist, so low that the effect is striking.

"You're a wizard," Qonna states. "You must be."

"I prefer 'sorcerer', actually."

"Why?"

"Because the term wizard implies wisdom and that is not quite my style," he says with a smirk.

"You're some sort of shapeshifter," Cisir croaks.

"I have, at times, been known to favour a different form. I'm much happier as a dog, though there are undeniable advantages to being a horse too. Never had much luck with birds—heights don't really agree with me." He lifts his right leg and watches his wiggling toes. The rain starts to darken his hair, sticking it to his scabby back and shoulders.

"You can obviously pass through the stones," she says. "Is that another one of your talents?"

He shrugs again. "When I have someone to open the gate for me." He gives Cisir an appreciative nod. "I think we can all be proud of what we achieved yesterday."

"Where were you born?" Cisir asks. "In which of the Eight Kingdoms?"

"We had many more than eight back then and the mossy pile of pebbles that passed for my mother's house has long since disappeared. You wouldn't know it if I told you."

Cisir shoots Qonna a warning glance.

*I have a right to know, and I will ask.* "I assume you're much older than you appear?"

"Being turned to stone will do that for you. The years might catch up with me eventually, but I really have no idea what's going to happen." He puts his hands on his hips. "It's getting wet out here. Weren't we supposed to be back in town?"

"Can you turn yourself back into a dog?" Qonna asks.

He starts to unknot the shawl and Cisir turns away with a yelp.

Qonna holds out her hand to receive her shawl and though she tries to resist, she can't help but get another eyeful. Teasel is beautiful—or perhaps it's merely the confidence he carries himself with. His freckled skin begins to shimmer as he crouches in the grass.

Qonna blinks, then stares at the dog, fully grown, who tilts his head at her. He's shaggy and massive, reminding her of a wolfhound but for the colour.

Cisir winces. "Can you be a puppy, please? Otherwise, we'll have a hard time explaining you to Qonna's brothers."

This time it's a quicker transformation and the familiar aspect of little Spark, snub-nosed and with a much shorter coat, looks up at them from the muddy grass.

"Let's hope he can't talk in this form," Cisir mutters.

They walk for most of the way in silence and Qonna can almost hear Cisir's thoughts rattling through his head. Perhaps she made a mistake, pestering him for a second kiss. Who knows how long Teasel would've waited to reveal himself otherwise? From time to time, she fights the urge to stare at the little dog toddling down the hill after them, trailing Cisir's heels. Within two days her whole life has been turned upon its head and it's exhilarating. With every step the amber statuette bounces against her thigh, and pushed in next to Sister Sun is her half of the golden shell.

She always knew there was magic in the world, but how on earth is she, Qonnamaris na Qes, allowed to touch it? Just a smidge of something extraordinary, but it gives her the rush she's waited for her whole life—the point at which her real existence finally begins.

While Cisir appears to be quietly panicking, she can barely keep from smiling. It makes sense that her auntie picked her to oversee *Pomegranates* when they have magic in common. Glancing at her father's secretary, she also knows that from now on, she needs to protect him with everything at her disposal.

They arrive at *Pomegranates* to a maelstrom of little carts, collecting and bringing in the goods Qonna's parents have taken into storage since the fire. It seems many people have decided to leave the city to wait out the rebuilding in the countryside. Cisir hesitates, then picks up Spark, protecting him from the heels and hooves, and as the puppy licks his chin, he grimaces but allows it.

Qitli greets them on the stairs. "I'll let Mother know you're back. She's been moaning about having no proper help." He bounds up the steps before them.

"You should try and touch him," Qonna says to Cisir. "You need to find out whether it's just me and Dad or if any of my brothers have it too."

"You mean, *you* need to find out if you're special," he mumbles.

She bristles. The second kiss shifted something between them, as if he's trying to play obstinate after the horse had already run away with him.

"Yes," she says. "You should want to find out as well. You might have to avoid a great many people in order to not constantly wreak havoc with the masonry."

"I don't plan on kissing a great many people." A corner of his mouth hitches up.

"You're already one up on me, and you've probably been licked by Spark a lot, so maybe two up?"

He blushes. "I don't think we can count him."

"Shame. He would be a colourful feather in your cap." She grins at the puppy in Cisir's arm and Spark stares back, narrow-eyed.

"Qonnamaris, what time do you call this? Where is your father?" Qonna's mother stands in what was her family's dining room, be-aproned and appearing more formidable than ever.

"He's gone straight on to the Red House, but he sent me and Cisir home."

Her mother takes her by the elbow. "What happened?"

Cisir ducks out of the way.

*Coward*, she thinks fondly. "It looks like Hevo will recover. He's started speaking."

Delight washes over her mother's features. "Praise the Star and all its gods in their infinite wisdom. That is the good news we needed on this day. We lost two people in the night, and I asked Qatt and Qov to organize the removal."

"Are a lot of them still coming in?"

"The Brothers sent over another four," her mother confirms, "but it seems that things have generally slowed down. We all need a break. Is Gia coming, and your other friends?"

"I think Noa is planning on it." *I can't wait to see her again. Even if I can't tell her about everything that happened.*

"Good. We also need every pair of hands we can get. Wash yours, Qonna, and come to the sick room."

"Yes, Mother."

"I put a clean apron in your room."

"Yes, Mother." How quickly she folds back into the space she's expected to occupy in the house. She shrugs off her wet shawl, the one that covered a sorcerer's nakedness.

Her room is swept and seems smaller to her. The bed is without a single crease. She takes up the linen apron and wraps it around herself, covering the slight smattering of mud stains on the hems of her skirts. The jug next to her washbowl is filled with water and she takes care to scrub between her fingers and remove the dirt from underneath her nails before drying her hands. It should depress her, but she carries the memory of the stones.

"I saw him this morning," Noa tells Qonna as she joins her in the sick room after midday. She seems tired, but enthusiastic. "And he does well, though Gia refuses to leave his side, as if she fears he'll fall back into darkness."

"Has he said anything to you?"

"He prays a lot." Noa sorts through the small clay jars on the table. "I can't blame him. He must've been terrified."

"Hopefully he'll calm in time."

"You seem awfully calm yourself after what happened yesterday, Qonna."

*That sounds as if she blames me.* "Perhaps I've always hoped for something like it. Something that gets me out of the house."

Noa glances over her shoulder to see Qonna's mother clean yet another head wound to prepare it for stitching. This one is on a young woman who clutches the edge of the cot, tears slipping down her face as she's treated.

"I'd say you got your wish," Noa says. "Though the gods didn't choose to be subtle."

They both look over to Eravis, who assists Qonna's mother, concentrating on the wound.

"Eravis has been stroppy about it," Noa whispers, "though I still think it was a good idea not to have her present at the stones. She talks a lot about resenting her position, but I don't think she's very gracious at all when others manage to get free. And it sounds daft, but I think she might also be jealous."

*Jealous? Oh, please.* "Of what?"

"Of me talking so much about you. I thought she would be pleased, because she suggested I bring you up the hill in the first place, but she's been sniping at me since we left the hall."

"Should I talk to her?" *Try to make her see sense?*

"You could try, but I'm not sure she's inclined to change her mind."

*She might. She might not. I wish I didn't have to play it so safe.*

Qonna sidles up to Eravis as she lays out needles and thread on the silver tray Qonna's mother has designated for her sick room treatments. "Tell me what's wrong."

"Nothing is wrong as such." Eravis is pale beneath her simple linen headdress. Exhaustion pulls at her eyes and mouth.

"Noa says I should talk to you."

"Maybe I'm disappointed not to be included." Eravis does sound a little bitter. "I'm aware your families share a history. I believed you to be my companion too."

"I am," Qonna protests, though weakly.

"It doesn't feel like it anymore."

Anger flares up. *I'm trying my fucking best!* "We are all in a situation that couldn't have been anticipated—and my mother is certainly lucky to have us all to help."

Eravis lifts a shoulder. "I hadn't planned on befriending your mother, Qonna. Somehow you've carved out a new position for yourself, gallivanting around the city with Noa's brother and getting mixed up in Company politics. You're clearly all too happy to leave me behind."

Qonna stares at her, taken aback. Noa said exactly that—Eravis doesn't want Qonna to have what she can't have herself.

"I'm sorry," she says, "but I'm not giving up my chance for another life to please you."

Eravis' gaze lifts to hers and Qonna sees wrath igniting in it, deep and nurtured by many old grievances. "I won't help you again," she snaps. "When all of this inevitably falls to ruin, I won't bend down to pick you up." She takes the tray and sweeps away. Eravis must have convinced herself Qonna is doomed to fail. She might pray for Qonna to stumble and crash. If the pen is too small, the pigs will hurt each other.

Qonna wipes her clammy hands down her apron and leaves the room. Her heart is pounding, and she can feel her own anger taking root. She shouldn't be in the sick room in her state, and she doesn't particularly care to see her mother sewing up yet another head. She leans against the back of the door, folding her arms.

*She'll calm down. We're all on edge after losing so much.*

# CISIR

## *both weird*

I hoped you'd be awake."

Qonna's voice startles Cisir, and he struggles up from the folding bed allocated to him. He hadn't been sleeping exactly, but it feels as if he was roused from deepest dreams. "Why?"

Behind her looms the curious face of her oldest brother. Qonna glances eagerly at Cisir.

"Oh no," he groans. "You want to do this now?"

"Qatt, help him up."

Qatt frowns but obediently leans in to grab Cisir's arm. All Cisir's muscles clench as he awaits the pain—nothing happens. Qatt's touch doesn't hurt at all. He sighs in relief.

"What?" Qatt asks, confused. "Why are you both looking at me like that?"

Qonna seems happy about it too. "Thank you, Qatt. You can go if you want."

"You're both weird." He snorts and storms off.

"We are," Qonna says softly and turns to the puppy curled up beside the bed, pretending to be asleep. She gives Spark a pat on the back.

"At some point you must speak to them." Cisir rises to his feet. "You should also rest."

"Tell that to my mother. Noa's here and she says Hevo is still doing well."

Cisir forces out a long breath. "That's good news, indeed. I don't particularly wish to repeat the experience."

"You might have to, if we find others in the same condition."

*No, please no.* "Qonna …."

"We have so much more to explore. Don't you dare try to take this away from me." Her brow is furrowed.

"Of course not," he says in an attempt to assuage her. "We need to be careful, and we certainly can't afford to antagonize all of your brothers."

It's a relief to know Qatt is out of danger; for whatever reason the gift has skipped him. It'll be awkward enough to face his master in the morning without that complication. Cisir tries to heed the order and after Qonna leaves, he stretches out on the bed again, but doesn't manage to drift off until dark.

He wakes with a jolt at eight bells the next morning, as *Pomegranates* comes back to life. Spark is squeezed in next to him and before he remembers who exactly is lying there, Cisir has cuddled the puppy to his chest, keeping his musty warmth closer for one more sleepy moment. Spark gives his elbow a long, lazy lick and proceeds to snooze until Cisir is dressed and ready to leave. Instantly the dog is up and determined not to let Cisir out of his sight again, all the way into the street.

Compared to the previous day, the road is cleaner. Order is slowly creeping back into town. Window shutters are thrown open once more. Servants sweep out the Eastown houses, some of them greeting him with waves or nods before returning to their tasks. Cisir wears a yellow tunic he pulled from the chest the Wolves brought with them to *Pomegranates* and finally unearthed. It's the first time since the fire that he's put on the uniform of the Sun. The tunic smells of herbs and has a stubborn ink stain on the right sleeve that won't come out. All the little scabs on his back rub against the undershirt and he wonders how Spark feels with his own pulling at his fur. The puppy keeps to his sight as if Cisir is holding a leash, and he knows Spark's presence is something he'll have to get used to.

When he arrives at the Red House, Rinald opens his mouth as if to protest the dog, but shrugs. "Do whatever you want," he grumbles. "Can't drag any more dirt in than the rest of them."

Since Cisir was here last, the yard of the Bulls has acquired the same messy aspect as *Pomegranates*; indeed, he feels as if he's seen some of the packages piled high back there before they were moved over. Some of the messenger boys huddle at the stable corner, dividing up letters between themselves.

"He's been waiting for you, mate," one of them calls. "He's in the house, corridor to the left, fifth door on the right."

Spark climbs the stairs next to him, panting, and Cisir feels a twinge of guilt. As a fully grown dog he wouldn't have a problem keeping up, but that would remind him too much of who Spark truly is, and how many questions Cisir needs to ask him before long.

Inside, the clutter has spread into corners, as if the rooms in the main house the First Bull had assigned to them have been hastily cleared to host the Suns. Rolled-up wall cloths and various chests have been pushed to the sides and baskets filled with folded mildew-speckled scrolls.

Cisir knocks.

"Come in!" his master bellows.

The First Sun and the First Bull sit across from each other—one dark, one silver-blond, both in their Company colours as if there's a pressing need to keep themselves separate and defined.

"Cisir." Qes' mouth shuts like a trap when he sees the puppy next to him. "Glad that you've found our new headquarters. We'll need a lot of help organizing our effects now we have a halfway-functioning office at our disposal. We're in dire need of paper, ink, and pens, so I'm afraid you'll have to liaise with Bjell's own secretary about the flow of supplies."

"Yes, Master."

Bjell da Relian squints at the dog. "Is that one bred from the na Eloven's kennels?"

"Probably not," Qes says cautiously. "Just a stray he picked off the street. It won't let him alone since."

"He looks expensive," Bjell remarks. "Have you had the scratches seen to?"

His master squirms. "Yes."

It's astounding that most people react so strongly to Spark with the unfettered urge to protect and soothe. The First Bull crouches down and offers his hand, and when Spark presses his nose into it, the leader of the Bulls appears to melt. "As long as he doesn't pee everywhere, we're happy to have him. Take care that you walk him every few hours."

"Of course, Master."

Bjell seems surprised to be addressed as such, though he quickly straightens and wipes his palm along his shin. "My secretary should be in my study. Go and find him for us, please."

"Certainly, Master." Cisir withdraws into the corridor. As he closes the door behind him, he turns to the puppy.

"Good boy," he says. Spark grins at him with a lolling tongue.

Unfortunately, the young Bull he's supposed to liaise with is far less disposed to lose his decorum over a pet. "Does he have to be in here?"

"The First Bull himself granted special dispensation."

"Obviously." Deep disappointment tints the Bull's voice. "No sense for propriety whatsoever."

"I am Cisir. I think we're expected to work together for the foreseeable future." Though he would rather be anywhere but here, he puts out a hand to shake.

"I'm not touching you after you've handled the dog," the Bull says. "Only the Star knows how many diseases that fleabag carries. I haven't survived the Big Blaze of Seagard to pop my clogs because of the mange." He shudders. "Or ringworm."

"He doesn't have ringworm!"

"He looks crusty."

"Because he was injured," Cisir protests, anger raising his voice.

"Anyway ... what do you need from me?"

Cisir squares his shoulders. "The First Bull has called you to the rooms of the First Sun."

The secretary rolls his eyes. "Fantastic. Keep the mutt away from me." He nearly bends himself into a knotted bun to avoid touching Spark as he pushes through the door. Cisir notices that his red tunic is spotlessly clean except for a splatter of ink down the right sleeve, exactly where he wears his own stain. The Bull's hair is the colour of clay and caught in a firm braid, and for someone mainly working around the offices, he has quite a broad back.

Cisir follows him down the corridor at some distance and hears Bjell call, "Can you order our guests a brazier and crockery to use, Rilk? I'm holding you responsible for making sure all Suns are treated with respect within these walls—and that includes the yard."

"Master." Rilk's voice conveys the impossible situation the order puts him in. "There will always be some who can't be persuaded to forget about decades of provocations …."

"And they will be punished," Bjell says icily. "By your own hand if necessary, though the command cuts both ways. Any Suns who take advantage will be made to pay." His gaze bores into Cisir. "We can't afford to lose time in getting business back up and running, and neither of us enjoys having to separate apprentices by the scruffs of their necks."

Qes nods behind him, biting down on a grin.

Bjell continues. "Show Cisir where the storerooms are, how to fill out our forms, and how to keep track of the ordered supplies." He makes a dismissive gesture Rilk answers with a shallow bow, and when Rilk steps back, he mutters something very inappropriate under his breath.

"Have you served long under Bjell's late uncle?" Cisir asks.

Rilk scoffs. "The Old Bull would never've stood for this nonsense. He didn't allow a single scrap of yellow cloth in the house and ranted every month about having been cheated by the Suns."

"You don't think that sounds the tiniest bit …? "

"Deranged?" Rilk adds. "Mad as a squid—but you could always count on him to do what benefitted the Red House most."

*And put all others at a disadvantage.* "The fire changed everything."

"No, it didn't." Rilk kicks one of the piles of baskets blocking his way. "The Company of the Sun will always be treated like an interloper, and there are enough families discontented by the reign of Crooked Hill to see the Sun for what they really are: a vanity project of a dynasty never meant to rule the south."

"Careful, now," Cisir says, stomach clenching. "You don't want to fall foul of your master's decree so quickly. I might enjoy you being ordered to punch yourself in the face, but it might confuse our colleagues."

Rilk gives the next basket a harder kick and steams ahead. Cisir grits his teeth and follows.

At the two afternoon bells, the storeroom that has been turned into the centre of the Suns' operation is stuffed with chairs, firewood, two small desks, and a new set of scroll shelves. Rilk complained with every breath, but no one could fault the execution. Most of the afternoon Cisir has been busy getting everything in its place and finding the best position for his master's desk to make the most of the light streaming in from the window. Out in the yard, throngs of Bulls appear from time to time to eat and drink before making their way out into Westown to continue the clearing process. *Will we ever grow together enough?*

The only Suns around are the messenger boys until early evening, when Qonna's two youngest brothers arrive with a cart to bring the last goods for the day from *Pomegranates*. They don't wear yellow, and still the Bulls in residence surround them in the same way they did to Cisir when he met them on the road all those weeks ago.

"Master …." Cisir warns.

Qes na Qarim spins around to face the window. "Oh shit."

When master and secretary arrive in the yard, followed by a yawning puppy who spent most of his day stretched out under the brazier, the shoving has already started.

Qov is red in the face and his fists are up. Cisir recognizes the Bull in front of him. It's the short one he fought himself—the one who obviously remembers his last humiliation all too well. As he spots Cisir next to the First Sun, his face distorts with hate.

"This is enough," Qes bellows, so loud that all the young men freeze in place. "What is the meaning of this?"

The short Bull spits on the cobbles. He's too far away to reach Qov's boots, but the direction is all too clear. "Fucking fire starter."

"Excuse me?" Qes growls.

"It's all over the Westown," one of the other Bulls jumps in. "Birklanders were seen to put a torch to a roof."

"That is nonsense," Qitli snaps back. "Everyone knows it was an exploding oven."

"Enough!" His father takes him by the shoulder. "We haven't had any official report yet, so all is speculation."

"They wanted to burn the temple," the short Bull says. "Everyone knows it's true."

"And yet the temple stands," Qov says. "Why would you think we had anything to do with that?"

"Your house didn't burn either."

"Lots of houses didn't burn," Qitli pipes up, "and most Birklanders lived in the quarters worst affected!"

"Don't try to appeal to their common sense," his other brother says. "None of them know what they're talking about. They're angry about being put to work."

"You need to get out there and listen," one of the Bulls yells. "Listen to the people, the citizens of Seagard who lost everything to the flames. There are enough witnesses to satisfy the most—"

"I said *enough*," Qes interrupts. "All of you. The royal family will soon announce their decision on how Seagard is to move forward, what will be rebuilt, and what help will be put in place for everyone. There's no need to panic."

The short Bull's face is a grimace of disgust. "Says the man who managed to swindle his way into the Red House."

Cisir's master scowls, but Qes na Qarim retreats across the yard.

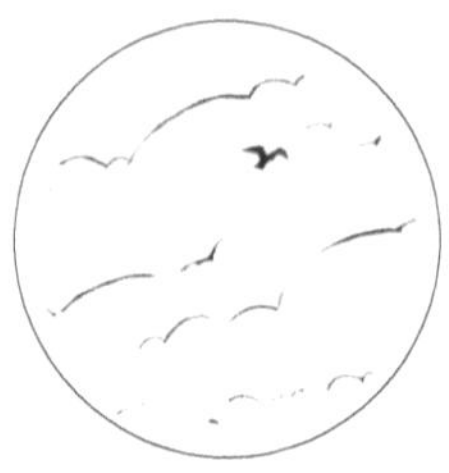

# QONNA

## *getting involved*

I hoped to find you here," Qonna says as she enters her father's study. Uncle Lauron blinks. "Why? What have I done wrong?"

"Nothing at all," Qonna reassures him. "I wanted to ask you some things about what happened."

It seems Gia's father has been hiding out, but his sleeves are dirty enough to suggest he spent most of his day helping shuffle goods about like her brothers. He pulls out a chair for her. "Sit. I don't think I can send you off with a few platitudes."

*Too right.* "Have you ever seen anything like it?"

Lauron shudders. "No." His mouth is set in a grim line. "And I never expected to. I mean, I always knew the Siblings were, for want of a better word, *real*, but that night was extraordinary and not something my fellow Wolves would take in their stride, either. I really can't stress enough that this isn't normal. Most of us must be content with much, much less." He lays his hands on his knees and Qonna puts her palm on his. "I'll never forget it as long as I live but it also upsets me."

"Upsets you, how?" He trembles beneath her hand. She's rarely experienced Uncle Lauron so vulnerable.

"That the same gods who granted us the success of pulling Hevo back from the land of the dead didn't prevent my family from losing the *Pear*." He swallows as if the movement causes him pain. "After so many years of barely making ends meet it felt as if we were finally getting somewhere. With more Suns lodging with us and a more affluent patron, and generally higher standards. Since last year I had finally started to sleep through the night again. Everything we clawed from the Triangle lies in ruins. I dare say many a man has lost his faith over less. Days later I'm made to witness the stones opening. Whatever this weird little dog is, it feels as if the Siblings have finally reached out to give me a painful flick on the nose." He pulls a face. "How do you feel, Qonna? Did it hurt to open the stone?"

"Maybe a bit, but I've already forgotten that part." *Not quite. It hurt and it drained me.* "Have you spoken to Gia? Was she scared?"

"You should ask her yourself. I know she's thrown herself into helping Hevo back on his feet, but she needs you too. There must be many things she wouldn't tell her parents but is keen to discuss with you."

Qonna averts her eyes. Sometimes Uncle Lauron hits too close to the bone. "I can ask Noa to take me to the manor tomorrow."

"That might be a good idea. We must all help each other, and in a way you both grew up in the same situation: expected to worship the Star but with strong ties to the gods of the old country. You might certainly be said to belong to both sets and that must be very strange."

"It is." Qonna leans back and removes her hand. "Especially as both our mothers hold such strong opinions about the Star. I wish it were less complicated, but I suppose that's also what makes it exciting." She smiles.

Something rumbles against the door of the study and Qonna's father squeezes through. "Bloody baskets … oh. What kind of strategy meeting is this, then?"

"I expect your day was as hard as mine," Lauron says. "You look like shit."

"Feel like it too. Things are coming to a head in the city and while I'm trying to sweet-talk the First Bull, I really can't charm every miserable sod in the Westown."

"Why?" Qonna asks. "What's going on out there?"

"What many predicted—the hunt for someone convenient to blame. Now the first shock is over, we'll have to come up with a plan to make everyone's situation better. Lilyis will start to move refugees up to the manor and we should consider setting up open kitchens to serve the citizens."

"Who do they blame?" Qonna asks.

"Everyone who looks like us," Lauron says with a sigh. "That's what you mean, right? Everyone who might reasonably be suspected to have a connection to another continent."

"Specifically, Birklanders." Qonna's father rubs the bridge of his nose. "It reeks of the temple, I'm afraid."

"I agree." Lauron clenches his jaw. "I'm not surprised they'd pull such shit after you took so many wounded off their hands. It's fucking typical. What do you want to do?"

"I don't think there's anything we can do, apart from making sure we always keep one of the princes between us and an angry mob. I had to save Qov and Qitli from being chewed up by Bulls, and they won't be the only ones targeted until the Westown calms down again. We need the crown prince to make a statement to draw the heat."

"Will he be amenable to that?" Lauron asks.

"He'll have to be. There's only so much hiding he can do. I'll meet him tomorrow to put pressure on him and the other princes."

It feels like the situation is moving away from her. She forces herself to take a deep breath. "Can I come with you? I'd like to be there."

"I'm sure Lilyis would approve including you, but Qonna, I can't promise you won't regret getting involved."

They set off up the hill after a quick breakfast in the kitchen. Qonna notices her father makes himself eat, chewing deliberately though he's a bit green around the gills, while she's impatient to get away from the sick room and keep the promise she made to Lauron.

When she finally coaxes Qes out into the yard, flecks of blue sky are visible over the Eastown and though the clouds carry a grey tinge, timid sunlight illuminates the streets. She's never walked through town this often, and sweat breaks out beneath her headdress as she pushes on past the hedge once planted around the city's burial grounds, now being prepared for the mass memorial.

Carts line up in front of its gates, which stand open, inviting Qonna to glimpse the many rows of stone markers anchored in the grass. Graves are being dug behind the hedge for many people she might've passed in the streets without knowing, while she, Qonnamaris na Lorian na Qes, can finally breathe. None of it feels quite real yet, although she carries the reminders with her, the figurine and half a golden shell.

At the manor, Qonna and her father arrive as the hall is set for the midday meal and are ushered into the living quarters before they can get in the way. The room the crown prince has commandeered for the length of his stay in Southclere is lavishly furnished, and beside the window his young wife and her new friends are busy embroidering, whispering to each other as they spot Qonna entering their sanctum.

"Master Qes." The crown prince pushes up from his cushioned seat. "And Mistress Qonnamaris—followed by my dear brother, I see."

Nivael da Nileon has joined them, in leather riding breeches and smelling faintly of horse. "Brother, can we get this over with? There are so many things that need to be taken care of today, I have not had time to take a piss."

"No need to be crass," Nurin da Nileon says with a scowl.

"Nian is bringing the first citizens up the hill as we speak, so expect all of us to get snappy by end of the week." Nivael's brow arches.

Qonna's father clears his throat. "Which brings me to the heart of the matter. Rumours are starting to make the rounds in town. Rumours that put many of your subjects in immediate danger."

The crown prince pulls a grimace. "Fine. Let's leave the ladies to their gentler pursuits and find a closet."

If the crown prince is surprised to see Qonna coming with them, he has enough sense not to show it, and she's absurdly grateful no one else tries to shove her away.

Nivael leads them to a private suite and into the smallest of its spaces—a rectangular room with a bench heaped with quilted cloths that could serve as a makeshift bed, a small table, and two well-used chairs with shabby cushions. Piles of hide-bound books and scrolls lie scattered around and behind the door hangs a soot-streaked cloak that Nurin studies with distaste. "You'd think you'd never set foot inside Crooked Hill."

His younger brother shrugs off the barb. "Excuse me for not indulging your personal taste in my closet, but as the last days have shown us, none of that is important compared to the suffering inflicted upon the whole of Seagard. You sit your scrawny arse down, brother."

Qonna suppresses a grin.

Qes starts off the meeting. "My sons were subjected to threats when they entered the yard of the Red House. While the Bulls at least try not to insult us Suns to our faces, my sons were nearly pounced on because someone deemed it convenient to implicate every single person of Birklandish descent in how the fire started."

"Someone?" Nivael sneers. "Fucking priests." Being exhausted makes Noa's father much more foul-mouthed. Qonna bites her lip again.

Nurin shoots him a warning look. "Is there any evidence these accusations originate at the temple?"

"Not that we know of—yet," Qes admits. "But we can all agree it suits the Star to single out families of our heritage, to blame the fire on our connection to old gods and the customs they always condemned. Granted, most of the Bulls are young men, easily riled and swiftly led, but we need to assume every citizen who's believed to have any Birklandish blood will need to be protected. I ask you to address your subjects, Nurin. Assuage their fervour."

Nivael and Nurin exchange a long glance that makes the hair at the back of Qonna's neck rise.

"The official burial would be a good opportunity," the younger prince says quietly. "You should give a speech."

"Aww shit. Why can't you do it? You're the one they associate with any action we take," the crown prince protests.

"You're the future king of the Hillakes and Southclere. At some point you need to step up and show them what kind of ruler you plan to be. Notwithstanding the general contempt you hold for everyone."

Nurin snarls under his breath, brow deeply furrowed. "Is it not enough that we open our park for them to destroy the grass and pee in the carp pond?"

"Brother …."

"I'm joking, of course." Nurin makes a dismissive gesture.

"Really?"

"No, not really. It sounds like the perfect opportunity for the masses to get out of hand and throw rotten food at me."

*He might have a point there*, Qonna thinks.

"There is not enough food to go around."

"Horseshit, then. There's always plenty of that. Calm down, little brother. I'll see what I can come up with."

"So we agree." Qonna's father uses his fingers to itemize. "You will speak to the populace, you will assure them that the true reason behind the catastrophe will soon be uncovered, and that you will punish everyone who attacks any Birklanders left in Seagard, stressing there is no reason to believe us involved?"

"I will mention a sufficiently gruesome penalty," Nurin consents, "but are you sure this won't come back to bite us? We can't afford to annoy the temples too much. I don't want them to get weird ideas about separating the south off again, just because one tiny place at its arse end decides to put up barricades."

"You can give me the first draft of your speech to read and I will tone it down," Nivael promises before turning to Qonna. "Do you have any comment to make, Qonnamaris?"

She straightens her back. "It would be good to find out if the temples are actually the instigators, or if the rumours stem from yet another disgruntled group of citizens. Whatever reason the Star has to fan the embers, they can't be the only ones reading the situation as an opportunity to create discord among the factions in the city."

"What other groups do you suspect?" her father asks.

"Are you quite sure the First Bull has changed his tune?" Qonna raises a brow, trying to look quizzical. It never served her to trust the Bulls before.

He winces. "I need to believe that at least the man in charge is trying to work with me, so for now I'm going to be careful, but not distrustful."

The crown prince yawns. "I think that's the best anyone can hope for."

"How is he doing?" Qonna whispers to Gia, trying not to wake Hevo.

"Sleeping more, which is good. But dreaming a lot and thrashing about." Her friend wrings out the bandages she's been washing before draping them on the inside of the window slats to dry. "I wish he would talk about what really happened to him on the other side. He must get tired of praying eventually."

Qonna sniffs. "Do you want to be with him until then? It might take him weeks to crack."

"I'm prepared to wait. He's been through a lot."

"So have you. You deserve to take a break and think about recent events."

Gia grits her teeth and flicks waterdrops from her wrists. "If I stop to think I get scared. At least when I'm so exhausted I'm ready to drop, I sleep easily and don't remember my own dreams."

"Do you pray with him?" Qonna glances towards Hevo's hunched shoulders buried in the blankets.

"Sometimes."

"Which god of the Star do you both pray to most often?"

"That's private, Qonna."

"I'm sorry. I hope you can get him to be at peace with his experience."

"Why does he need to be? Because you found new hope in it?"

Qonna shakes her head. "I don't understand how you choose to ignore all the things that happened that night and hang yourself on the neck of the Star when you both had proof the old gods have welcomed us." If Gia can just feel like she feels about that night, maybe it'll start to make actual sense.

"They might have welcomed *you*," Gia says sourly. "They left me right where I've always been."

# CISIR

## *the pertinent facts*

When Cisir wakes up, Teasel sits with his naked back against the door, his dirty grass-stained feet stretched out before him.

"You're ignoring me," he says when Cisir rubs the sand from his eyes.

"Trying my best to." Cisir winces. Seeing the shapeshifter in his human form rattles him. He spent too much time getting attached to Spark not to feel betrayed.

"Why?"

"Because you're not supposed to be a man—you're supposed to be a puppy."

"Why can't I be both?" Teasel asks, tilting his head.

"Because a naked man in my room is something very different than a naked puppy," Cisir replies flatly.

"Give me something to wear then."

Cisir flings his blanket, which Teasel artfully drapes over his loins. "This is dangerous," Cisir admonishes the self-professed sorcerer. "Right now all strange people are kept under supervision."

"Strange people—including yourself?" Teasel arches a rust-coloured brow.

"And everyone who looks different from what the citizens imagine the average Seagarder to be. Don't play stupid. You were there."

"Nothing ever changes." Teasel sniffs, scratching the back of his head under the thick locks. "People always need to find someone to hurt. Sometimes innocent civilians, sometimes not quite so innocent men."

"Meaning yourself?" Cisir asks.

Teasel stares at him, which he takes as a clear answer. Cisir pushes his hands beneath his thighs to soften the edge of the cot biting into him. "When you said your name describes your personality—are you interested in plants?"

"Not exactly. I have a tendency to hang around. And be somewhat prickly. And insufferable too."

*You don't say.* "How long ago were you turned into stone?"

"I've lost count of the years, but back then the land was mostly covered in forest and the houses much smaller. There was a lot more magic about, though I don't know if anyone could've made sense of you and your ... friend. *Is* she your friend?"

"Yes," Cisir replies without hesitation.

"Are you more than that? She wanted to kiss you badly enough."

Cisir scoffs. "Because she believes something magically happens when we kiss."

"It did," Teasel says.

"Maybe," Cisir concedes. *It absolutely did. You know it.*

"There is no 'maybe' about it—it's like two pieces fitting together. Two halves of the nutshell, so to speak. I've met my fair share of sorcerers during my services, but none of them depended on the collaboration of another."

"What kind of sorcerers?" *More of his sort?*

Teasel pulls a face. "The hugely annoying kind. Every man who aspired to call himself a king dug up a moth-eaten wizard—and every queen." His brown eyes widen. "In fact, the queens were often much less discerning. I don't want to talk about that. I'm hungry and the bells will soon call us to town."

"That's what we experienced? A kind of collaborative magic?"

Teasel jumps up and the blanket falls to the floor. When he turns around to retrieve it, Cisir's eyes are drawn to the scabs covering his freckled back. They've gone nearly black and are peeling away at the edges. Teasel heals quickly, suspiciously so. "That sounds about right. There were a lot of female sorcerers in my time, by the way."

*Like Qonna?* "Truly?"

"Talent doesn't fall where it's convenient. Many of the queens preferred a wizard they could integrate into their household without their husbands getting squirrelly about it. And you—you might never have learned what's awry with you."

*If you hadn't fucked up your engagement. If you hadn't been sent away from Windyhill.*

"It might've been an easier life," Cisir mutters.

Teasel twists his hair into a coil. "Oh, undoubtedly. None of what follows will be easy."


The sun glares on the washed cobbles in the yard that is finally clear of debris. The Bulls have already been dispatched to the Westown and the Red House lies strangely quiet. The only one to greet Cisir on his arrival is old Rinald, who sits on the stairs of the main entrance, mournfully contemplating the last bite of a piece of bread.

"You're later than usual," he comments. "They're all gone but you might be able to catch up with them."

"All gone where?"

Rinald shrugs. "To meet with the Brothers to plan the memorial service."

"Ah. I'll think I'll wait for them here." Just thinking about getting close to the temple again makes him break out in goosepimples. Whatever doubts he might've had before, now the situation has truly changed. Hiding himself and Spark away in the Red House shouldn't feel safer, but it does.

He retreats into its dark corridors like a badger into its set and has barely planted his arse on a chair when Rilk's head pops through the door, checking for any evidence of Spark. When Rilk discovers him safely tucked away between the wall and the chair, he draws nearer. "What's your excuse for not running after them?"

"Qes na Qarim won't need me to bring his point across, and I have too much to do to get the office into shape."

"Huh. Maybe you can be of help to me. I've spent the morning combing through Bjell's correspondence regarding the exact terms of this arrangement." He waves his hands around the cluttered room. "I'm supposed to draw up a proper contract, but I'm not certain about some of the terms our masters discussed among themselves. Is it only use of the rooms and you're responsible to supply your own food? Or are we supposed to invoice you for—your eyes are glazing over."

"Apologies, I did have a few stressful days." He rubs his brow.

Rilk snorts. "It won't get better. Bjell always comes up with weird little ideas to keep me occupied." He glances at the snoozing puppy. "Is it true you're engaged to your master's daughter?"

The blood drains from Cisir's face. "What? No. What gives you that idea?"

"Because he wouldn't parade her around town without having a firm idea of who'll take her off his hands afterwards—and you strike me as woefully progressive."

"What do you mean?"

"Who else would want someone with such tainted blood?" Rilk says with a perfectly straight face. "Word is, you've been extremely friendly towards her. I must admit, it's not a bad play, going for your master's dependents. If Bjell were married, I'd probably try something like that."

"Tainted blood?" His fists close.

"You might regret attaching yourself to someone like her, now all those things about the fire are coming to light."

Cisir pushes his heel into the puppy's side. "Spark—bite him."

For all the suspicion he harbours towards Teasel, the puppy is up and at Rilk instantly. The growl escaping from him is deep and resonant, his teeth longer than they should be.

Rilk blanches and retreats, throwing the door closed behind him.

"Good boy," Cisir says as Spark comes back and sits down, rewarded with a pat on the head. "The next time he comes anywhere near us, you have my permission to maul him without waiting for him to open his mouth. I think we need to expect everything that comes out of him to be hateful filth."

Spark leans into his hand, his tongue lolling once more in a wide grin.

"I heard about what happened," Cisir's master says.

The delegation returned after the midday bells and Rilk immediately complained. Qes na Qarim pulls his ochre-yellow cloak off with a sigh. "I know you wouldn't have set the dog on him without good reason. What did he say to make you so angry?"

"I don't want to repeat it, Master."

"Cisir, I should know," Qes insists.

Cisir grits his teeth. "He said things about Qonna."

His master's patchy eyebrows rise sharply. "Qonna?"

"About the fact people have started to talk about her moving freely through town."

"Right. You think she should return to the duties her mother has set out for her?"

*That feels like a trap.* "No, I think … it doesn't matter what I think, does it? Any discussion with the likes of Rilk will get me deeper into trouble."

"Hmhm. People are picking up on the bond between you. I can't promise you it won't get complicated."

"It's already very complicated," Cisir admits. "I am afraid we'll need help."

"All the help I know of is six weeks' worth of sailing to the west of here. But I agree. Lauron confirmed he's out of his depth with the whole situation."

"He doesn't have all the pertinent facts, either." Cisir pinches himself. *Don't chicken out now. Qes deserves to know.* "What happened at the stones that night is only half of it."

His master freezes in place. "Do you believe Qonna is in danger?"

"Yes—but me as well, same as you. We're all in *terrible* danger, because I'm sure things will start to happen in the city that we won't be able to keep quiet forever."

"What exactly are you talking about, son?"

"I think your suspicions about the trinkets your father collected and brought into the Yellow House were warranted, and it might be a good thing that all but the doorstopper burned with it. It might have saved us from more difficult situations."

"Just say it, please." Qes sounds weary.

"He might look like a dog, but he isn't a dog."

"Yeah, no shit."

"The name he uses when in his human form is Teasel. We should probably check the prince's library to see if he's mentioned in any old court documents."

"What kind of a name is 'Teasel'?" Qes asks.

"Most likely one he chooses to hide behind."

They both stare at the puppy, who does his best to charm them with big, sad eyes.

Qes clears his throat. "You've seen him in human form?"

A picture of a very naked Teasel rises in front of him. "Yes."

"He's a human man choosing to be a dog, not the other way around?"

"That's how it seems, Master." Cisir expected Qes to explode or, in the best-case scenario, to laugh at his concerns. To find Qes so ready to discuss the situation flusters him.

Qes inclines his head. "There are stories in the old country of bears who shift into human form when the moon goes through its various phases, so it isn't such a foreign concept. Werebears are part of the legends I grew up with. I think the best approach is to send you to Birkland." Cisir gasps. "Believe me, I wish there was a way around it, but waiting for Sloe to come here would literally take twice as long. When Lilyis leaves for the far west, you should go with her. Both of you."

Cisir swallows painfully. *Don't get your hopes up. Ask him to clarify.* "You'd allow Qonna to go?"

"I prepared myself a long time ago for the possibility and seeing her grow up in a town that places such restrictions on her has been hard. I always thought if she had the chance to explore her Birklandish heritage, she should be allowed to, and I dare say her mother will someday come around to the idea."

"Has Qonna said anything to you?"

"Not for a while, but when she was younger, she often asked for stories. She loved the idea of visiting her family on the other side of the sea. I can't imagine she ever forgot those old wishes, and it sounds as if it would be the best option to gain clarity."

"You don't want to know about yourself, Master? If you too would be able …."

"No." His master's face closes off abruptly. "I've seen what exposure to the Siblings did to my father. I spent many decades building another kind of life. I reserve the right to make a choice—but I also know I'm in a privileged position. My daughter might find the only way to come to grips with what the world can offer her is to see it for herself. The Sun has an established network in Birkland; I'm not sending her into the wilderness. Whatever the Star tried to tell you about the old country, they based it on a plethora of misconceptions."

"I know," Cisir says. "Since I had the fortune to meet Lauron Wolf and his family, I've been aware that the Windyhill village priest didn't know his arse from his elbow, though I must be honest and confess one of the reasons why I had the idea of applying to the Sun in the first place … it was because it featured from time to time in his sermons and when … when my engagement came to an end, my betrothed accused me of having been infected with the *Birklandish disease*." He whispers the last words. He's never talked about it before, about the last altercation before she announced the transfer of her affections to his brother.

*The disgust on her face. The hatred she could barely contain.* The memory hurts like a stab to the neck.

Qes na Qarim breathes out slowly. "I'm sorry. For both of us. I had no idea people talked about us like that, and if you ever find yourself in doubt: nobody has the right to tell you that wanting to kiss someone as ravishing as Jark is wrong or shameful. Of course you hoped to find yourself among friendlier people in Seagard. Given how your own family treated you, you could only hope for something better. What do you think? Do you want me to talk to Qonna first?"

Cisir starts to shake. He expected hate, to see his master recoil from him. Having someone voice understanding is almost too much to bear. "Please," he whispers. "Qonna needs to decide."

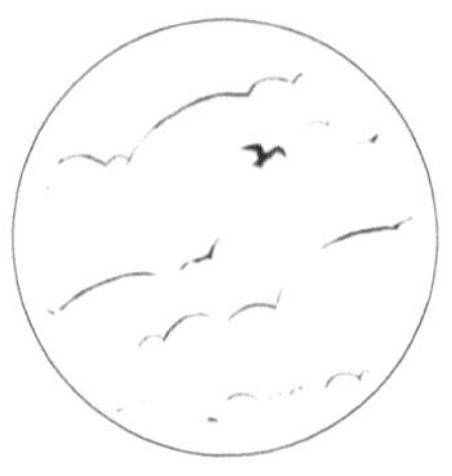

# QONNA

## *a passionate heart*

I really thought she'd handle it better." Her father looks as mortified as he should be after his wife burst into angry tears and slammed the door to the sick room behind her.

Qonna knew they were making a mistake as soon as he asked her mother to enter, but it's so unbelievably painful to feel the hope die within her. "Do you think she'll calm down?"

"I don't know." He slumps into the chair as if all the air has been sucked out of him. "I'll try to bring it up later. She must be utterly exhausted with everything going on around here, and since we moved the office into the Red House, I'm not here enough to pull her away from the patients."

Qonna presses her nails into her palms, trying to hold on to her anger, her disappointment. "Would she react in the same way to the prospect of Qatt and Qov, or Qitli going to the old country?"

"She's had many years to get used to the thought of them eventually being let loose in the world. It wouldn't mean too many changes for them. They would go as members of the Company of the Sun, with the full support of the royal family at their back, while you accompanying Lilyis would be a much more private arrangement."

Qonna blinks. "Dad—why do you call Nian da Nileon 'Lilyis'? Has he asked you to use the name?"

"Yes. It's the name she will be using in the old country."

"Ah." Qonna takes a while to think through the implications. "Since when …?"

"Since the Company was founded. You'll get used to it. There are so many more possibilities in the west, and she found a way to make use of them."

"No wonder she wants to spend so much time in Birkland." *I would, too. Being a woman in the Eight Kingdoms is not an enviable position.*

He smiles at her. "Hopefully, you'll find all you need there too."

*At least* someone *is rooting for me.* "I will, if Mother lets me go in the first place. Perhaps you should tell her what really happened."

"Not quite yet."

"She'd be less inclined to refuse if she knew."

"You should try to find out more about it first, and from what Cisir has told me, you'll have a lot to explore. He's been asking me for permission to search through the prince's libraries at the manor to find out more about a certain sorcerer."

Qonna sucks air in through her teeth. "He told you about the dog?"

"Yes, and I'm glad he trusts me as much. In all the legends I've ever heard, I can't recall coming across the name 'Teasel'. I wish your grandfather was still alive; he'd be sure to have an opinion on the situation. He could tell us why he brought the doorstopper into the Yellow House and where he found it."

"I don't think he came from overseas," Qonna says. "He talked of times when all the hills around the stones were covered in trees."

"Do you trust him?"

Qonna thinks back to the freckled face, the twitching smile. "No. But I believe he spent a long time in the stone, and that he has no one but us. Bringing him to Birkland will help him too. Auntle Sloe might welcome the challenge."

"Or not. Whenever Lilyis speaks of their life there, it sounds as if they're dreadfully busy holding the whole of wizardkind together. Your arrival would be a complication, to say the least." He yawns and rubs his palms over his face. "But if life has taught me anything, it's that hunkering down and hoping your problems will simply go away will cause more pain in the long run, so I promise I'll do my best to persuade your mother."

Noa and Eravis arrive in *Pomegranates* the next day to resume their duties in the sick room. "Hevo seems to be doing better," Eravis reports. "Gia sticks to him like a burr." She sneers in a way that sets Qonna's teeth on edge. "If I didn't know better, I'd say she's taken a shine to him."

Qonna sorts through the clean bandages on the table. "Why shouldn't she? They've spent a lot of time together."

Eravis gifts her a sour smile. "Because her parents surely wouldn't want her to marry someone like him? Hevo might've found his way into a guestroom at the manor, but he comes from the poorest part of the Westown and Gia's parents will doubtlessly have a lot to say about it."

It seems strange to think about such details when wounded people are lying about the room, some fitfully sleeping, some staring at the ceiling, waiting to be checked and fed with broth. Qonna wipes her clammy hands down her apron, unsure how to respond to the woman she can't quite consider a friend anymore.

"I hope they've fallen in love," Noa says with a dreamy expression. "*Passionately*. I need some good news, with all the frightful rumours making their way through the people staying in tents in our garden. They're all muttering about evil plans and what bad things will befall them next. Many of them don't want to attend the memorial for fear of an attack."

"An attack by whom?" Qonna's mother steps in, her face drawn and grey, her eyes hard like flint beneath the folded edge of her linen headdress.

"I don't know." Noa blushes and shrugs. "Mother says they've all been frightened out of their wits, thinking that the fire was either meant as a punishment sent by the gods or started by Birklanders to eradicate the population. They all come up with different reasons."

Qonna's mother's voice is icy. "They should be grateful to be taken under the wings of the princes, housed as best as they are able, and fed. This is no time to indulge in speculation but a time to help each other survive. Qonna—a word?"

Qonna swallows. She's taken care to avoid her mother since her earlier outburst. *You can't fuck it up now. Breathe and use the right words.* "Yes, Mother."

Her mother leads her into the study. The small space with its dusty books has always served as her father's sanctuary, and her mother doesn't make any effort to sit down. She turns to her daughter and opens the conversation. "Your father has set his heart on you going to Birkland. You are now old enough to understand that it would spell ruin for your future. When I married your father, things were different, and my family saw the chance to connect us more firmly to the da Nileons. I believe your father's heritage made them curious, and they thought the riches of Birkland would come flooding into our own coffers." A muscle tics in her cheek. "Since the temple has been established at the heart of the city, our outlook has shifted and the increase of hostilities ... you know what your brothers face every day when they help to clean up the Westown, and people have always been quicker to criticize and condemn a young woman for the same reasons. You'll be subjected to disgusting claims and exhausting speculations. You won't be able to marry into any of the families I had earmarked for you. It will change whatever future you've envisioned for yourself."

"I understand, Mother." *At least I hope so. But if I don't grab my chance now, I'm going to regret it for the rest of my life.*

"No, you don't, otherwise you wouldn't behave as you do. You wouldn't so much as consider setting foot on a ship. It might be difficult to believe, but I was once in the same situation, and I wanted to take a risk—marry the dashing dark-haired man who astonished the whole town with his unprecedented rise to favour, to be mistress of one of the most beautiful houses in Seagard, and to claim his adventures as my own. Twenty years of being despised for a choice you made with a passionate heart grinds you down, Qonna. There will be little left of you by the end."

It is indeed difficult to picture her mother as anything else but the stern-faced woman who tries to restrain her. "I do understand—and I'm willing to chance it."

Her mother's face distorts. "Why? Why are you so eager to throw away all hope of a successful life in Seagard?"

"Because when you married Dad, you took a gamble in more ways than one, and now all your children are connected to a place beyond the seas. While Qatt, Qov, and Qitli might be able to fulfil their wishes and ambitions here, Seagard is already too small for me, Mother. You've sent me to attend countless dances; you know as well as I that I don't belong here in any way that would make me happy. It feels so wrong to say it, because just thinking it goes against all the lessons I've been taught, but I need to go and find a place where I can breathe. Where I am allowed to be more. You know I'll find my way back eventually." Qonna fights the rising tears. "I'll finally miss *Pomegranates* when I'm allowed to leave it for a while."

Her mother makes a pained noise. "You'll fall under the influence of dangerous people. Much more dangerous than the wayward prince. Birkland isn't like the Continent but with fewer rules to inconvenience you. It is wild and unholy forces abound."

"You mean magic," Qonna says accusingly.

"I know it sounds exciting, but magic corrupts. The wayward prince is the best example at hand. You would blanch to hear all the rumours that have made the rounds concerning his marriage and objectionable relationships in Birkland, not least with the person you wish to find."

"You mean Auntle Sloe."

"Yes," her mother admits.

"The very one by whose generosity you live in this house."

It's her mother's turn to blanch, but the colour rushes back in, burning two patches on her cheeks. "Qonnamaris na Lorian na Qes …."

"It's true. *Pomegranates* has never been ours, and every man who would agree to take me off your hands would be deceived about what he was getting himself into. *Pomegranates* has been loaned to us and put us into a debt we don't want anyone to know about, because Dad's famous rise to favour came with more than one condition attached. This is the hold the royal family has over us, and what we can't let anyone discover is that it came about exactly because of those unholy forces. Our whole standing in the city is based on magic—and, in case you didn't know, magic comes through the blood."

Her mother flinches as if Qonna tried to hit her.

"You know," Qonna realizes. "You know all of it, and you've been afraid of any of us showing signs of it. Good news, Mother—so far it seems as if your sons have been spared, but your daughter …." *You can't back down. You need to go through with it.* "Your daughter has been the one chosen to carry that particular burden too."

For a heartbeat, it feels as if she's going to pass out; the walls of the study close in on her and Qonna stamps her foot to make it stop. "It's merely a little drop—and, as I'm finding out, also comes with conditions. I won't burst into blue flames anytime soon, but it's enough of a worry for me to want help. My voyage to Birkland isn't meant to be frolicking around to indulge my curiosity—it's necessary for me to find out more about the trouble it could cause for all of us."

Her mother shrinks against the shelves, as far away as she can get from her daughter.

It's petty to continue, but Qonna can't help herself. "You once made your passionate choice for the dashing, dark-haired man—this is the result."

After Qonna fled the study, it took her until the late afternoon to calm her heart. She tried walking circles in the yard, then pounding the shit out of soiled linens in the laundry, but nothing really helped the regret settling its claws into her.

With one stream of desperate words, she unleashed the secrets her father had asked her to keep. With a few cries she threw open so many barred doors, destroyed so many plans—and on top of it, she left her friends short-handed in the sick room. Even if some of the wounded recover enough to leave, they're replaced by new arrivals who come in with injuries they sustained while clearing the rubble. *Pomegranates* has become the place to go and be cared for, and while it will certainly help to secure some citizen's affection for the house, it also means all supplies are running short, and soon every single jar of salve will have been used up, down to the ones Noa liberated from the manor's stores.

When Qonna catches up with her as she and Eravis prepare to leave, she notices Noa's exhaustion, as if, in addition to her days of gruelling work, she hasn't slept well either. "Let me walk you up the hill," Qonna begs. "I'm climbing the walls waiting for my mother to decide on my punishment."

So close to Shortest Night the evenings are long and mild. The guards the princes sent to escort the women back to the manor are sweating in their armour, and their mail makes a faint melodious sound with every step. Whatever they think about being ordered to serve as armed chaperones, they are all duty, and Qonna wishes that sometimes her own life could be so deceptively easy. Could she ever do what she's told?

*Obviously not.*

Her father will be so disappointed she couldn't manage to keep her trap shut. He'll have to deal with his distraught wife and the complications of the Suns being dependant on the Bulls for at least a few more months, and all the pushing and shoving that's part of it.

As they reach the walls surrounding the manor grounds, Noa sneaks her hand in Qonna's. "Whatever you said to your mother, it will work itself out. It always does when I'm mean to mine."

Qonna barks out a bitter laugh. "She has no reason to go easy on me. I was extremely out of line."

Eravis addresses them both. "This is a time when everyone comes to the end of their tether. There are bound to be misunderstandings."

"It was the absolute opposite of a misunderstanding," Qonna says through clenched teeth. *Don't patronize me. Don't make my fears sound stupid.* "It was a clarification, and however overdue it was, some of it was not mine to say. I've failed not just myself today."

Noa clasps her hand tighter. "In all the stories, honesty is always the best principle to follow."

"Yes, but the world we live in is too complicated to wrap up in one neat little package. It will have consequences for me, mark my words."

She's beginning to leave her friends behind. Neither Eravis nor Noa will ever be able to comprehend what she'll have to deal with from now on. She slowly pulls back from Noa's grip.

*Some paths are meant to be walked alone.*

# CISIR

## *different obstacles*

It's only taken a few days for the manor grounds to look like a well-established campsite, with communal areas and large cooking fires. The tents are furnished with all the odd bits saved from the Big Blaze. For some reason the camp has divided itself into similar factions as the town. Most of the refugees coming from Westown have pushed the people from the harbour quarter further down the hill.

Cisir can make out a contingent of royal guards keeping an eye on them, poised to subdue any animosities before they get out of control. Children run around the old trees; some sit on the small jetty next to the boat house and dangle their feet in the water, splashing each other. At least they seem happy to be there.

The first thing Cisir does after his arrival at the manor is check on Hevo and Gia. They sit in front of the window, Gia hemming a tunic while Hevo tries to focus on a small booklet stitched from rough paper that looks like something the village priest in Windyhill would preach from. Seeing him concentrate so hard on the pamphlet, resentment bubbles up unbidden in Cisir's chest. "How are you feeling, Hevo?"

Hevo lifts his gaze, but it seems as if Cisir's presence doesn't fully register. He doesn't reply.

"What are you doing up here?" Gia asks, leaning forward to let Spark sniff her hand.

"I managed to get dispensation to do some research in the prince's library. For half a day only—the Red House is still in shambles." He clears his throat. "I'm sure you've heard that we relocated the office?"

Hevo glances nervously at the puppy. "Yes. Some news can't be escaped."

"It causes new and unexpected problems every day, but what we could salvage from the Yellow House has been packed away and some orders have started to come in. Not all houses in Seagard burned."

"My father's house did," Hevo says flatly. "With him in it."

It's the undeniable truth and Cisir tenses, trying not to flinch from it.

Gia takes up the tunic again. "Have you heard that the official memorial will be held on Shortest Night? I think the crown prince felt it to be more auspicious. From this year onward, we'll think of everyone we lost and send our prayers to the Heavens for them on that night."

Hevo sighs. "It won't be enough. It'll never be enough to wash away the guilt they brought upon themselves."

Gia squirms on her chair, as if Hevo has made quite a few similar pronouncements since he regained consciousness.

Cisir decides to ignore him. "The timing makes sense," he says. "Gia, have you spoken to Qonna?"

"She came to visit a couple of days ago. She seems busy with everything going on in *Pomegranates*."

"Yes. I haven't seen her at all recently."

"Maybe she's hiding from you," Gia says with a smile.

"She ought to," Hevo proclaims.

Gia angles herself away from him. "As I understand, she had a big fight with her mother. Who's a good boy?"

Spark leaps up to get his paws on her lap and again she abandons her sewing to scratch his ears and let herself be licked.

Cisir watches Hevo's face and the pure disgust that fights to its surface. *You can't mourn what is so absolutely lost.*

The room Cisir is given access to is little more than glorified storage, long and narrow, as if it had been created by splitting off part of another, and though there are some cushioned chairs standing around, it reminds Cisir of the record section of the Yellow House, without ornament and purely practical as befits the private taste of Nivael da Nileon.

Apart from a dozen volumes of Rosegardian poetry that seem strangely out of place, the main focus points of the collection are histories and maps, painted on enormous scrolls and stored in a shelf modelled after the inside of a well-populated bee skep: many round openings close to each other that offer the best protection for the precious parchments pushed into them, each label made from leather and hanging out to be easily accessible without pulling the whole thing free. Multiple Birkland maps are among them, but Cisir doesn't risk unrolling any. Instead, he concentrates on the histories.

Most of them concern other continents; he can only locate a handful about the Eight Kingdoms, and most of them look like dry, scholarly works written fairly recently. No one would dare to openly discuss magic in these times, and Cisir opens many books searching for a copy of older manuscripts.

All he knows of the magic once practiced on the Continent stems from the fairy tales he was told by his nurse, where grey-bearded men in ankle-length robes carried staffs and powerful jewels around and posed incredibly annoying riddles to all heroes they came into contact with, and the sorcerers you were supposed to hate were called 'witches' and were all in love with a demon or two, so much so that they traded the souls of innocent people for sexual favours.

It takes him almost the whole morning to find something useful in one of the volumes, while Spark sleeps next to the door as if nothing about the search has anything to do with him. Cisir stares at the words, written down so many years ago the letters have faded into the parchment. The manuscript is small and has been rebound to match the books it stands among, but at one point it suffered considerable water damage. Some pages are ripped in half, causing Cisir's stomach to drop in frustration and dismay. Who knows how many of the elegant leather bindings conceal similar evidence of precious pages being mistreated?

The manuscript he holds was clearly written by a single person. The same idiosyncrasies appear on every page: the little squiggle for abbreviated words, the same spellings for unusual ones. Compared to most of the other books it is without much ornamentation, and on some pages the script slants across as if it had been written under less controlled circumstances, perhaps while travelling.

Most of it is in short paragraphs, and some of the headings convince him it's indeed a collection of legends and older tales: *ye dragon and ye beartrapp, south~bleakheath, but also west~heath*—as well as *ye waterhors' revange, hillakes (east~)*.

Given the multitude of regional markers, the author must have journeyed to all corners of the Continent. Cisir also finds inserted notes cross-referencing other stories. On some of the later pages, the small paragraphs disintegrate into hasty scribbles set on repurposed parchment, with the underlying text sanded off as best as possible, as if someone grabbed two piles and combined them into one.

Cisir returns to the beginning of the small book. "Does the name 'Yuzan' mean anything to you?"

Spark sniffs, then gives a weirdly human shrug as if to say, *There were many Yuzans about in my day*.

"Yuzan of Riverclere?"

Spark hides his nose between his paws, something Cisir hasn't seen him do before.

"You do know him, then?"

Spark pretends to be asleep, which is as good an answer as any.

"You're going to talk about it later," Cisir warns him, before unpacking his own sheets of grass paper, the reed pen, and ink container fashioned from the tip of a cow's horn, stoppered with beeswax. The princes would never allow him to take the manuscript out of the library, but if the writer lived long enough ago to be Teasel's contemporary, this is the best start Cisir is going to find. He's barely made it through the first ten stories when the door opens.

"They said you'd be around." Jark kneels next to Spark and rubs his belly. He seems freshly washed, and a cloud of reddish dog hair descends upon his damp arms. "Just finished my watch and thought I'd come find you."

It's been days since they've seen each other. Cisir can barely stop himself from flinging the book away and jumping up. Instead, he awkwardly comes to his feet, beholding the first man he ever kissed and the puppy rolling around on the floor. Spark playfully nips at Jark's hands.

"He looks happy." Jark smiles up at him.

"He should be—all he does is sleep."

"We should be so lucky." Jark's dark eyes shine with joy as he reaches out to Cisir and pulls him into his arms.

Of all the rooms in the manor, the library is the most perfect for them; standing behind the door they can block anyone from walking in, and they are conveniently far away from the only window in the room, which is covered in hide to protect the books from sunlight. It's strange to hold Jark without his leather armour; he seems to fuse to Cisir's body as their kiss intensifies, so much that Cisir's shoulders brush up against the door and a little groan escapes his mouth as Jark's hands wrap around him—in the middle of his back and well below his belt. Cisir grows hard against him as Jark's fingers begin to explore, never breaking the kiss, and he's so warm against Cisir, so blissfully solid, though soft at the same time. He shivers in the knowledge that all they're doing to each other, all they're making each other feel, are some of the worst sins in the Star's book. The pleasure is sharp-edged and laced with shame. He notices that Jark tries to hold in his breath, to quieten himself as much as possible before he steps away and studies Cisir's flushed face, the trousers straining to contain him.

"Are you all right?" Jark asks.

"Very much so." But then Cisir's gaze falls on the dog, sitting up and staring at them with a creased brow. It feels as if icy water crashes over his neck. He has a witness to everything Jark does to him.

"Would you rather wait?" Jark asks. "It might not be the best idea, doing that here, in the manor."

"I don't mind so much about the manor—I mind him gawping at us." Cisir gestures towards the puppy.

Jark laughs. "You can send him away."

"I don't believe it works like that, sadly. He does what he wants to, and at the moment he's sticking to me like sap."

Jark frowns. "You need to train him."

"Good luck with that. Look at those eyes—could you send him out?"

"Gladly, if it gives me the opportunity to finally rip the clothes off you." Jark starts to kiss him again, but the wild abandonment has passed.

Cisir pulls away. "I'm serious. I don't want him to watch us."

"He's just a dog."

"You're telling me you like an audience?"

A deep line appears between Jark brows. "Well, that was uncalled for."

"I'm sorry, but I don't want to be watched. By anyone."

"Why? What are you afraid of?"

"I already have a hard time accepting it. I don't need any witnesses to what I … wish to do."

Jark takes a step back. "You feel shame about wanting me?"

"How can you not?" As soon as it's out he knows he's made a mistake. No one likes to be told they're a guilty secret. A secret it would be so much easier to live without.

Jark blinks. "I made my mind up a long time ago. Whatever the Brothers try to tell me, I know the gods in the Heavens wouldn't have granted me so much if it was evil. It wouldn't feel as right if it was truly wrong."

"I don't have the luxury of so much confidence," Cisir whispers. "I spent too much of my life afraid that even if it feels like coming up for air, I still have to face the consequences."

"Not if you're clever about it."

"You've done it that many times?"

"Often enough," Jark replies, with a new bite to his voice. "And I won't stop just because you're scared."

"Fine. Leave me be, then. Find someone else."

"I don't want anyone else."

"Yet."

"You don't get to do that," Jark snaps. "Pushing me away and then making me feel awful because I let myself be pushed. I know you want to give in—you're halfway there already." His gaze drops to Cisir's crotch and something in his face makes Cisir bristle.

"My body and my head are two different obstacles to overcome," he grits out. "Perhaps you've never been caught, and you've never had your parents glare at you with such disgust, merely for mentioning to your fiancée that sometimes you feel there's too much you want to give, that you have terrible suspicions about yourself—and then she can't keep the secret and the whole bloody mess blows up in your face."

"You're right." Jark crosses his arms. "I was only beaten half to death and spat upon—nothing like being sent to bed without any dinner by my nurse."

They stare each other down. Cisir manages to say, "Probably a good thing I'm about to leave for Birkland."

Jark's arms sink. "You're going away?"

"Almost certainly, yes. My master is trying to get a place for me on the next ship the prince sails back to the west."

"Why didn't you tell me?" It sounds like an accusation.

"Because we haven't seen each other for a while. It's quite a recent development."

"I don't want to fight." Jark's shoulders slump. "I want to spend time with you, show you there's nothing wrong with being together." Jark steps into his arms again and their foreheads meet.

Cisir wants to sob with relief, but he can see Spark sitting on his haunches, his eyes fixed on Jark's back, on his hand cupping Cisir's face. Cisir's heart jumps and stutters, but as happy as he feels when Jark's arms are around him, it doesn't take anything away from the danger they've put themselves in.

"I don't want to fight either," Cisir says softly as he takes Jark's wrists and pulls him off. "But unfortunately, that doesn't seem to be enough."

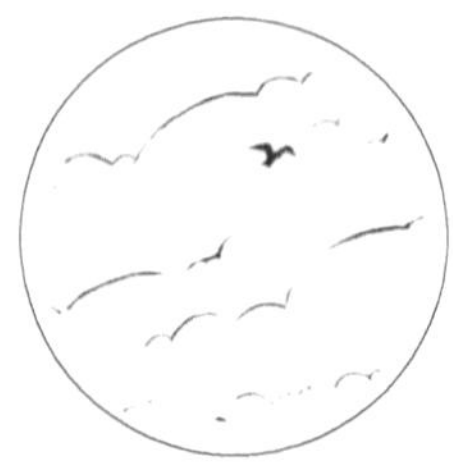

# QONNA

## *sit out the pain*

Gia gives the sheet a last shake to make it fit snugly around the mattress. The window shutters and slats are open and sun streams into the guest room she's spent so much time in since Hevo was brought up the hill. Qonna has already helped her change the bedding and sweep the floor before giving the bedframe a scrub. Leather buckets with the dirty water stand close to the door and the whole room is clean and ready for its patient to return.

"He spoke of the temple a lot in the last few days." When Gia shooed Hevo out into the corridor, he appeared close to tears, unsure where to go for the next few hours. He must dread the day when the princes take away his bed, the space where he hides from the world, while half the town sprawls itself out in the manor gardens.

Qonna pulls the bed curtains back into pleasing folds. "Hevo hasn't said anything to you at all? He doesn't have anywhere else to go, has he?"

"He could find somewhere in the Red House, I suppose." Gia sniffs. "I understand why he's apprehensive about going back to the city, but it's not as if he's very relaxed here, either."

They both glance out onto the gravelled yard. Hevo sits on the water trough in front of the stables, his back turned towards the park where children play among the stones. A gaggle of small girls with flower crowns chase each other around the birches standing guard.

It could be an idyllic sight, if it wasn't for the smoking cook fires and huddles of dejected-looking people at the bottom of the hill.

Hevo hasn't tried to go among the Westowners to find anyone he might know. He sits with his gaze glued to the gravel, although the sun is out and a soft breeze rustles through the ancient trees lining the property. The girls laugh and shriek as they trail dandelions and daisies and try to snatch the crowns off each other's brow.

Given what they've been through, Qonna should be enjoying these sights and sounds, but she understands all too well why Hevo doesn't want to see any of it. Her own world is in the process of reordering itself too, and not all aspects of it are painless. Her mother still hasn't talked to her.

"I'll get out of the way, if you want to fetch him back," Qonna says.

"I think you should go and tell him the room is ready." Gia flashes her a grin. "We shouldn't make it too easy for him."

Hevo pales as he realizes Qonna is coming straight for him, her hand lifted to shield her eyes against the sun, her steps crunching on the gravel.

"I'm not going to bite you," she says drily.

"That remains to be seen." He rises from the trough, clutching at his thighs, as if his legs have long since started to cramp and he tried to sit out the pain.

"I haven't done anything but try and help you. So has Cisir."

Hevo's face softens for the blink of an eye. "It's not about your intentions," he hisses. "It's about the method."

"We did what we had to do to get you back."

"I wish you'd let me die."

His words feel like a slap across Qonna's face. "Let you die? Why? What did you see on the other side?"

"I don't remember." He lies. He must lie, because why would he behave like he does if he doesn't recall what happened? He presses his eyes shut. "The only thing I know is that it hurt. A lot. As if you're being boiled and can't get out of the pot. It would've been kinder to make it stop, not to force me back, to make me a witness to what you did."

Qonna detects so much misplaced insinuation in his words that she shivers. "We only held the stones open."

"I saw you both glow." He trembles with hostility. "Normal people don't *glow*."

"I might have a little magic. Why must that be a bad thing?"

His laugh holds a bitter edge. "Do you truly believe it's going to be like in the stories?" He pushes the dark hair from his face. "One word to the Brothers and they'll lock you away. They're already keeping an eye on you and your family, and if you give them the slightest reason to doubt your heart, they'll have sufficient evidence to declare you a witch."

"A witch?" The words sound sour in Qonna's mouth. Wizards are people to be feared—witches are people to be despised. "I don't think I'm a witch."

He walks away from her with a cold sneer on his face. He seems fragile and shaken, but if his last words have shown her anything, he believes he has enough power to make her life extremely difficult.

*If I let him.*


Qonna finds Noa in her father's library—a long, narrow room hidden away in the family quarters that has only one window and shabby chairs. Nivael's daughter has opened one of the big maps on the floor, its edges restrained with cushions to keep it from rolling up.

Birkland covers quite a few floorboards; the ink is colourful enough to assume this map was only recently commissioned. On the west coast, the dark silhouette of a fortress carries the label *Tower of the Sun*, and many other places are marked.

The map must be based on the older one destroyed with her father's office, on which he made many revisions or updates in his own hand. Qonna sees the blue splotch of the Golden Lake dominating the middle lands and a long ridge of mountains in the east.

Noa lies before it, her elbows on the floor and her chin in her hands. "I wish I could come with you," she says dreamily.

Qonna's heart skips a beat. "What?" How wonderful would it be to experience Birkland with Noa, together?

"Nian said your father asked about suitable accommodation for you on a voyage west, and that he was looking forward to showing you around the Stoneharp." She gazes longingly at the Tower of the Sun. "Father says I'm not old enough to come with you, that I need to give it a few more years, but you're not that much older than me. I bet when the time comes, he'll find another excuse to keep me from sailing. I've been on a ship before. I know I don't get seasick."

Qonna kneels next to her, in front of the eastern mountains. "When have you been on a ship?"

"Only for a quick trip around the coast, up to Eastbay to see my aunt Nuvalis in Whiterivers. Mother threw up all the way, but I didn't feel so much as a twinge."

"That must've been exciting. I've heard Eastbay is one of the grandest cities you could visit."

"It's fine." Noa shrugs before reaching out and tracing her fingertips across the Golden Lake. "Very big and very austere, full of spiteful little cousins who call me names because they think my mother should never have become part of the family. I counted the days until we could go back onto the ship." She grimaces. "There were some nice things. Did you know Eastbay has the largest and oldest temple on the Continent? That was quite impressive. And there were a lot of dogs everywhere, because they have a dog on the city flag, one of these thin, silver-grey hunting dogs, nothing sweet and cuddly like your Spark. The food was boring though, and they made us sit through more services than I care to remember. We weren't allowed to go to the big temple, so I don't recommend Eastbay, really. It might be more fun to go as a merchant. I've never seen so many ships in one place, and so many storage houses—a whole quarter of them! I wonder if that's what the Stoneharp is like? Nian says most of the Suns in Birkland are stationed there, but some are on the south coast too, here in Foalstones, and they're in negotiations to open a post in Goldenlake directly, not only in Coldharbour on the east coast of the lake." Her fingers again rest on the little dark blue waves the map maker used to denote the vastness of the waters. "You might get to see it and meet other wizards."

"Maybe. If I really get to go."

Noa looks up at her in alarm. "Why wouldn't you?"

"I'm not sure my mother will agree in the end. We haven't been on speaking terms the last week and she has a stubborn streak."

Noa crawls back on her heels and carefully brushes down her dress. "There's something I want to give you. I started it when you first came to the manor, before the fire." She pulls something from the long pocket hidden in her skirts.

It's a neckerchief, made from the finest linen Qonna has ever touched. At first glance it seems covered in a floral pattern, but when Qonna brings it close to her face, she sees that what she thought to be sprigs of blue flowers are tiny unicorns, rampant, with their horns lowered. It must've taken Noa uncounted hours to create something so delicate.

"Oh." Tears rise to Qonna's eyes. "That is so beautiful."

"To make you think of me in Birkland," Noa says with a satisfied grin, "and make you bring me back a present."

"I don't know how to thank you, Noa." *With a kiss?* No—somehow the idea of a kiss feels wrong.

"I just told you how. Should you want to return to the west one day, you could put in a good word for me, so I'm at least allowed to be with you on your next adventure. Unless you find an overwhelmingly handsome wizard to marry, someone who sweeps you off your feet and keeps you in Birkland."

"I don't think I'll ever find someone strong enough to sweep me up," Qonna says. "I like my feet to stay firmly on the ground."

"Then you might find another princess you can do that to." Noa pushes the cushions off the edge of the map and it rolls up with a *snup*.

Qonna forces out a deep breath. "What do you mean?"

"I see how you look at Gia sometimes. Have you ever spoken to her about it?"

"No, and I don't think that's what I really want, either." Not in that way, at least. Not like Gia wanted Jark. Not like Cisir so clearly wants him.

"It would be beautiful, though," Noa says.

"How can you speak so calmly about things like that?"

Noa shrugs again. "I have a brother who's a sister in Birkland. Father never tried to keep that from me, and he always told me there are many things about which different rules exist on the other side of the sea. He said in Birkland I would be allowed to rule, and all my daughters with me, and that I could marry a man, a woman, or someone Other like your auntle. So you see, the idea that a princess of the Birkland families would fall head over heels in love with you isn't so far-fetched at all. I hope you remember to write to me when you're happy ever after."

"Is that what you want for yourself?"

"Maybe? I don't know yet. I think I'd love to have the option. Apart from the fact that being a Queen of Birkland sounds like a sweet deal to me. You know, coming from a minor Princess of Crooked Hill who'll never get within sniffing distance of the throne." Noa smiles sadly. "I'm sure I'll find out one day."

"What the fuck did you say to him?" Gia grips Qonna's arm hard enough to hurt.

"To whom? Ow, Gia!"

"To Hevo, of course. He sat on the bed for a while and then stormed out!"

"I didn't say anything to him, at least nothing … nothing mean. *He* called me a witch."

"Qonna …." Gia growls.

"Where do you think he went? There's nothing left of the Westown and by now most of it must have been cleared anyway."

Gia bites so deep into her bottom lip she must be about to draw blood. "How can you question it? He'll run straight back to the temple, after all the work I had with him." Anger flashes in her dark eyes, making Qonna's hackles rise with guilt. "That will teach me to sacrifice so much time on someone."

"Do you want me to go after him?" Qonna asks.

"What good will that do? He'll only see his worst fears confirmed, that we'll do our utmost to keep him from the healing only the Star can give him."

They stand in front of the open door, peering into the newly empty room, prepared for someone who finally made up his mind to flee.

Qonna sighs. "Good riddance, I say. If he can't appreciate how much care you've lavished on him, he isn't worth any tears."

Gia lets out a bitter laugh. "Why must they all run away? Every man I give the slightest bit of attention to, they all take the first opportunity to get out. Why must I lose everything? I don't have my home left—all those hours scrubbing the walls, sweeping up the ashes, scouring pots to make the *Pear* into a presentable house, while *Pomegranates* still stands."

Qonna knows she has a point, that everything the gods dished out has come to land at Gia's feet. "*Pomegranates* will become your home."

Her friend clenches her fists. "That is so much more easily said than done. If the temples could be persuaded to take in women, I might try and hide with them too. Make a whole life devoting my labours to the Star; maybe that would give me more reward in the end."

"Really?" Qonna asks, horrified.

"No, not really," Gia concurs.

"I can ask my father to let you come with me—if I'm allowed to go. Would you want to go to the old country with me?"

Gia blinks. "You know what will happen if I do that? We might have some adventures and I might see a bit more of the world, but when I come back, people will point at me and say I've tasted too much freedom, that I've spoilt myself. I was supposed to be a tavernkeeper's daughter, respectable and helpful to all the community. To make a marriage that pleases both me and my parents and spawn enough brats to secure the future of the establishment, to make the hard work we put into the *Pear* pay off."

"I understand why you're angry."

"Somehow, I doubt that. I never wanted to leave Seagard as badly as you, Qonna. I would've been happy with attending the Braid Makers' Annual Dances and having my pick from among their apprentices. If I come with you to Birkland, people will say I believed myself too good for it."

"Fuck them."

"What?" Gia sounds genuinely shocked.

"Fuck every one of those people. We don't need any of them." *They can all go and die.*

Gia's face scrunches up, as if she's about to burst into tears. "Fuck them," she repeats, but her voice shakes.

# CISIR

## *not that kind of magic*

He what?" Qes na Qarim asks. It's late and the sun is about to set over *Pomegranates*. Still, Cisir's master seems ready to jump up and run out again to retrieve his aberrant apprentice.

Cisir frowns. "Qonna said he left for the temple, and as her information came straight from Gia, I think we have every reason to believe her."

"That's not good news," Qes mumbles. "After all we did to get him back last time …." The First Sun gnaws at his fingernails.

It's been a long day in the service of getting both the Suns and the Bulls off their knees, and Cisir and his master are in need of food and a wash. Most of the patients left in the sick room are asleep and only Gia's mother is up to watch over them, all other women having taken the chance to finish their duties and retreat.

Qes balls his fist and tucks it away. "Have you two come up with a plan yet?" He glances at Cisir, then at the puppy.

Spark shakes his head.

"I'm not sure how much interference is advisable, Master."

"I can't put my tail between my legs and cower before the Brothers," Qes says, "and I think we both know they wouldn't send him back voluntarily. They're glad for every man they lure away from us and the influence of the princes. I'm not looking forward to getting the royal family involved again, but if that's what it takes, in these times when the Companies do their best to work together …. I'm tired."

"I don't want to sound mean, but you *look* tired, Master."

"So do you. How did your afternoon go, son?"

"Fine. Rilk kept his distance today, so everything was much easier."

"Please don't let him get to you. There'll always be Bulls who don't understand what we're trying to achieve and that Bulls and Suns pooling their strengths can only be a good thing in the end. Clearly, winning the First Bull around is just the beginning. You know what? I need sleep. We'll deal with Hevo tomorrow. Was your time in the library worth the effort?"

"Sort of. I might've found something that could be of help, but the manuscript is too fragile to take it from the manor."

"I'm sure the princes could use some help up there, keeping control of the citizens. You could make yourself useful to Lilyis in whatever form she requires. It doesn't make much sense for you to run all over town each day, only to be bullied by Bjell's odious secretary."

"That is kind of you, Master, but my work …."

"Whatever you can find concerns my daughter," Qes interrupts him, "and as my secretary I can send you where I please. Continue your research in the manor library. Is Gia still up the hill?"

"No, she returned to *Pomegranates* today. Qonna made space for her in her bedroom."

"At least there's that. Under these circumstances it will also make sense for you to keep an eye on things at the manor, now the memorial will be held on Shortest Night and tensions between the princes are bound to occur. They always start to quarrel at the least opportune moment." Qes tries to suppress a yawn but ultimately gives in. "Right. Go get some sleep and wait for me in the morning. We need to talk strategy."

Cisir struggles awake after a night of sticky, confusing dreams, only to find that Spark has not crammed himself into the cot for once, but lies stretched out in front of the door, as if sniffing all coming and going in the corridor. When someone knocks at the door he barks once, low and threatening.

"Tea is ready!" Gia calls.

Cisir joins the Wolves and his master's family for breakfast. The only one missing is Qonna's mother, who still prefers to eat in her room. Everyone at the table is bleary-eyed and strung out from nearly two weeks of incessant work, but Gia is particularly grey around the mouth. She likely blames herself for not being able to keep Hevo from absconding, when the guilt lies so obviously with— Cisir pinches himself to cut off the thought.

Qonna pours out tea for him and slides sideways on the storage chest to make room between her and Qitli.

"Right," her father starts off. "I think we've all become aware things are beginning to heat up." He glances at his sons, who glower back. The altercation at the Red House was surely not the only fight they've dodged in recent days. "I want to clarify that *Pomegranates* will remain open to anyone requiring help, but especially to anyone experiencing hostility based on their perceived heritage. If you come across anyone who needs protection, bring them here. The gods were gracious enough to spare this house, and so it must serve."

"What exactly are we preparing for?" Qatt asks, bending sideways to rub Spark's ears before sneaking him a bit of sausage.

"I expect Hevo to confess." Qes na Qarim's voice sounds gravelly. "To whatever he thinks he saw the night he woke up properly."

The only confused ones at the table are Qonna's brothers.

Qitli swallows thickly. "What does he think he saw?"

"Something that scared the shit out of all of us," Lauron Wolf grunts, "but that hopefully no one will believe."

"The city is buzzing with rumours," Qatt interjects. "If it's not completely inconceivable, people will jump on it like flies on rotting meat."

Qes winces. "Qonna, what do you think?"

Gia grabs Qonna's hand as she takes a deep breath and answers. "I believe Hevo will try to make things as difficult for us as he possibly can. I'm sorry, Cisir, I know you think of him as your friend, but the last time I spoke to him … it didn't go well, maybe leave it at that. So yes, I think he's too scared to think beyond the relief of getting it off his chest."

"What the fuck happened?" Qov bursts out.

Qonna shrugs a shoulder. "You know that Auntle Sloe is called a wizard? It seems like some talents run in the family."

Her brothers draw in a collective breath. All three make the same jerky movement to scoot away from their sister. Qatt, Qov, and Qitli are so much alike, they look like the same man getting bad news across different years.

"What did you blow up?" Qatt asks.

"Nothing! It's not that kind of magic. I'm probably nowhere near as gifted as Sloe. It's just a tiny, tiny bit." Her eyes lock onto Cisir.

He manages a wobbly smile.

Qov squints at his sister. "Did you set fire to the city?"

"No! But I'm sure in one way or another that's exactly the conclusion the priests will reach, especially as they're so eager to implicate Birklanders. This is why I'm hoping to visit the old country soon."

"We should come with you," Qitli says. "To protect you."

"That's sweet of you," her father jumps in, "but you will be needed here. We'll expedite the start of your apprenticeships to increase the Sun's numbers."

"You can't let her go on her own," Qov says with a snort. "Mother would never allow it."

"I'm well aware," Qes says, "and Qonna won't be alone. She needs your support, boys. Because her name could well come up in anything the Brothers proclaim next."

During the day, the campsite at the bottom of the hill is much emptier; most citizens have become involved in the cleanup of once bustling streets and squares, but they leave a few women to watch children too small to help, and as Cisir assists Jark and other royal guards, lugging baskets of cabbages and bags of flour freshly arrived from the closest village mill, he sees many worried faces around him. Lilyis gets swamped immediately, beseeched with questions about butter and milk and more blankets. As some with lesser injuries have returned to their families, there's also need for salves, bandages, and calming teas, and clothes have to be kept clean somehow.

Cisir is glad to be used only for his strength and that none of these people recognize him as someone who can decide anything. They look at him as if he belongs to the royal guard, and it's a relief. A few girls chase Spark to give him cuddles, and his yips echo across the park.

"At least one of us is having fun." Jark takes up the rungs of the hand cart they brought down the hill. "You're nervous again. You don't look forward to vanishing into the library as soon as we're back at the house?" His chin points to the tower on which climbing roses have bloomed; they give it a soft outline, as if it's beset by pink butterflies.

"It's the calm before the storm." Cisir wonders if his pronouncement sounds too gloomy. The pits on the burial ground have finally been closed. No more dead have surfaced and the same village the flour came from has provided a stone mason to finish a memorial marker that will inform future generations of what was lost during the Big Blaze, how many citizens died and how many houses burned. Why Seagard will never be the same again and why some quarters will have many new buildings, while others won't.

The grounds of the manor won't bear any scars once the camp is disbanded. Grass will grow back, and the same flowers will emerge next spring. If no one gets any dangerous ideas in the meantime.

Jark huffs with effort and some of his comrades push the empty cart to make the ascent easier. They have many more deliveries to make today before they'll relieve another contingent of guards in the city. The crown prince has ordered more guards to arrive for Shortest Night and until then Jark will undoubtedly be kept busy.

Spark bounds up the hill and grazes Cisir's calves as he overtakes him. There's not a single moment Cisir is truly alone; he can't go for a pee without the puppy sitting and waiting, probably listening to every grumble of his guts. This close to the beginning of summer, the more sculpted gardens around the main house are awash with flowers and powerful scents; lilacs are coming into bud and rose hedges breaking out in glorious swathes of loosely filled blooms, from icy white to darkest red. All this might be gone one day, destroyed or simply forgotten, the stones of the tumbling walls repurposed, the rose shrubs exploded into a tangle of thorns around the ruins. He shakes his head to dislodge the image.

Spark waits for him to catch up, his eyes narrowed in suspicion.

"Do wizards have visions?" Cisir asks him, and Spark employs the doggy version of a shrug, which Cisir takes to mean, *Some.*

"I don't need visions," he groans.

Another shrug.

To his right, the guards have reached the yard and Jark waves at him to say farewell. He'll spend the rest of the day away. Something in Cisir heaves a sigh of relief.

*You can't afford to be tempted again.*

He enters the manor through a side door and wipes his brow as he takes the stairs to the living quarters. As he steps into the library, he almost stumbles onto the map on the floor.

"What the …?"

"Oh, sorry. I didn't want to startle you." Noa lies on her stomach, her naked feet folded over each other.

Spark jumps on her to lick her face, and she screeches in delight.

Cisir glances over the map. It's colourful and beautifully drawn, showing the same lands as the one nailed to his master's old study wall. "What are you doing?"

"Dreaming about sailing with Qonna to the west," Nivael's daughter admits, trying to push Spark off her neck, while he tries his best to stick his tongue down her ear.

"Get off her," Cisir cries, and both puppy and princess freeze. Spark finally retreats.

Noa rolls around and folds her legs under her skirts. She's flushed but smiles up at him. "And you?"

"Research. We're trying to find out more about … the stones."

"Then you'll probably want to check the oldest books. I can show you which—and the Riverclere collection."

"Oh, I think I found that one the last time I was going through the shelves."

"There's more than one volume. Father has a weird shelving system; sometimes it takes ages for me to dig out the books I need. Mother has good reason to keep her own books separate."

"I'd be grateful for your help." Spark whines and crawls back towards the door, as if he knows now that Cisir has a guide to the library's treasures, he'll find what he needs, will find out things about the man who calls himself Teasel.

"Help me pack the map away," Noa says, "and we can get started."

Cisir takes a last look at the squiggly west coast above the towers marking the Stoneharp and the Tower of the Sun. There might be a chance for them yet. If Noa believes Qonna will sail, her family might already be in on the plan, and something tells Cisir if Lilyis gets an idea into her head, it won't be easily dismissed.

The map slots back into its space among the others. Noa turns the label out, then takes three steps to a section Cisir hasn't yet searched. She pulls four thick volumes free. "This is where we start," she says with an excited grin.

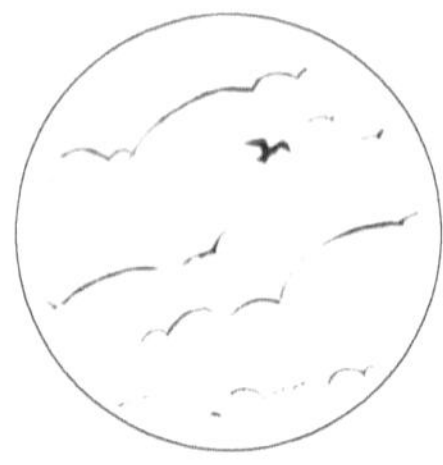

# QONNA

## *break through the form*

The next morning the whole front of *Pomegranates* is covered in horseshit. Someone went through the trouble to pick it off the streets and smear it all over the carvings, and the door is mottled with it, whatever didn't stick piled up before it.

Qonna's mother loses all colour as she stares at her befouled house, the same house she's opened to so many citizens since the fire. While her mother is close to tears, Qonna is ready to rip someone's head off.

"It's just the start," Uncle Lauron prophesies as he carries leather buckets of water from the well house. "When I first took over the *Pear*, many people found it necessary to show their disagreement in the most unhelpful of ways. Be glad that it's horseshit. There are so many smellier kinds."

Qonna's brothers follow with brushes and brooms, all three blotchy with outrage, while their mother vanishes into the depths of the house.

"Go inside," Lauron says to Qonna and his own daughter. "You shouldn't be out here while we clean this up." He makes a weird gesture towards Qonna's father.

"He's right," Qes says. "Go help your mother. We'll talk about it later."

"Dad—"

"Later, Qonna."

An icy fist clenchs around her stomach. *He couldn't be any clearer. It's your fault. Why else would your brothers look at you like that? They know. Everyone knows.*

More people are collected from the sick room, and in every face Qonna reads embarrassment and sheepishness, as if none of them wishes to be beholden to a Birklandish family. As if they can't get out of *Pomegranates* fast enough, dragging their loved ones away from the evil that lurks in the Eastown.

Qonna's mother works quietly, her face a mask, but her eyes burn with indignation, the same Qonna felt before shame and guilt caught up with her. Qonna clears away the empty cots, the sheets and blankets that are to be washed. She should be riding across the city, or helping Cisir find out more about Teasel, not hiding away, waiting to be smoked out by a mob of priests.

Her father discovers her as she stuffs the last laundry basket to carry it into the yard.

"I'm due at the Red House," he says. "But we need to talk first."

"Yes. Please, let's talk."

Her father's study has a half-abandoned look now the Sun's effects have been brought over to the Bulls. "None of it is your fault," he says as he pushes the door closed behind them. "Even if Hevo spilled the peas as soon as he reached the temple, this befoulment was planned longer, and I don't believe the Brothers would stoop so low as to rake shit off the street to make their point. It was meant for all of us." He speaks calmly. "I don't want you to burden yourself, Qonna. It means *Pomegranates* has been recognized for what it is: a sanctuary for everyone under threat. We'll post watches if we have to. I bet there are some royal guards we could ask to be assigned, and things will have to get a lot worse before citizens openly attack the royal family. That's not to say it won't happen, but not for a while yet."

He shudders. "There's something else you should know."

"What is it?"

"Back when we first took possession of the house, both my father and Sloe made sure it was well protected." Qes studies her face as if to search for signs of fear. Or more outrage. "Sloe brought guardstones from the north and we placed them to amplify the wards that surround *Pomegranates*."

"Guardstones?"

"The castle of Crooked Hill sits atop a reservoir of them, and it ensures that magic can't harm its inhabitants. It probably made sense after the sorcerers of old were chased off—but for *Pomegranates* my father prepared a different kind of ward. This house has been blessed by the Tall Gods and the Small Gods. It will not fall to a few pitchfork-wielding bigots." He steps forwards and takes her hands. He still bears traces of the fire, though his brows have started to grow in again. On his neck is a patch of rough, reddened skin where he was burned and a scab mars his hairline. "*Pomegranates* will stand, so you don't need to worry."

Qonna isn't prepared to let it go yet. "Do you mean the whole Eastown could've burned down around us, with only *Pomegranates* left?"

"Probably. Brother Flame is one of the gods standing closest to your auntle. I don't think he'd want to take the blame for going against the wards."

Qonna's shoulders relax, and her forehead smoothes. "That's good to hear."

"Whatever happens to us in the future, this house has been singled out. It's the safest place for any of us—though I agree you should sail to the west, find out what you can do. I'll talk to your mother again and try to make her see sense in letting you learn about yourself."

Cisir returns in the late afternoon, strangely giddy and clutching a bag bursting with paper. Ink smudges his cheek and Spark slinks behind him, swerving around Qonna, as if he expects to be scolded once they're inside.

"Noa was a great help," her father's secretary bursts out. "She knows both her father's and her mother's books like the back of her hand."

Qonna ushers him into the study before her mother can realize exactly what they're talking about. Spark whimpers as she gently pushes him through so the door can close once again.

Cisir lays out the scraps of paper on her father's desk.

"Did you actually find him in the records?" Qonna asks.

"There are a few candidates in the accounts Noa showed me, but there's also a story of a wizard who was imprisoned after conspiring behind his master's back. He kept running away, so they brought in other wizards to enact punishment."

"Turning him to stone?"

"Exactly. It's a story from when the Hillakes were a patchwork of tiny kingdoms, and the writer who collected them noted that he heard variations of the tale in the Hillakes proper as well as where the borderlands are today."

"You mean, close to Chillyhill?"

"Windyhill," he corrects her. "Though Chillyhill is very apt." Cisir's mouth hitches up at the corner.

"You might be related to Teasel."

They both stare at the puppy, who shuffles and whines in discomfort.

"Very distantly related if so," Cisir says. "All it really tells us is there were quite a few wizards about, and they must've left traces in the local population."

Qonna sighs. "You can't expect all of them to live chastely, I suppose. But he hasn't given you his opinion on any of it?"

Cisir shrugs. "No, but he also hasn't run away, though he clearly wants to. Which makes me think there might be a strange kind of bond in place."

*Please, no.* "A bond?"

"I wonder if he understands it himself."

Qonna crouches down next to Spark. "You don't care to enlighten us?"

Spark tries to lick her face but doesn't show any sign of changing form. Qonna hugs him. "If you don't mind us developing our own theories, keep being a dog. But don't complain later when we've built our own story about what happened to you. You bear the mark of shackles, and getting turned into stone by your peers hopefully wasn't an everyday occurrence back then. Does the writer give a name for the wizard in question?"

Cisir checks a scrap of paper. "He calls him the Red Wizard."

"His hair is quite red."

"A disciple of the Burnfoot, whatever that means."

Excitement grips her. "Have you cross-referenced 'Burnfoot'?"

"Noa widened the search for it, though she can't recall having come across it before."

"You still have nothing to say?" Qonna asks the puppy, who's gone motionless. He doesn't even blink.

"I guess a shapeshifter wouldn't have a lot of trouble escaping his chains many times," Cisir murmurs. "From the name of Burnfoot we can infer an affinity towards Brother Flame. Do you think we could turn him back into stone if he doesn't start talking?"

The puppy makes a strange sound, as if something rips apart deep in his throat, and then it says, quite clearly, "You have no fucking clue."

"Would you be so kind as to explain?" Qonna asks.

Between the smear attack on *Pomegranates* and her father's disclosures, a dog speaking doesn't impress her half as much as it should. Perhaps she's always suspected Teasel could break through the form.

"The Burnfoot is not a single *sorcerer*," he says pointedly. "In this case it's a whole group of masters, all with strong opinions on what behaviour is seemly for a young acolyte."

"Like a wizard's council?" Cisir asks.

"Sorcerer," Spark snaps. "The word is sorcerer."

"Why?" Qonna interjects.

"Because it denotes a gift given at birth, not something that's taught. So whatever's going on with you two, you're not wizards—not yet, anyway."

*Being called a sorcerer is better than a witch.*

Cisir blinks. "Interesting."

Qonna nods slowly. "In Birkland, wizards are supposed to study a lot; even the ones who don't ascend to come face to face with the Siblings. We might be able to make sense from all that eventually. Are we correct to assume a Burnfoot is named after their connection with Brother Flame?"

"Yes," Spark grumbles. "But they teamed up with Rockfoots to imprison me."

"Do all Tall Gods have these sorcerer communities at their disposal?"

"They did back then. It happened an awfully long time ago. Every single one of those people has long since been eaten by the earth and blossomed in a thousand generations of flowers."

"Our assumption that Cisir might descend from one of them is probably not far off, then?"

"Listen," Spark spits, "there must be thousands of descendants roaming about this continent. There's no reason why the gift shouldn't pop up in a random boy from the arse end of the Hillakes. I don't make the rules. I learned from my mistake hundreds of years ago, and I'm still being punished for the stupid ideas I may have entertained in my wayward youth. All this? Having to put up with you two dimwits and your ridiculous notions of what could be happening to you? That's *torture!*" The last word comes out like a bark.

Qonna's shoulders tighten. "Then teach us. Help us."

"Every sorcerer has their own journey to make," Spark says. "Everybody's gift is different. I could as soon try to teach a pig to sing."

"You're a horrible person," Qonna blurts out.

"Sorry to be the one to tell you, but they don't put someone in stone for being sweet-tempered and helpful."

Since Gia moved in with Qonna again, the tiny room weirdly seemed tidier than before, though there should be more clothes, more stuff in it—but Qonna is on her best behaviour, not wanting Gia to know how much chaos she can spread at the drop of a dress. The room smells better too, like rosemary and lavender, the soap her best friend favours.

Gia looks up from the piece of cloth she's working on. "I've started something new. The fabric isn't as fine as the neckerchief Noa gave you, but I thought if no one else is going to give me something to remember them by, I'll make my own."

Qonna bends over the small portable frame. The first pattern pieces are small rosy-cheeked pears. "This is beautiful, Gia."

"I know. At least it won't remind me of some random ungrateful twat."

"Hevo might still change his mind."

Gia scoffs. "The Brothers won't let him out of their sight. Having someone at hand who left the Sun because he was uncomfortable with rituals practiced under the supervision of the First Sun *and* the princes? It's gold to them, Qonna, you know that. They'll cling to his every word and whatever he chooses to tell them will surely come back to haunt us. All of us present at the stones will be implicated, and if he wastes a thought on the effort we spent on getting him back on his feet, he'll shrug it off and move on."

Both Gia and Qonna flinch as someone knocks on their door. They exchange a glance before Qonna says, "The door is open, come in."

She can feel her heartbeat in the tip of her tongue as her mother enters. She's shed her apron but is still clothed in the simple dress she wore to her duties all week, the one that has a rip in the hem and blood spatters on the elbow. "Qonna, I need to talk to you."

Gia jumps up. "Of course, I'll …."

"I think it would be good for you to stay. You might understand what I am trying to achieve," Qonna's mother says.

"Mother?" Sweat breaks out at Qonna's hairline as her mother takes a seat on the edge of her bed, glancing around the clean room with subdued satisfaction while the lines on her brow carve even deeper.

"What happened this morning …." She takes a deep breath, then reaches for Qonna's hand. Her fingers are dry but cold, and they shake slightly. "It might've been the last piece of the picture that fell into place. Since we spoke, I haven't stopped mulling over the dangers waiting for you out in the world, but Seagard is changing too, and a burned city where people fight each other for food and shelter is not a space I wish you to live in, either."

"You'll really let me go?" A spark of hope kindles in Qonna's heart. Who knew the befouling of her home would work to her advantage?

"I am coming around to the idea," her mother admits.

"But …," Qonna prompts her.

Her mother squeezes her hand. "I can't let you go alone."

Qonna's voice is squeaky as she turns to her best friend. "The prince will be with me, and Gia too, right?" Gia nods enthusiastically.

Her mother releases her. "If you sail, you will have to get married first."

# CISIR

## *painted a target*

I can see where she's coming from," Gia says. "But the plan hinges on one important element."

Cisir swallows. "Qonna doesn't want to marry. She was clear about that." He didn't expect to be waylaid by Lauron Wolf's daughter this morning. His eyes are gummy with sleep, and everything sort of smells like horseshit around the house— enough to put him off the slices of toasted bread the cook brought up for breakfast.

Gia rubs her face. "Believe me, after her mother left we talked at length about all that, and you know there's only one viable solution."

His skin crackles with apprehension. "Did she send you ahead to sound me out?"

"Yes, she did." Gia yawns. "So what do you say?"

"I think I need to talk to her myself." Cisir feels numb. When he woke on his folding cot, he'd been looking forward to another foray into the manor's book collection. The prospect was almost enough to let him forget there could wait more humiliation, more shit or harsh words from Bulls he might meet on the way up the hill. He didn't foresee the danger coming from inside the house. From Gia, of all people. It tastes like betrayal.

Gia must know it would be so easy for him to love Qonna, but Qonna doesn't want him. Not truly. Not for what he can give her apart from completing her magical talents.

"If you mean to be horrible to her, I can't let that happen," Gia says, taking a deliberate sip of tea.

"I'm not going to be mean to her."

"It wasn't her idea."

"I know, but this is a situation I've been in before, and one I'm never going to enter lightly." *I'm not ready to take on such pain again.*

"Which gives you credit, but you'd also be responsible for ruining it for all three of us if you don't. You see, I have a vested interest in your betrothal too." She flashes him a sly smile.

*A vested interest?* "Gia?"

"How will I ever get to Birkland, if not with you both? I don't have brothers who can accompany me and I'm not allowed to join any of the Companies."

"Of all the men in Seagard, I'm the last Qonna should marry."

"She is aware—but your name was the only one that came up. You're bound anyway."

"We're not bound," he protests.

"You are, and you have quite a few witnesses to that." As she glances over his shoulder, Spark sits up, his brown eyes glued to her face. "If I understand correctly, any magic you can do is conditional on you working together. I would call that 'bound.'"

Cisir turns around to face the puppy, who is doing his best to fade into the background. "Fuck."

"You should probably talk to Jark too," Gia says, and there is the tiniest glint of glee in her eyes, a sure sign of what he thought he detected before: the satisfaction of stabbing someone in the back.

Cisir doesn't want to think about it but can't help himself. When he first met his master's daughter, he would've fallen over himself in haste to agree to such a match. So few weeks ago, his whole world was different, and he so desperate to be accepted by someone beautiful. When their names were first connected, when they started speaking to each other .... He kicks a stone from between the cobbles, and perhaps it is because he looks down so much, or because suddenly his future looms bright and terrifying, that he doesn't realize he and Spark are being followed.

When Spark presses against his calves, then nips at his trousers to catch his attention, Cisir blinks and comes to a halt. He passed the fork going down into the Westown and there are other people on the road with him, carts drawn by donkeys and heavy horses, transporting timber and clay into quarters where people have started to rebuild. But he can feel eyes on him, as if he's being touched.

One of them walks behind a cart but glances over every other step. Another one is coming up behind him; the hairs rise on Cisir's neck with his approach. They're not dressed in a specific way, ordinary-seeming men in work clothes, but chances are they saw him leave *Pomegranates* and rightly assume he's involved with the Birklanders. And he wears the yellow tunic—he can't pretend not to be affiliated. He marked himself clearly as a Sun, as someone who belongs somewhere.

Spark pushes against him, steers him into the middle of the road. He hadn't noticed how far he'd drifted to the side. This time, all the thoroughfares he could've used to hide are burned to ash.

He starts to walk faster and yes, the man next to the cart picks up his pace. He looks young but for a deep crease cutting his left cheek, and his palms are dirty. He bares his teeth at Cisir. They're pointed like a ferret's. Should he draw his knife?

*Fuck, fuck, fuck. If I live though this … if I live through this, Qonna and I might have to get married. She might have to throw herself away on me.*

He stops so abruptly that Spark runs into the back of his legs and lets out a frustrated bark.

"What?" Cisir snaps at the man who crosses the cobbles to get to him. "What do you want from me?"

He can feel the other one drawing closer too, and there's a third man, greasy-haired and with the same nasty grin. He might wear dirty clothes, but his nails are clean, and there's a pale line around his neck as if he usually wears a pendant. He isn't the one with the blade, though.

Cisir grasps the hilt of his own eating knife, but his palm is sweaty and he nearly drops it.

Spark growls, his ruff bristling.

"They said you'd hide behind your cur," the man with the blade says before he springs. He's on Spark in a flash and when Cisir hears the sudden high-pitched whine, he throws himself forward. He has no thought left but to save whoever this is hidden inside the puppy. The man screams as Cisir's knife punches into his thigh, as he rips the small blade out again to slash backwards and take out the priest in disguise. The man crumples against him, crashing to the cobbles and tripping up the third man, who catches himself at the last moment, going into a practiced half-crouch.

A noise like tearing silk makes Cisir gasp as Spark goes for the first man's throat with teeth that should never fit into the mouth of such a young dog. Cisir stares at the edge of the knife wielded by the third attacker, doubtless the most used to violence. He holds it point down like a chisel, and it's well-oiled and sharpened to the finest of points—the tool of a professional. However many hours Cisir spent in Windyhill, being forced through weapon forms by his tutors, he knows the only way he can get out alive is—

The man stumbles back as an arrow punches deep into his neck, red-fletched to match the blood. The man goes down like a sack of turnips.

"Not so clever now," the archer calls out.

A whole herd of Bulls is approaching, and at the front, waving a short bow, is none other than Rilk. He's not the only one armed. Between them, the Bulls carry more weapons than Cisir has seen outside of his father's armoury.

Rilk beams at him, but the effect is ruined by him hopping on one leg to ward off the puppy with the bloodied maw. "Get him away from me, for fuck's sake!"

Next to him walks the short Bull, who doesn't seem quite convinced saving Cisir's skin was a good idea.

Cisir takes Spark by the scruff and hauls him back. "What are you doing here?"

"Keeping an eye out for marauders," Rilk huffs, "and getting hapless Suns out of trouble, apparently. Where's your personal guard? Didn't you have one of them?"

Cisir croaks out, "Not anymore."

"Might've been useful." Rilk finds his grin again. "Can't believe you're stupid enough to wander about alone, as if all Westowners weren't out for your blood. Bo, have you seen any of them before?"

The short Bull bends over the dead man with the arrow in his neck. "Not this one." He turns the one with the ferret teeth over with his boot. "Him neither. That one seems more familiar, though." Bo kneels by the last attacker and rifles through the man's pockets. "Hah!" he calls out as he holds aloft the silver Star pendant, its chain the exact width of the pale line around the corpse's neck.

He glances at Cisir. "All jokes aside, you did good work."

The arrow that felled the final man is poking upright from his body, like the mast of the *Buttercup*. "You saved my life," Cisir says.

The five Bulls glance at each other. "Don't get weird ideas," Rilk says. "That doesn't mean we like you any better. We can't have priests and assassins jumping on Company members—Suns or Bulls."

For the first time, Cisir feels as if he could have something in common with this man. "You're a very good shot."

Rilk frowns. "All of us are. Let's get them out of the way, boys."

Quite a few carts have stopped, and their drivers are staring at the blood pooling on the cobbles.

The knife makes a clanging noise as it falls, bouncing off Cisir's boot. It wasn't just Rilk. Cisir killed one of them and wounded another badly enough for Spark to finish off. He might've cut a few people, deliberately or by mistake on the training field, but never had he spilled more than a few drops. Now blood congeals on the cold stones and his knees start to shake.

"Hey!" Bo props him up. "You're fine. No need for hysterics."

"Fuck, he's about to drop." Rilk hands the bow to another cousin. He and Bo usher Cisir to the side of the road, lean him against one of the houses. A carved bunch of grapes presses into Cisir's back as he doubles over, clutching his knees. Bo stays with him while the other Bulls carry the bodies to the other side of the street, worryingly familiar with such a gruesome task. The first carts start to roll again, as if nothing extraordinary happened.

"You're an odd one," Bo says, shaking his head. "Setting your dog on a guy to rip out his throat but going into meltdown straight after?"

*He's right. That was monstrous.* "How can you stay so calm?" Cisir grits out between forced breaths.

"Oh, we've always known there would be some kind of war," Bo says with a shrug. "That's what we've trained for since before the Bulls became the Bulls. You're lucky our uncle died in time for a new Bull to turn the ship around."

After the Bulls manage to commandeer a cart, they push Cisir onto the edge of it, and while the dead men's boots bump against his kidneys with every turn of the wheels, Spark runs behind the vehicle with flying ears. He's licked the blood off his face and appears once more like innocence personified. When they reach the Red House, the Sun's messenger boys throng to them, calling out in excitement, and suddenly there are more Bulls and laughter, Suns and Bulls patting each other's backs.

"Cisir?" His master comes at him in long strides. "Are you all right?"

Bo snorts. "Who can say?"

"Help me get him to his feet."

Bo looks as if he wants to protest but grabs Cisir's shoulder. Qes wraps a scarf around his hand before touching the other arm;  Bo's brow creases in confusion, but Cisir is grateful for the protection against the inevitable zap. It's still painful enough that he grits his teeth against it.

"I'm sorry." Cisir avoids his gaze. "This wasn't at all how this day was supposed to go."

"I'll say. I think he's good." Qes signals to Bo and the Bull retreats with a scowl.

"We think one of them might be a priest." Cisir points his chin back to the cart. "And I wouldn't—I couldn't ...." He draws a trembling breath. "I killed him. I killed a priest." Saying it out loud makes it real. Saying it out loud, he knows he's going to all Eight Hells.

"It seems you had to."

"I don't know."

Qes watches the Bulls and Suns milling around the cart. "It might have served some purpose," he mutters. "I believe this incident has put the Companies firmly on the same side."

The First Bull is once again in full regalia, complete with brooding snarl. "Do you believe these two occurrences to be related?"

"That's difficult to say," Qes admits, "but it feels as if someone has painted a target on our backs. My sons tell me it took three hours for them to wash the facade. Someone really wanted the shit to stick."

Bjell makes a noise against the roof of his mouth. "You won't mind me saying that today's attack seemed not so much directed at your family but your secretary?"

"Yes," Qes says with a sigh. "I think you might be correct. And I need to come to terms with the fact that soon we will have more assaults launched at specific people. We suspected Hevo would confess sooner rather than later."

"Confess to what?"

"To what happened to him."

Bjell's pale brows knit together. "Wasn't he hit on the head? I know of many cases where head injuries led to certain complications, at least for a while. People regularly lose their memories after such incidents. The Brothers saw him out cold with their own eyes. How do they know what he thinks he saw really took place?"

"Because they cling to everything that serves."

"You say this renegade of yours has become a threat to the Red House?"

"I'm afraid so."

"How can we kill him?"

Cisir gasps. "I don't want him killed!"

"The time for sentimentalities has passed." Bjell's thunderous face has its own beauty, but his words hit Cisir like a slap. "If we can extricate him from the temple, we will. We have quite a few cousins in the Star, and someone will be happy to put family before fervour."

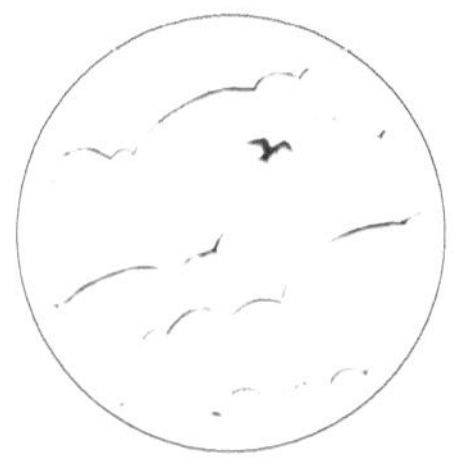

# QONNA

## *guard our hearts*

Footsteps thunder up *Pomegranates'* stairs. "Have you heard?" Noa bellows, her voice so loud it hurts Qonna's ears.

"What?" Gia flings the linen towel away, all too happy to be saved from yet another day of drudgery in the sick room.

"We could see it from far off this morning; my mother woke me early." Noa bounces up and down. "You need to come—we can't miss it!"

"What on earth are you talking about?" Qonna asks.

"The *Primrose*, of course! If we don't hurry, we'll miss the first people coming to land. Just in time too—my uncle announced he'll leave Seagard after the memorial and I was afraid he'd make Father come with him, but now we can be part of the arrival celebrations!" She pulls Gia out of the door. It's before the midday bells, but they're far from the only people making their way down the hill. *Pomegranates* might've been the last house to get the news. There are more carts on the streets than usual, many of them with drivers wearing pieces of red or yellow—a sign they've been hired by the Companies.

It feels amazing, rushing downhill in a group of three, a wonderful, timely distraction from all the unanswered questions taking over Qonna's life. Here is the ship that carries not only her father's hopes but her own. Even with so many people crowding the empty spaces once covered in warehouses and taverns, the vessel brought into the harbour is huge, like a floating house, its yellow sails furled tightly.

Its crew line up at the rail, waving so hard they're surely about to pop their arms from their sockets, though some faces are streaked with tears. Perhaps it's the view of the fire's aftermath or merely the prospect of reaching the safety of the harbour that makes the men so emotional, but Qonna fights a lump in her own throat. Among so many people, her own relief is eclipsed by the shouts around her. Noa cheers and jumps up and down, her headdress fluttering in the breeze. They might get in trouble for abandoning *Pomegranates* and their stations, but on that ship, its ochre-yellow paint stripped off its bulge by the wind, salt, and waves, lies the key to the Sun's resurrection.

Qonna and Gia manoeuvre Noa through the mass of citizens receiving the ship with deafening joy. Every cask of syrup, every pelt stored on board will contribute to the city's rebuild, the investors will be rewarded, and the Suns on board will not be added to the list of people lost at sea. Skins of wine make an appearance among the onlookers, passing from mouth to mouth.

"Time to back off," Gia yells in Qonna's face. "Let's get out of here before it's too late."

They both reach forward to drag Noa away by the shoulders.

"Wait, for fuck's sake, the ramp hasn't gone up yet," the princess yells.

"We'll see more from further away and not get trampled," Gia says.

"But ...."

"We shouldn't be out here in the first place," Gia states firmly, before they pull Noa up the hill. More and more people flock to the quay, and where a week ago the bodies of the fire's victims were collected, people are cheering ever louder. A great noise rises like the swell of a wave as the ramp is finally lowered into place and the first Suns climb over. From up the road they appear rangy and shaggy, as if they battled more than the elements on their voyage. Amidst the carts pushing through the crowd Qonna can make out more yellow tunics. She spots the dark curls of her father as he shoulders his way to the ramp.

Arrival days have always been celebrations, but this time the whole city glories in the survival of the *Primrose*. Qonna's father embraces the Suns, his face bright red.

Noa starts to bounce again. She seems to be the only member of the royal family at the scene, and likely shouldn't represent her father's interests on such a momentous day, when the first shreds of hope appear like streaks of sunlight splashed across the skies after Longest Night.

"Right, we're going," Qonna decides. "Back to *Pomegranates.*"

"Awww ...."

Gia nods her approval. "This might get out of control. We need to keep you safe, Noa."

As they push through people uphill, Qonna can't resist turning around one last time. The *Primrose* gently moves up and down with the waters, like a living thing breathing in and out. If she can overcome the obstacles thrown at her, she'll be the one climbing that ramp, making herself familiar with the layout of the decks and the smells, good and bad.

Qonna finds Cisir sitting at the brazier, a bowl of tea cradled in his palms. Spark lies at his feet, chin on paws, glancing up at Qonna accusingly.

"I thought you'd be down at the harbour," she says.

"Your father thought it better for me to keep my head down." It's the first time they've come face to face since Gia volunteered to put the all-important question to him. Qonna should've been the one to ask but sending Gia into to the breach gave her the opportunity to think the whole situation over.

Cisir sits hunched, as if he wants to make himself smaller, his hair bunched up in a careless knot. His bare neck is stippled with small red marks left over from sparks and splinters.

"Cisir, I'm sorry. When Gia offered to test the water with you, I was too relieved to refuse. I should've asked you directly."

"Yes, you should have." He takes a sip of tea. "I understand. I think I would've tried to wiggle out too."

She leans in. "Have you thought about it? I mean, you know I wouldn't ask you if I saw another way forward, right?"

"Did your mother specify it must be me?" he asks.

"No. But of all the people I know, you're the only one I can see myself getting married to, and whatever contracts my mother wants us to sign, I would make sure we go into our understanding with eyes wide open and our own set of rules."

"The last time I tried to be honest, my engagement blew up in my face," he murmurs.

"I know it's hard for you. It's hard for us both." She wishes he could see that she's giving up something too. "We're starting off from a very different point. With you I'd be sure we could give each other the space to breathe, that we're friends, first and foremost."

"What about later? What if we meet other people we want to be with?"

*Or if we've already met them?* "Clearly we would work out rules about that too."

"What about Jark?" His voice hitches.

"You're welcome to keep him."

"Truly?"

She looks into his eyes. "Yes."

He exhales a shuddering breath. "I need more time to think about it."

"Of course."

Something in his cheek twitches and Spark glances up abruptly, as if he senses a shift.

Qonna sits next to him. "You weren't hurt, were you? When they came after you again?"

"No, but it was a close call. Very close. Whatever positive developments will come from it … I killed someone, Qonna. I've never done that before."

*I wonder if I could bear it easier.* "I'm sorry. I wish I had the right words to make you feel better about it."

"I don't expect you to," he says quietly.

"I know, but I wish to help you." She touches his shoulder. The sensation that floods her, floods them both, feels like sun falling across her skin, warm and soothing. As if she stepped through a door into a space where she feels at home.

Cisir makes a low noise of surprise, his eyes wide and starkly blue. He lifts his arm, covering her hand in his, and light wavers around their fingers like pale flames dancing. His touch becomes a caress across the back of her hand, and then their fingers weave together.

Spark gives a worried yip as the power surges between them, as yet undirected, soft and oddly benevolent for something that could so easily flip towards destruction.

Nearing footsteps rip them from the moment. One of the maids enters to collect more laundry. Now that the sick room grows ever emptier, the old tasks slot back into place. On her face Qonna reads disapproval, as if she'd caught them kissing, not just sitting close. Uncomfortable silence vibrates in the room until she leaves with the overflowing basket on her right hip and pulls the door closed with force.

"She's going to tell the cook," Qonna says, "and soon Mother will know."

Spark whines and Cisir turns to him. "You have something to say—say it."

The puppy's outline flickers, slowly revealing Teasel, sitting with his legs pulled up against his chest and with no apparent concern for his modesty.

Qonna wills her eyes upwards to his face. The sorcerer seems thinner than the last time she saw him in human form, with none of the puppy's softness left.

"You're up to your necks in the mess," he rasps. "It makes no sense to fight it now." He pulls his legs under him. "As I understand it, your names have long been brought up in the same breath. It's too late to step back."

"No," Qonna interjects with a rush of desperation. "It's not too late if we decide that we can't come to a solution that works for us both."

"You felt it," Teasel says sternly. "You're settling into your strength. It will mould itself with every touch between you. As little as I understand your specific kind of magic, it is not that difficult to grasp the principle."

"It has nothing to do with marrying each other," Qonna replies, her throat beginning to close.

"It will mean a life spent in proximity, whatever you choose to do. Get it over with. All this hemming and hawing would bore the strongest man to tears." He drags his hair away from his face. "Fuck each other, don't fuck each other—*nobody cares*."

Lying next to Gia, Qonna can't drop off to sleep. There are only five patients left. The others have joined their families in the camp on the hill, and it feels as if they're finally allowed to draw breath.

"You've been turning like a millstone ever since we went to bed," Gia grumbles. "How am I supposed to rest with that going on? Are you thinking about this morning? We got Noa out, safe and sound. I don't think anyone knew who she was. We might've stayed longer."

*Keeping Noa safe. Somehow that's the most important thing of all.* "I know, though the thought of all of them getting drunk around us frightened me a bit."

"We need a reason to celebrate," Gia says, "and what better opportunity than such a great success for the Suns—and the Bulls, seeing that they'll profit off storage and transportation fees?"

"That's not really what I'm fretting about."

"What then?"

"I think Cisir will agree to my proposal."

"Isn't that a good thing?" Gia asks, nonplussed.

"Whatever promises we make to each other, we're bound to clash."

"Because he wants to have Jark and you want to have ...." She waggles her brows suggestively.

"Exactly. It looks like a simple solution, but it will become so complicated if we want to make sure neither of us gets hurt."

"You care enough for each other to worry about that. I'd say it's a good beginning, better than most people are granted. You might come to love him one day."

"I think I might already, in a way. Right now I don't have a particular interest in anyone else. What happens if I fall head over heels in love one day? He might change his mind quickly."

"He might—and you might find that you experience more jealousy than expected too. Don't forget, Qonna, if he agrees, you'll join Nian da Nileon on the *Primrose*. You'll sail to the old country and bring back stories of great adventures."

"If we survive," Qonna mutters.

"If the gods grant it." Gia folds her elbow beneath her head to study Qonna's face. "If you go, I can go too. We can all get out of the city and be among people we share blood with. Somewhere we're accepted."

*To be accepted. That might be too tempting to consider.* "True, but we'll also bring something with us, something that might frighten the most stout-hearted of Birklanders. Something none of us understand yet."

"It's a quest for knowledge," Gia pronounces. "Like in the old legends. Dad told me so many of them when I was little. Monsters running free in the forests and curses carried through generations by blood. I really liked the gory ones, until one day I only ever wanted to hear about heroes falling in love and fighting against all odds to be together with the ones they love."

"I liked werebear stories too," Qonna recalls, "though Mother deeply disapproved of them."

Glancing over Gia's shoulder, Qonna can see the outline of the little box in the dark—the box in which she now stores the likeness of Sister Sun and her half of the golden shell during the night.

Gia notices and takes her hand. Her voice sounds raw as she whispers, "Sister Sun, guard our hearts. Grant us strength for the things ahead, to make the difficult decisions without regret and to open our minds for the eventualities that might scare us at first. Do you want to go on, Qonna?"

Gia's hand is warm and her hold calms Qonna enough to pick up the prayer. "Sister Sun, please protect my family, my friends, and this city. Whatever happens, whatever opportunities you send our way, we aim to follow your will."

# CISIR

## *inside out*

For several nights, Cisir dreams of Windyhill. Of being small and lost within its walls, of his tutors screaming at him and his father's silent disdain. Every morning, he wakes covered in sweat with Spark's paw on his shoulder, as if the puppy couldn't bear to see him writhe in his cot for a moment longer and has shaken him awake.

He starts these days with the unmovable knowledge that though his father did his best to teach his oldest son how to kill as soon as Cisir was able to run unaided, he would also hate Cisir for the disgraceful way he handled the attack on the street, how he wasn't skilled enough to get out of a brawl without spilling that much blood.

It doesn't help that while Cisir's head knows he was merely defending himself against attackers, at least one of them trained, his stomach tries to turn itself inside out as soon as he sets foot on cobbles. Each morning it's a fight to get out of the house. He leaves as early as possible, and though his master offered to arrange for a guard again, Cisir knows he couldn't stand walking with someone other than Jark, and if Jark volunteered his services, it would be even weirder.

The early hours protect him, as does the knowledge of what kind of teeth are hiding in Spark's soft muzzle. The puppy who trots next to him on big paws keeps a watchful eye on every citizen they pass so close to sun-up, when most of the population is barely awake.

Before Shortest Night there should be some preparations underway to hint at the festival to come. In Windyhill—or Chillyhill, as he's started to think of it—there would be piles of wood along the road ready to be stacked into a gigantic bonfire, and the smell of baking would waver through the village, its communal ovens not allowed to rest for weeks on end. Piglets would be selected for slaughter, and most of the young women would be busy talking about their dresses for the night and if the travelling musicians still had the handsome drummer with them, the one granted more favours than the local men, who took them with an easy smile, much used to being admired. No one would suggest having a bonfire in Seagard this year and there are barely enough houses left to decorate. Whoever tried to hang a garland across the door would likely deal with the same horseshit debacle as *Pomegranates*.

Even the manor sports no sign of the upcoming festivities; the guards posted at its gates greet him with bleary eyes. They expect him to be here, to walk into the house as if he works at the manor. He can hear snoring in the living quarters as he lets himself and Spark into the library.

With Noa's help he's collected everything they've found so far in one corner of the shelving. He takes off his cloak and folds it for Spark to sleep on before pulling the books out.

"I saw you coming up." Jark pushes the door open. He's not yet in his armour and clearly put his shirt on in haste. All its seams are showing. "You look awful," he teases.

Cisir doesn't have the strength to play. "I haven't been sleeping well."

"No one sleeps well anymore." Jark glances at the pile of volumes. "You appear to have a full morning ahead of you. Do you have time for me? For a quick talk?"

*Into the breach.* "Yes. I think we have to."

"Now that the *Primrose* is back and being made ready for another journey, I heard Nian da Nileon speaking to the crown prince about his plans. Are you still preparing to go with him?"

"Yes."

Jark's eyes are red-rimmed, as if he's rubbed them raw. "Have you decided yet, if … if you'll agree to the marriage?"

It feels as if Cisir's guts are being pulled out through his throat. "How do you know about that?"

"It turns out Nian is well informed. He certainly seems to think there was no other way to allow Qonna to come, and without her … I don't know why, but you're connected in some way. As a good friend, I believe you'll make up your mind to give her this chance at getting out of the city. And since you're living at *Pomegranates* now, you must have many opportunities to get close to her. You're seeing a lot more of her than of me, and I wanted to be clear about … if you need me to step out of the way …."

"No! No, Qonna would never ask you to do that."

Jark's shoulders fall. "Are you sure? I don't want to come underfoot."

Cisir's knees shake and he sinks to one of the stools close to the hide-covered window. Sometimes having rules in place is easier and being given a choice—a true choice—impossible. Spark runs to him, licks his hands, and Cisir can almost forget who he is. He leans in; the puppy's coat is impossibly soft against his face.

"I'm sorry." Jark hovers close, as if torn between the wish to touch him and the desire to get out of the situation as quickly as possible. "It must be overwhelming."

"Yes, it is. But Nian is right. Qonna's mother was extremely clear with her conditions. I owe them all, more than I wish to think about. I'm aware being married to Qonna would be a different arrangement than my previous engagement, but I can't help but remember …."

Jark pushes the other stool close with the tip of his boot. When he sits down, his right knee almost presses into Cisir's thigh, but he takes care not to let it. "You're right. Qonna is kind, generous, and open-hearted. She would not wish to cause you pain."

"She will, nonetheless. And I'll hurt her too. There's no way around it. Qonna deserves a well-thought-out wedding, but under these circumstances there won't be more than a few weeks to scrape everything together. She shouldn't have to compromise."

Jark reaches out to scratch Spark's chin. "I'm sure these reservations do you credit, but I think you know she only needs the priest to race through the rituals so she can jump aboard."

Having Jark so close makes his body ache. He so wishes he could be reckless enough to—Jark's hand slips from Spark's shoulder to Cisir's knee, his palm burning through the fabric as it slides higher, deeper, then cups him so gently Cisir knows he expects to be pushed off.

"I wish …," Cisir manages to croak out. "I wish it were that simple."

"You said yourself there isn't much time before you'll be given away—and if you allow me, I would very much like to be the first to claim you, despite all that is set to come your way."

His fingers dig in harder, and a little yelp breaks from Cisir. "Yes?" Jark asks, not waiting for him to get his courage up to speak.

"I … I can't, not in front of the dog. Or the books."

"They've built an improvised hay store behind the stables. You can meet me there."

"Yes?" It comes out like a question and Cisir hates himself for it.

Jark smiles and releases him. "Wait a bit before you follow." He jumps up.

Cisir tries to catch his wrist, but Jark is out the door before he can be held back, leaving Cisir blinking at Spark as the door snicks shut. Apparently, from now on, everything will happen much too fast.

*He's probably used the hay store before. You can't be the only one he keeps on with—he didn't hesitate. You shouldn't have agreed. You're weak and he knows it.*

Spark nudges his leg as if to encourage him. As if this unhelpful hesitation is something else he can't bear to watch.

"Don't," Cisir says sternly. "I shouldn't do it."

Spark gives one of his doggy shrugs, and the situation is so incredibly absurd Cisir can't help but laugh. He also can't deny that he wants to sleep with Jark in the hay store. Every priest of the Star would blanch at how clearly defined his dilemma is, and still, the grasp of Jark's hand lingers.

"Can you please stay here?" he asks.

Spark gives a short shake of the head.

"Thought as much. But could you sit at a distance—keep watch?"

Dogs can't actually grin, but Spark gives it his best attempt.

"Fuck it." Cisir's trousers are still painfully tight, but thankfully the cloak is long enough to hide his arousal. He abandons the pile of books.

The manor is waking up and there's no time to lose. He darts out the side door, gravel pulling at the soles of his boots as he does his best not to sprint across the yard.

*This is everything you were warned about in Chillyhill—the temptation of the Cities. You're proving them all correct, all the words they spat at you.*

The hay store seems to be a repurposed shelter for horses grazing around the stables, enclosed with hazel-rod hurdles and strewn with last year's leftovers. In a few weeks it'll be packed solid, but for now it's dry, empty, and out of the way as can be. No one has any reason to check on it.

Cisir's heart hammers, his knees shaky again with fear but also with the overwhelming want to not think about the future all the time, to be swept away by someone who's been there before, who knows where the path leads.

Spark falls more and more behind. How strange that having the sorcerer's blessing makes it easier. *Of course he approves. You already know he's a degenerate criminal. Don't act so surprised.*

"Jark?"

*He's not here. It was a joke, a test to see if you're desperate enough to fall for pretty words.*

The shelter's corners are filled with trampled hay and the damp smell left after winter. His heart shrivels.

Someone comes up behind him—someone Spark doesn't intercept.

Jark's arms wrap around him, and his mouth is on Cisir's neck. The relief of not having run into a trap, of Jark being here, with him, is enough to melt Cisir's last resistance. Jark's hands burrow under cloak and belt. "I wasn't sure you'd actually come," he whispers, before pulling the shirt away and kissing Cisir's shoulder. "I need to be up and ready for my shift soon, so we won't have as much time as I would like."

"Fine," Cisir says. "That's fine."

He turns around and their bodies collide. Jark swallows his moans as he pushes Cisir against the hurdles, then goes to his knees, taking Cisir's belt and trousers with him.

Cisir stares down at him, confused, but then Jark's mouth moves onto him and all he can do is clutch at the rough wall and not curse.

"I was about to sort the books away," Noa says reproachfully.

Blood shoots into Cisir's face. "Sorry, I was caught short."

"That must've been some shit." The Princess of Crooked Hill grins, making him freeze. "What? Did I say something wrong?"

"I don't think your father would appreciate that kind of language." Cisir ducks his head to hide the blush.

"My father doesn't but my mother adores it. Believe me, both have heard worse from me. Did you manage to find out something new before your … distraction?"

*This princess is too clever for her own good.* "No."

"Then aren't you lucky you have me? I expect you to sing my praises to Qonna when you get home." She spreads her notes in front of her, absentmindedly petting Spark's head as he pushes in. "I found a story in the Riverclere manuscripts about two brothers who only were able to work spells together."

"Really?"

She pulls one of the ratty-looking books closer. "Here. *Two Owls for a Tree.*"

"But Qonna's family are Badgers."

"Your family sigil is an owl."

"Noa …," he warns. He doesn't want to hear that the family he felt hard done by could be the reason behind the gift, behind being one half of Qonna's magic.

"Families pick their sigils for a reason. We da Nileons carry the sun because once we were given our right to rule from the Heavens, or so they said. Qonna's mother likes unicorns because … I actually don't know why. Maybe one of her ancestors killed a bunch of them."

"Why are they called Owls in the story?"

"Because they were in the habit of travelling on the wing. They could only do the transformation together and when one of the brothers was killed, the other was forced to remain a bird forever more."

"Are there many stories that feature shapeshifters?"

"Quite a few." Noa's yellow eyes glance in Spark's direction. She saw him cross the boundary into the land of the dead; she must have her suspicions. "Is that what we're dealing with here?" she asks. "A wizard who shifts?"

Cisir lifts a shoulder. "I think so, yes."

"But he licked my face," she shrieks.

"Yes."

"Do I have to count that as a kiss?" Noa sounds horrified.

It's all too much—the memory of Jark's mouth wrapped around him, his tongue working in tight circles, and the thought of how many times Spark slobbered on his hands. Cisir laughs. "I don't think so, Noa."

"Thank the Heavens. I always wanted to have my first kiss with someone special." She narrows her eyes at Spark. "But not that special. Bad dog—bad, bad wizard."

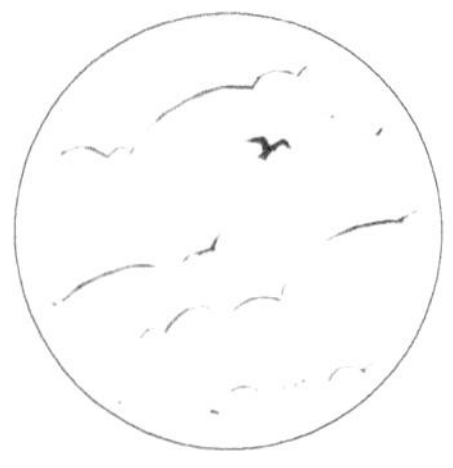

# QONNA

## *short notice*

Cisir's hand is sweaty and Qonna can sense the underlying tremble. It echoes her own. She smiles at him.

"Mother!" Qonna calls. "We have something to tell you."

The relief on her mother's face is stark. "Yes?"

"Cisir has agreed to marry me." It was supposed to sound more triumphant but comes out squeaky.

"That took you long enough." Her mother rises from the edge of the patient's cot, then leans in and kisses first Qonna's cheek, then Cisir's, and for once he doesn't blush; his mouth only sets in a line. "I hope you managed to think through all eventualities."

"I tried," he admits.

"Dad?" Qonna turns to her father, whose eyes have gone suspiciously shiny. "Would you like to congratulate us?"

"Of course." He jumps forward but thinks better of touching his future son-in-law. He swerves to Qonna instead.

"I hope you didn't feel as if I pushed you to it," he whispers.

Qonna can feel her mother's stare on them both. "Don't worry about it." She hugs him back.

"We'll celebrate as best we can at such short notice."

"Qes," her mother interrupts. "We talked about this. We'll have a quick ceremony now and something grander after you return."

Her father nods, holding on to Qonna. "To ensure everyone in Seagard is aware you've married into an ancient, noble family." He gives her a kiss on the cheek and steps back. "For now, I hope you're happy with a private celebration."

"Of course."

Her mother smiles coldly. "I've already contacted Brother Rago to get things underway."

Resentment bubbles up in Qonna's chest. "You have? Before you knew we were going through with it?"

"I knew you'd find someone willing," her mother says bluntly. "You've always been the most headstrong of my children." For once her statement is filled with pride.

Qonna feels numb. Suddenly the future is crashing over her head. She stands in her room, staring at the floor.

"What dress were you thinking of?" Gia asks.

"I don't know. I'm not sure I care."

"Well, I care," her best friend huffs, "and if you're not getting married in blue, I'm going to revolt."

"Can I leave you in charge?" Qonna mumbles.

"Don't be ridiculous. It might only be a private ceremony, but you should feel good about your choices. Will you keep your hair covered?"

"Yes, of course."

"As you wish." Gia makes a quick note on a scrap of spaper. "What about jewellery? Has your mother kept something back for the day?"

"What?"

"My mother always promised me her pearl combs for my wedding day."

"That's not something we ever talked about." *Perhaps I should've seen that as a sign.*

"I'm trying hard not to get frustrated with you. Why aren't you more excited?"

"Because I'm overwhelmed. This … this is the means to an end, Gia. Nothing more, nothing less. I need to get it over with to set foot on the *Primrose,* and that's as far as I want to think."

Gia narrows her eyes "You don't want to have a wedding night—of sorts?" she presses.

"No." The realization hits her like a boulder crashing through water. "No, I don't want a wedding night, and to make sure there are no misunderstandings, I need to start on the contract."

"Which contract?"

"We need documentation. It was one of Cisir's requests and I think it's a good idea. Something we can both point to later."

"Hmhm." Gia frowns, clearly unhappy with something so mundane taking centre stage before the wedding. "What are you afraid of, Qonna?"

"The last thing I want is lose his friendship because he's too timid to protest. My mother is correct in one thing: I am headstrong, and sometimes I can't help but go through the wall. He needs to have some protection. Blue dress, then. I probably need a fancier head covering. Hopefully Mother has something hidden away, if she already put advance orders on the priest."

"Hmhm. I thought I'd be wildly jealous of this arrangement, but now I wish you were more enthusiastic."

*It must be a joke. How can anyone be jealous of being sold off?* "Give me a day or two to adjust, and maybe I can manage a squeal."


"Congratulations."

"Awww," Qonna says. "Fuck off, Teasel."

The sorcerer has the gall to look hurt. "I only wanted to …."

Cisir sighs. "Without you we probably wouldn't be in this situation. Cut her some slack."

Teasel puffs out his freckled chest. "Without me, your friend Hevo would've died, and you would have to wait for another set of unlikely circumstances to find out you both carry gifts—or at least half of a gift each. Without me—" He leaves off with a growl.

"Go on," Qonna presses. "What were you going to say?"

"Without me, you both might never have been born."

Qonna nearly swallows her tongue.

"What? Why?" Cisir leans forward on his seat.

"Because the smallest things can have the biggest consequences, and no decision a sorcerer makes is ever unimportant. I've done many things in my time, in the service of the most powerful queens of the age. If I hadn't, none of the Eight Kingdoms might exist as they do today, and you'd be living in a very different world. If I hadn't been imprisoned at the time I was, maybe the whole continent would've exploded and *bam*! Seagard would never have been."

Cisir snorts. "*Bam*?"

Teasel crosses his arms. "Yes. You're lucky I found myself disposed to help your friend. I'm not obligated to do anything nice for anyone. Thankfully, I happen to believe that it's never too late to try and make up for past mistakes."

Qonna finds it strange that she's starting to look forward to the times when Teasel appears in his human form. By now she's almost able to ignore that he seems unaware that he's not wearing clothes, or maybe she's fine with it because, apart from her initial curiosity, she feels no attraction to this scarred slender man, while her future husband is noticeably uncomfortable and blushing at random moments in the conversation.

They only have a few hours left in which they can both consider themselves unattached. She'd tried to push any thought of the truth of her situation away, had been so happy to sacrifice her freedom for the chance to get out of Seagard. She should've thought it through in its entirety, not the welcome side effects, but the actual relationship she'll embark on. Tomorrow … how on earth can tomorrow be the day she gets married?

"You look stunned." Qatt pushes into the room. He's dusty, his forearms streaked with dirt. "I'm sorry it all happened so quickly. No one should get married on the day of the memorial."

"It's also the day of Shortest Night, but I know what you mean."

He holds the door open behind him and Qov and Qitli follow, as if they sent Qatt in first to test the situation.

"Can we hug you?" Qitli asks, "or is that weird?"

"Not weird at all." For the first time since Qonna broke the news to her parents, tears well up. Each of her brothers waits patiently until it's their turn to be embraced. They smell of smoke, but also a bit mouldy, as if they spent their whole day grubbing through rotting planks. Whatever happened, however resentful she felt towards her brothers in the past, she knows she'll miss them.

"We'll have a really big party when you're back east," Qatt promises. "Seagard won't know what hit it."

"You three will be proper Suns by then," Qonna warns. "Everything will be different."

"Have you heard about the plans for the harbour bridge?" Qov asks.

"No—what's going to happen?"

"Dad wants something purpose-built, and it seems the Bulls might join in the redevelopment. The Company Houses might be the first buildings everyone will see when approaching the city. They had the site properly measured today, lots of people running about and shouting numbers at each other." Qatt grins.

"I'll miss all of it," Qonna says.

"Only if the Bulls decide to move forward soon," her eldest brother replies. "If they dig in their heels, it might all come to nothing."

"Dad seems to have established a good rapport with the First Bull," Qonna says.

Qov shrugs. "Which also can change."

"You don't need to assuage me. It's not as if I'm going to have much time to bemoan my plight."

"Sailing can be boring, though," Qitli says. "Even if you're newly married and have your best friend with you."

"I'm sure we'll find something to talk about."

Qatt sniffs. "Just be careful no one catches you practising. Seamen are famously superstitious, and they probably won't develop a sudden sense of humour about witchcraft and sorcery overnight."

"I'll be careful." She clings to her brother's arm. "I promise."

It's the first time she feels part of the group, all children who were born in *Pomegranates*, who lost and gained significant parts of their future since the fire spread through town.

When Gia storms in, arms heaped with a mass of diaphanous sky-blue linen, it takes Qonna a while to disentangle from her brothers.

Qitli wipes tears from his face. "Do you want us to pray for you?" he asks, his voice thick.

Qonna smiles at her youngest brother. "Please. Whatever gods there are, I could use as much good will as possible."

The next to drop by are Noa and her brother, and while the wayward prince seems excited by the prospect of his plans forging ahead, Noa's mood is much more subdued.

"Where's the groom-to-be?" Nian asks as they push the seats around to make her father's study as comfortable as possible for their visit. Looking at him—or her—Qonna wonders what will change in their relationship once they reach the old country. Will Lilyis treat her the same as Nian?

"Getting his affairs in order," Gia mutters through a mouth full of pins. "Noa, what do you think?"

The princess eyes the sky-blue folds. "Remember that the construction needs to live through the memorial first."

"Won't there be time for a change and adjustment?" Qonna asks. "I'd rather not turn up at the burial grounds like a ship under full sail."

"Good point," the prince says. "Is there tea?"

"You find us in great disarray this morning," Qonna lets out a long sigh. "But I'm sure we can get something from the kitchen for you."

"Don't bother," Noa says. "We won't stay long. We wanted to check in on you."

"But ...." Nian gives a frustrated snort.

"They're obviously extremely busy," his sister scolds, "with a wedding to be organized at a mere moment's notice."

"I'm sorry, Noa. It wasn't supposed to be such a hurried operation, but we're doing our best to work to your schedule."

Nian nods, the corner of his mouth twitching. "The *Primrose* has been nearly emptied of its load and will start to take on fresh water after Shortest Night. Thankfully, we don't have to wait for significant repairs to be made, though I have asked for it to be painted. I don't fancy arriving at the Stoneharp in a ship bleached like an old apple crate. We need to give them something impressive."

"The Stoneharp …." Images of impossibly high walls and a multitude of towers rise in front of Qonna's inner eye. She's heard stories of the Stoneharp for as long as she can remember. "I can't quite believe this is where we'll land."

"Unless Sister Storm has different plans for us." Nian turns over paper scraps and pens on her father's desk as if searching for something. "Though during all my crossings, I only remember being blown off course three times, and the *Primrose*'s navigator is one of the most experienced in Birkland's waters."

"You're probably looking forward to getting back." Qonna holds Gia's half-pinned creation in place with one hand.

"Very much so. I always enjoy autumn in the west. Especially as we should have enough time to reach Goldenlake before its peak season."

"Goldenlake?" A couple of pins fall from Gia's mouth, and she curses. "You plan to bring us so far over land?"

"There aren't many wizards left in the Stoneharp these days, so our best chance is for the Golden Lake to provide," the prince says. "If you truly want to explore the potential of your connection. I mean, we'll have to check with Sloe first, but I'm quite sure this will be what they'll say. Are you having second thoughts, Gia?"

"Thank you," Gia says to Noa, who's crouched down to retrieve the pins before they get lost between the floorboards. "Not as such, but there are many days' travel between the west coast and the shores of the lake. Territories of a lot of different families."

"Birkland has changed a fair bit since your father left its steppes," Nian reassures her. "There are many more posts, many more Suns happy to help us across the land."

"Will there be werebears?" Qonna asks, a bit breathless.

"There might be—though nowadays they've withdrawn much deeper into the forests."

"I wonder how Spark will react to them."

The prince blinks, and—for the first time—seems nervous. "We can but wait and see. Do you really want to attend the memorial, Qonna? No one would be surprised if you gave it a miss."

"Many who will be honoured tomorrow gave their lives for the Sun. I'm sure my parents expect me to come with them."

Nian shudders. "My uncle has been practicing his speech for days. I can't wait for it to be over, all this show of piety and sorrow for people we never knew."

"You knew Yoren," Qonna says.

A cloud falls over the prince's face. "You're right. I forgot about him."

"This is why I need to go." She studies the prince, the person her father calls Lilyis. He—soon to be she—bites his lower lip, as if there are many things to add, but nothing that wouldn't hurt her.

# CISIR

## *running towards the gods*

The procession forms on the cleared main road leading up from the temple. Despite grumblings and ever louder criticism around the Westown, the city has come out in force, as if no one is willing to risk slighting the gods of the Star on this day, even if the crown prince has never been a popular person around these parts.

The Suns and Bulls have their own divisions to walk in, quite close to the head of the long line of dignitaries, and what's more, no one is on horseback, by royal decree. The whole da Nileon family walks with the citizens, and though they're flanked by their guards in their best and most colourful attire, with Jark somewhere among them, their gesture of humility surely isn't missed.

The atmosphere is sombre as is befitting, voices hushed, and necks bent. The guilds of Seagard march behind the Companies, each proceeded by a standard proclaiming their trade. Walking behind the Suns and Bulls are the Goldsmiths, the embroidered cloth hanging from their standard slightly burned at its left edge, rescued in the nick of time. There are the Bookbinders, Bakers, Dyers, and obviously, the Braid Makers, and these are just the delegations within Cisir's sight. All have lost members to the fire and many of the attendants are limping or sporting bandages and burned-off brows.

In his own division, the Companies have sorted their members into one row of yellow tunics followed by a row of red, repeating through the ranks. Both the First Sun and the First Bull lead their stripy throng uphill. Even Spark wears a collar of yellow and red braid, as well as a broad leash he puts up with under protest.

Cisir's tunic is freshly laundered, but he's already sweating through it. Summer has taken its cue to begin strong. Perhaps it was to be expected Sister Sun would bless the day, though it's not nearly as appropriate for the kind of ceremony Cisir needs to get through first.

The streets are lined with people watching the procession and joining in as soon as it passes them. The queue slows somewhat on the steepest part of the hill, before the thorn hedge surrounding the burial grounds juts out from the side of the road, covered in feathery leaves and the remnant of blossoms. The gate is festooned with da Nileon banners, new and blazing, the grim-faced depiction of the sun a reminder that it's a privilege for each citizen to come this close to the ruling family.

Noa and her mother are among the women who went straight to the burial grounds and are watching behind their veils as the rest of the attendants arrive.

Cisir spots Qonna and Gia, and both their mothers too, quite close to the royal delegation. The woman who will marry him in a few hours stands tall, her shoulders squared, as if the memorial is a mere inconvenience to get over. In front of the women, the long pits have been filled in and covered in turf to make it seem as if they've long since grown over. Among them stands the marker, commissioned by the crown prince and shaped like a writhing grey flame. It's much larger than Cisir expected. His gaze finds Qonna's. He can't be the only one who's reminded of the stones on the grounds of the manor, anchored deep in the hill to stand upright. The lead trembles in his clenched fist.

A group of priests makes its way through the guard, past the members of the royal family. In their long robes of unbleached wool, they stick out from the citizens dressed in their flamboyant best, and people shrink back from them, give them much more space than needed. Perhaps they're unaware of the irony as they gather around the flame hewn from stone to begin proceedings, but though Cisir and Spark stand quite far away, Cisir can see the smirk on the crown prince's face, which almost distracts him from the fact that behind the priests, more men dressed in muted colours have started to appear, all wearing expressions of penitence.

One of them stands at the furthest edge. Hevo's dark hair is clipped severely, baring the angry red scar across his scalp. It seems as if Hevo isn't the only young man running towards the gods, while so many others lie buried at their feet.

"… and by the grace of the Star …."

The voice of the crown prince echoes around the grounds. Whatever rumours have made the rounds while the old king has continues clinging to power, no one can fault Nurin's technique. While his face becomes slightly sun-burned, he calls to his future subjects, "… that every one of us who is able to praise their names, will always keep these days in their heart—when the city of Seagard was almost broken, but refused to be. When we look back in remembrance, we will always mourn the people who gave their lives to ensure the city's glorious rise."

No one applauds—it's not that kind of ceremony—but Cisir hears pleased muttering around him as Nurin da Nileon, future king of the Hillakes and Southclere, withdraws, sweaty and inconvenienced.

Next to him, his young wife is crying into her veils, her companions drawn around her like a protective wall—among them Qonna's older friend, though her face shows only disdain.

Cisir flinches as Spark pushes his wet nose against his hand. He hadn't noticed his fists were balled, that his joints hurt from holding on so tightly. He forces himself to breathe out.

No one in their right mind would use this day to launch an attack. It's Shortest Night, one of the dates in the calendar when the Heavens are closest to earth, where the gods' attention is particularly drawn to all people beneath its canopy. There might be no bonfires this year, but there will many prayers, and every wish uttered this night brings with it increased urgency.

Cisir stares at the last of the Star's penitents. Hevo should've walked with the Suns and Bulls today, clothed in their colours, but instead he wears a dust-grey tunic and linen trousers. He's barefoot, as befits his new status.

Spark pushes Cisir again, then nips at his thumb to drive the point home.

"What?" Cisir hisses.

The puppy leans against his leash.

"We can't move yet. We need to wait."

Rilk shoots Cisir an irritated glance for interrupting the baleful atmosphere, but Spark keeps tugging, like a tow boat guiding a sailing ship into harbour, and when Cisir finally relents, his fellow Suns tut in annoyance. At least he has a puppy to blame for being dragged away before the proceedings have properly ended, before the attendants disperse in an orderly fashion.

"Sorry, sorry, sorry!" He jostles against more people than he can count, and with every leap, Spark seems to grow more powerful. Cisir can barely keep up, and when he finally stumbles and nearly falls, the leash slips off his wrist. Spark can't very well yell at him around so many people, but he circles back immediately.

"I'm walking as fast as I can," Cisir protests. "What is wrong with you?"

Instead of an answer, Spark steers him out of the enclosed grounds. Many people are standing around on the road, all who couldn't fit between the hedges, who didn't get to hear the speech. When Cisir snatches up the trailing lead again, Spark heads straight for the bottom gate in the manor wall.

With every royal guard required at the ceremony, it's been locked for the day, or at least it should've been. Spark jumps up with his broad paws against it and it gives way.

The campsite sprawling at the bottom of the hill lies deserted, its fires quenched, and as soon as Cisir pulls the gate closed behind them, Teasel stands up and rips the leash off, although the collar holds fast.

"We don't have much time," he says. "Get a fucking move on."

"Why?" Cisir is so out of breath his mouth tastes like blood. "What are you doing?"

"Shortest Night," Teasel grunts, taking Cisir's elbow and continuing to pull him, nails digging painfully into flesh. "It should be both of you but there's no chance of getting Qonna out without causing a scandal."

As he runs, Teasel's long hair flies into Cisir's face, and he's so close to the fresh scars on Teasel's back he can see the older ones beneath. They could be claw marks or left from being whipped—tortured.

When they finally make it up to the clump of birches guarding the stones, someone is waiting for them in the shadows of their leaves. He's as tall as his son and has the same big nose with the bump.

"No …." Cisir tries to pull away, but Teasel's grip is relentless.

"He wears his face, but he's not your father."

The man standing up from the fallen stone has the same wavy grey hair bound back from his long face, the same frown, but his eyes … they're the wrong colour. They should be blue, like Cisir's own, but instead they're the same amber hue as Qonna's little statuette.

"We finally meet," he rumbles. Even his voice is borrowed from the father who banished Cisir from Windyhill. "Well done, Burnfoot."

Teasel throws himself down in the trampled grass. Cisir can hear him sobbing.

The man who looks like Cisir's father makes no attempt to get Teasel back to his feet. He leaves Teasel cowering as he turns to Cisir. "This seems to be an effective form to take. Have I got it right?"

"All but the eyes," Cisir manages to say.

"Ah. The eyes are always tricky."

"Why are you doing this, Brother Flame?" The name he guessed at brings an ashy taste to his tongue. *Eight Hells. Eight Heavens. None of it means anything now.*

A smile ghosts the Sibling's mouth, so unlike his father Cisir feels the cringe to his bones. "Because I have no choice. You see me as you want to see me, and the same goes for your friend Teasel Burnfoot. Stop crying, son. You would've been released at some point—it merely happened earlier than expected."

"So," Cisir says. "I'm a Burnfoot, like him?"

"It seems that way."

"And Qonna?" Her name tastes odd on his lips. Sweet, almost.

"Lightfoot, maybe? This is not a situation we encounter every day, and though we've become more accustomed to working with each other since the Order of the Eight was founded, it will mean some adjustments around you two."

"The Order of the Eight?" *Eight Siblings? Eight Kingdoms?*

"You'll see," Brother Flame promises. "You'll meet them soon."

"Is this why you wanted to see me? To bestow a blessing, or to rattle me?" Cisir's voice wavers as he speaks to his god.

"Both?" Brother Flame laughs with his father's voice, and Cisir nearly pisses himself. "I thought it might calm you to know you will reach your destination unharmed," the Sibling admits. "That it might make the next hours easier for you to deal with. You carry it, don't you?"

"What?"

"Don't play dumb, boy. Your half of it."

Cisir's mouth opens and even Teasel ceases howling and looks up at him, his face covered in tears and snot. Cisir pats the pocket where the golden half of the shell rests. His fingers shake as he pulls it forth to offer it to the old god on his palm.

"Don't lose it." Brother Flame appears tempted, but he doesn't touch the shell. "One day you'll have to explain what happened that night and it will serve as precious proof. You should also take care of your companion." Brother Flame crouches down and ruffles Teasel's hair. "He's always been a most valuable asset, despite his obvious shortcomings. And his emotional outbursts." He leans forward to kiss the sorcerer's brow. "He'll need help to find his feet in a world that has changed beyond measure. Many tasks wait for you at the other end of the world, for you and your soon-to-be wife. Just don't strangle the priest today."

"Which priest? Oh, you mean …."

"The one who's about to arrive at the house, full of dark misgivings about the family he pretends to serve. Your mother-in-law trusts him, and he will die soon enough."

Cisir blinks. "You know that he'll die?"

"You all do, boy, though he will take his time to suffer. The tumour is not yet big enough to affect him."

"I don't …." Grief hits him, as well as a ghastly rush of self-pity. "I shouldn't know that."

"Agreed. It is a small taste of what waits for you. I must be grateful to my sister for granting me the use of this place. She guards it jealously, and having too many people learn of its potential would be dangerous. I am glad I was able to meet you today. Now put your dog to its leash and run down the hill. You don't want to miss your own wedding."

"We need to talk," Cisir says as the puppy slinks away, tail clenched between his legs. "How many other important things are you keeping from us?"

They weave their way through the citizens returning from the memorial, but no one gives them a second glance. Many walk in silence, busy with their prayers for the people buried around the grey flame. Cisir should be engrossed in remorse about the loss of Hevo and the priest he killed, but he feels light-headed, as if he's rushing through a dream.

"Where were you?" Gia runs towards him, skirts flying. "Everyone thought you got cold feet."

"I didn't get cold feet. I might've if I had one single breath to myself."

"No time now. They're all waiting and if you don't show your face quick, Qonna will bite all her nails down." She grabs Spark's collar and hauls him forward.

Qonna's brothers hold the door open for them. "Thank the fucking Star," Qov says. "We don't need to kill you for jilting our sister."

The whole house smells of lavender and rosemary, as if they were scrubbed into its smallest creases, and suddenly Cisir is aware that he's bathed in sweat and more sunburned than the crown prince, while Qonna's brothers are almost as clean as *Pomegranates* itself, and handsome with their tight braids and eyes sparkling with excitement.

"There you are." His master bursts into the corridor, glowing with relief. "We can't let Brother Rago wait much longer."

"No, we really can't." Cisir's stomach twists with guilt.

The room that housed so many wounded people has been cleared and draped in garlands made from wild roses, and around its walls, clutching cups of wine, stand most of the royals he saw at the memorial. Noa waits with her family, including Lilyis. Qonna is half-turned away from him, in a blue headdress he's never seen before. It's folded into an elaborate shape and the pins that hold it in place are topped with pale moonstones, close in colour to Qonna's eyes.

"Don't gawp." Jark steps into the room behind him. "They've taken a lot of trouble."

"Why are you here?"

"The First Sun invited me, and I didn't have the good sense to refuse."

"But you can't be here."

"Of course I can." Jark lays a hand on his elbow, like he did when they first met each other. "Walk with me."

The priest, younger than Cisir expected, assesses him, mouth distorted in disgust as if he can smell Brother Flame on him. "Can we start?"

Qonna's mother nods. "Yes." She pulls her daughter in front of the priest, but Qonna ignores them both. "Are you all right?" she asks Cisir. "You look flustered."

"Well—yes."

"Do you still want to go through with this?"

The room holds its collective breath until Cisir nods. "Yes." He can't well say, *Brother Flame insists on it.*

When Qonna takes his hand, it's cold and clammy for the first time. She seems so calm, but they're both shivering.

Lilyis darts forward and pulls the hem of Cisir's yellow tunic straight as the priest is already starting to declare "… under the unending number of stars in the Heavens, the grace of the gods …."

Qonna squeezes his hand so hard he can hardly stifle a groan. Their strength runs over his skin like a wave of tiny spiders, tickling, teasing. He wants to spin around; he wants to turn to Spark or Jark for assistance, for support, but Brother Rago speeds through the vows, unstoppable at this point. "… and hold him accountable for all the sacrifices, promise to never forsake his heart, to honour the gods of the Star in all their eternal glory?"

"Yes," Qonna chokes out. "Yes, I promise all that."

How often has the priest spoken the required words? He doesn't seem to think about it, the sounds blending into one single sweep. "… in all their eternal glory?"

"Yes." It comes out squeaky. Cisir clears his throat. "Yes, I promise all that."

"Thank fuck," Lilyis says, barely audible, but loud enough for the priest to glower in her direction before he seals their fate. "Then with this moment you hold yourself for each other, as man and wife, blessed by the gods of the Star and all who have entered into the same union since the beginning of time, to be beholden to each other forever after."

The spiders have reached the small of Cisir's back, and the sensation is more than he can bear. He pulls Qonna close, waits for her to give him a small nod, then kisses her for the third time while her brothers whoop and clap, and Noa and Gia fall into each other's arms.

"Wait." The First Sun signals to his wife and she ushers the priest from the room.

Qes na Qarim draws something from his cloak—the sheath of a knife, longer than the daggers Cisir learned to fight with, its pommel etched with a sigil not used by any of their families: a kestrel in flight, its wings curved into the shape of a bow.

Qonna pulls Cisir's hand forward and together they grasp the sheath.

"A promise to the future stewards of this house," Qes says hoarsely. "And all you need to prove your claim." He smiles first at his daughter, then at his secretary. "Welcome to the family."

**The Sun & Flame duology continues in**

## EVERYTHING THE FLAME HEALS

**more information on www.cmkuhtz.com**

# AUTHOR NOTE & ACKNOWLEDGEMENTS

When I began to plan a new duology, I knew I wanted to start it off with a one-setting volume, and use a medieval-ish urban backdrop to do so.

It made sense to have the story take place in Seagard, the first city in the Eight Kingdoms I had a really firm grip on. I'd recently listed to the audiobook of Ian Mortimer's *The Time Traveller's Guide to Restoration Britain* (in my opinion the series is one of the very best resources for fantasy writers!) that has a section on the Great Fire of London—and suddenly I saw the city I had built so carefully go up in flames. It was both heart-breaking and freeing—this is the paradox at the centre of every unexpected occurrence of destruction I wanted to explore with this story, especially in Qonna's case. It mirrors my experience with the COVID-19 pandemic, a horrific censure in my own life, that nevertheless created a few unexpected and more positive results.

The pandemic caused me to think through my life's direction and deciding on going all out on founding an indie imprint as well as to finally take my mental health more seriously. The moment of crisis was an undeniable moment of opportunity—though it took me a long time to see it in this light.

One of my favourite tropes is the 'marriage of convenience', but I have seldom read a book that dealt with the topic in a sufficiently complicated way. I wanted the two people caught up in the situation to enter it because both had really good reasons to, and that one of those reasons was a friendship straddling the border between romantic and platonic.

Cisir and Qonna are very different people, but they are connected in feeling at odds with the world around them. I wanted to pick two rather unlikely heroes, characters who might be pushed to the back of the scene in more mainstream fantasy stories. I've long been interested in the lives of clerks and other office workers during periods in history where every word needs to be written by a human hand—one of the reasons why I asked My Lan, who created the stunning cover, to give Cisir a quill to hold. As someone who writes all their first drafts by hand, this was important to me. I also longed to write a male main character who is fundamentally kind-hearted, sometimes to his own detriment, and very aware of his own privilege without becoming a doormat.

In contrast, one of Qonna's main feelings is anger—about feeling stuck, about being unfairly treated, about not knowing her own heart. For me, she radiates strength. She isn't your typical 'strong female character' but someone infinitely more interesting and complex— and things are just getting started!

As always, there are so many people who need to be thanked:

Friends without whom I would not have the strength to write: Isa, Marlen, Dorit, Diana, Nicole, Bouke, Elena, Lorna, Claudia, and Jenna.

Fellow writers and alpha readers who partake in the peculiar madness that is a writer's life: Gobion, Hannah, and Ariadne.

River, for making this book so much more beautiful (and coherent!) than it was before they wielded their magic.

My Lan, for bringing Qonna and Cisir to life in such a stunning way. Wait until you see the cover for volume two!

Ken, for the beautiful illustrations that mirror the interior life of my characters.

Aliya, Lindsey, and Britt, beta and sensitivity readers extraordinaire. My parents and my brother Henry, who are the kernel of my soul nut.

And lastly, you—dear reader—for joining me on the adventure.

*What if the Chosen One doesn't get chosen?*

Sloe Moon, youngest child of the ruler of Tall Trees, has always wanted to follow in their father's footsteps and become a famous wizard. Instead they are expected to marry for the good of the Moon family and uphold an age-old alliance.

When the opportunity arises for them to travel to the famed wizard council of Goldenlake, Sloe and their best friend Qes set off on a journey that will not only put them in the path of mortal danger but also entangle them with the fate of the Moon's allies, enemies, and the mysterious men from the Eastern Cities, who have come to the land of the families with their own agenda. With so many odds stacked against them, will Sloe be able to fulfil their destiny?

*Sloe Moon: Tall Trees* is the first volume of a six-part queer fantasy series with a fat, nonbinary protagonist.